the
TRUE
LOVE
EXPERIMENT

ALSO BY CHRISTINA LAUREN

Dating You / Hating You
Roomies
Love and Other Words
Josh and Hazel's Guide to Not Dating
My Favorite Half-Night Stand
The Unhoneymooners
Twice in a Blue Moon
The Honey-Don't List
In a Holidaze
The Soulmate Equation
Something Wilder

THE BEAUTIFUL SERIES

Beautiful Bastard
Beautiful Stranger
Beautiful Bitch
Beautiful Bombshell
Beautiful Player
Beautiful Beginning
Beautiful Beloved
Beautiful Secret
Beautiful Boss
Beautiful

THE WILD SEASONS SERIES

Sweet Filthy Boy
Dirty Rowdy Thing
Dark Wild Night
Wicked Sexy Liar

YOUNG ADULT

The House
Sublime
Autoboyography

CHRISTINA LAUREN

the
TRUE
LOVE
EXPERIMENT

G

GALLERY BOOKS

New York   London   Toronto   Sydney   New Delhi

G

Gallery Books
An Imprint of Simon & Schuster, Inc.
1230 Avenue of the Americas
New York, NY 10020

First Gallery Books hardcover edition May 2023

GALLERY BOOKS and colophon are registered trademarks of Simon & Schuster, Inc.

For information about special discounts for bulk purchases, please contact Simon & Schuster Special Sales at 1-866-506-1949 or business@simonandschuster.com.

The Simon & Schuster Speakers Bureau can bring authors to your live event. For more information or to book an event, contact the Simon & Schuster Speakers Bureau at 1-866-248-3049 or visit our website at www.simonspeakers.com.

Interior design by Davina Mock-Maniscalco

Manufactured in the United States of America

10 9 8 7 6 5 4 3 2 1

Library of Congress Control Number: 2022952426

ISBN 978-1-9821-7343-2
ISBN 978-1-9821-7345-6 (ebook)

*This one is a blatant love letter to our genre.
There be romance in these pages.*

*And for Jennifer Yuen, Patty Lai, Eileen Ho,
Kayla Lee, and Sandria Wong.
There's a piece of each of you in here.
We are so grateful that you shared yourselves,
and we hope we've made you proud.*

FIZZY

was born the first of three children, but I joke that I'm like that first pancake." A smattering of laughter ripples across the assembled crowd and I smile. "You know what I mean? A little messy, slightly undercooked, but still tastes good?"

The laughter intensifies, but mixed in now are a few bawdy cat-calls, and I burst out laughing in realization. "See, and that wasn't even meant to sound saucy! Look at me trying to be professional, and I'm still a mess." I glance over my shoulder and grin at Dr. Leila Nguyen, the provost of UC San Diego's Revelle College and my former creative writing professor. "I guess that's what you get for inviting a romance author to give the commencement address."

Beside Dr. Nguyen sits another person struggling to smother a smile. Dr. River Peña—close friend, hot genius, and unconfirmed vampire—is also a special guest today; I guess he's receiving yet another honorary degree for being some type of sexy prodigy. He looks like he belongs up here: stiff collar, perfectly pressed suit pants visible below the hem of his full doctoral regalia, shiny dress shoes, and an air of austerity I've never been able to master. Right now, I can see the knowing amusement light up his smug, thickly lashed eyes.

When I first received the invitation to speak at this ceremony, River immediately slapped a twenty-dollar bill down onto the table between us and declared, "This is going to go completely sideways, Fizzy. Convince me otherwise."

I'm sure he and my best friend, Jess—his wife—expected that I would get up onstage and deliver *The Vagina Monologues* to the academic masses, or pull out a banana and remind everyone while I rolled a condom onto it that safe sex is still important in this here year of our Lord Harry Styles—but I swear I can play the part of a buttoned-down literary type when the situation calls for it.

At the very least, I thought I'd make it further than one line into my speech before dropping a double entendre—and that one wasn't even intentional.

I turn back to the sea of black, blue, and yellow–clad grads that stretches far across RIMAC Field and experience a wave of vicarious, breathless anticipation for all these youngsters taking flight. So many opportunities ahead. So much student loan stress. But also so much great sex.

"My younger sister is a neurosurgeon," I tell them. "My little brother? Yeah, he's the youngest partner in his firm's history. One of my best friends, sitting right behind me, is a world-famous geneticist." There's genuine applause for biotech's It boy, and once it dies back down, I go in for the kill: "But you know what? Despite all their accomplishments, none of them wrote a book called *Cloaked Lust*, so I think we all know who the real success story is here."

Smiling at a fresh wave of cheers, I continue. "So listen. Giving this kind of speech is a big deal. Most people invited to send off a group of young superstars like yourselves will list concrete ways to find your place in an ever-changing culture, or encourage you to amplify your impact by reducing your carbon footprint. They would tell you to go out and change the world, and of course yes—*do that*. I support those ambitions. Global citizen: good. Ecoterrorist: bad. But Dr. Nguyen didn't invite an inspiring climate scientist or charismatic and acceptably neutral politician. She invited me, Felicity Chen, author of books full of love and accountability and sex-positivity, and frankly the only professional advice I'm qualified to give about being eco-conscious is to support your local library." Another muted wave of laughter. "In fact, the only thing I care about—the one thing that matters most in the world to me—is that when every single one of you gets to the end of this crazy ride, you look back and can truly say you were happy."

It is a perfect day: bright and blue. Eucalyptus trees sway at the edge of the field, and if you breathe in at just the right moment, on the perfect gust of warm San Diego breeze, you can smell the ocean less than a mile away. Despite that, my stomach feels a little tilty at this next part of my speech. I've spent a majority of my adult years defending my profession, and the last thing I want to do is sound defensive. I'm standing up here in my own cap and gown with a lecture that I typed up and printed out so I wouldn't start winging it, derailing the whole thing with penis jokes exactly the way River expects me to. I want them to hear the sincerity in my words.

"I'm going to tell you to live your life like it's a romance novel." I hold up a hand when those smiling graduates begin to titter, but I don't blame them for thinking it's a joke, that I'm being coy. "Listen." I pause for effect, waiting for the laughter to subside and curiosity to take over. "Romance isn't gratuitous bodice ripping. It can be, and there's nothing wrong with that, but in the end, romance isn't about the fantasy of being wealthy or beautiful or even being tied to the bed." More laughter, but I have their attention now. "It's about elevating stories of joy above stories of pain. It is about seeing yourself as the main character in a very interesting—or maybe even quiet— life that is entirely yours to control. It is, my friends, the fantasy of *significance*." I pause again, just like I practiced, because all these babies have been raised under the dreary cloud of the patriarchy and I consider it my mission on earth to smash that with a proverbial hammer. The truth that we all deserve significance needs time to sink in.

But the pause stretches longer than I'd planned.

Because I didn't expect my own thesis to hit me like a thunderbolt to the center of my chest. I *have* lived my entire adult life like it's a romance novel. I've embraced adventure and ambition; I've been open to love. I enjoy sex, I support the women in my life, I actively think of ways to make the world around me a better place. I am surrounded by family and close friends. But my own significance is primarily as the sidekick bestie, the devoted daughter, the one-night stand they'll never forget. The real meat of my story—the romance plot, including love and happiness—is one gaping hole. I'm tired of first dates, and I suddenly feel so weary I could lie down right here at the podium. I am aware, in a jarring gust, that I have lost my joy.

I stare out at the sea of faces pointed at me, their eyes wide and attentive, and I want to admit the worst bit: *I've never made it past the first act of my own story*. I don't know what it feels like to be consistently significant. How can I tell these fresh babyadults to go out there with optimism because everything will be okay? The world seems intent on beating us down, and I don't remember the last time I was genuinely happy. Everything I'm telling them—every single hopeful word of this speech—feels like a lie.

Somehow I manage to put the glowing Fizzy mask on and tell these kids that the best thing they can do for their future is to pick the right community. I tell them that if they approach their future with the optimism of the world's boyfriend, Ted Lasso, things will turn out okay. I tell them that if they put in the work, if they allow that there will be blind curves and ups and downs, if they allow themselves to be vulnerable and loved and honest with the people who mean some-thing to them, things really will turn out okay.

And when I step away from the podium and take my seat beside River, he presses something into my palm. "You nailed it."

I stare down at the crisp twenty-dollar bill and then discreetly hand it back to him. Plastering a big grin on my face, aware that we're still facing an audience of thousands, I say, "But what if it's all bullshit?"

one

FIZZY

Approximately one year later

I f you aren't deep in a daydream about the hot bartender, then you have no good excuse for not reacting to what I just said."

I blink up across the table at my best friend, Jess, and realize I've been essentially hypnotizing myself by stirring the olive in my martini around and around and around.

"Shit, I'm sorry. I spaced out. Tell me again."

"No." She lifts her wineglass primly. "Now you must guess."

"Guess what you have planned for your trip to Costa Rica?"

She nods, taking a sip.

I stare flatly at her. She and her husband, the aforementioned River Peña, seem to be connected constantly by a vibrating, sexy laser beam. The answer here is very obvious. "Sex on every flat surface of the hotel room."

"A given."

"Running with wildcats?"

Jess stills with her glass partway to her lips. "It's interesting that you would go there as your second guess. No."

"A tree house picnic?"

She is immediately repulsed. "Eating with spiders? Hard pass."

"Surfing on the backs of turtles?"

"Deeply unethical."

Guiltily, I wince over at her. Even my Jess-Fizzy banter well has run dry. "Okay. I got nothing."

She studies me for a beat before saying, "Sloths. We're going to a sloth sanctuary."

I let out a gasp of jealousy and drum up some real energy to effuse over how amazing this trip will be, but Jess just reaches across the bar table and rests her hand over mine, quieting me. "Fizzy."

I look down at my half-finished martini to avoid her concerned maternal gaze. Jess's Mom Face has a way of immediately making me feel the need to handwrite an apology, no matter what I've just been caught doing.

"Jessica," I mumble in response.

"What's happening right now?"

"What do you mean?" I ask, knowing exactly what she means.

"The whole vibe." She holds up her wineglass with her free hand. "I ordered wine from Choda Vineyards and you didn't make a joke about short, chubby grapes."

I grimace. I didn't even catch it. "I admit that was a wasted opportunity."

"The bartender has been staring at you since we got here and you haven't AirDropped him your contact info."

I shrug. "He has lines shaved into his eyebrow."

As these words leave my lips, our eyes meet in shock. Jess's voice is a dramatic whisper: "Are you actually being . . . ?"

"*Picky?*" I finish in a gasp.

Her smile softens the worry lingering in her eyes. "There she is."

With one final squeeze to my fingers, she releases my hand, leaning back. "Rough day?"

"Just a lot of thinking," I admit. "Or overthinking."

"You saw Kim today, I take it?"

Kim, my therapist for the past ten months and the woman who I hope will help me crack the code to writing, dating, feeling like myself again. Kim, who hears all my angst about love and relationships and inspiration because I really, truly do not want to drop the depth of my stress in Jess's lap (she and River are still relative newlyweds), or my sister Alice's lap (she is pregnant and already fed up with her over-protective obstetrician husband), or my mother's lap (she is already overly invested in my relationship status; I don't want to send her to therapy, too).

In the past, when I've felt discontentment like this, I knew it would ebb with time. Life has ups and downs; happiness isn't a con-stant or a given. But this feeling has lasted nearly a year. It's a cyni-cism that now seems permanently carved into my outlook. I used to spend my life writing love stories and carrying the boundless opti-mism that my own love story would begin on the next page, but what if that optimism has left me for good? What if I've run out of pages?

"I did see Kim," I say. "And she gave me homework." I pull a little Moleskine notebook from my purse and wave it limply. For years, these colorful journals were my constant companions. I took one everywhere I went, writing book plots, snippets of funny con-versations, images that would pop into my head at random times. I called them my idea notebooks and used to scribble things down twenty, thirty, forty times a day. These scribbles were my deep

well of ideas. For a few months after my romance brain came to
a screeching halt in front of a thousand fresh college grads, I continued carrying one around in hopes inspiration would strike. But
eventually, seeing it there in my purse stressed me out, so I left
them in my home office, collecting dust with my laptop and desk-
top. "Kim told me I need to start carrying notebooks again," I tell Jess.
"That I'm ready for the gentle pressure of having one with me, and
even writing a single sentence or drawing a doodle in it will help."

She takes a second to absorb this. The phrase *even writing a single sentence* hangs between us. "I knew you'd been in a slump," she
says, "but I don't think I realized how bad it was."

"Well, it doesn't happen all at once. For a while, I wrote, but it
wasn't very good. And then I started to worry it was actually pretty
terrible, and that made me think I'd lost my spark. And then thinking
I'd lost my spark made me think maybe it was because I'd stopped
believing in love."

Her frown deepens, and I press on. "It isn't like I woke up one
day and thought, Wow, love is a lie." I stab the olive in my drink,
then use the toothpick to point in her direction. "Obviously you're
proof that it's not. But at what point do I acknowledge that maybe
my love life isn't going to be what I think it is?"

"Fizz—"

"I think I might have aged out of the majors."

"*What?* That is—" She blinks, her argument dying on her tongue.
"Well, that is actually a very good metaphor."

"It's the classic chicken-and-egg dilemma: Has the writer's block
killed my romance boner, or has losing my romance boner killed my
actual boner?"

"There are a lot of boners in this situation."

"If only! And once you're single for so long, you aren't even sure whether you're suitable for a relationship anymore."

"It's not like you've wanted to be in one," she reminds me. "I don't know who Felicity Chen is if she's not treating dating like it's an extreme sport."

I point at her again, energized. "Exactly! That's another fear I have! What if I've depleted the local resources?"

"Local . . . resources?"

"I joke that I've dated every single man in San Diego County—and inadvertently some of the married ones—but I don't really think it's that far off from the truth."

Jess scoffs into her wine. "Come on."

"Remember Leon? The guy I met when he spilled a huge tray of Greek salad on my foot in the Whole Foods parking lot?"

She nods, swallowing a sip. "The guy from Santa Fe?"

"And remember Nathan, who I met on a blind date?"

She squints. "I think I remember hearing that name."

"They're brothers. *Twins.* Moved out here together to be closer to family. I went out with them two weeks apart." Jess claps a hand to her mouth, stifling a laugh. "When Nathan walked into the restaurant and approached the table, I said, 'Oh my God, what are you doing here?'"

Her laugh breaks free. "I'm sure he and Leon get that all the time, though."

"Sure, but then I went out with a guy last month named Hector." I pause to underscore the weight of what I'm going to say next. "He's the cousin the twins moved here to be closer to."

To her credit, this laugh is more of a groan. This shit used to be funny. It used to crack us both up—and dating like this was a blast. The Adventures of Fizzy used to give me unending inspiration— even if a date went terribly, I could still play it for comedy or even just a tiny spark of an idea for dialogue. But at this point, I have six books partially written that get just past the meet-cute and then . . . nothing. There's a roadblock on the way to the "I love you" now, a NO ACCESS sign in my brain. I'm starting to understand why. Because when I see Jess light up every time River walks into the room, I must admit that I've never shared that kind of reverberating joy with anyone. It's made it increasingly difficult to write about love authentically.

I'm not sure I even know what real love feels like.

Jess's phone vibrates on the table. "It's Juno," she says, meaning her ten-year-old daughter, my second-in-line bestie and one of the most charming small humans I've ever met. Kids are mostly a mystery to me, but Juno somehow translates in my brain like an adult would—probably because she's smarter than I am.

I motion for Jess to take the call just as my gaze locks with that of a man across the bar. He's gorgeous in such an easy and immediate way: messy dark hair falling into a pair of light, penetrating eyes, jaw so sharp he could slice my clothes off as he kisses down my body. Suit coat tossed over a chair, dress shirt stretched across broad shoulders and unbuttoned at the neck—he's got the disheveled appearance of a man who's had a shitty day, and the famished look in his gaze that says he'd use me to forget all about it. Men who deliver that kind of eye contact used to be my catnip. Past Fizzy would already be halfway across the room.

But Present Fizzy is decidedly *meh*. Is my internal horny barometer really broken? I tap it with a mental reflex hammer, imagining pulling that Hot CEO from his barstool and dragging him by that open collar into the hallway.

Nothing.

Look at his mouth! So full! So cocky!

Still nothing.

I tear my attention away and turn back to Jess as she ends her call. "Everything okay?"

"Coordinating dance and soccer," she says with a shrug. "I'd elaborate, but we'd both be asleep by sentence two. But back to Hector, the cousin of—"

"I didn't sleep with any of them," I blurt. "I haven't slept with anyone in a year." I did the math a couple of days ago. It feels weird to say it out loud.

It must be weird to hear it, too, because Jess gapes at me. "Wow."

"Lots of people don't have sex for a year!" I protest. "Is it really that shocking?"

"For you, *yes*, Fizzy. Are you kidding?"

"I watched porn the other night and there was barely a clench." I look down at my lap. "I think my pants feelings are broken."

Her concern intensifies. "Fizz, honey, I—"

"Last week I considered going jogging in flip-flops just to remind myself how sex sounds." Jess's forehead creases in worry and I deflect immediately. "The answer here is obvious. It's time for bangs."

There's a tiny beat where I can see her considering battling this redirect, but thankfully she hops on this new train. "We have a strict agreement that no crisis bangs will be approved. I'm sorry, it's a no from the best friend committee."

"But imagine how youthful I'll look. Quirky and up for anything."

"No."

I growl and turn my attention to the side, to the bar television, where the previous sportsball contest has ended and the local news is reeling through the headlines. I point to the screen. "Your husband's face is on TV."

She sips her wine, staring up at two-dimensional River. "That will never stop being weird."

"The husband part, or the TV part?"

She laughs. "TV."

And I see it all over her face: the husband part feels as natural as breathing. That's because science, specifically River's own invention—a DNA test that categorizes couples into Base, Silver, Gold, Platinum, Titanium, and Diamond love matches according to all kinds of complicated genetic patterns and personality tests— essentially told them they're as compatible as is humanly possible.

And I'm more than happy to take credit. Jess wasn't even going to try the test that matched them—the DNADuo—until I shoved an early version of it into her hands. Where are my rightfully earned karma points for that? River turned his decade-long research on genetic patterns and romantic compatibility into the app and billion-dollar company GeneticAlly. Now GeneticAlly is biotech's and the online dating industry's gold-star darling. River's company has been all over the news since it launched.

It's a lot of blah-blah-yapping-hand when he gets really sciencey about it, but it really has changed the way people find love. Since the

DNADuo launched about three years ago, it's even overtaken Tinder in number of users. Some analysts expect its stock to surpass Facebook's now that the associated social media feed app, Paired, has launched. *Everyone* knows someone who's been matched through GeneticAlly.

All this is amazing, but for someone like River, who prefers to spend his days facing a fume hood rather than leading investor meetings or fielding questions from reporters, I think the frenzy has been a drag.

But, as the nightly news is reminding us, GeneticAlly isn't River's problem for much longer. The company is being acquired.

"When does the deal close?" I ask.

Jess swallows a sip of wine, eyes still on the television. "Expected Monday morning."

I really can't fathom this. The GeneticAlly board has accepted an offer, and there are all kinds of subrights deals happening that I don't even understand. What I do comprehend is that they're going to be so rich, Jess is absolutely paying for drinks tonight.

"How are you feeling about it?"

She laughs. "I feel completely unprepared for what life looks like from now on."

I stare at her, deciphering the simplicity of this sentence. And then I reach across the table and take her hand, fog clearing. Her right wrist has the other half of my drunken, misspelled Fleetwood Mac tattoo: *Thunner only happens* and *wen it's raining* forever binding us together. "I love you," I say, serious now. "And I'm here to help you spend your giraffe money."

"I'd rather have an alpaca."

"Dream bigger, Peña. Get two alpacas."

Jess grins at me, and her smile fades. She squeezes my hand. "You know the old Fizzy will come back, right?" she asks. "I think you're just facing a transition, and figuring that out will take time."

I glance across the bar at the disheveled hot guy again. I search my blood for some vibration, or even the mildest flutter. Nothing. Tearing my eyes away, I exhale slowly. "I hope you're right."

two

CONNOR

Some bloke on a podcast once philosophized that the perfect day comprises ten hours of caffeine and four hours of alcohol. I might agree with the caffeine bit, but the mediocre beer in front of me feels more like liquid sadness than escape. Oddly fitting for the day I've had.

"Pivoting over to reality television might be fun," my mate Ash says distractedly, eyes glued to the basketball game on the TV above the bar. "It's sort of like what you do now, just sexier."

"Ash," I say, grimacing as I rub my temples, "I make short docuseries on marine mammals."

"And dating shows are short docuseries on *land* mammals." He grins at his own cheekiness, looking at me and nodding. "Am I right?"

I groan, and we fall silent again, turning our attention back up to where the Warriors are obliterating the Clippers.

Rarely have I had such a horrendous day at work. Having started from the bottom in the shark tank of big Hollywood, I know I have it good working for San Diego's comparably tiny production company North Star Media. There are the obvious frustrations that accompany working in a small shop—limited budgets, the uphill battle of distribution, and the simple fact of being 120 miles away from Los Angeles among them—but I also have autonomy in my projects.

Or did, until today, when my boss, one Blaine Harrison Byron—a man whose office decor includes a huge slab of graffitied concrete, a life-sized statue of a naked woman, and the newest addition, a gleaming saddle—told me the company was making a major pivot from socially conscious programming to reality television. Is it possible for a man named Blaine Harrison Byron to not be a giant, pretentious wanker?

(I see the fair point to be made—that a man named Connor Fredrick Prince III should not be so quick to cast stones—but I didn't just sideswipe the lives of my entire staff on a whim, so I'm standing firm.)

"Let's talk it out," Ash says when a commercial for Jack in the Box comes on. "What'd your boss say, specifically?"

I close my eyes, working to recall Blaine's exact wording. "He said we're too small to be socially conscious."

"Out loud?"

"Out loud," I confirm. "He said that people don't want to sit down after a hard day's work and feel bad about the ziplocked sandwich they took for lunch, or how much water is wasted to make the electricity to charge their iPhone."

Ash's jaw drops. "Wow."

"He said he wants me to go after the female demographic." I sip my beer and set it down, staring at the table. "He said Bravo was the number one rated cable network in prime time among women ages eighteen to forty-nine because of their two top reality franchises, and that demographic spends the most. Ergo, the executives are going after premium ad revenue. They've already got one of my colleagues, Trent, working on some mash-up of *The Amazing Race* and *American Gladiators* they're calling *Smash Course*. And they want me to spearhead a reality dating show."

"So, like, women competing to get some oiled-up hunk to choose them," Ash says.

"Right."

"Half-naked Gen Zers locked in a big house together trying to get laid."

"Yes, but—"

"Hot women marrying some average dude they've never seen."

"Ash, there is no bloody way I am doing that."

He laughs. "Put your British manners away. Pretend you're American." When he sets his beer down again, I notice his shirt is misbuttoned. Ashkan Maleki can be counted on to be untied, unzipped, or otherwise disheveled at least fifty percent of the time. It's endearing, but I have no idea how he survives in a room full of unfiltered six-year-olds every day. "Every job has downsides. We just have to keep at it."

I met Ash when my daughter, Stevie, was in first grade and he took over her class halfway through the year. It also turned out we went to the same gym and kept running into each other. We immediately hit it off, but hanging out felt a little like secretly dating my kid's teacher. Thankfully, when the school year ended, Stevie moved on to another grade and my friendship with Ash stuck.

"You love being a teacher," I say.

"Most days. The kids are great," he clarifies. "It's their parents who are a mess."

I give him a humorously dark look.

Ash grins as he pops a fry into his mouth. "Nah, you and Nat were fine. I got the usual kid gossip from Stevie but nothing too bad." He leans in and lowers his voice. "You wouldn't believe some of the stuff kids tell me. Some of these parents are nuts. I had one physically threaten me when their son lost the school spelling bee. They were worried about his academic career."

"What career? He's *six*."

"The word was *thwart*."

"I can barely spell that now."

"Exactly." His attention is drawn to the TV again when the crowd around us collectively curses at something happening in the game, and my work malaise returns.

When Natalia and I divorced eight years ago, we agreed on shared custody of our daughter. This means Stevie, now ten years old, spends the weekdays at her mum's place and the weekends and most school holidays at mine. It's usually not a problem, but because of this evening's disaster meeting with Blaine, I missed my pickup window. At some point, I'd done the Southern California mental calculation of:

$$(\text{time of day}) \times (\text{motorway construction})^{\text{It's Friday}}$$

and told Nat to just carry on the evening without me.

She had to take Stevie to run errands and wouldn't be home for a few hours. Now not only is my career in the toilet, I'm missing out on time with my favorite girl, too.

Restless, I glance around the bar, my eyes wandering back to the two women I saw earlier. One of them's got her back to me, but the other, the one I made eye contact with shortly after I got here, is so gorgeous I can't stop stealing looks at her. Petite and willowy, with inky black hair that gleams in the light above their table, she's in a formfitting black dress, legs crossed and one thin, spiked heel resting on the leg of her barstool. Everything about her screams *cool*, which is an odd way for a grown man to describe another adult but it's true. She's animated while she speaks, making her friend laugh often. I should stop staring, but it's nice to be distracted by a beautiful woman rather than obsessing about work.

If I were wired differently, maybe I'd walk over and see if we could distract each other somewhere else for the night. But I'm jerked from my daydreaming when Ash's hand absently paws at my collar in reaction to something on the screen.

"What the— *Ash*."

"Get it . . . Get it!" he shouts. His expression crashes. "*Noooo*."

He slumps back into his chair.

"I just lost five bucks." He reaches into his pocket for his phone.

"Five whole American dollars?" I ask, grinning. "You'd better watch that gambling habit."

"I don't know how she does it, but Ella is a shark and never loses."

"You lost to your wife?"

He looks up from where he's typing her a message. "I'm considering taking her to Vegas."

"Definitely do it before the baby is born—pregnant ladies love smoky casinos."

He ignores this and slides his phone onto the table. "Let's get back to your job crisis so I can go home. I know this will hurt your do-gooder soul, but I think you need to bite the bullet and do the reality show Blaine wants. Spend the rest of the year making candy, or whatever he called it, and if it's successful, you'll have leverage to make what *you* want after that."

I begin to protest, and he holds up a hand.

"I know you hate this. I know your work matters to you. Thanks to you I haven't thrown away a gum wrapper or used a plastic water bottle in two years. I'm going to be using cloth diapers, man."

"I must be a lot of fun at parties."

Ash steeples his fingers under his chin. "I say this because I know how much you want to stick to your principles here. You want to make stuff that matters. But I also know you can't lose this job. You only missed a few hours with Stevie tonight. Imagine what you'd miss if you had to move back to LA."

I turn my gaze down to my beer. The thought alone makes my stomach twist. "Yeah."

"So do it and move on."

"I'm not sure it's that easy."

"Come on. We're smart guys. Bounce some sexy show ideas off me."

I press my fingers to my temples, trying to will a million-dollar idea into existence. "That's the problem, I don't have any. I'm certain the world doesn't need another one of these things."

"Well, while the world may not *need* another, it certainly wants it: Ella watches every single one. What you need is a new angle." He turns to glance around the bar, and when he does, I see the dry-cleaning tag still attached to his collar. Has it been like this all day? With a sigh, I reach over and pluck it off. "Huh," he says, examining it before placing it on the table and looking back to the TV.

I follow his attention to where the game has finished and the nightly news is on. It's too loud in the bar to hear the voiceover, but the captions inform me that GeneticAlly, the biggest dating app in the world right now, has been bought by Roche Pharmaceuticals.

"Holy shit," Ash murmurs, then narrows his eyes to read something on the screen. "That is an absurd amount of money."

My jaw is on the floor. "No kidding." Remembering something, I look over at Ash. "GeneticAlly—isn't that how you and Ella met?"

He nods. "We're a Gold Match."

A couple to our right has just taken their seats. The vibe between them is heavy with disappointment. A bad first date. They glance at each other only when they think the other isn't looking, and an accidental brush of hands leads to bursting apologies but no shy smiles. No spark. It's presumptuous of me, but I could walk over there right now and tell them they've got no chemistry, no chance. Couldn't we all? I'm not overly familiar with GeneticAlly, but I know they developed a system that matches people for compatibility based on signatures in their DNA. I'd give this couple a zero.

Lifting my chin, I say to Ash, "Think they're a Gold Match?"

He glances over and watches for a handful of seconds before raising his drink to his lips. "Nope. No way."

I look back up at the TV and an idea tickles the edge of my brain. I'll have to make a few calls. Maybe having time to kill will be a good thing after all.

three

CONNOR

Two hours later, I pull up in front of Natalia's house. It's a beautiful place—I should know; I cosigned the loan. The Realtor called it Spanish Colonial Revival, with white stucco walls, a low-pitched tile roof, and a gated courtyard Nat always goes all out decorating for Halloween. But where there was once a tricycle in the yard and pastel chalk animals scribbled on the sidewalk, now there's a ten-speed and a row of potted orchids leading up to the front door. Natalia took up gardening after our divorce. Post-divorce she's thriving, and so are the orchids.

Waiting for me on the front step is Stevie's chocolate-brown labradoodle, Baxter. We are absolutely those parents who got their kid a consolation divorce dog. He barks cheerily to alert the house that an intruder has entered the premises and, tail still wagging, promptly rolls over for belly rubs.

"All that money for puppy camp and you are still a terrible guard dog," I say, bending to pet him. "Where is everybody? Where's Stevie? Can you go fetch her?"

The door is slightly open and Baxter nudges it with his nose and goes up the stairs.

"Hello?" I call out. It's cool and quiet inside. Stevie's homework is spread out on the coffee table and a basket of folded laundry sits on the couch. The walls are filled with photographs, some of Stevie and Natalia, a few with me. We've taken photos of Stevie in the same location and in the same pose on her birthday every year, and seeing them grouped together is like a time lapse of her childhood. She's tall for a ten-year-old, and rail thin. She has her mum's olive complexion and dark hair, but her eyes—my eyes—are as green as they've ever been.

Footsteps pound on the stairs and a second later, a body collides into mine, skinny arms wrapping around my waist. Baxter is right behind her. "Finally," Stevie says into my stomach.

I bend, pressing a kiss to her hair. "Sorry, boss. Meeting ran late. Did you have fun with your mum?"

She flops onto the couch dramatically. "We drove *everywhere*. We went to the dry cleaners and to drop some things off at the post office for Abuelita and then to Mom's nail appointment. I forgot my book, so she let me watch videos on my phone and we ordered Chinese food."

Guilt—my constant weekend-only-parent companion—raises its ugly head.

"I'm sorry, Sass."

"It's okay. I got my nails painted." She holds up a hand and wiggles her pink-tipped fingers. Stevie will pick pink everything if given the opportunity. "And I know you're super important at your job."

I sit on the coffee table facing her. "There were some things that couldn't wait until Monday."

"I bet they were a really big deal," she says slyly. "You have the *best* ideas and make the *best* documentaries."

I'm suspicious. Much like her mother, Stevie is a master negotiator. The problem is that I rarely know we're negotiating until I've already agreed to something. "What's the angle?"

"No angle. You're just really cool, that's all." She pauses. "But I almost forgot!" She sits up, miraculously rejuvenated. "Wonderland is coming here!"

Wonderland, Stevie's current obsession, is a pop group that's taken over every chart and award show in the country. For birthdays, Christmas, and every minor holiday involving a basket, treat, or wrapped parcel, Stevie has asked for Wonderland merchandise. The members' faces are on so many of her T-shirts I could spot them in a crowd without any trouble.

"Coming here as in for a concert?"

"Yes! Could we go? Please?" She takes both my hands in hers and makes her eyes as wide as moons. "It could be for my birthday."

"Your birthday was in January. It's May."

"Hmm," she says, recalibrating. "If I get straight A's?"

"You already get straight A's."

Her wry expression says it clearly: *Exactly*. A sucker, I am. I pull out my phone. "Okay. Where are they playing?"

Stevie's vibrating intensity dials up. "The Open Air!"

"Calm down," I say gently. "I'm only looking. Did you talk to your mum about this?"

"She said it's fine if you take me."

"Of course she did." When the site loads, a giant banner fills the top of the page: WONDERLAND: THE FORBIDDEN GAME TOUR. "A title like 'Forbidden Game' leaves me with many questions."

Stevie rolls her eyes. "Dad."

I scroll down to the San Diego dates and spot the red SOLD OUT flag over the buy link. I turn the screen to show her, and she immediately deflates.

"I'm sorry, Sass. Maybe next time round? Besides, it doesn't even start till eight and you're dead asleep by eight thirty." Her bottom lip juts out and I bend to meet her eyes. "We'll check if it's streaming and maybe we can watch together."

She's disappointed, but rallies anyway. "Can we get tour shirts and order pizza?"

"Absolutely. Now go fetch your stuff so we can go."

She leaps off the couch, long, coltish limbs propelling her to the stairs. I swear she's taller than when I saw her on Sunday. The dog races behind her.

"Where *is* your mum, by the way?" I call after her.

"She was outside. Insu is building a shed in the garden and she's watching." She looks down at me from the top of the stairs. "He's really strong."

"I've noticed."

Insu is Natalia's boyfriend. He's twenty-six . . . so there's that. It took us a few years to iron out the kinks of divorced co-parenthood, but the care and respect we show each other now is better than when we were married. Watching Nat fall in love again eased a weight I hadn't fully realized I was carrying. Having that person practically be a teenager (a slight exaggeration, but I'm the single one here, so let me have this) is a flavor of joy I couldn't have anticipated.

Stevie's footsteps sound overhead and then she falls silent, presumably throwing things into a bag. In the quiet, I pace the living room, and my mind rolls back to my work dilemma.

I could make some hybrid of eco-conscious and reality programming, but the truth is that I don't really want to bump up against my documentary colleagues in this setting. It's taken me years to build the credibility I have, and I suspect one adventure race through the jungle will squash all of it in a single go. Besides, Blaine wants something salacious and sexy, and nothing in my current repertoire could be described as such.

I'll have to think outside my current box. Dating shows have been done ad nauseam, so a new show would need a hook to make it stand out above the rest. I'm an amateur in a very well-traversed space, but the more I sit with it, the more I keep coming back to the idea I had at the bar after hearing the GeneticAlly news. My gut says there's something there, but I'm still missing a piece . . .

I find myself in front of one of Nat's many bookcases. Without question, Stevie got her fangirl genes from her mother, but where my daughter loses her mind over pop stars, Natalia is an avid romance reader. Upon inspection, I register that the shelf before me has over two dozen books all by the same author. I pull one free.

Ravenous on the High Seas by Felicity Chen.

The cover features two beautiful people wrapped up in each other on the deck of what appears to be a pirate ship. It's a great photograph—sweeping, sexy, atmospheric—and when I open the cover, there's an even more detailed version inside. I glance at the summary: a lost heir, a sword-wielding heroine, a country on the brink of war, and hidden treasure that could save them all. When I flip open the back cover, I freeze. The author photo staring back at me is the gorgeous woman from the bar.

Over at the family computer, I enter the password and type

Felicity Chen into the search bar. The screen instantly populates with results. Publication interviews, fan edits, social media accounts, retail sites, and her publisher's page. I click on one of the news hits and see a commencement address at UCSD Revelle College.

By the time footsteps sound on the wood floor behind me, I've watched the commencement address and half a dozen short interview clips, read three *Entertainment Weekly* reviews of her work, and scrolled through much of her Instagram feed. Felicity Chen is funny, charismatic, smart, and great in front of a crowd. She would be a natural on TV . . .

Natalia is suspicious. "Why is my favorite author's face all over that screen?"

I spin in the chair to face my ex. "What do you know about her?" Felicity's bio is frustratingly lacking in personal details. Wikipedia isn't any more helpful. "Is she single?"

"If you date her and break her in some way and I don't get her next book, I may have to kill you."

"I don't want to date her, Nat."

"Do you want to date *anyone*? You don't have to live like a monk, you know."

"This again."

"The thing with Stevie walking in—"

I stick two fingers in my mouth and let out a sharp whistle. "Yellow card, Garcia."

Nat bursts out laughing. This little troublemaker knows I am legitimately scarred after four-year-old Stevie walked in on me going fully at it with a date's ankles on my shoulders. It was the first and last time I had someone over while Stevie was staying at my place, and I'm not sure I'll ever recover. I swear I am only waiting for the day that memory surfaces and my daughter can never look me in the eye again.

"Sorry," Nat says, sounding not sorry at all. "Just put a bell on her door. Works like a charm."

I hook a thumb over my shoulder at the computer monitor. "Can we focus?"

Her eyes drift past me to Felicity's face on the screen. "Yeah, I'm pretty sure she's single. She's talked about dating in past interviews. Why?"

"I want her for a show."

Nat's eyebrows drift upward. "Like a documentary on romance and feminism or something?"

I laugh. "No."

"What's the laugh about?" she asks, scowling.

Careful, I think. Nat has busted me in the past for giving her shit about the kind of books she reads. I don't want to step on a land mine here when I need her help. "Sorry, no, it's just that I might be making a dating show."

Her eyes widen. "A—*what*? What is North Star's brand? Sitcoms and Lifetime movies, to environmental documentaries, and now dating shows?"

"It's Blaine," I say by way of explanation, and Natalia requires nothing more. Blaine bounces from one thing to another, depending on who's currently got his ear, and right now—understandably— it's the executives holding the purse strings. Odds are good I was hired because a now-ex-wife was worried about marine mammals. "And nothing's set in stone yet, just exploring some options." I don't want both of us worrying about this, so I change the subject. "How's Insu?"

"Wonderful," she says, draping herself across the couch in the exact way our daughter would. "He's taking me to dinner tomorrow night for our anniversary."

"Oh cool, did he get his driver's license?" I grin at her. "They grow up so fast." In truth, I like Insu—he's far more mature than I was at that age, he adores Natalia, and Stevie likes him, too—but I'm not going to pass up a chance to take the piss a bit.

"You know he's only seven years younger than you."

"Which would also make him eight years younger than you. I hope you're locking up the drinks cupboard."

A cushion connects with the side of my head just as Stevie makes it downstairs with her things, Baxter and his own weekend bag in tow.

"Ready to go, Sass?"

"Yep. I sent you a link to the tour T-shirts," Stevie says. "You don't want to wait because they might sell out."

I reach for my phone again. "Yes, Captain."

"Would this happen to be Wonderland related?" Nat asks.

"Sadly, the concert was sold out, but we'll get some goodies to soothe the ache."

Nat gives me a little *what a relief, huh* look over the top of Stevie's head as she hugs her goodbye. And for a handful of seconds, regret cuts sharply through me. I'm sure I miss a thousand of these ordinary and sweet moments every day. I could have lived this life with the two of them. It would have been platonic and passionless, yes, but stable and loving. I'd assumed there had to be something more out there, but really, it's not like my love life is any more electric than it was when we were married.

But it's too late to start over again, and the truth is, I'll miss all of this and far more if I don't figure out what the fuck I'm going to do about work.

four

FIZZY

The first time I ever met a producer to discuss adapting one of my books into a film, I was so excited I barely slept the night before. I spent hours picking out what I would wear. I told every person I knew that my book was being adapted into a movie. I gave myself five hours to drive the 124 miles to Los Angeles and then paid forty dollars to park so I'd have a place to wait because I'd arrived three hours early. I sat there and thought about what I might wear on the red carpet, who might be cast as the hero, and how it would feel to see him on the screen for the very first time. I walked in with big smiles and big plans and big hopes.

That collaboration didn't go anywhere, and neither did the next meeting, or the next, and the meetings that *were* productive were about projects that eventually languished in predevelopment for years. I had to learn the hard way that everyone in Hollywood is excited about a project until it's time for the wallets to open. Now I know this song and dance; the meeting my film agent set up for me this morning at the unknown-to-me North Star Media doesn't even register as a blip with my adrenals.

North Star's administrative assistant is a sweet twentysomething cutie-pie who offers me coffee and a doughnut from a pink mom-and-pop-shop box on her desk when I arrive. I consider answering a few DMs while I wait, but what my readers want is an update on the book, and I've got nothing for them. I put my phone away and busy myself with a doughnut instead.

Looking around, I must admit the vibe in this small San Diego production company is much beachier and chill than all the glossy glass-walled or intentionally industrial bluster of LA. But when the dude I'm meeting steps out of his office, I'm reminded that Hollywood is Hollywood, even in San Diego.

I think I know him from somewhere, but I can't place where—this is not a man who would hang out in any of my favorite coffee shops or bars. His hair is so perfectly coiffed that from a distance it looks like a Lego hair block. I'm distracted by his height, so I don't catch his name, but I smile as if I did. White gleaming teeth, glimmering eyes that would get the sparkle sound effect in a cartoon, and muscles bunchy and flexing under his white dress shirt. He is hot in a very obvious way. If I were writing this book, I'd immediately cast him as Hot Millionaire Executive. Sadly, my mental Rolodex tells me three important things about this hero archetype: He will talk a lot about whatever sport he played in college. He is, at best, a performative feminist. And, relatedly, he does not enjoy going down on women.

But I follow him into his office anyway because if I stay in the waiting area, I'll eat a second doughnut.

Hot Millionaire Executive's office is tidy and sparse. Unlike many other film executives' workspaces, it doesn't have a framed collection of signed rare comic books, a coffee table book about vintage sneakers, or a vanity wall of film posters. He has a few framed black-and-white photographs of what looks like the Central California coastline, some other framed photos facing away from me on his desk, and then nothing but clean walls and surfaces.

The hot, boring man gestures that I should sit in one of the expensive leather chairs grouped around a low wood coffee table, and I really do try to fall effortlessly into the seat, but the rip in my jeans hits at the worst place in my knee and the second I sit it makes an audible tearing sound. A moment passes where I can see him debating whether he should react to it.

He seems to decide against it, smiling instead. I add *nice smile* to his character description. "Thanks for coming in today, Felicity."

"Oh. A Brit." I feel the first, tiny pants flutter in ages and update my mental archetype Rolodex.

"Born and raised in Blackpool."

"I don't know where that is, but it sounds piratey."

He laughs at this, a low, rumbling sound. "Northwestern England."

I nod, looking around, trying to figure out how a man looking like that left his pirate hometown, ended up in an office this bland, and eventually found his way to my books. What a journey. When my eyes return to his face, I can't shake the feeling that we've met before. "Do we know each other?"

He hesitates, mouth briefly forming one word before it takes a different shape. "I don't believe so. But my ex-wife is a huge fan."

An indelicate laugh rips out of me. "I'm going to say that's the weirdest compliment I've ever received."

Even his wince seems too perfect to be real. "Sorry. I guess that's a strange way of saying that I was impressed by you. Natalia has discerning tastes, and she owns every one of your books."

I feel an eyebrow point sharply skyward.

"She's made a fan out of me, too," he admits, and oh no, now he's gone too far. It would be so refreshing if one of these dudes would just say, *I haven't read your books and I like to mock the genre with my bros, but romance has the largest readership in publishing, and I want to make money off it.*

I smile, flashing my teeth. Time to catch him in a lie. "Which book is your favorite?"

"I know you probably expected me to say *Ranger's Castle* or *At the End of the Road* because of the action in both of them, but I'm going to say *Base Paired*."

Ah, so his adorable assistant is good at the Google. That must be why I'm here. "*Base Paired* it is."

Hot Brit spreads his hands magnanimously. "It's a clever idea, Felicity, and the timing was great."

Or maybe he's not so good at the Google: anyone who knows me either personally or professionally knows that the only people who call me Felicity are my former schoolteachers, and even then only on the first day of class or when I was in trouble.

Anyway, despite his patronizing tone, he's right—the timing *was* great. I wrote *Base Paired* just as GeneticAlly launched the DNADuo app, and its publication dovetailed perfectly with the rising hype of the technology. That book, about two sworn enemies who turn out to be a Diamond Match, spent a long time on the bestseller list. But after a small production company failed to sell a series, I got the rights back last month.

"Listen, Ted—"

"Connor."

"—I'm going to be honest," I say, rolling past this because, frankly, his name doesn't much matter. "The rights are available, and I'm not opposed to working with someone to adapt it into a film or series, but this project is special to me for a lot of reasons, and I'm wary of—"

He holds up a giant man hand. "Sorry to interrupt. It's just— that's not why I asked for a meeting."

I am immediately confused. And maybe a little annoyed with myself for skimming my agent's email. "What?"

"I'm not interested in adapting *Base Paired*." Hot Brit shakes his head. "I'm curious whether you're open to being cast as the lead in an upcoming show."

At this, I frown, concerned. "I'm an author."

"Yes."

"I felt like we were on the same page for a minute." I wave a finger back and forth between us. "But that question took us to different genres."

He laughs, and not only does it seem to come from some sexy depth in his chest, it also reveals a small dimple, low on one cheek.

Tall, British, *and* dimpled? Never trust a cliché.

"We'd like to offer you the role of the central character in an upcoming reality dating show."

I stare blankly at him. "Me?"

"Yes."

"A dating show?"

"Yes."

"One where *I'm* dating?"

"Yes."

"Is this a joke?" I am immediately suspicious. And then it clicks. I went on a couple of dates last year with a community theater director who insisted he had lots of connections in the feature world. Maybe I shouldn't have been so obvious in my disbelief. "Did Steven put you up to this?"

"Steven?"

"I don't remember his last name," I admit. "But picture the hot guitar-playing college heartthrob archetype, then add twenty years to his jawline."

Hot Brit frowns. "I don't— Yeah, no. There's no Steven involved in this."

Oh. Of course. "Billy? He used to work at Paramount." I mime muscles. "Gym rat? Shaves *everything*?"

He shakes his head, bewildered. "It's coming from—"

"*Evan.*" I slap the arm of the leather chair. "Goddammit, of course!" I look at Hot Brit. "He loved a practical joke. I broke up with him because he had a Bart Simpson tattoo low, and I mean *really* low on his hip, and I couldn't go down on him without thinking *Cowabunga, dude.* It was a mood killer."

"I—"

"We got into this big argument at the end, but he still reminded me to turn my clocks back an hour that night for daylight savings." I laugh. "I basically told him his terrible tattoo ruined our sex life, and he was like, *Wow, that's a bummer, but also don't oversleep.*" I turn my attention back to Hot Brit. "So now that I'm thinking about it, he might be too nice to have done this. You can tell me if—"

"It's not coming from any of these men," he says slowly. "I am developing this very real show, and you are the first person I've approached for it."

I am utterly speechless.

"But are—are any of these men your *current* boyfriends?" he asks.

"I'm never sure when to use that term," I admit, rolling past the thin film of disapproval in his voice. "Is a boyfriend someone you have sex with more than once? Can you have a one-night boyfriend? A weekend boyfriend? Or is it necessary to have the boyfriend-girlfriend talk after a specified amount of time spent dating? Regardless, no, none of those men are current boyfriends by any definition."

Hot Brit clears his throat, reaching forward to straighten a book on the coffee table. "Okay."

I watch him, fighting a smile.

"Would you like to hear the show premise?" he asks once he seems to have finished clutching his pearls.

I'm willing to let him run through the entire ruse if he's so well prepared. "Knock yourself out, Colin."

He takes a beat before speaking, and when I look at him, I see flat disappointment in his gaze. I don't know what I did, but I'm delighted anyway. If I could get paid for disappointing white men in suits, I would be a gazillionaire.

Regrouping, he begins, "I've always been fascinated with the idea of arranged marriages—"

"Oh boy."

"—in that most in the modern day are quite successful."

Okay, that is not where I thought he was going with that.

"When we let people who know us well choose our partner, they generally do a pretty good job. But then I also had the thought the other day that most of us have seen so many portrayals of love—in person, on-screen, in literature—that we should be good at identifying real emotion. Don't you think?"

I shrug. "Actually, I'm amazed at the often limited capacity of emotional intelligence in adults."

"What if we put you in a house with twelve men—"

"Well, now I'm definitely listening."

"—who are each trying to win your heart—"

"Keep talking."

"—but instead of you choosing who gets to stay in the competition each week, we'll have the audience live vote over the twenty-four hours after the episode airs on who stays and who goes. The eliminated contestant or contestants will find out at the start of the next episode."

"So you let the audience vote on who they want me to end up with? I have no say?"

He tilts his head from side to side. "Yes and no. The audience will have to gauge your reactions. But I am hoping there will be some great options in there, because here's what I think could make it really interesting: We'll cast the contestants based on your DNADuo compatibility scores. I assume you're familiar with it?"

It feels like my heart stops. That's River's technology. "Oh, I'm familiar."

"Some scores will be low, some will be higher," he says. "But we'll make sure there is at least one Gold Match or better in the cast. The twist is to see who can better find your soulmate: technology or the audience."

I struggle to hide my shock. "You're serious."

Hot Brit nods. "Your books are international bestsellers, Felicity. You have readers in every age and socioeconomic demographic—and your biggest fans are right in the heart of the reality TV audience. This overlap could be very advantageous for your book sales as well as our ratings."

I stare out the window. I was wrong: it isn't satisfying to have him be so forthcoming that the bottom line is why I'm here. He wants me because my brand—happy romance—would play well with audiences. This man would have no way of knowing I'm no longer happily romantic, but given his industry, he'd tell me that doesn't matter as long as I can put on a good show. It all makes me feel even more pessimistic about love.

"I know a lot of these dating shows are manufactured or cynical," he continues, oddly reading my mind, "but I think this could be different. Because it's *you*. I'm drawn to you, and we've only just met; viewers will feel the same. Your readers will *want* you to find love."

This one is like an arrow to the heart. My sweet readers do want me to find love, and it appears to be the one thing I cannot give them. Well, that and a new book.

Hot Brit leans in, green eyes earnest and soft. "I truly believe that women want to watch other women find happiness."

As I blink back over to him, something cools in my blood. "That seems like such a nice thing to say, so why does it sound ironic when you say it?"

He looks taken aback for a second, his expression crashing. "I— No, I truly mean it."

I push to stand. "Thanks for making the time. I'm not interested."

five

CONNOR

Felicity leaves so abruptly the whiplash slaps my thoughts against my cranium and I simply stare after her, mute. I was fifty-fifty on whether a woman as stunning and successful as she is would be into the idea of starring in a reality show, but by no means did I expect the offer to outright piss her off. If I can't even pitch this show without getting it horribly—and mysteriously—wrong, what hope is there that I'll be able to make it a success?

"The fuck just happened?" I ask the empty doorway just a moment before a head pops into view, and my boss flashes a set of bright white veneers at me.

"Got a sec?"

I glance at my watch. "I need to be upstairs with Shazz in five."

Blaine steps in, sliding a hand into a pocket and jiggling some change. "Just got off the line with Bill," he tells me. Bill Masters is the CFO, and one of the few people Blaine is afraid of. "The C-suite really wants to make this dating show happen." He pauses for dramatic effect, half of his mouth lifting in a cocky grin. "They're giving you a million and a half."

"Dollars?"

"No, Connor, hookers. Yes, of course dollars."

The meaning of what he's said finally penetrates. "They're giving me $1.5 million for this, but won't give me $40K for my biodiversity doc?"

He pulls a whistling breath in through his nose, drawing it out, like his patience is a dangerously cracking top layer of ice. "Like I said, kid, we all really want this to happen. By the way, Barb in programming must know where a body is buried because your time slot will be prime time on ABC." And then he amends, "Saturdays."

There is literally nothing prime time about a Saturday night time slot.

Reading my expression, Blaine says, "Listen, with this timeline we're lucky we didn't land on Friday. There was some scuffle with their new procedural, and we got to them before they filled the slot. Now give me some good news. I heard you were meeting with a possible lead?"

"I was," I say, lifting my chin to indicate that she's gone. "She wasn't interested."

"Not enough money?" He's incredulous. To Blaine, that would be the only logical reason someone would turn this down. "Some people are too dumb to see an opportunity when it's right in front of them."

"We didn't even make it to the money part. Wasn't the right fit, I guess." The reality that she's blown me off is settling in and I'm more disappointed than I would have expected. For a minute, while she was sitting across from me, I couldn't believe the wild kismet that the woman I spotted at the bar last week would end up in my office. And, of course, I realized how nice it would be to be able to work with a sexy, successful romance author for once rather than a group of sun-ravaged, disheartened scientists.

"It's your job to find the right fit," he says sharply.

"I was hoping to find someone uniquely beloved by the demographic," I explain, trying to redirect away from his irritation and toward something productive, "but maybe I was thinking too far outside the box. I might have to go a different route."

"Just go the regular route: legs, boobs, lips."

Ah, Blaine. A generation of walking lawsuits. I clear my throat in response.

"Female shaped and willing." He doubles down. "That's all we need. Keep me updated." Blaine raps a knuckle on my desk. "I gotta jet."

And just as quickly as he appeared, he's gone.

"This fucking day," I say to the empty doorway, and only a split second later, another head pops into view, scaring the shit out of me. "Jesus Christ."

My producing colleague Trent Choi extends an arm, showing me his watch. "We have that meeting with Shazz in three."

Poor Trent. He is without question the only person who gets to meetings on time around here. "Right," I say. "Was just chatting with Blaine."

"Oh?" He quickly glances back over his shoulder. "Do you have a second?"

"Course."

Stepping in, Trent closes my door until only a small slice of hallway is visible. "I'm starting to freak out that if *Smash Course* doesn't work, I won't have a job."

I grimace at him in commiseration. "What did Blaine say?"

"That if this show doesn't work, I'm out of a job."

"Seems like you've got a good read on the situation." He winces and I try to soften it. "If it makes you feel better, I'm in the same boat. He's got me doing a dating show."

"At least those are successful. Who even watches extreme sports challenges?"

"Literally everyone, Trent." This poor, bookish wanker.

"I'm going to be on the road for six weeks," he complains. "Six weeks on a bus with sweaty, testosterone-fueled weekend warriors who want to kill each other, and then I have to come back and edit the footage to make it look like a good time."

"Sorry, mate." I gently slap his shoulder. I do get his angst. These shows certainly get attention, but I don't know if it's the kind of attention we're prepared to take on. If my dating show sucks, I'm fucked. And if it doesn't suck, I'm not sure how smoothly I can pivot back to the kind of programming I care about. I guess there's some consolation that I'm not the only person stuck bottom feeding.

"I'm sure it will be fine. One thing at a time, eh? Right now I've got to find someone"—I hold up air quotes—"'female shaped and willing' and just get through this."

six

FIZZY

There's always a risk of misinterpreting something when hearing the tail end of a conversation, but in this case, there's no room for a mistake.

. . . find someone female shaped and willing, and just get through this.

I'd returned for a parking validation, but I immediately forget again as three simultaneous explosions take place inside my skull. The first is over the wording, which is so terrible that Hot Brit immediately stops being a hero in any form and is now only a villain over whom I must triumph. The second realization is that he's going to make this show no matter what I do. He will use River's app to spread this garbage, and he will happily paint the central woman as desperate to find her soulmate like she isn't completely fine all on her own, because reality television executives have not updated their view of women in forty years.

The third explosion is the most powerful. For as much as I now dislike this man, I cannot ignore that he's offered to hand me the mic. How many times have I idly wondered why, if men want to know what women want, they don't just—oh, I don't know—*ask women directly*? Hot Brit has given me the chance to ensure this show isn't a disaster for every woman who hits Play on episode one. I can choose the vocabulary and the format and the discussion around what it means to date and fall in love.

I walk right up to the producer's door, push it the rest of the way open, and witness his expression morph from irritation to horror as he registers that I've just heard him.

"How badly do you want me for this?" I ask bluntly.

He swallows, glancing to the other man in the room, who seems to want to be absorbed into the wall. Hot Brit considers his words carefully. "I suspect you are the only person who could make this project worthwhile."

I can't tell if that's ignorant or thoughtful. "It occurred to me in the elevator that perhaps my answer was too hasty."

He stares at me, not understanding.

"I'll do this show, but only on my terms."

"Terms?" he repeats. "Such as?"

I work to not break eye contact. I . . . have no idea what my terms are. "I'll send my ideas to you through my agent. If you want me for this, you'll agree to incorporate what she sends over."

He wears silence easily, doesn't rush to speak, and I begrudgingly acknowledge that I respect this about him because it's something I've never mastered.

"Can I trust that you'll choose these terms in good faith?" he asks at last. "You'll keep the audience in mind?"

Holy shit, this condescension. "Literally the *only* thing I care about is this audience." The edge to my voice is so sharp it could draw blood. "I don't think you have the same priority. Other than some of them being 'female shaped'—whatever the fuck that means—I don't think you even know who this audience is."

"Felicity, what you heard—"

I hold up a hand. I don't need to hear his excuse; I'm not doing this for him anyway. "It's a yes or a no, Corey. Your call."

He blinks away, giving me a view of the defined jawline, the long neck. Finally, he turns back to me. "Yes, then."

I reach out for him to shake on it. "Good." With understandable hesitation, he reaches out and wraps his hand around mine, giving me a very perfunctory British handshake.

Shifting my purse on my shoulder, I turn to leave, but he speaks again. "One more thing, if I might."

I turn back around.

"My name is Connor." He doesn't smile this time when our eyes meet. "Not Ted, or Colin, or Corey. Connor."

This jerk has just passed me the baton. He doesn't have any fucking clue what he's agreed to. I'll call the poor guy anything he wants.

After all, his name is the least of my concerns. Because now I must figure out what my terms actually are, how I'm going to make time for this reality TV circus when I'm already three months late on my manuscript deadline, and how on earth I'll reconcile the way his solid, warm grip and steady, attentive gaze didn't feel at all like those of a villain.

seven

CONNOR

A ny news on scheduling?" Natalia asks from the kitchen. "We've put a deposit down on that cabin in Yellowstone, but I don't want to take Stevie if you're going to have a window of free time then."

Next to me, dressed in her new Wonderland tee and crowned with a pink tiara, the child in question searches through dozens of tiny grayish-taupe puzzle pieces, intent on finding the corners of an elephant's ear and the tip of a lion's tail in our African Wild After the Rains jigsaw puzzle. I wonder about the chances that an elephant and a grown lion would stand this close to each other, but it seems a minor quibble.

"Unfortunately, no," I say. It's already June; our holidays would normally be parsed out and set in stone by now, but with my filming schedule still up in the air, summer plans are as well. "And I'm sorry, Nat, I know it's a pain. I've been going back and forth with Felicity's agents for weeks. Just make your plans and I'll work around them."

Nat crosses the room and sets down lunch for each of us before taking a seat on the floor across from me. Normally my daughter and I would be at my place for the weekend, but Stevie's social circle seems to be ever expanding, with a birthday party tonight and another in the morning. Co-parenting means compromise, and I'm happy to hang out here if it means time together.

The food doesn't hurt, either. It smells amazing; for the two years Nat and I were married I was deeply spoiled by her cooking. When we split, I had to get my shit together—I couldn't feed my toddler ramen and Happy Meals every weekend. Now I appreciate nothing more than food I don't have to prepare myself.

"How's everything going with her?" she asks, pulling my attention up from the steaming bowl of pozole.

I haven't shared much with Nat because there isn't much to tell. Felicity has been communicating with me through her intermediaries—attorney and agents. She has me by the balls and knows it.

I swallow a too-hot bite, wincing. "She's tentatively accepted."

"What are the conditions?"

"Her agent is supposed to be sending them over."

"You sound thrilled."

I wipe my mouth with a napkin. "Let me ask you something. Weeks ago, I asked her to do this thing. I offered—she could have turned it down but didn't. Isn't it weird that she still seems to be . . . sort of . . . questioning my commitment a bit?"

With a little laugh, Nat takes a bite and pokes at her bowl with a spoon. "I don't know that much about her in real life—I mean, she shows us what she wants us to see. She seems playful and funny and adventurous, but a reality show doesn't seem like something she'd do. There must be a reason she's considering it, and if she called you out for seeming less than enthusiastic, you'd better get your attitude squared away." Natalia looks at me straight on. "You're a wonderful guy, Conn, but you've been acting a little snobby, like this is beneath you."

I turn back to the puzzle. "How is it snobby if it's accurate? I would never do this if Blaine wasn't forcing me to."

I know it's a mistake as soon as the last word is out of my mouth. Even Stevie pushes a somber whistle through her teeth.

Natalia stares at me. "Connor, do you think I'm dumb?"

"What?" I say, horrified. "Of course not. You're the smartest person I know."

"Well, *I* watch reality TV. I read romance. And when you say stuff like that, it's belittling." She tilts her head toward Stevie, and the unspoken *Especially when you do it in front of our daughter* lands like a mallet.

"I just meant that it's not *my* bag. Of course it's cool if it's yours."

Her eyes go round. "Wow. Thank you."

"That is not at all—"

She waves this off. "Have you watched any dating shows or read any of her books since you agreed to take this project on?"

"I ordered them."

She looks unimpressed.

"*And,*" I continue proudly, "I had Brenna do write-ups on Felicity's five top sellers."

Stevie shakes her head again. Natalia gives me a disappointed frown.

"Okay, I hear how that sounded," I say. "I'm the arsehole executive pawning my work off onto my assistant, that was shitty. But, Nat, the show isn't even about Felicity's books. It's about *her*. About how charismatic she is, how good she is in front of people. It's about the audience rooting for her."

"Are you really so thick not to see that her audience roots for her *because* of what she gives us in her books?"

Before I can answer, she continues. "If you told me you didn't like Wonderland's music, I'd say, 'Fine, to each their own.' You've heard all their songs at least a hundred times, so you would be making an informed opinion. But you've never even read a romance novel or watched a reality show and have formed this opinion based on what you *think* they are."

I slip another piece into place, bridging a large elephant ear to its head. "C'mon, Nat, you've got to admit romance novels are a touch predictable."

"Why? Because the couple ends up together?"

"Exactly."

"That's a rule of the genre, Connor," she says. "Which you would know if you'd bothered to even google it."

I wave her on, hearing the way she's frothing up over this. "Go on. Get it all out."

"You describe them as my 'guilty pleasure.' Do you have any idea how condescending that is?"

"Well, don't they bring you pleasure?" I ask, confused. "How is that condescending?"

"Yes, but why should I feel guilty for reading something that makes me happy?"

I open my mouth to respond, and she pins me with a look so clear in its meaning it might as well be a warning shot fired over-head.

"You treat the things I love as if they're silly or something to be indulged," she says. "My point, Conn, is this: You asked me if it was weird that she's questioning your attitude. But if I see your condescension—and I'm someone who knows what a good man you are in a million other ways—what do you think she saw, when she doesn't know you at all and her entire career is centered around something you believe is beneath you?"

I close my eyes as this one settles in. I worked on a project once where an expert said intolerance is a failure of curiosity, and it's always stuck with me. Am I being quick to judge things I know next to nothing about? "Okay. Yeah."

"Read one of her books." Nat picks up her spoon again. "Keep an open mind and you might even like it."

I know that she's right, and I'm about to tell her so when my phone buzzes on the table with an incoming email. I open it, and immediately my brain locks up. "What the fuck?"

"Dad." Stevie glares at me.

"Sorry, but—" I gesture to the phone. "It's the list of Felicity's conditions." I do a quick scan of the text. "She wants to keep shooting to four days a week." I look up. "I thought it was standard to keep people sequestered or something on these shows. To keep the results hidden."

"They are on *The Bachelor*," Stevie offers.

Nat reaches to adjust Stevie's tiara. "It's almost like knowing how these shows work would make his job easier."

Stevie giggles.

"Okay, you," I say, and continue scrolling through the email. Looking at all this I immediately know it'd be easier to cast someone who's only concerned with fame and exposure. But if I'm stuck doing this, I'd rather do it with someone who has something to say.

I realize I expected her terms to read like a rider—requests for time away from the cameras, a list of dietary demands, marketing money, or specific stylists, as much promo of her books as possible—but there's none of that. Her list of conditions reads strangely like a dare. "She's given me a very specific casting list." I look up at Nat. "What the hell does 'cinnamon roll' have to do with casting?"

"Oh," Natalia says with quiet thrill. "*Oh*, Fizzy Chen, you are my goddamn *hero*."

"*Mom*. Language."

I frown down at my phone. "Himbo? Is that a typo?"

Nat doubles over, absolutely howling in laughter.

"And it's going to take forever to get clarification. I'm supposed to go through her ag—" I break off when I reach the end of the scanned PDF and spot a handwritten note from Felicity near the bottom:

Text me if you have questions. Good luck! I suspect you'll need it.

eight

FIZZY

Honestly," Jess says across the table from me at Twiggs, "if I was this nose-deep into something on my phone, you'd tell me to share the porn or put it away."

In ye olden times, it was our routine to meet up at Twiggs coffee shop a few days a week to work. I would write like a madwoman and Jess would do numbersy things. We were (usually) very productive. These days our work sessions are more ceremonial: Jess is taking the summer off, and I'd be more likely to grow a third ear than write a compelling kissing scene. But even though the vibe is more casual than business, Jess's words are my cue to slide my device into my purse and return to bestie time. Sadly, even if Oscar Isaac were standing tableside naked, I'm not sure I could look up from this text exchange. It's like watching Connor Prince III's slow spiral into insanity.

Darcy? he texts. I don't even know what that means.

I smother a laugh with a hand, typing, Think taciturn.

"Felicity."

Shaking my head, I tell Jess, "I don't think you want to know what I'm doing." My phone vibrates again.

"Phone sex?"

"Better."

What's a hot nerd?

Do you really need me to explain that one to you?

Fine. Silver fox?

Daddy kink.

Vampire?

A laugh rips out of me and a few of the other regulars toss a dirty look my way. I'd forgotten that gem. But this time I've come so close to spraying a mouthful of coffee across the table at Jess that she finally tries to reach for my phone and I have to dodge her grasping fingers to finish typing my reply.

Be creative.

Gingerly, I put my phone down. "Hello, friend."

"Are we not even pretending to work today?"

I look at the chair to my right where I set all my things when I came in a half hour ago. I haven't even bothered to unpack my laptop. No wonder I can't get anything done. Grinning at her, I say, "I promise this is work related."

"Uh-huh."

Jess knows I've been avoiding social media and work emails like the plague, so she's understandably skeptical. I elaborate: "My terms for the show landed in Hot Brit's inbox this afternoon, and he's got some questions."

Jess frowns. "What did you do?"

"What do you mean what did I do? Why am I immediately the bad guy?"

"Let's see," Jess says, cupping her hands around her flat white and leaning closer. "There was the time you talked me into going to the nude beach for your birthday before realizing we were walking around naked on private property."

"Blame GPS, not me."

"You handcuffed me to the bed for research and then realized the key was back at your house."

"You were only alone for, like, a half hour, and I made sure you had plenty of water!"

"Okay, how about when you set me up with the guy who was out on parole?"

"For tax fraud! It's not like he killed anybody."

"Really, Fizzy?"

"Well, it sounds bad when you say it all together!"

She waits patiently.

Finally, I nod because: *fair.* "I'm just trying to make a good show here." The skepticism deepens and I remind her, "You didn't want to hear about the TV show because you didn't want information you'd have to keep from River." Who, predictably, flipped out when I mentioned over burgers a couple of weeks ago that I'd been approached to star in a reality dating show based on his very serious scientific research. There was some intense staring down at his plate followed by some agitated pacing. I'd assured him that there was no way North Star Media would ever agree to my terms once they saw them, and River had been slightly mollified. But he'd also requested to hear no more about it.

Which means I can't tell Jess anything, either, or she'll internally combust over having to keep anything from her husband. And which is why she's pretending to be uninterested.

The thing is, if you *ask* Jessica Marie Davis Peña what her favorite TV show of all time is, she'll say *Breaking Bad* or *Downton Abbey*, because those are socially appropriate answers. No one says their favorite show is *Married at First Sight*, just like nobody says their favorite restaurant is McDonald's. But *somebody's* buying those 550 million Big Macs a year. Jess eats those shows up, feeling smugly entertained with a globe of red wine in her hand on her giant sectional in the living room. No matter what River wants to happen, Jess is intrigued by this. Dare I say she is secretly thrilled.

Which means I can count down to the moment when she breaks.

In three . . . two . . .

"I'm almost afraid to ask what your terms are," she says, tapping a casual finger on the side of her laptop. "Knowing you, they're insane."

I lift my drink to my lips and realize it's gone lukewarm. "Is this you asking?"

She adjusts her computer glasses. "No."

"Okay."

I glance down at my phone to find a new string of texts.

> You want at least 2 of the heroes to have experience knitting?

> I don't understand the exclusion term re: poets.

> Felicity, my understanding was that you would enter this negotiation in good faith.

> Are you free to talk?

I giggle, typing as gleefully as if I'm sexting.

> Sorry. I'm slammed at the moment.

> When is a good time?

> That depends. Are you in or are you giving up?

A plastic clatter echoes across the table as Jess tosses down her glasses in defeat. "Just tell me everything."

"But it's about the dating show. River might not like it."

"He can cry into his giant bags of money."

"You're right," I say in a burst. "Well, in case you didn't realize this already: I am a genius."

"And so admirably grounded."

"Listen," I tell her. "The more I get into this idea, the more I like it. The Hot Brit executive wanted me to do a dating show, right? Put me and twelve dudes in a house, roll me out in a push-up bra, and let the audience decide each week who should be eliminated."

"Right," Jess says, nodding.

"The gimmicky piece is, of course, that they'd use the DNADuo to find a range of matches for me," I say.

She leans back in her chair, crossing her arms. "Three weeks ago, you didn't even want to date one man. Now you're going to live with twelve?"

"Twelve prime-of-their-life dongs just walking around looking for a Fizzy to hide in? I am only human, Jess. How do I say no to that?"

She shakes her head at me over the top of her coffee cup. "Do you hear the things you say? Like, at all?"

I ignore this. "Real talk here: Twelve might be too many. Even for me." I pause. "I can't believe I'm saying that. But I am. So, I'm going to suggest cutting it to eight. I also don't like the idea of being totally sequestered in a house with these guys for the duration of the shoot, so I told Hot Brit I'd give him four days a week to shoot, and during those days the Heroes and I will just . . . date. Each week audiences will eliminate a couple of them, and I'll go on new, more elaborate dates with the ones who remain. We'll get to know each other the way we would in real life, with the rest of life happening around us."

Jess frowns. "Will they go for that? Isn't the point of these shows for it to be this intense, forced-proximity experience, and if you're let back to your real lives you might talk to your families about the show and get tips and feedback?"

"Yes, but that's how dating works! If I went out with one of them in the real world, we'd go home after and talk to our people about how it went. Especially if it went well, we'd want to talk it out and include our community in the excitement. I'm tired of these portrayals of romance in a vacuum, making people think once you find that special person, you don't need anything else. That isn't a healthy take on love! I want to date the guy who has the support of his family and friends the entire time, not the one who tells his loved ones they have to accept this new person they know nothing about who he swears he's in love with after three weeks. Haven't these people ever read a romance novel? A supportive community is, like, half of the happily ever after!"

"Oh my God, Fizzy, take a breath."

I pause and take a calming sip of my tepid vanilla latte. "But that—the dating structure is easy. Do you want to hear the best part?"

"No, of course not. Boring details only, please."

"I sent over a list of romance hero archetypes that Hot Brit has to cast if he wants me."

Her expression flattens. "I'm sorry, what?"

"I sent him a list of twenty archetypes—hot nerd, professor, rock star, Navy SEAL, et cetera. He'll cast eight Heroes that fit those categories." Off her dubious look, I add, "It's not that hard."

Jess waves her fingers for me to hand it over. "Let me see the list."

I pull it up on my phone and pass it across the table. Jessica's blue eyes scan the screen, widen, and then she starts again from the top, reading some of them aloud. "A prince?"

"Or royalty more generally," I say, casually examining a fingernail. "I'm not fussy."

A pause, then she snorts. "Scottish rogue. Fizzy, my God."

"Keep going."

"The One That Got Away?" She laughs. "Talk about casting a wide net. You sure you want that?"

"Frankly, I didn't want any of it, but if they managed to pull this together it would be amazing. I can't write a damn word lately, which means the 'Coming Soon' page of my website is getting about as many visitors as my vagina. But if I can reach a romance audience with this, it would make my readers—and Amaya—happy." My literary agent, Amaya Ellis, is a badass worth more than her weight in gold and absolutely does not deserve the headache I have been for the last year.

"Amaya thinks this is a good idea?" Jess asks, skeptical.

"I don't know if I'd go that far, but both she and my film agent think it could be great exposure. And since I have literally *nothing* else going on, I was 'strongly encouraged to consider it.' She also reminded me that the whole reason I did the DNADuo in the first place was for research and I should go into it with that mindset."

She briefly looks up. "And, you know, the whole possible soulmate thing . . ."

"Yeah, yeah, sure," I say, watching her absorb the list and work to keep her shit together. "So, what do you think? I put some real thought into it."

"That much is clear." Her gaze snags. "Vampire? You expect them to cast a vampire?"

"Hot Brit tripped on that one, too. How they do it isn't my problem, is it?"

Her eyebrow points skyward and she looks over the top of my phone at me. "Dom?"

"Gotta respect the genre."

She reads some more, smothering her smile with a hand. "Twenty percent or more need to have gone to therapy, thirty percent are required to have a female friend they have never had sex with? Fizzy, you're such a troll." She shrieks briefly: "No poets."

"This might be the greatest idea I've ever had. Unfortunately, it's never going to happen."

She tilts her head side to side, a *maybe, maybe not* gesture. "What do you do if he agrees to your terms?"

I wave this off. "I won't get my hopes up. And even if he did, I'd really have to wrangle my shit into order and bring my A game." That truth sinks in. I hadn't actually imagined a situation where Hot Brit would agree to these preposterous terms. There's been safety in my outlandish demands; literally any other woman on planet Earth would make this show easier than what I've just requested. To think, even briefly, that I might end up doing this makes my stomach clench. I'd have to be funny, and engaging, and—shit—convincingly fake being open to love.

"There's absolutely no way he wants me bad enough to say yes to all of this."

"I'd tend to agree with you." Jess hands me back my phone, nodding to the screen where a text has landed from my new contact labeled British McHotpants. "Except I think he just did."

nine

CONNOR

The next time Felicity Chen walks into my office, she shows up ready to play. Instead of ripped jeans and boots, she's wearing a black tailored suit and an expression that leaves no doubt she's planning to oversee everything from this point forward. She politely passes on Brenna's offer of coffee and crosses the room to where I'm standing in front of my desk to greet her.

"Felicity, it's good to see you."

She gives me a handshake alongside her wide smile. Amazingly, she makes the ballbuster aesthetic look like a good time. "Call me Fizzy. No one calls me Felicity, except the guy at the DMV."

I laugh. "Fizzy it is."

Instead of sitting at a chair at my desk, she settles down onto one of the small leather sofas framing the coffee table. I remember reading once that confident people use furniture wrong. They sit sideways, they loop an arm over the back of an adjacent chair or sit on the edge of a desk. Fizzy isn't doing any of those things, but she's still a portrait of confidence. Her posture is relaxed, one leg crossed over the other, hands casually crossed at the wrist, one index finger and thumb tapping as if she's counting down to something. Her shoes are bright blue suede with heels at least four inches tall. It takes more effort than I'm comfortable with not to let my eyes linger on the tiny glimpse of her exposed ankle.

"How are you?" I ask, dragging my eyes away.

"I'm great."

I sit down across from her, working to look as casually confident as she is. Normally, I am. Normally, I'm hard to fluster. But the duality of the intensity of her demeanor and ease in her body is distracting.

"Thanks for taking my meeting," she says. Her hair is up in a bun; a few tendrils have come loose, and they fall softly against her long, delicate neck. She wears minimal makeup, I guess, but her lips are this perfect, soft red. However much of a shit show this program will end up being, this woman is going to be beautiful on-screen.

"Absolutely." I swallow, trying to get my voice to sound less strained. "We still have a lot to hammer out." An understatement. The requests her agent sent over read like a foreign language, but Nat told me to trust her so here we are. I feel like I'm stepping into a dark, foggy alley with nothing but a rolled-up newspaper to defend me against surprise knife attacks. This will be either an inconvenient but brief project that gets me what I want from Blaine, or the worst mistake of my professional career. "But before we get too deep in the details," I say, "I wanted to ask if you have any experience with the DNADuo. Past user profiles are obviously confidential, but our legal department needs to know if we have any previous Gold Matches we should filter or add to the list for The One That Got Away."

"I'm familiar with the app," she says, smoothing a hand down her thigh to straighten a soft wrinkle there. "And, uh, I stopped checking my matches before I ever saw any Gold ones."

"Okay." I jot down the note, sensing there's more beneath the surface there, but she doesn't elaborate. Closing my notebook, I meet her eyes across the table. "Well, if you think of anything that seems worth discussing, let me know. We don't need to know your dating history, but also don't want to put you in an awkward position with someone you've met and didn't like."

"Thank you." She keeps nodding but doesn't take her eyes off my face.

Needing something to do under her scrutiny, I sit forward in my seat, reaching to pour us each a glass of water from a pitcher on the coffee table. "Is there something you wanted to discuss?" I ask.

"I can't quite figure you out."

"What would you like to know?"

"What's your background?" She runs a thoughtful finger beneath her full lip. "North Star's website doesn't go very deep. Google doesn't tell me much about you. All I know is you usually make documentaries and grew up a young pirate in Northern England."

I laugh at the callback to our first meeting. "Blackpool. That's right. Had to quit the looting-and-pillaging industry at fifteen, when my American father brought me to the States."

"Fifteen." She winces. "That's rough."

It was, but no reason to linger. "I went to USC for film and ended up here. And yes, until recently I've worked on documentaries. Coastal climate change, marine animals, you know."

"USC for film but ended up in San Diego at a small production company," she says. "Either you aren't very good at your job, or you have a personal reason for being here. It seems like an important distinction if I'm your newest collaborator."

I smile, not rising to the bait. "I had a very good job at Sony, in LA. I moved here because my ex-wife got a job and I wanted to be close to our daughter."

Her expression falters—softening—before she reaches for her water. "Why did you agree to take on this show? Coastal climate change to a reality dating show? Not really a natural transition."

"It was assigned to me."

"So, you're being forced."

I go for honesty. We barely know each other, but I can already sense I don't want to be caught lying to this woman. "It wouldn't have been my first choice, no."

"Are you at all excited about it?"

I reach for my water, taking a sip as I formulate an answer that is both honest and encouraging. "I'll say this much: I'm truly glad you came on board."

This makes her grin widely, brightly. "I know you are. You said yes to all my ridiculous requests."

"If you thought they were ridiculous," I say, setting my glass down, "why did you make them?"

"Because they're hilarious. They'll make the show different. Fun. We could all use a little more fun." I can't disagree there. "You said at our first meeting that one of the reasons you've brought me on is because our audiences intersect almost entirely. Tell me a little about this audience."

"About eighty percent of the people watching dating shows identify as female ages eighteen to fifty-five, but about half of them are over forty-five. This is similar to the readership of romance novels. A third of all fiction sales are romance, and about forty percent of that market is women over forty-five, meaning a whopping twelve percent of all pure fiction sales are women over forty-five reading romance." I pause, wondering what else she wants me to say. "It hasn't been my demographic, historically, but I'm trying to learn."

Fizzy's gaze has an intensity I've seen in some of the most powerful executives in Hollywood. "What does that mean?"

She isn't being harsh, but I still don't like being put on the defensive, don't like how carefully I need to tread here because she hasn't officially signed the contract yet and I need this before I let her leave today. After going over Fizzy's ideas, Blaine gave me two months of preproduction, with five weeks of filming, the finished episodes airing at the end of each week. That means crash editing every week. I've never made something with this kind of editorial pressure before. We've already spent so much time waiting for her terms and running everything through our legal department. I can't start over again.

"It means I'm learning this the way I learn about any new audience," I tell her. "Market research. In this case, studying what other things that audience does in their free time."

She stifles a smirk and I lean back in my chair, inhaling deeply, getting my bearings. "Ask what you really want to ask me, Fizzy."

"I don't want to sign up to do this if your only research here is reading Nielsen reports. The documentaries you've made help convince me that your heart is in the right place, but why you? Why this? Why you *for* this?"

"It seems the company is taking a new direction." I shrug, choosing transparency: "We're small. There are only a few of us. That's probably why me."

"Have you read anything I've written, or did you ask me because your ex-wife had some of my books on her shelf?"

"I'm finishing *Base Paired* right now. It's funny, sexy, creative, and . . ." I trail off, searching for the word that eludes me. I began reading per Nat's instructions, looking for what it is about romance she loves so much, trying to find that kernel that has built such a huge following for Fizzy. *If I can understand it,* I think, *I'll be able to unlock what we need to make this show a success.*

"And?" Fizzy prompts sardonically, like she's expecting an insult to wrap up my list.

"Joyful." It comes out in a burst. "There's a lot of joy in your writing."

I can see I've hit something important. She leans forward, happier now. "Yes. Now we're getting somewhere. Romance *is* joyful. What brings *you* joy?"

"My daughter. My work, historically speaking." I dig around for something that makes me sound more dimensional, but sitting here with this bestselling author talking about joy and connection makes my life feel like a lather, rinse, repeat of arid routine. "Watching footie. Mountain biking. Exercise."

As I speak, I see her point: none of this really qualifies me to speak specifically to this audience. It's true that, other than my time with Stevie, nothing in my life brings me outright joy anymore. Most of it, I realize, is a way to pass time when I'm alone, and none of it is about seeking connection.

I think about the chapter in her book I read last night. It was a love scene where, afterward, the heroine admitted that she was afraid of how fast things were moving. It wasn't that this type of conflict felt groundbreaking, but the way it was written with such vulnerability and self-awareness after the most scorching sex scene I'd ever read left me feeling pensive all night. Fizzy is the playful, wisecracking alter ego, but I'm beginning to see that Felicity Chen is smart—brilliant, clearly—and I must give her more than just a confident smile and measured responses. She reads people expertly, and right now she needs to be convinced she won't be stuck with a two-dimensional Hollywood stereotype.

"I sound like a boring git." I laugh. "There's something about reading your book that has made me hyperaware of the sterile banality of my current life. I am," I admit, sifting through words because I rarely get personal with relative strangers, and never with colleagues, "a bit of a workaholic. But I am not an egomaniac. I brought you on because I know you are connected—literally and figuratively—to this audience. I want this to be a success."

"I want that, too." Fizzy's posture eases and she leans back. "Listen, Hot DILF. I need to confess something. I'm good friends with someone involved in the DNADuo technology. He's not thrilled about this show happening, but because of the way the deal was structured, he doesn't get a veto on media use."

"Will that be a problem?" I ask, ignoring for the time being that I think she's just called me a Hot DILF, or the fact that I wouldn't have understood that phrase a few weeks ago.

"No. But this show needs to be smart. It needs to be delightful. It needs to be irreverent. It needs to be sexy, and real, and relatable."

"I agree."

An edge of vulnerability appears in her next words: "The problem is, even though I've just interrogated *you*, I must admit I am a little worried about whether I'm even the right person to do this."

Oh.

The power in her posture, the shine in her eyes—both of those things have dimmed without me noticing. I sort through the words in my head. "I completely understand that you'd want to do right by this technology, given your personal connection to it, and I wouldn't expect you to do all the heavy lifting here. But even knowing you just the tiny bit that I do, I know you will absolutely delight the viewers. You have a magical quality that is rare, Fizzy. I'm sure you know that—it translates in your writing, and it translates in person, too."

"Well, thank you. But no." She reaches up, pressing the heels of her hands to her eyes. "I used to be fun. I used to have a million ideas. I used to be spontaneous and playful and sexy and inspired. I haven't felt any of those things in ages."

My pulse slows and then rocket-launches up my throat. "So— what are you saying?"

Did I really go through all of this for her to back out now?

"Joy," she says behind her hands, and then drops them onto her lap.

"What?"

Fizzy takes a deep breath, and then exhales slowly. "I'll sign the contract on your desk under one condition."

"What's that?"

"In the two months we have before this show starts filming, you and I get out of this office, away from our keyboards, and rediscover joy."

ten

FIZZY

So much for joy. I tug off a black-and-gray-striped sweater and hurl it with just a touch of rage onto the mountain of clothes forming on my bed.

"I must be insane." I'm headed to my first book signing in months. I'm not feeling myself, I'm worried my mojo has permanently abandoned ship, I'm going to have to face my readers and be as perky and excited about the next (still nonexistent) book as I can be, and in a moment of weakness, I invited Hot Brit DILF along on some impulsive quest to find our joy. Like we're buddies.

"*God.* Tell me why I told this television executive to come pick me up for my signing tonight instead of just driving myself."

In my bedroom doorway, my little sister shoves another handful of chips into her mouth and crunches loudly through them before answering. "Because you seek out power struggles with men to avoid being vulnerable?"

"Wow, drag me, Alice." I reach for a sheer-sleeved black dress in my closet.

"Am I wrong?"

My answer comes out muffled as I wrestle my way into the dress. "No."

"Also, Amaya called again while you were in the shower."

Grimacing, I brace myself. "Did you pick up?"

"No way. I don't want to get yelled at."

I duck back into my closet to dig for shoes. "She's cool with me doing the show, and we got an extension on the manuscript, but I need to give her some more concrete timelines and I just don't have them figured out."

"You're really going through with this reality show?" Alice asks, badly feigning a totally chill vibe. My pregnant, overachieving sister had been told to cut back on work and take it easy, and is already painfully bored. This explains why she's following me around my house instead of relaxing with her feet up in her own. I suspect she cares less about this dating show being successful than she does about it being the greatest rubbernecking opportunity of her lifetime.

"I signed the contract, so yeah."

"Do Mom and Dad know abou—"

I emerge in time to cut her off. "No, and let me tell them."

My gut immediately clenches at the thought of that conversation. Thirty-seven years old and I still stress about disappointing my parents. They emigrated from Hong Kong in the early eighties and have obviously lived here long enough to have grown comfortable with many Western ideals. But given how my mother still considers my romance novels to be training wheels for the literary masterpiece she's sure is yet to come, I can't really imagine how she'll react to the news that I'll soon be dating eight men on reality television. Pointing to the bed, I remind Alice, "You promised to relax."

She finds an empty sliver of mattress and settles down. "Isn't Dad going tonight?"

I pause, struggling to find the zipper pull and realizing that's why I haven't worn this dress in so long. "Oh, good point."

"So get this producer guy to tell Dad," she says, "and let Dad tell Mom."

None of us would have predicted that the man whose sex-ed talk with his teenage daughters consisted of him finding us while we were doing dishes one night, putting a hand on each of our shoulders, and awkwardly muttering, "Your virginity is sacred," would one day be the very proud father of a steamy romance author. He retired two years ago and—much like Alice and her doctor's orders to slow down—was immediately bored out of his mind. A former workaholic, instead of putting in seventy hours at his lab at Scripps every week, Dad now spends his weeks reading three books, walking a cumulative thirty miles, helping my baby brother, Peter, restore his vintage Karmann Ghia, playing chess with friends, and keeping his garden meticulous. Not to mention bringing Alice whatever pregnancy concoction Mom finds at the market and dropping off meals for any of his three children that his wife tells him to deliver when she's on a cooking spree.

My dad is also a beloved fixture at almost every signing I've had in the Southwest. Readers love taking pictures with him and getting him to sign their copies of my books, too. Some photos of him cheekily pretending to read *The Pirate's Darkest Wish* or *Dirty Deeds on the High Seas* have gone viral online.

So Alice's idea is smart: introduce Dad to Hot Brit, let the Brit do his flashy sales pitch, and let Dad take the information home to Mom. Boom, genius.

"Tell me about this guy," Alice says, watching me fiddle with the broken zipper. "What's he like?"

"Tall." I think of some other adjectives. "Uh. Dark hair. Well dressed."

"I mean is he *nice*?" she asks, laughing.

"I guess?"

"Is he excited for the show?"

"Not overtly."

"How long will you be filming?" she asks.

"Five or six weeks, and then I pick who I want to take on some flashy trip at the end."

"Oh my God, what about Peter's wedding? Can you still go?"

Our baby brother is getting married in a matter of weeks, and it promises to be an opulent circus with the most ridiculous menu I've ever laid eyes on. Brother or no, I wouldn't miss those eight courses for anything.

"I'll be there, ah mui. This won't interfere with any of that."

I stand in front of the mirror, surveying. The dress is fine—it does great things for my boobs and is super comfy. But the problem isn't really the clothes. It's knowing this is my first public event in six months, that I have to face my readers and smile and pretend like everything is fine and the next book release is right around the corner, that the producer dude will be there watching, and that it was my idea for him to come pick me up.

It's weird that I did that. He'll be coming over. Will I invite him in? I don't need to, right? It's been ages since anyone other than Jess, Juno, or my family stepped foot in my house.

"Mui mui, does my place look like the home of someone who lets their cat casually stroll around on kitchen countertops?"

Alice sits up. "Did you get a cat?"

"I mean the overall vibe."

"Um. No?" Alice returns to the plush array of pillows and digs back into the chips. "But can we talk about this show? What *is* it?"

"It's me going on dates with some guys they've screened for DNADuo compatibility, and the audience gets to vote on who they think I'm most compatible with— Will you stop eating chips in my bed?"

She ignores me and angles a few more into her mouth, speaking around them. "Why do you need to go on a dating show, though?"

"I don't *need* to. I—" I break off, unclear how to best explain to the most competent woman I know that I'm stuck in my writing, stuck in my dating, how the only thing I'm sure about is that I love my readers, my family, and my friends, and doing this show takes care of two of those things. I am the floppy wind sock in a family of sturdy street signs.

My sister and her adorable belly follow me into the kitchen, where I've just pulled open my nightmare of a junk drawer to find a safety pin for the broken zipper pull. I spot the shiny foil corner of a sealed condom and pull it out from beneath an avalanche of paper clips and broken pencils.

This moment feels like a perfect metaphor.

"You keep condoms in your junk drawer?"

"Ask that again," I say, "and realize how funny it sounds."

She snorts behind me, and I feel a wave of protectiveness. Alice's life has never been out of whack for even one second. When she was fifteen, she made a milestone list, complete with goals, ages, sometimes even locations:

. . . *Begin Stanford at eighteen, graduate at twenty-two, medical school at Johns Hopkins, residency in San Diego, marriage at thirty, first baby born at thirty-five* . . .

So far she hasn't missed a single one except for *maid of honor at Fizzy's wedding at twenty-eight*. (She dutifully crossed that one out with a thick black marker a few years ago and we celebrated my book hitting the *New York Times* list instead.) But pregnancy hasn't been her favorite experience, and I wonder if she's feeling even a tiny bit of what I do right now, like she's facing a future with unknown complexity, wicked blind curves, scary blank spaces.

"Have you ever felt like you've lost track of yourself?"

She points to her big, pregnant belly. "This kid isn't even here yet and I don't remember who I was six months ago. Did I really used to run every morning? For fun?"

"I've been so aimless lately," I admit, and I'm sure it's weird for her to hear. "I feel like this show might be a way to get back to myself. Even if it's a colossal failure, at least it's something *different*."

"I get that," she says wistfully. "I've been having skydiving dreams lately."

"You?"

She nods. "Sometimes I'm skydiving into an ocean of Oreos. Last night it was beer."

This makes me laugh, and I turn to wrap my arms around her middle. "Tell me I'm not making a huge mistake doing this."

"You're not. In fact, I wrote it on my list, don't you know? 'Fizzy does a crazy romance reality show when she's thirty-seven and has the time of her life.'"

eleven

FIZZY

An unexpected upside to bringing a Hot DILF to my first sign-ing in months is that readers are much less concerned with when my next book will be published and much more interested in who the giant man lingering in the background is. There were a few murmurs and glances during the Q and A portion of the event, but by the time the signing starts, every person in line is trying to figure out who the six-foot-five piece of ass over there talking to my dad is.

I know this because they're all breaking their necks trying to keep track of him as the line weaves around bookshelves. Several have come right out and asked me. My answers have ranged from "He's my security detail" to "He's my mail-order groom."

Listen, I get it. Catching sight of the Casual DILF on my door-step earlier caught me off guard. Gone was the man in the starched shirt sitting in a pristine office. This version of Hot Brit looks more like a hot lumberjack, in a soft faded flannel shirt and worn jeans with much-loved sneakers. His hair falls over his forehead; his eyes seem unbelievably bright for someone standing in the dark corner of a bookstore. In *One for the Road*, I described the eyes of the hero, Jack Sparling, this way—"illuminated from within," I think it was—but I've never really seen it in person.

Except—

I'm mentally jerked backward, tunneled in reverse to the moment with Jess a couple months ago in the bar when I looked across the room and met eyes with the man in the suit, rumpled hair, jaw like a blade. He'd looked at me like he wanted to meet in the hallway and fuck me into next month.

Is this really the same guy? I can't believe all this was hiding under that stiff, gelled hair, a bright toothpaste-ad smile, and a crisp black suit.

I look down at my lap, daring the flutter to linger. But it fades out, and I'm dropped back into the present day when the reader in front of me asks me if I'm okay.

"Gas," I tell her with a grin, and she laughs a familiar *oh, Fizzy* laugh and takes her signed books. But I'm still feeling the echo of interest in my lower torso. Was the pants flutter because I was thinking about Jack Sparling? His sex scenes *were* some of the most fun to write, that dirty little rascal.

Or was it . . . from *him*? Intrigued, I look up across the room at Connor again.

He's so taken with my dad he's barely seemed to register how much mental salivation is being aimed in his direction. I knew he'd get along with the unstoppable Dr. Ming Chen. My father is an objectively charismatic man with a million stories for every situation and has the most infectious laugh you've ever heard in your lifetime—it's this sort of bursting belly laugh that honestly should be recorded and trademarked as Happiness™. But what surprises me is how much talking Connor seems to be doing. I don't see Dad waxing poetic, telling jokes, doing all the heavy conversational lifting. When I glance over in tiny, furtive glimpses, I see Connor doing much of the chitchatting and Dad is cracking up. Almost like Connor's got stories.

Almost like he's . . . *interesting*.

He's also grinning, and the way it exaggerates the lines around his eyes and softens the angles of his face makes a flutter happen up near my chest, too.

But the heart flutter is doused by a cool, reactive flush spreading across my skin, panicky and jarring. *Wait,* my brain screeches. *I don't want to actually* like *him*.

"Who is that guy over there with Papa Chen?" a reader asks, and slides an impressive stack of books onto the tabletop. A quick inspection tells me the only ones she's missing are from the High Seas series, which, honestly, is full of fantastically filthy pirates, and it is a truth universally acknowledged that pirates are not for everyone. I won't hold it against her.

"He's my dad's new boyfriend," I answer, and this earns me another *oh, Fizzy* laugh, especially because Dad chose this moment to come kiss my cheek and tell me he's heading home. Clearly, if he heard me announce that he has a new boyfriend, he knows to ignore it. He gets an enthusiastic burst of applause as he ducks out of the bookstore.

"Who is he really?" the reader prods, leaning down so I can confide in her.

We haven't announced anything about the show yet, so it's not like I can tell her specifics. But saying he's a friend would raise too many eyebrows.

"He's on the publishing team." I give an apologetic wince like I know she wants a juicier answer. But the time it takes to make my way through her stack of books gives me the perfect opportunity to work past my weird *ew, emotions* moment.

This is good, actually, I tell myself, signing my name with a flourish. *This isn't about emotions! You're just experiencing a long overdue Fizzgina reawakening. You need to get the flutters back if you're going to have any success on this show. You need to get the flutters back if you have any hopes of writing romance again! It's okay that Connor is good-looking. The fact that you notice means you're one step closer to being back to the old Fizzy!*

The pep talk works. When I hand the hefty stack back to the woman, I feel the twinkle of a real smile in my eyes.

I find Connor after the crowd has thinned, standing alone in the horror section, awestruck as he turns a gilded hardcover over in his hands. He looks like he's about to lick it.

"Do we need to run a DNA compatibility test between you and that special edition of *'Salem's Lot*?"

"I didn't know they released this," he says, running a long finger down the spine. "This was one of the first books I can remember being unable to put down. This edition is gorgeous."

Why is it so sexy when he says *gorgeous* like that? Like he's staring down at a lover, overcome? I was hoping the power of his attractiveness would lessen, up close—bad skin, weird odor, yellowed teeth that I'd somehow missed—but I'm irritated to discover that none of those things are true. He smells like yummy man and the trace of whatever deodorant he's wearing. I bet it's called Ice Zone or

Sports Hero or Silver Blade, and I'm disgusted with myself for liking it. I can't even locate the Hot Millionaire Executive archetype in Connor anymore. He is all soft and brawny. Soft Lumberjack is his new name. Why does he ever approach that head of hair with even a drop of gel? I might have to take one for the team and pretend I know him well enough to advise him on styling.

I wonder idly, on a scale of *Get It Girl* to *Only If You Never Want to Work Again*, how bad it would be to sleep with my reality romance show producer. Get back on the horse and whatnot.

Squeezing my eyes closed, I do a hard mental reboot. I'm glad to see the old Fizzy rearing her head, but she's a bossy one, and even I know that hooking up with Connor Prince III would be not only professionally brainless but probably astonishingly mediocre. It would have to be, right? His hot lumberjack vibe today is likely a one-off while his suits and Lego hair are at the cleaners. My first sex after the dry spell should leave me walking with a limp and recuperating for an entire weekend with a giant bottle of Gatorade and Nancy Meyers movies for company.

"Why are you staring at me like that?"

"Like what?" I ask, immediately swapping out whatever my expression was doing for a relaxed smile.

He frowns, his gaze doing a brief circuit of my face, searching for whatever he saw a moment ago. "Never mind."

Redirect time: "Did you have fun today?"

"I did," he admits. "You're funny. Your readers are so enthusiastic. I can tell you genuinely love being with them."

He's right, and in hindsight I'm annoyed with myself for being so nervous on the way over here. Sweaty palms, bursting, too-loud answers to his polite questions in the car, overexplaining as we entered the bookstore. Connor was calm and easy at my side, this steady, sturdy presence to my jittery stress. But the second the room filled, my pulse slowed and I came home.

"Romance readers are my absolute favorite brand of human." I grin at him. "You see how much they love what they love. They show up—it's a Monday, and see how many decided to leave their houses and fight traffic, maybe find child care, just to come here?" I gesture to the now-empty bookstore. "You had everyone here tonight. Homemakers, attorneys, hourly employees, scientists, retirees, students."

He whistles, looking back at the checkout counter as if remembering. "I saw someone with two copies of every one of your books."

"And I've signed those three times before, but she still shows up for every local event to say hi and get them signed again."

"She didn't buy a book?"

"She bought one tonight, but not one of mine." Off his surprised expression, I add, "Fangirls show up, Connor. Those are my people."

He nods, studying me. "I'm seeing that."

With a smile, I say, "I'm glad you took a break from flirting with my dad to study your show's demographic."

Connor's energy dials up a few notches. "I did, but it was hard. Your dad is *great*."

"He's literally the cutest human to ever exist."

"By the way, I didn't realize you hadn't told him about the show yet. Hope I didn't make that weird for you with your parents."

"No, I was completely using you as a shield."

He gives me a mock-stern look that I like more than I should.

"He was into it," Connor says. "But he said he's not telling your mum."

"*Shit.*"

Connor laughs. "We need to find a way to get him on."

A cold flush spreads down my arms. "On—on the dating show? My dad?"

He nods, thinking it over. "Family visits with the final contestants, maybe."

My stomach tilts. "Whew, that's . . ." I'm about to say *that's terrifying*, because just the idea of bringing multiple men over to my mother's house for her to inspect makes me want to roll into traffic. But for the first time since we started talking about this, there's a light in Connor's eyes that looks genuine, and if hanging with Papa Chen did that for him, who am I to pour water on the fire? "That's a great idea," I say with a limp smile.

Connor laughs. "Don't worry, we'll figure it all out. Right now, we're just suggesting loads of things to see what sounds right."

Adrenaline seems to dissipate all at once from my bloodstream and I lean against a shelf, exhaling slowly. Signings are the strangest paradox: the most energizing, fulfilling experience, but also the most exhausting. I want everyone who comes to the table to feel like the most important person in my life, because for those handfuls of minutes, they are. But keeping that energy up can be draining. Add to that the stress about not knowing whether I'll ever release another book and I'm absolutely wiped.

And *starving*.

I press the heels of my hands to my eyes and feel him lean in. "You okay?"

Taking a deep, steadying breath, I— Shit. I really, really like the smell of his Ice Zone Sports Hero Silver Blade deodorant.

"I'm great." When I drop my hands, light pops into the periphery of my vision. The only tiny hit of adrenaline remaining is the one I get when I stare right up at him, towering over me, soft and lumber-jacky and flashlight-eyed. "But I'm about to be even better."

I tell myself not to be too interested in the way he flicks one curious eyebrow, saying, "Do tell."

"If you trust me, then let's go."

twelve

CONNOR

I get the strong sense that the types of directions Fizzy gives are the ones we warn our children not to blindly follow: trust me, sign here, eat this. And yet, here I am, following her out of the bookstore and into my car, where she directs me twenty minutes south to a taco joint in San Ysidro, just on the Mexican border.

In an unremarkable parking lot in front of an unremarkable building, she climbs out, stretches long, happily groaning, and then grins wickedly at me. "Are you ready to have your world changed?"

"Uh, sure?"

As she moves with ease toward the building in her black dress and heels, there's something thunderous about her. Objectively slight, Fizzy has the ability to take up space in a way I've never mastered. I was always relatively tall growing up, but having been raised by a single mother, I felt conscious not to appear imposing in any way. It was this tendency of mine that drove my father insane on the rare occasions when he would visit. He would lecture me about entering a room with power, about the importance of claiming space. By the time I'd turned fourteen and was well over six feet tall, and taking up space was a foregone conclusion, he turned to other things to criticize: my lack of ambition, my deference to others, my protectiveness of my mother. Later it was my career choice, my shotgun wedding, my job title.

But as much as my father exhausts me, I can't help but think that admiring Fizzy would be one thing we'd have in common.

"I'm going to order for us," she says over her shoulder. "I'm going to put joy in your mouth, Sexy Lumberjack. Trust me."

"Is trust required?"

She ignores this, stepping up to order for us, and I look down at my outfit. From Brit to DILF to Sexy Lumberjack. I can't know for sure if this transition in nickname signals a good wardrobe decision on my part, but I changed three times before picking her up today, prompting Stevie to ask me whether I was going on a date.

It's not a date. I mean, of course it isn't. But there's something about being this close to Fizzy that makes me want to impress her in the same way.

As she orders, I hear the words *lengua*, *cabeza*, *buche*, and *tripa* and am aware that I'm going to be eating some things I have never before put in my mouth. With a bulging paper bag in one hand, two drinks in a cardboard tray in the other, and a little nod for me to trust her yet again, we climb back into the car and drive a few minutes to a small road leading us to a coastal wildlife refuge.

At a weatherworn metal table overlooking an empty stretch of beach, Fizzy opens the bag and lays out an enormous selection of tacos. "Take your pick." She points to each, describing what's in it—from grilled beef and cactus, to pork belly, to tripe, to beef head, to tongue. And as I take my first bite of the pork belly, she watches me with anticipation, waiting for a reaction.

Letting out a low, involuntary groan, I feel my eyes drift closed.

The sharp tang of fresh cotija and bright lime, with crisp bits of meat and a soft, handmade tortilla—this is easily the best taco I've had in my entire life.

It takes a minute for my senses to settle and I realize she's still looking at me.

"You like?" she asks, smiling happily.

"Bloody lovely." I wipe my mouth. "Are you just going to watch?"

She breaks her stare and blinks down at the selection in front of her, choosing what I think was the lengua. "I like seeing you like this. Outside of that office and that suit. This is a good vibe." She motions to my clothes. "Still DILFy, but without the uptight CEO thing going on."

"Not sure a coworker has ever called me a DILF before."

She shrugs. "You didn't bring me on because I lettered in propriety."

"Fair." I smile, taking a sip of my fountain drink. "But you seem awfully intent on pegging me."

She barks out a laugh. "I don't think that means what you think it means."

"Jesus Christ." I flick my eyes upward in mock exasperation, and then finish the small taco. "You know what I meant."

It's a struggle not to stare at her while she eats. She hums happily as she chews, licks a tiny bit of salsa from the side of her mouth, and studies the food in her hand with pleasure-drunk eyes. So far in only this first outing alone I've seen two very different sides to Fizzy: effusive and public facing, and this more intimate, quietly playful version. Both charismatic, both sexy, both mesmerizing. First, I was resentful to be assigned this, then I was resigned. Now I feel a flicker of excitement over the challenge of capturing her brand of magic on-screen.

You're going to be setting her up with other men.

The reminder crashes into the forefront of my thoughts, and I blink away. "I had a thought about the show."

She glances up at me and laughs. "I hope you've had more than one."

"This is specifically about the title. What do you think about calling it *The True Love Experiment*?"

"I think I'm mad I didn't come up with it myself."

A sunburst of pride spreads quickly through my torso. "Brilliant." I reach for a mystery taco. "So, to recap: We'll cast the eight Hero archetypes. Filming will be Monday to Thursday, with Friday for crash editing, and a Saturday broadcast. Voting will take place over twenty-four hours after the episode airs, and the following Monday we'll reveal to the cast who has made it through each round."

She mumbles a happy sound around a bite.

"And," I continue, "I think we should go in with the understanding that the show won't be so heavily produced. I don't mean from an aesthetics angle, but the actual story lines. I've been thinking quite a bit on this, and I really want to do something different, as much as we can. From what I gather, some of these shows are plotted out from episode one, which makes me question the sincerity of any relationship that comes out of them. Since viewers will be voting on our outcome, we want to give them the truest possible narrative we can."

She nods, licking her lips again, and it splits my focus into foggy tendrils. I squeeze my eyes closed for a beat to recapture the thread.

"Because it's a limited series, you'll only really be tied up for about five weeks."

"Tied up, huh?" Fizzy grins. "Sounds fun."

"You're trouble."

She laughs. "I think that's why you chose me."

"I *chose* you because you're beloved by your fan base. But yes, I am excited to do this in part because you're also a bit mischievous."

"Excited?" She drops her balled-up napkin and plants her elbows on the table. "That's a new development."

I take a bite, chew. "What can I say? I am continually evolving."

"I see that."

"I know this matters to you," I tell her. "I want you to know it matters to me, too."

Fizzy takes a long breath, opens her mouth to speak, and then seems to change track. "You said you moved here when you were fifteen?"

A flicker of unease quells the vibrating hum in my blood, and I take a bite to delay what I suspect will be a gentle but surgical interrogation. "Yes, that's right."

"And your mother is the Brit?"

I nod. "She lives with her parents now, just outside Blackpool, but she met my father when she was studying abroad in the States. She got pregnant, and my father wasn't interested in being a father yet. He'd visit every year or so to pop in and tell her what she was doing wrong."

"Wow, sounds like a nice guy."

"He's a mixture of unbearably selfish and unremittingly dutiful."

She laughs at this. "Why'd you go live with him?" I narrow my eyes at her, calculating whether I want to get into it, and she smiles under the inspection. "What?" she asks. "Is this story *escandaloso*?"

"Perhaps a bit."

"Oh, well now you have to tell me."

"My mum and I were in a very bad car accident when I was twelve. We were both fine, eventually, but the entire thing really shook her up."

Fizzy's expression straightens. "Oh no."

"For . . . a few years," I explain, "Mum didn't leave the house. I had to for school, of course, and to take on odd jobs. But she suffered from a great deal of anxiety. This whole period is when I got into film, so I can't resent the solitude, but in hindsight I do see how much I missed of my adolescence." Before this can veer too bleak, I wrap it up: "Anyway, my father visited when I was fifteen and didn't like what he saw. By then he'd married and had a couple of kids with my stepmother, but eventually Mum conceded that I needed a change of scenery and agreed to let him take me until I was ready to go to university."

"Do you ever go back to England?"

"Of course," I say. "I spend some Christmases there. I speak to my mother regularly. I'd planned to move back after I'd graduated uni, but life had other plans."

"And what about present day?" she asks. "Are you remarried? Out every night, living the hot single life?"

I clear my throat, frowning as I adjust the napkin on my lap. "I— no. Neither," I admit. "My daughter is still quite young. I only have her on weekends, and I work late most weeknights—so I haven't. I don't. That is, I don't date much." I hear the stumbling clutter of my words and squint past her, to stare at a flock of birds picking at something on the sand.

"What's her name?"

I'm grateful that she's letting me move on. "Stefania Elena García Prince." Fizzy bites back a smile and I laugh in understanding. "I know. My last name always sounds like the sad friend at the party. She's a trip, though. Part princess, part evil mastermind."

"She sounds like my kind of girl."

"I genuinely fear the day you two meet. I think Nostradamus wrote about it."

When I look up at her, I register that she's been studying me. Her dark eyes are wide and gently set on my face.

"Anyway, we should be talking about you, not me."

She doesn't look away as my gaze holds hers. It's this, and the way her voice goes a little hoarse when she says, "I'll tell you anything you want to know," that make me suspect I am absolutely, irrevocably, and undeniably fucked.

thirteen

FIZZY

I assume we all have the proverbial angel on one shoulder and devil on the other, but in my case, they're very real, and the devil is a shouter.

I know that it is stupid to flirt with Connor. I know how absurd it is to develop sexy desires for this man in particular, but it's been so long since I've been attracted to anyone that I feel like a starving dog staring at a T-bone.

Connor licks his lips, pulling them in between his teeth, and I realize he's reacting to the weight of my stare. Blinking away, I focus my attention on the waves crashing into the smooth sand instead.

I need to get my shit together. As much as I'm glad I'm a butterfly coming out of the cocoon of sexual stagnation, I probably shouldn't fly directly to the first flower I see. Especially if that flower's professional goal is finding me a soulmate.

"Well," he says after our odd, lengthy showdown, "let's start easy."

I stretch, pretending to crack my neck.

"Tell me what you look for in a guy."

Taking a deep breath, I look out at the waves in the distance, thinking. "Have you ever gone to the grocery store hungry?"

Connor laughs in understanding. "Yes."

"Cheese plate, carrots, chips, salsa, Cocoa Pebbles, and sugar cookies. Whatever sounds good at the time."

"Right."

"I'd describe my dating energy a little like that. I don't have a type, exactly, but maybe that's part of the problem."

He nods but doesn't take this opportunity to speak. Again: hot.

"I initially did the DNADuo for fun," I say. "You know, to try out the technology from a romance research perspective. I got matches and went out with everyone. I wanted to see if a Base Match *felt* different from a Silver."

"Did it?" he asks.

"It did, but in romance, love is often about getting past our core assumptions. So if someone told me I had a Titanium Match, wouldn't I subconsciously work harder to make it successful than I would with a Base Match? That's always the question with this technology."

He hums, nodding. "That makes sense."

"I think doing this show is the perfect way for me to get back into the dating scene. I won't know what kind of matches I have. I won't overthink it. I'll just have to go on how we vibe and let the audience worry about the rest. I mean, I'm not having any luck on my own, why not let a bunch of strangers give it a shot?"

"And you never went back to the app? You haven't used it at all in the past couple years?"

"Oh, I haven't had much interest in dating for a while. My desire to find a partner crashed and burned entirely around the same time I was doing my DNADuo dating spree—unrelated to the app, I should add."

He seems to chew on his next words before finally asking, "What's the unrelated bit?" Connor smiles. "If you don't mind me asking."

"Ah. Well . . ." There are very few things I hate discussing, but high on the list are the word *moist* spoken aloud, people who use *FML* or *LOL* in actual conversation, and my tumultuous yet brief relationship with a man named Rob. "Around the time the DNADuo was launching, I went to a party with a friend and met this guy. We were together for a little while and I thought things were really going well until I found out he had a wife."

His expression crashes. "Oh."

"It was awful. I was devastated, all of the expected things from a situation like that. But then a little over a year ago, she confronted me."

Connor winces. "What happened?"

"It wasn't on purpose—or, well, she didn't intentionally seek me out. I was on a date and we happened to be in the same place. She recognized me from some photos that had been on Rob's phone, I guess, walked over to my table, and said she'd divorced him and that I was free to have him if I still wanted him."

"Fuck," he mutters.

"In any other situation I would have clarified that no, I absolutely did not want him—that I hadn't even known Rob was married when we started dating—but I was totally frozen. It's one thing to have made a mistake and live with it in an abstract way. It was totally different to see the fallout right there in front of me."

"That must have been awful. I'm sorry that happened, Fizzy."

"I had spent so much time wondering what happened to them.

Did she forgive him? Did they split up? So it answered those questions, at least. Anyway . . ." I pick up my drink and the ice rattles against the Styrofoam as I raise it in a toast. "My therapist was able to remodel her kitchen with the money I paid to work through it, so I guess there's a silver lining."

Connor smiles a little at this. "I get why you were scared off dating for a bit, then. But what about now? Are you ready to be in a relationship?"

A long stretch of silence follows his words as I run into this question like it's a brick wall. I've known that finding me a match is the entire goal of the show, but I haven't internalized it at all. If Connor and I are successful, it will be more than just entertainment for my target audience. I could end up with a lover, a boyfriend, a soulmate. A chill climbs up the back of my neck, and Connor sees the shiver pass through me.

"I think so," I say, willing it to be true.

Connor balls up the last taco wrapper and drops it into the paper bag. "When you met those Base and Silver Matches, tell me what you were looking for. What worked for you? What didn't? Basically, who am I looking for when I start casting tomorrow?"

"Well, I want to know who they voted for and where they stand on several political and social issues. I know I'm supposed to say that I can look beyond that, but I know I don't work that way. There are some things that are nonstarters for me, and overt political questions aren't on the DNADuo intake forms."

He nods and pulls out his phone to write in his Notes app. "I agree."

"And I guess I want what most women want: someone who makes me laugh and doesn't take themself too seriously. Someone who's ambitious but good, who's supportive of me and the things I love. But mostly, I want us to be head over fucking heels for each other."

I look out over the water and think of Jess's face when River walks into the room. It's the same way my dad's eyes light up when he sees my mom; it's how completely whipped my brother-in-law is for Alice. I know what love looks like—and I've written it so many times—but I've never felt it myself.

He looks at me across the table. There's no judgment in his eyes, no pity, only empathy and compassion. "Those seem like pretty reasonable requests."

"I have no idea what this will be like, but I hope I end up being what you wanted for the show. I'd started to wonder if maybe I was going to find peace with being single. I was wrapping my head around that when we first met that day in your office, you know?"

"Yeah," he says with gentle understanding.

"I also think we both said yes to this project for reasons that weren't all about us."

His eyes meet mine and I see unspoken agreement there.

"I was worried North Star had no idea what they were doing," I say. "I thought you were a dick."

This time his "Yeah" is carried on a laugh.

I grin at him. "See? Core assumptions. I don't think that anymore, if that helps."

Connor offers a knowing smirk. "It does, thank you."

I don't say the other part out loud, that not only do I not think he's a dick, I'm actually deeply attracted to him and wonder if I can ignore it for the sake of the show.

I know myself. It's unlikely.

We gather our things and I use the public restroom while he waits for me nearby. When I return, he's ending a call. "Everything good?" I ask.

"Just saying good night to my daughter." He motions for me to lead the way as we head back toward the car. It's one of the most beautiful nights in recent memory. The air is warm, heavy with condensation; the briny ocean breeze feels like a gentle cloak.

"This weather is so perfect," I say, taking this last moment to soak it all in. I'm finally coming back into myself and the beast part of me wants to throw myself into his arms just to thank him, to tell him he has no way of knowing that he's helped me just by being attractive and laid back and a good listener. But I manage to contain the impulse, continuing only to say, "I want to stuff this happiness in a pie crust and eat it with ice cream." I close my eyes, pretending to take bites of the sky, "Nom, nom, nom."

When I look back at him, he's staring down at me with an unreadable expression.

A haze of electricity settles around us and I don't know where to look. My eyes keep getting dragged back to him, to his throat or lips or shoulders or those massive hands. I'm never in the gray area like this, where I'm attracted, and I think he's attracted—but I'm not sure—and even if he is, I don't think we're supposed to do anything about it. My romantic life before, I realize, has been so black-and-white. Accept or refuse. Take to bed, or don't. No subtlety, nothing nuanced.

At his car he reaches past me, and it's only after I've tilted my face to his that I realize he's not coming in for a kiss. He's unlocking the door for me. But then he doesn't pull back immediately. He stares down at me, looking a little lost.

"Should we head home?" he asks.

"I guess."

Even coming from San Ysidro, the drive is too short, and I watch out the window as the car slows at my curb. Connor looks at me across the console, and it suddenly feels like making out, this eye contact, the way his gaze softens and makes a circuit of my face. But then he sucks in a sharp breath, turning and bursting out of the car.

Okay.

I follow him out and we make a slow death march to my front door. "You okay?" I ask.

"Great."

"That was some night, huh?"

He laughs but doesn't say anything.

Now we're on my porch. "Are we gonna pretend it didn't totally feel like a date?"

He turns to face me. "Good practice for you," he says lamely.

I reach up, daring him to dodge my touch, but he doesn't. He lets me brush his hair off his forehead. "Wear your hair like this more often."

"It's messy."

"It's great."

"It gets in my eyes," he says, more quietly.

"It's sexy."

He closes his eyes. "Fizzy."

"Come inside."

Slowly, he opens his eyes again and his gaze dips to my mouth. "What for?"

"You know what for."

He laughs, but it's not out of amusement or mockery. It's a laugh of defeat. It's agreement. And for a flash I'm elated.

But then he says, "You know we can't."

"Technically we can. My contract prohibits me from dating or any outside romantic involvement only during filming. I checked."

"Fizzy. We absolutely cannot."

He shoves his hands into his pockets. And they're hidden but I remember them like they've been imprinted in my retinas, and all I can think about is those big hands gripping me, walking me backward, bossy and directed, pushing me up against a wall or down on a bed. His strong arms bracing over me, those long fingers exploring. I want him above, blocking out every light source. I want to know nothing but the heat and scent of his skin, the rough sounds he makes when he comes.

"Why not?" I aim the question at his throat and it bobs with a swallow.

"You know why. Our goal is to find your soulmate. I already—" He breaks off. "We can't."

"The show hasn't even started yet. Consider it more homework." I reach forward, rest my hand on his side. God, he's so solid under my touch. "Finding joy. I promise you'll enjoy it."

"That's not what concerns me."

"It's been so long," I admit. "I'm so relieved to *want* this. I—"

"Fizzy."

"Trust me. I'm great at compartmentalizing."

"That's the thing," he says, and bends to press a soft but definitive kiss to my jaw. "I'm not."

fourteen

CONNOR

What does a man do after being propositioned by one of the most beautiful women in San Diego and then turning her down?

1. He considers slamming his head into a wall because he's an idiot for deciding casual sex doesn't work for him.

2. He has a wank so many times imagining it that he wakes up a bit chafed the next morning.

3. He goes to work—where he has been tasked with finding the soulmate of the very woman he wants, and who apparently also wants him—because his livelihood and access to his child depend on it.

4. He makes a mental note to get very drunk afterward.

And a plan for drinking later is wise considering the once-familiar office I walk into suddenly looks like a beefcake sweet shop.

There are men everywhere: in the lobby, clustered in conference rooms, and just casually—albeit attractively—leaning against cubicle partitions. In front of me stands every possible male phenotype—

businessmen in suits, surfer dudes in shorts, inked-up blokes in torn jeans, cuddly-looking lads in jumpers—and each has the potential to be Fizzy's soulmate. Wonderful.

My phone rings as I round the corner near my office. I take a calming breath, unsure whether I'm ready to put out any fires yet this morning, but relax when I see a photo of Nat and Stevie filling the screen.

"Hello—"

"I have a favor to ask," Nat says immediately.

"Go on then."

"Insu was asked to speak at a convention in Vegas this weekend and invited me to go. I'd have to leave Thursday, so I was wondering—"

"Of course. You know I'll always take her early."

"Thank you," she says on a relieved sigh. "Stevie mentioned you had a date last night, and I didn't want to assume anything."

"I *told* her it wasn't a date." I told her several times, in fact. I should probably be concerned that my ten-year-old is getting this invested in my love life, but I'm neck-deep in twenty-six-to-forty-eight-year-old eligible bachelors and just do not have the time. "It was a work thing," I say, and then add, "With Fizzy."

The line goes quiet; I can practically hear Nat's grin. I regret the clarification immediately.

"Ah," she says. "So it's Fizzy now."

My first instinct is to tell Nat it was nothing, but I've never been able to keep anything from her. We turned into adults together. We're forever connected through Stevie. She's seen me at my best and my worst, knows me better than anyone, and loves me anyway. Ducking into a vacant office, I close the door behind me.

"It's not as exciting as it sounds." Then why is my heart beating like I walked the eight flights up here instead of taking the lift? "All right, maybe it is, but it shouldn't be. We spent the evening together after her book signing and talked about the show over dinner. Then she, uh . . . she invited me to spend the night."

"Are you telling me that you and *Felicity Chen*—"

"I said no, Nat." It sounds just as stupid the second time. "I told her I couldn't. I'm the producer on her *dating show*."

"Okay," she says, processing. "Right. I get that, but—"

"There's no 'but.' Even if I wanted to, I can't."

"*Do* you want to?"

"The easy answer is yes. The answer that's based in reality and the way my life works right now . . . is more complicated."

"How did she take it? Was she upset?"

I'm not about to flatter myself into thinking Fizzy's proposition was anything more than a moment of mutual attraction and wanting to scratch an itch. But it's nice to know I wasn't imagining it. "I don't think she was too upset." Fizzy can have any man she wants. I'm not going to delude—or torture—myself into thinking it was anything more than it was. "Anyway," I say, searching for a change in subject, "I can absolutely pick Stevie up and keep her however long you need. More time with our kid is never a hardship. I'm sure I'll have to pull in a few favors myself once the show starts. Speaking of which"—I check my watch—"I need to get going."

"Thanks, Conn. This speaking thing is a big deal for Insu. And in Vegas! There will be buyers from all over the country."

"Tell him congratulations, really." Insu and a friend started a fledgling software company a few years ago and have been working on a VR game. He must be over the moon at this opportunity. "I'm not sure he's old enough to gamble, but you kids will have fun either way."

"Didn't you say you had work to do?"

We ring off, and I continue to my office, pausing as I stop outside my door.

My hardworking, straight-from-Kansas assistant has two very fit-looking young men moving her desk from one end of her workspace to another.

"Good morning, Brenna," I say.

She spins around, cheeks flushed. "It certainly is!"

Trent rounds the corner, briefcase and car keys still in hand. He looks as tired as I feel.

Confused, he surveys the chaos around us. "What in the fresh hell is happening?"

"Casting," I tell him. "We're narrowing down the final contestants for my dating show, *The True Love Experiment*."

He continues to look around, and I imagine his bewildered expression looks much like mine did barely ten minutes ago.

"What are you doing here, anyway?" I ask. "I thought you were on a bus for six weeks."

He runs an exhausted hand down his face. "I've got to meet with some lawyers and fly right back out tonight. I've barely slept in four days; these contestants never shut up, and there are just so many rules! Did you know there are insurance clauses about different protective cups for this type of show?"

Brenna tilts her head, confused. "Different . . . oh."

"Right." He nods. "I'll never forgive Blaine for putting phrases like 'testicular degloving' in my vocabulary." At both our horrified expressions, he adds, "It's absolutely as bad as it sounds. Learn from my mistakes and don't google that one."

Brenna gently turns Trent back toward the kitchen. "Why don't we get you some coffee before your meeting?" Trent continues to mumble about penis dislocations as they move down the hall.

"Be grateful you got a dating show, Connor," he says over his shoulder.

———————————

Later that morning, I'm set up with Brenna; the casting director, Kathy; and our director, Rory, in North Star's largest conference room. We've successfully signed on a viral YouTube sensation named Lanelle Turner to be the show's host—an intermittent role requiring her only to pop in at the beginning and end of each episode—but the bulk of the day's work stretches ahead of us, with a call sheet approximately seventy beefcakes deep.

Fizzy insisted that she doesn't have a physical type per se, but having walked through the halls of North Star Media today, I think it's safe to say these men are *everyone's* type.

Our first possible Hero is Isaac Moore. He's tall and fit, Black, with short, cropped hair and a smile so arresting it makes Brenna flush from head to toe when he shakes her hand. Isaac has two sisters, collects vintage board games, and works in AI modeling and development.

I make a note, checking a box next to Hot Nerd.

"What does that mean exactly?" Kathy asks, looking at him over the top of her tortoiseshell glasses. She's in her midfifties, with curly red hair and a diamond on her ring finger that's so large I'd imagine her left arm is significantly stronger than her right. Kathy has been brought on as a consultant; she doesn't usually cast the kinds of things I make—obvious, perhaps, given that the kinds of things I make usually feature marine mammals—so we've never worked together before. "AI modeling and development?"

"I work with artificial intelligence systems that build and implement engagement algorithms. Specifically, I program the ethics and accountability that come with those systems."

"So, like . . . dealing with trolls on Twitter?" Kathy asks.

"Exactly." His smile morphs into a small laugh. "Yeah."

Brenna giggles again and I catch her eye. *Keep it together.* Even Rory, who rarely cracks a smile, glances up from her notes. Rory is also new to me, though not by reputation. She's worked on some of the most popular unscripted shows of the last few years, and seems to be nice enough, if a bit intense. She has a reputation for things getting a little dramatic on set, but once her name came up, Blaine was like a dog with a bone until we had her signature on the dotted line. She also wasn't cheap, but thanks to North Star's new flair for throwing money around, that wasn't a problem, either.

Together we go over Isaac's questionnaire, ask about his family, his reasons for doing the show, his political leanings—per Fizzy's request. I listen to all of it, taking more notes and asking my own questions while the camera silently captures everything in the background.

"Isaac, what do you think men want in a partner?" I ask.

He tilts his head thoughtfully, tenting his hands on the table. "I think most men want someone who's smart, loving, and kind. Open to adventure. What I want is a companion. Someone to share the good and the bad, to laugh and hang with, to respect and support and share all the things that make us who we are."

He's perfect. Charming, interesting, thoughtful, and supportive. He even manages to pull off a sweater vest. Fizzy will love him.

It's irrational, but I hate him already. He's in.

Man number two is in skinny dark jeans, a distressed black band tee, and worn black Converse. Is this what Fizzy meant by Vampire? Somehow I don't think so. As soon as he's gone, I write *no* next to his name.

The next few hours are pretty much the same—a lot of caricatures with a couple of keepers along the way. Some are quick no's: the potential Tattooed Bad Boy who is obviously just here to be on television; a Darcy who'd one hundred percent show up at a white nationalist rally. There's a terribly cliché Millionaire CEO who looks like he intentionally put white powder under his nose to really nail the trope.

I'm very interested in the names Fizzy gave us for The One That Got Away. I'd like to say my motives are altruistic, but even my sweet mum wouldn't believe that. In the end, however, these interviews prove to be mostly anticlimactic. There's no common thread or characteristic I can pinpoint in any of the men we meet from the list. Some are good-looking, some are not. A few have money and some don't. Most of them are nice enough. No great Fizzy mystery is unlocked, and I am just as bewildered and fascinated by her as when I started. We do end up putting one Evan Young into our A group, however, and it takes me all of two minutes to realize he's the bloke that Fizzy mentioned during our first meeting. The one with the terrible Bart Simpson tattoo.

He's apparently picked up the pieces of his Fizzy-less life: he's gone back to school to get an engineering degree and, when not in class, works as a barista part-time in a small coffee shop. Evan is also attractive and charming and, just like Fizzy said, incredibly nice. He has nothing but glowing things to say about his ex-girlfriend.

I cannot wait to see her face when he walks in. I'm tempted to whisper, "*Ay, caramba*," into her earpiece.

By the end of the day, we've narrowed our top picks down to seven, with all Fizzy's highest-ranked archetypes included but one: the Cinnamon Roll.

Our final guy is Nick Wright. After a long day of waiting, he's got to be as tired as the rest of us, but he walks in with a bright, bashful smile. On paper he's six three, 182 pounds, likes basketball, and has a small veterinarian practice in Orange County. In reality, he looks like he stepped out of the pages of one of Fizzy's books. We've seen a lot of good-looking men today, but there is an audible gasp from both Brenna and Kathy when Nick walks into the room. We go through the standard questions, and he has all the right answers. He was engaged, but it ended when she wanted to move abroad, and he felt he owed it to his staff and clients to stay. He's the oldest in a family of five, feels like marriage is the one thing he's missing in his life, and he knits while watching BBC procedural dramas to unwind from a long, stressful day. Houston, we have a Cinnamon Roll.

"Nick, what do you think men want in a partner?" I say, reaching the final question.

He smiles down at the table, paradoxically looking both shy and like a lab-created hybrid of Chris Evans and Bond-era Pierce Brosnan. "I think most people would say men want someone who makes them feel good about themselves," he says. "But I want someone who challenges me." He rests his very tan, very toned forearms on the table. "My grandparents have been married for over sixty years, and when my grandma walks into the room, my grandpa looks at her like he's still nineteen and trying to figure out how the prettiest girl in school is giving him the time of day." He laughs. "I want that. To be as head over heels in love at eighty as I was at thirty. To be together and just . . . feel joy."

I wonder how it's possible that *this* is the moment all of this finally feels real. The show will start, Fizzy will meet and eventually date these guys, and if all of our efforts pay off, it will be a success. Fizzy will fall in love, and I get to keep my job and stay in San Diego.

When I blink back into the moment, everyone is standing. Kathy shows Nick out and closes the door behind him. "Holy shit," she says, eyes wide in disbelief. "That was great, right? He was really great?"

"I don't think I blinked the entire time he was talking." Brenna stands and rounds the table. "Can you imagine him on-screen with Fizzy?"

"Can you imagine her with Dax? Or Evan? Or *Isaac*?" Kathy says. "I've never seen a reality show with a group like this." She turns to Rory. "And we've done DNADuo screenings on them already?"

Rory nods. "They've all been binned. We've got a good spread."

"They all feel so . . . *real*," Kathy muses. "Genuine, I mean."

"If Fizzy doesn't marry one of them, I'm going to." Brenna turns to me. "Connor, this could be huge."

Rory is still staring at the door Nick just walked through. "I had my doubts, but . . . we might actually pull this off."

They're right, I think. The pieces are coming together, and if my gut is correct, it could be good.

I got exactly what I wanted. And I have nobody to blame but myself.

fifteen

FIZZY

Whether or not I ever have children of my own remains to be seen, but what can be stated without ambiguity is that I am the most embarrassing adult to ever attend a child's soccer game.

Even Jess and River don't want to be seen with me. They march ahead onto the field, lugging chairs, a cooler, and a sunshade to a point that seems like the farthest distance from where we parked. I know the marching can't be because they're grouchy that I've declared myself to be JUNO'S BIGGEST FAN with bold black letters on a fluorescent pink shirt, because it's objectively true: only Juno's biggest fan would wear this in public. But my sweet little dancer has decided to try something new, and even if she's too mentally sturdy to tremble in fear, rumor has it she hasn't been sleeping well in the nights leading up to her first soccer match. So if I can be a bigger idiot than anyone else out here, then maybe Juno won't worry so much about whether she'll mess up. I have pom-poms in my tote bag, but they're a "break in case of emergency" kind of thing. Hopefully it won't come to that.

But once we're set up at the sideline, I think I might have overcompensated. This entire operation doesn't seem that intense. Of course there is the one kid in high-tech gear with shiny new cleats and ribbons in her hair that match the uniform. Her parents are easy to spot, too; they're the ones taking a million pictures of warm-ups and shouting encouragement/instructions across the field. But this is, after all, a group of ten-year-olds, so there's also the kid who's obviously in her older sibling's shorts, which are cinched tightly at the waist and balloon out past her knees, as well as the kid whose parents must be as sporty as I am because they've sent their daughter to a soccer game in jeans.

I spot Juno in a small group of girls gathered around a sequoia of a man who's bent and drawing something on a clipboard. He's too far away for me to ogle properly but has dark hair and upper arms that seem to test the physics of his T-shirt sleeves.

"*Hello*, sir." I make binoculars out of my hands and pretend to zoom in. "Ahh*woooo*gah."

I have been a mess since dinner with Connor. An absolute horndog. I haven't mentioned it to Jess because I think she's so unsettled by my admitted loss of sex drive and inspiration that she'll be the worst enabler. It's been hard enough not texting Connor a daily *How about now?* The last thing I need is Jess's brand of ride-or-die yelling "*You deserve good sex!*" in my ear every day.

"That's the coach," Jess says, pushing up one of the arms of the shade tent and clicking it into place.

"Let me tell you, my kid would never miss a game."

She laughs. "He's one of the parents, actually. Stevie's dad."

Stevie is one of Juno's newer friends, and although I've only met her a few times, the two of them are hysterical when together. Too smart and cute for their own good and more fun than many of the adults I know. Who knew they were making kids so great these days?

I adjust my imaginary binoculars. "Well, Stevie's dad is a hot piece."

"He is, indeed."

River ducks inside the sunshade with the three folding chairs in one big hand. "Who's a hot piece?"

"You." Jess stretches to kiss him. "And Connor."

I think River gives this fair consideration. I *think* he says, "Stevie's dad? I could see that." But I'm not entirely sure because all motion in my brain has halted.

"Did you just say Connor?" I ask, stomach falling.

Jess is distracted by a folding chair that won't open. "Yeah, Connor Prince? He's the coach you're checking out."

"No."

Jess slowly looks up at me, sensing danger. "Yes?"

"Absolutely *not*." I immediately shove my imaginary binoculars away.

"What's wrong with you?" River asks me, laughing.

"That's—that's *Stevie's* dad out there?" I point in the distance at the giant whose shadow now, I admit, looks strikingly similar to the man I wanted to bend me over the kitchen counter the other night. "Adorable Stevie who told me the sad story about global warming and sea turtles, so I threw a bunch of money at the Oceanic Society?" Oh shit, that actually tracks.

I groan and sit in the chair Jess has just coaxed open.

"Have a seat," she tells me wryly, opening another and sitting down beside me.

"This is a plot twist I should have expected," I grumble. "Am I a writer or a block of wood?"

"Is someone going to tell me what's going on?" River asks.

Jess holds up her hands. "Don't look at me."

"Do you know what Connor does for a living?" I ask them.

Wincing, Jess admits, "I think Juno said something about conservation?"

I look over at River. "What about you?"

He presses a surprised hand over his chest. "Me?"

"Yes. You out of any of us."

"Why 'of any of us'?"

"Because Connor Prince III is the creator and executive producer on my upcoming dating show, the one that uses your life's work as its central hook."

Jess presses her fingertips to her lips, speaking from behind them, "Oh my God, you've been fucking with *Connor* this whole time?"

"I've been nicer lately. I invited him inside after the signing."

Jess's wince tells me she's read this right, but she gives me an out. "Please tell me you mean inside for a cup of coffee."

"No, inside my *vagine*."

River coughs out a sip of water.

"Sadly for him, he turned me down."

River's low, mournful whistle says *Awkward*.

"It's fine," I say. "Honestly, it's probably good one of us had our heads on straight. I was just feeling sexy for the first time in forever, and he was conveniently there."

Nice one, Pinocchio.

My best friend nods dubiously. "Right, he was just *there*, just a hulking, muscled Adonis that you were attracted to purely because your dry spell has gone on so long."

"I'm glad you get it," I tell her with exaggerated gratitude.

"Sorry, wait, it's just sinking in." Jess presses her fingers to her forehead. "You propositioned the guy who's running the show where you try to match with a *soulmate*?"

"It was just a mood," I insist. "One and done."

"I've interacted with Natalia more because she's got Stevie during the week," Jess says. "But Connor seems like a really sweet man. He doesn't strike me as one and done."

"Are you suggesting sweet men can't also have moods?" I swing my smirking eyes to River. "They can, right, Hot Genius?"

He busies himself with opening the cooler, saying a distracted, "Sorry, just a sec."

"I just mean," Jess continues, "you thought this guy was an asshole. You called him Hot Millionaire then Hot Brit—" She cuts off, narrowing her eyes at me. "You did the typecasting thing with him, didn't you?"

"In my defense he is very hard to pin down. He had a different vibe at first—he was absolutely a Hot Millionaire Executive the first time we met."

"Connor? Not even a little," she protests.

"I mean, obviously I'm not going to win this argument today when he's showing muscular thigh in shorts and wearing a T-shirt that's, like, four sizes too small, but you just have to take my word that first-impression Connor was a mix between Kendall Roy and a Lego figure, including the hair."

As usual, my mouth is moving too fast. These last words come out just as I register the long shadow in front of our chairs isn't from the sunshade.

"Well," Connor says, "at least tell me I'm Lego Batman or the Hot Lifeguard."

sixteen

CONNOR

I'm sure I'm imagining it when I see her across the field. But here she is, ten on a Saturday morning: Felicity Chen, ranting about my shirt being too tight and my thighs being too . . . there. I'll ignore the Kendall Roy jab, but I'm taking the muscular thighs comment to my grave.

Before today, I would have thought she was impossible to ruffle. Fizzy says what she thinks, takes what she deserves, and makes no apologies for either. But when she finally turns to face me, she's visibly flustered.

"Batman is a bit too toxic masculinity for me," she says, and brushes the hair from her face. I think it's supposed to be one of those casual and carefree gestures, but I remember her doing it at the bar that first night and wonder if it's something she does when she's anxious.

"But Lifeguard Lego could work," she continues, eyes moving over my entire torso. "You're both hard workers and clearly have great upper-body strength."

"Thank you . . . I think. And for the record, this shirt is not too small."

The corners of Fizzy's mouth turn up, all traces of embarrassment gone and replaced with the spark of challenge. "It wasn't a complaint."

"There's technically nothing inappropriate about any of this," someone says, "but it still feels like we should cover all the kids' eyes." I follow the woman's voice, and it's only then that I notice the couple watching from the side: Juno's parents, Jess and River. I read the words on Fizzy's shirt, and it suddenly makes sense.

"Wait, you know Juno?"

"I do." She throws an accusing look at Jess before turning back to me. "What I didn't know was that *you* know her."

"She and Stevie just started on the same football team." I pick up the whistle hanging around my neck. "I'm the coach."

"Hi, Connor," Jess says, abandoning all pretense of not listening and coming right over.

"Hi, Jess." Awareness lands. "Ah. River must be the friend Fizzy mentioned is involved in the DNADuo technology. I get it now."

"And you must be the hot TV guy Felicity hasn't shut up about." Jess turns to Fizzy with an exaggerated grin. "I get it now."

I bite back a smile, sensing backstory here and that Jess is getting some long-awaited revenge.

"Okay, Jessica," Fizzy says. "Take your gorgeous husband and just sit down over there."

Still grinning, Jess waves and ducks back into the sunshade.

River extends a hand and I meet him with a quick shake. "Connor," he says.

"River."

He opens his mouth, but with a quick glance in Fizzy's direction, he seems to recalibrate. "Good luck on the game," he says instead before joining his wife. I don't know either of them well; Jess has always been friendly and is the first to volunteer rides for the other kids and snacks. I've seen River once or twice, but we've never spoken at length.

When it's just the two of us again, the silence feels loaded.

"You called her Stefania," Fizzy says accusingly.

"Stevie is her nickname," I explain. "Yelling 'Stefania Elena Garcia Prince' around the house would be rather a mouthful, don't you think?"

The silence stretches. It's not awkward exactly, but *aware*. I might have said no on Fizzy's doorstep, but I suspect we both know I wanted to go inside. How do we move on from this?

A breeze darts across the field, ruffling the trees and sending umbrellas and blankets tumbling along the grass. When I reach up to push my hair off my forehead, Fizzy's eyes follow the movement. I'm reminded that she said I should wear it like this more often, that she likes it.

I clear my throat, ready to steer us in a less dangerous direction. "I forgot to tell you: callbacks were great. I think we've found our Heroes."

Her entire face brightens. "Oh my God, tell me everything. Wait, first tell me they're all insanely hot."

I mentally stumble at the shift in her enthusiasm, and just how much I dislike it.

"Ratings-through-the-roof hot," I say. "I don't want to say too much because nothing's finalized, but we narrowed it down to eight men. All approved archetypes."

She's about to reply when there's a blur of movement and two small tornados collide into our bodies. Stevie looks up from where her arms are wrapped around my waist. Juno is hugging Fizzy.

"Can we have ice cream after the game?" Stevie asks.

I bend to kiss the top of her head. "Sure. Can you say hello to Fizzy? She's starring in the show I've been working on."

I turn her around and Stevie tilts her head back to look up at me. "I already know who Fizzy is," Stevie says. "She's walked us home a few times."

Fizzy reaches over to twirl the end of Stevie's long hair. "Sometimes we stop for hot chocolates on the way. Sometimes for cocktails. Depends how the day went."

Both the girls giggle, but then something catches Stevie's eye— a sticker on the back of Fizzy's phone—and she steps forward to examine it. "You never said you liked Wonderland!"

"She loooooooves them," Juno says.

"How have we never talked about it?" Fizzy says. "They are my happy place!"

I look closer at the small holographic logo, wondering how I missed it when there's a similar one attached to fifty percent of Stevie's belongings. Probably because when I'm with Fizzy, the last thing I'm looking at is her phone.

"Have you seen them in concert?" Fizzy asks.

Stevie shakes her head. "I've never been to a concert before."

"They're coming in two weeks! You should go!"

"It's sold out," I say.

Fizzy swats this detail away. "I could get us tickets. I dated an executive over at the stadium, and let me tell you—" She stops, noting my apprehension over what might come out of her mouth, and settles on, "I know a guy."

"That's a pretty late night." I'm already imagining carrying a sleeping Juno and Stevie across a mile-long parking lot. "They'd be exhausted the next day."

She scoffs. "It's summer! Besides, being exhausted after a night of screaming your face off is a fangirl rite of passage." She gives me a silent, pleading look, adding quietly, "Joy, remember?"

I exhale, unable to resist any of these females and their sweet persuasion. "If Fizzy knows a guy . . ." I hesitate long enough for my common sense to rescue me. It doesn't. "I guess we're going to see Wonderland."

"We *are*?" Stevie and Juno scream in unison, already jumping up and down.

"We are!"

"You're the best dad," Stevie says, and throws her arms around me.

"Thank Fizzy, not me, love."

And while I watch Stevie embrace Fizzy next, I can't help but think this is a terrible idea for at least a hundred reasons. The last thing I need is to spend *more* time with Fizzy. Happy time, joyful, enthusiastic Fizzy time. My guts twist in dread and anticipation.

"It's going to be great," she says as the girls sing and dance around us. She gives me her widest smile, the one that makes me think of words like effervescent, sparkling, *fizzy*.

seventeen

FIZZY

I can't even complain to Jess that this entire debacle just landed in my lap, since she was there when I very explicitly said I would take two ten-year-olds and a Sexy DILF Coach to a Wonderland concert. But the lines of people waiting to get into this venue are so horrendous I would love to have someone other than myself to blame. I check Instagram while we stand. I reply to reader DMs and dutifully avoid my inbox. But with every passing second the number of bodies around us grows. There are only eight entrances, and thirty thousand people trying to cram through at the same time. With no barricades or even any real signs about where a line begins or ends, the unending strings of people wind and weave, snaking around posts and crisscrossing with each other until we are essentially trusting that the person in front of us believes that the person in front of them is in the right place.

And going off the way his jaw looks tight, Connor is thinking the exact same thing. I'm sure he can see over most of the heads in the crowd, but I definitely cannot, and Stevie and Juno seem tiny in the middle of the giant mass of bodies, their eyes big and round with confusion. As the clock ticks down, there's a vibrating undercurrent of panic, as if the crowd is sensing that Wonderland is about to take the stage and we are all potentially going to miss it.

I tug Connor's sleeve, urging him down so I can tell him, "Put me on your shoulders."

He leans in closer, not understanding. "I'm sorry, what?"

"So I can see where this line goes. I'm worried it's a giant clump of people up there pushing their way in, and I am not letting our girls miss this."

He doesn't hesitate, crouching down into a squat, and with giggling Juno and Stevie steadying me, I climb on those broad, muscular shoulders. Connor stands seemingly without effort, sending me well over six feet into the air.

I let out a terrified squeak, clutching his jaw with both hands. "I take back every wish I ever made to be tall."

Connor laughs. "Relax, I've got you." He curls his hands around my bare shins, gently coaxing me to hook my legs back, tucking them under his arms. I'm now aware not only of the chaos ahead of us, but of the warm solidity of Connor's neck between my legs and the unreal stability of his shoulders beneath me. I wonder if he feels the heat of me, too, and if he's thinking what I'm thinking, which is how great it is to have his head between my legs.

I could obviously stay up here all night, but duty calls. "Okay, I've got it. You can put me down."

He does, staring quizzically at me once we're both standing again. "Helpful?"

"Very." I put my hand atop Juno's head and bend to meet her eyes. "I'll be right back."

And with that, I duck into the crowd.

Twenty minutes later, we are inside, holding beers in the small suite the venue executive who once asked to be called Doctor in bed booked for us, and watching a delighted Juno and Stevie dance on the glass-enclosed balcony to music being piped through the speakers before the show begins.

Connor is smiling at me like I'm a superhero, but really all it took was dragging the bewildered security team to the entry gate where an enormous cluster of people were cutting in line and wedging in ahead of everyone. Once they sorted that situation, concertgoers started filing in, happily organized.

"You could have been trampled," he says now.

"Unlikely." I sip my beer, wiping away the foam on my lip. "When I'm determined, I look much bigger. I bet I was at least six foot two walking through that crowd."

"Aren't you afraid of anything?"

I laugh when Juno and Stevie begin pretending to twerk. These tiny dummies. "No." And then I reconsider, looking up at him. "Wait, yes. I'm afraid that at some point in the past I've accidentally Face-Timed someone while masturbating and they are too mortified and polite to ever tell me, so I will live out the rest of my life not knowing whether I actually did that but always suspecting that I have."

Connor stares blankly down at me.

"What?" I ask. "Don't you ever worry about that?"

He smiles, shaking his head as he tips his plastic cup to his mouth.

A rare flush of self-consciousness takes root. I know I'm a lot to take, and I suspect if Connor found me unbearable, he wouldn't ever let on. He couldn't. He'd grin and bear it, maybe just like he is right now. He has to put up with me because he wants this show to work, and he wants this show to work because if it doesn't, he's out of a job and likely has to move two hours away from his daughter, this tiny bundle of barely contained energy, dancing over there like a sparkler on New Year's Eve.

"Sorry," I mumble into my cup.

"For what?"

"The masturbation thing," I whisper, and then add with a smile, "And the Kendall Roy joke at the soccer game. You are not nearly that broken."

This makes him laugh. "Don't be so sure. And now I'm wondering if *I've* ever accidentally FaceTimed someone during a wank."

I look over at him, grateful at his attempt to ease the tension, but emotionally obliterated by the mental image that's now being projected in HD in my brain.

Connor shrugs, taking another sip of his beer, and affection clutches at me as I register yet again how easy he is to be around and how much I genuinely like him.

The words are out before I've given them time to marinate: "Sorry about the other night, too."

"The oth— *Oh*." And now tense awareness falls like shrapnel from the sky. Connor contemplates something in the distance, squinting. "Yeah, no. You don't have to apologize for that."

"Yes, I do."

I do everything I can to not fill the answering quiet with jokes or innuendo or even remarks about the weather. I just stew in the awkwardness of it, wanting him to know that I'm capable of gravitas and sincerity, even if I am outwardly terrible at both.

"I declined for several reasons," he says finally, and my mortification bottoms out to dungeon levels.

"Please don't feel obligated to list them."

He turns to face me, expression sober. "But none were because I wasn't interested. I'm sorry if I didn't make that clear."

"Oh." I have to break eye contact from those hypnotic, fresh-leaf eyes. Suddenly my brain is nothing but the static white noise of a thousand sexy songs blaring over each other. Connor has no idea that he's toying with barely controlled fire, that flirtation is my love language, and that I haven't gotten laid in a very, very long time. Frankly, I was just being polite by apologizing.

"Tell me about Jess and River," he says, blessing us both with an escape route. "How do you know them?"

"Jess and I have been friends forever. River used to come into our coffee shop every morning and they'd do this whole *Pride and Prejudice* flirt-but-not-flirt thing. It was entertaining but ultimately exhausting. I forced her to do the DNADuo. I'm telling you, if it wasn't for me, she'd still be single. I should get a finder's fee."

"I wasn't really paying attention to the technology yet when the company first launched," he says, "but they had a very high match, right?"

"Diamond—a score of ninety-nine, in fact, still the highest score in company history. The executives actually paid her to get to know him. Honestly, I couldn't have written a better happily ever after myself."

I make the mistake of letting my eyes wander down the length of his body. He seems strangely fidgety, and when he pulls his sweater up and over his head, folding it on the back of his chair, my brain short-circuits for at least a second.

A new emotion invades my blood: soft fondness. I blink at his chest and the five grinning male faces there beneath WONDERLAND in the branded, swooping font. "You're wearing a Wonderland T-shirt?"

"Stevie and I got some merch when you and Juno were stuck in that abysmal porta potty line earlier."

I laugh-whisper, "*Merch.* You've got the lingo."

He grins at my slack-jawed awe. "We are on a quest, right? A quest for joy? Do I not need to attain certain knowledge?"

For a beat, I'm speechless. I have a tight feeling in my chest, like twine around my lungs, seeing him in this T-shirt. And not just wearing it, but proudly wearing it. I've agreed with Jess about how hot it is that River is such a good dad to Juno, but it's a truth I can't look at straight on. I celebrate it for her obliquely, on the sidelines. I want a family, of course, but who knows what that will look like for me. The *meet someone + love someone + be together long enough to want to have a kid together* math isn't really mathing for me. I assume my role is being the auntie everyone comes to when they need to learn how to do the perfect winged eyeliner, hide a hangover from a parent, or cry about their first broken heart. I think every child needs someone who adores them unconditionally but is not biologically obligated to. Being attracted to a proud dad is doing weird, painful things to my breathing.

It's only attraction, I remind myself. *Don't make it into a big deal.*

"I didn't realize their merch sizes went up to giant," I say, pushing my voice out past the cork of emotion in my throat. I make the mistake of reaching out to touch the shirt absently, curiosity guiding my movements, and realize how firm his body is underneath. "At least this one doesn't look like it came from the kids' department." Holy bicep. I jerk my fingers away like he's on fire.

"The sizes are confusing," he admits.

I take a small step back, willing my skin to cool down. "I bought a shirt in women's large a while ago thinking I'd have something to sleep in. It fits me like a wetsuit."

He laughs. "I assumed that's why this one was available. The woman said it was the last size to sell out. Most of their fan base—" He holds up a hand to stop me from correcting him. "No. I *thought* everyone would look like Stevie and Juno." Connor motions for me to follow him to where the girls are standing at the edge of the suite, overlooking the crowd. We see a group of women fully decked out in Wonderland merch below us. The suite to our left has three thirty-something couples, standing at the ledge like we are, laughing and sipping cocktails. The one to our right has a group of teenage girls and a lone dad scrolling on his phone. And throwing my gaze out farther I see a large group of women of all ages, a group of men in LED necklaces singing along to the preshow playlist, a pair of white-haired older women taking photos in front of the giant screens. "It looks like one of your signings," Connor says.

"Just a little bigger," I say, laughing.

"Only for now." He looks over at me, his eyes dropping only briefly to my mouth. "Once the world sees you, Fizzy, they're going to fall in love."

eighteen

CONNOR

Stevie has always been an exuberant child, driven by her emotions. She dances around the house, does cartwheels in the aisles at the grocery store, and was so overcome when we brought Baxter home that she held him and cried into his silky puppy fur for a full hour. I'm familiar with her squeals of delight when we get the back car on Big Thunder Mountain, and the nonstop giggles that come from her room during a sleepover. But I have never seen my kid like this.

The show hasn't even started yet, and Stevie and Juno are already up on their feet, dancing and singing along to music videos with the rest of the audience. Fizzy wasn't kidding when she said that she had an in. We are in a suite, high enough to see the arena, but still reasonably close to the stage. There is also complimentary food, drinks—*booze*—and our own private toilet. We may never leave.

And Fizzy . . . I can't seem to keep my eyes off her. Logically I know it's self-sabotage to entertain thoughts about how good she looks or how tempting her neck is with her hair pulled back like that, but my brain doesn't seem to care.

When she climbed up on my shoulders outside the arena, it was like a pin being pulled from a grenade. I could feel the heat of her through her shorts; the strength of her thighs gripping my neck sent a sharp bolt of desire through my body, one I'd rather not experience in front of a few thousand people. I wanted to be alone with her, to run my fingers up the inside of her thighs, feel that heat pressed against my hand. I wanted to drop to my knees and show her with my mouth just how much I had regretted going home alone the other night. Job? Who needs a job?

But of course, we weren't alone. It only took one glance at Stevie—her eyes locked on Fizzy and shining with absolute awe— for reality to come screeching back.

Thankfully, it's the erupting screams that break me from my swimming thoughts, as the lights are snuffed out and the arena explodes into a blast of unbelievable sound. It's nearly overwhelming. I know that sound doesn't have color, but when I close my eyes, stars pop yellow and red on my lids. It is deafening, a tangible thunder that moves through my chest, rattling the ground beneath me. Stevie and Juno are jumping up and down, joining in a growing chant of the group's name.

Fizzy pulls me close, her hand clutching my forearm. I see her lips move but can't possibly hear her in the cacophony as she nods to the girls. When I shake my head, she stretches and I lean in, feeling her lips move against my ear: "I am so happy you're here to see this."

"I'd like to put a pedometer on them and see how many calories they burn by the end of this thing."

"Just wait till it starts."

She's so close I wonder how I'll be able to think about anything else, but when the first note rings through the dark, it easily yanks my attention away. I have never voluntarily listened to a Wonderland song, but it is impossible to be in the middle of all this and not be affected by the collective anticipation around us. This is the joy that Fizzy talked about. The shared adrenaline, everyone here for the same thing. Even the dads near us have decided to stand, some with arms folded across their chests as they observe, others shifting from foot to foot to get a better view, curious to see what all the fuss is about.

Fireworks erupt from the stage and the group emerges to a thunderous reaction. When the first song starts, Fizzy, Juno, and Stevie know every word. I'm surprised to realize I know most of them, too. The girls lose themselves to the music and the euphoria of the show. Fizzy dances where she stands, entirely unselfconscious. Somehow Stevie knows every beat of the show before it happens. She knows the set list, when the members will venture out into the audience, and at exactly what point they'll pass right in front of us. I'm so caught up in it that when she attempts to hold up her small sign, I'm ready to take over and hold it up higher.

During the final intermission, sweaty and surprisingly exhausted, I walk from the balcony and through the suite to use the loo. When I step out again, Fizzy is making herself a drink. We can still see the girls, but the glass walls close us in, dulling the noise from the show.

I join Fizzy at the bar, refill my water bottle, and close my eyes as I take a long, cold drink.

When I open them again, she's watching. "So." She leans casually against the countertop. "What's the verdict?"

"To be honest, I expected noise and traffic and two tired, cranky ten-year-old girls—which I'm sure we'll still get—but I was also sure I would hate every minute. I was wrong. You may now gloat."

"You were dancing," she says with a grin.

"I was *swaying*."

She lets this one slide. "I'm pretty picky about who I'll bring to a concert, but you were a good sport, Hot DILF. I may invite you again if I find myself needing a concert buddy. But know there are usually fewer ten-year-olds, more booze, and the occasional bad tattoo at the end."

"I look forward to it," I say, and glance back at the girls, unexpectedly struck by Fizzy's praise. The group launches into another song and Stevie looks over, searching for me. This one's her favorite, the song that plays on my way to work every Monday morning because it was the last one Stevie played Sunday night. She excitedly points to the stage before turning back to watch.

"She totally adores you," Fizzy says.

I don't know why that word in particular stings the backs of my eyes. Most kids love their parents. I don't like my dad, but I do love him in my own way. It's a love tangled up with grief and hurt and a messy pile of other complicated emotions, but it's there. To *adore* is to cherish, to treasure, and for Stevie to visibly feel that for me after all the ways I've fallen short fills me with so much pride it's almost hard to breathe.

If Fizzy catches any of this, she's polite enough not to say anything. "Thank you for bullying me into bringing her," I say. "I've never seen her like this."

Fizzy gazes at both the girls fondly. "She's definitely in her element."

"How did she know everything that was going to happen? The set list, even what they'd be wearing. Where'd she learn all that?"

"It's what fangirls do," Fizzy says with a shrug. "It's the same way you know when a new Shimano derailleur is coming out for your fancy mountain bike."

My attention snaps back to her and I grin. "Look at you talking about bike parts."

She reaches for a cookie and breaks it in two, handing half to me. "Some might say I'm an expert at typing things into the Google search." She studies her cookie. "Even went hunting for pics of you."

"Me?"

"You know, on set, mountain biking." She pauses, shrugging causally. "With girlfriends."

"And?" I lean against the counter at her side, smothering a smile. She is so bloody obvious. "What did you find?"

One side of her mouth turns down into a frown and carves a small dimple in her left cheek. "Nothing. Your Instagram name is a bunch of random letters and numbers that I was only able to track down because I know Jess who knows Natalia who happened to tag you in something, like, five years ago. You have four followers and two posts. It was both a relief and disappointing."

"We're supposed to be focusing on *your* love life, Fizzy."

"Just feels unfair," she says, and her smile is easy but her eyes are tight when she looks at me, "now that we're becoming friends, that we're only focused on finding someone for me and not you."

I look out to where the show is winding down and Wonderland is saying their final goodbyes. Nothing good can come from this. We both know it and yet we keep ending up here. "Well, I'd be surprised if there are photos of me with women anywhere. I don't date much these days."

"Have you ever tried DNADuo?"

"Me? Definitely not," I say, shaking my head. "It's not that I don't believe it or anything, I just . . . if I had a match, I'd want to take it seriously, and I just can't right now."

"Jess was the same way. With Juno," she says, clarifying. "She wasn't interested in getting involved with anyone until Juno was in college."

"Sounds familiar."

"I'll tell you what I told her: that makes for a boring fucking book."

"Well, maybe one day," I say. "I tried dating a few times when Stevie was younger, but any woman worth pursuing wants more than the occasional weeknight together. Plus, whoever I'm involved with gets me, Stevie, and Nat."

"How long have you been divorced?"

"Stevie was two."

"Oh wow. She was so little."

There was a time when a comment like this—no matter how well-meaning—would have sent me down a rabbit hole of guilt. Stevie *was* young and going through the divorce was the hardest thing I've ever done, but that doesn't mean it wasn't the right thing to do, either. "She was."

"But you and Nat are close now? I've heard Stevie talk about her a few times, and I'm pretty sure I've seen her at the school during pickup. She's hot."

I laugh. "She is. And she has a very young, also very hot boyfriend whom I expect to propose to her any day now."

"How nice for her." The moment stretches out, tense and

knowing. I expect her to look away; she doesn't. Instead, she clucks her tongue sympathetically. "Too bad for you you're no good at compartmentalizing."

I decide to stop dancing around it. "Specifically, I'm not good with casual sex."

The word *sex* flares out between us like a flamethrower and she grins. "Yes, actually I meant too bad for *me* that you're no good at compartmentalizing."

I laugh at this. "You are an honest-to-God menace, Felicity."

"You like it."

I pretend to think about it, and she comes right up on tiptoes, growling in my face.

Finally, I relent. "You are tolerable."

She sets back down on her feet and leans against the counter beside me. "Delightful," she says.

"Bearable."

"Gifted and charismatic."

"Pushy and opinionated."

"Your new best friend. Say it."

Her hand rests near mine. My pinky twitches, brushing against hers. If I move away now, I could pretend it was an accident. But I can't, and instead shift my finger so it rests on top of hers.

She curls her finger around mine. Heat spears through me, and the urge to turn into her, to press her against the counter, lift her up, step between her legs, and—

I pull in a slow, deep breath. "My new best friend."

nineteen

FIZZY

Juno is no longer a tiny child.

Which means when we pull up outside Jess and River's house, and both girls are passed out like sacks of flour in the back seat, there is no way I can carry Juno to the doorstep.

Truthfully, I'm not even sure I could get *myself* to the door right now. Not to toot my own horn, but I've written sexual tension that could peel wallpaper, and none of it comes close to the last twenty minutes in the car with Connor.

"I've got her." Connor ducks around me, bending to unbuckle Juno's seat belt.

His thighs flex beneath his jeans and his shoulders strain against the soft cotton of his new T-shirt as he easily lifts the floppy kid from his back seat. "I really don't think my ovaries can take any more," I mumble.

He turns, adjusting her weight over his shoulder. "What's that?"

I cough delicately into a fist. "Clear night, don't think there's rain in store."

Connor looks skeptical, but seems to trust that if I'm filtering myself, it's probably a good thing. He turns and heads up when I gesture that he should lead the way.

The door opens as we approach. Jess stands in the frame, backlit by a warm, golden glow, and seems to entirely miss the mental flare gun I repeatedly fire into the air. River comes up behind her, reaching to take Juno from Connor, who murmurs a soft "Got her?" as he passes her off.

My heart launches itself out a tenth-story window.

The little girl reveals her level of consciousness by snaking her arms around her dad's neck and mumbling, "Thank you, Mr. Prince."

I get it together enough to frown in feigned offense. "Hey, what about *me*? Ticket hookup, hello?"

Her response is a sleepy grunt as she's carried down the hall to her room.

With Juno situated and Stevie asleep in the back seat, Connor jogs down a couple of front steps, and then looks back at me expectantly. "Ready?"

I start to follow, propelled like there's a silken rope connecting us, but hesitate. I think about the warmth of the car and the soothing mood of the music. I think about Connor's big hands wrapped around the steering wheel, gripping it like it was a vine tethering him to the top of a cliff. I think about his forearms that are corded with veins and muscle, and how when he's two steps below me we're finally at eye level. I think about how his eyes lit up with joy tonight watching his daughter in her element, and I think about how his shoulders felt beneath my legs earlier when he lifted me. I think about the defeated growl of his *My new best friend* and I think about being in the front seat beside him for one second longer and I'm not sure I can do it. I am but a mortal woman after all, and once again

I want Connor Prince III to crush me beneath him like a delicate flower under a fallen tree.

But sexily.

"I think I'll crash here tonight," I tell him.

"It's not out of my way," he assures me. "Really."

"It's not that."

His eyes narrow. He gets it: I am very specifically not going with him because it's not the kind of ride I want him to offer.

Instead, I am going to go inside and tell my best friend all about this suffocating chemistry between us.

"If you're sure . . ." he says, smirking.

"Oh," I say, "I'm sure."

With the smirk still in his eyes, he says good night to Jess and then jogs his hot body back down the front steps.

We watch him, rapt, like it's the final few moments of *Squid Game*, and then I exhale fifteen metric tons of air from my lungs. "Jesus."

"You're doomed."

I follow her inside, kicking off my shoes. "I am not doomed. I'm awakened. I'm revitalized."

"Sure."

"Jessica, hear my words: Connor is a catalyst. A spark. An amuse-bouche for the libido. Aren't you glad? I've been an emotional robot. That doesn't make for interesting television."

Jess collapses on the couch. "Do you remember when I fake-dated River?"

"Of course I remember. Every time he walked into Twiggs you looked like you were going to eat his face."

"And still, I swore I wasn't into him."

I see where this is going, but I disagree with the parallel. "Yes, but you were delusional. You were already halfway in love with him."

"Like you right now with Connor."

"Absolutely not," I reply. "You were falling for River. I just want to ride the hot producer's dick."

Having just entered the room to join us, River makes a quick U-turn at this, disappearing back into the hall. "Good night," he calls.

"Come back! I value your opinion!" The only response I get is the sound of his footsteps echoing away. I grin over at Jess. "Whoops."

She shakes her head in exasperation. "Why do you always insist everything is just casual sex?"

"Because my last relationship was with a dirtbag, and for the past three years I'd rather eat a literal bag of dirt than risk breaking up someone's marriage again?"

"You say it like you're joking, but it's true. Rob *was* a dirtbag. He was the monster. You didn't do anything wrong."

It is true. I know it, intellectually, even if it took all this time to really feel the truth of it in my gut. I'm finally over the fatal sting of his duplicity (even if there will always be a fiery asterisk beside his name). I sit down beside her on the sofa. "I know."

"Not every guy is a Rob."

"Well, I certainly hope so, because I'm supposed to be optimistic that my soulmate will appear beside me on camera soon."

She stands, crossing the room to the ornate bar cart and pouring us each a small glass of whiskey. "So you're confident that Connor's team has done a good job casting?"

"Seems like it." I take the tumbler with a smile and sip, letting the heat trail down my throat and settle gently in my stomach. "I get the sense that he's been very, very picky."

"That's good." She swirls her drink. "He seems like a thoughtful guy." A long, quiet pause. "I wonder how this is for him. I got the sense tonight that maybe he's into you, too."

"I mean, I think he's attracted to me." I tilt the glass, letting the light catch the amber liquid. "He admitted earlier that he didn't turn me down because he wasn't interested."

"Of course not, look at you."

"Now that I'm in Connor-free air and can think clearly again, I sort of wish I didn't know, though," I admit. "Knowing he's attracted to me, too, has made me into a demon. I want what's in his pants."

She shakes her head at me. "Focus on the show. When does filming start?"

"Five weeks."

"And did you settle on a schedule?"

Nodding, I take another sip of my drink before answering. "He sent it over this morning to see if I had any notes. The first week is coffee dates. We all do testimonials about how it went, then the show airs and the audience votes to eliminate two based on who they think I vibed with most, and so on. The final two contestants will meet my family. I'm pretending that part isn't happening." Jess makes a sympathetic *good luck with that* face. "After that is the finale, where we find out if the audience picked my soulmate as predicted by DNADuo.

The winner of the audience vote gets $100,000, and then I get to choose who goes with me on a trip to Fiji. So yay."

"Funny, that doesn't sound like excitement I'm hearing."

I dig around in my head and my gut, searching for a convincing reply. "Sure, I'm excited."

"Fizzy, this is such a cool thing you get to do! You get to have eight romance heroes compete for your heart!"

"I know," I whine. "But Connor's thighs could crush me like a grape. I want that, just once before I meet a different kind of prince." Jess laughs as I lean my head back against the couch, sighing. "I swear, I just need to get him out of my system."

"That is literally your least favorite romance trope."

Lifting my head again, I lament, "Yes, but who knew it was a real thing!"

"No one!" she yells back. "Because it isn't!" She throws up her hands. "Okay, seriously. No more of these dates with him."

"They aren't dates," I argue. "They're *joy excursions*."

"Fizzy. Be serious."

"What! I am being serious! He does ocean conservation documentaries. I wanted him to know *this* audience."

"Do you feel like he does now?"

A shiver spreads through me, warm but still unsettling. "He does, and watching him not only open his eyes to this side of the industry but also enjoy it has been . . . I mean, it's been really nice. It isn't just that he's hot. I like being around him. He's fun. He's funny. And maybe my favorite thing of all is how he isn't cowed by my shit. I daresay he might like it."

Gross. Feelings.

"That's important for a producer, too," Jess says.

Groaning, I fall sideways into the couch beside her. "If he would just fuck me, I'd be over this already."

Jess runs her fingers into my hair, scratching gently. "Actually, I don't think you would."

twenty

CONNOR

I should have foreseen that extremes are the norm with Fizzy, and that our time together would be the most fun I've ever had with someone but also the most torturous. Over several weeks, *The True Love Experiment* begins to take shape, and Fizzy and I skive off every Friday in our continued search for joy. We take the train to the Broad Museum and talk about quiet, introspective joy. We visit the Last Bookstore nearby, where she buys me a collector's edition of *'Salem's Lot*, and I buy her a framed cover of one of her favorite romance novels. The following week, she treats the entire crew to tickets to a live showing of *The Rocky Horror Picture Show*. I get home that night and drink more than I probably should, all in an effort to clear my head of the way her entire being lights up inside when she's letting loose, how badly she sings and how much I adore that she does it with gusto anyway, how she takes the adoration from the crew and returns it to them, doubled, and how I'm beginning to abhor the prospect of her finding true love in only a handful of weeks.

Shooting officially begins tomorrow, but even knowing my workday will likely begin before dawn, I've got one more place I want to take her.

Fizzy and I blow down the freeway, windows open, wind whipping. The orange globe sun hangs heavy and seductive at the horizon. It's our last joy outing—at least the last one we've planned, and I'm sure the plan I've made is actually quite daft. We will be alone, it will be dark, with the sounds of crashing waves all around us. I can already imagine Fizzy running barefoot on the sand, tackling me, pushing through the pathetic restraint I'm clinging to.

Torrey Pines is a four-and-a-half-mile stretch of coastline located between Del Mar and La Jolla. Traffic is uncharacteristically light, and we make it to the parking lot just as the sun is beginning to dip into the water. As I park and meet Fizzy at the front of the car, I'm unprepared all over again for the sight of her in simple jeans and a T-shirt, sneakers, and a fuzzy sweater tucked over one arm.

There is so much riding on the show, but there are moments like this when I look at her walking toward the sand and can't remember what any of it is. When she talks about something she's passionate about or bursts out laughing, when she hands someone their ass or lets her tiny fissures of vulnerability show, I find myself rationalizing the reasons I should just give in. Maybe it's inevitable. Maybe nobody needs to know. Maybe I'm overthinking and it *won't* ruin everything. We're both adults; we've both had sex with people before and it was just sex. Maybe I *can* compartmentalize.

During the day, gliders and parasailers launch themselves from the red sandstone cliffs in the distance, and sunbathers, surfers, and swimmers crowd the beach. Tonight it's mostly empty, with only a few stragglers along the shore or straddling their boards in the ocean, bobbing along with the incoming tide. The sky seems to change by the second, a melting canvas of blue to purple to red to orange.

"So." Fizzy stretches, revealing a swath of skin between her shirt and the waist of her jeans. "The beach."

I smile at the disdain in her voice. "Not a fan, I presume?"

"Oh, I get it, it's beautiful." She sits on the sand. "But it's a little like sex on your period. It sounds like a lot of work, and you definitely don't want to do it every day, but once you get going, you're like, 'Hey, this isn't too bad.'"

"Oh my God, Fizzy," I say with a small laugh.

She looks up at me. "What?"

I sit down next to her, swallowing down the way infatuation rises like a sleeper wave in my chest. "I'm not even going to touch that one, I think."

She laughs, slipping off her shoes and wiggling her toes into the cool, damp sand. "Now that we know how I feel about the beach, tell me what we're doing here."

"Well, I grew up on the water, so I brought you here because I feel very peaceful at the shore, but tonight's not about the beach specifically. It's a moment."

She tucks her knees to her chin, wrapping her arms around her legs as she listens. Around us the sun has dipped below the horizon, the sky darkening like a bruise.

"My weekends with Stevie can be pretty routine," I explain. "We go for a bike ride, take Baxter to the park or somewhere he can run and play, we watch movies and do homework and cook together. Basic stuff. When she was about six, Baxter had surgery on his paw and couldn't come with her for the weekend. We decided to try something different. We packed a picnic and came to watch surfers and ended up staying most of the day. We should have gone home once the sun set—it was getting cold, and I knew she'd be a bear the next day—but she was having so much fun just running around and doing cartwheels in the surf that I decided to stay a bit. It got dark and we were just getting ready to leave when I saw this blue spark in the water, and then another. When the waves crashed it was like there were hundreds of fireflies in the surf."

"Oh, I know this one." She snaps her fingers, trying to recall the word. "Bioluminescence. It's algae, right?"

"Right. Some types of algae use bioluminescence to avoid predators, so when it's disturbed by something moving through the water, or even something getting too close, it produces this burst of blue light to scare them off." I point. "Look over there."

She leans in and follows my gaze to where a surfer is leisurely cutting across the surface on their way to the shore, leaving a swirl of blue light in their wake. "It doesn't look real," she says.

"I remember the amazement on Stevie's face and how I wanted to bottle that moment and experience it over and over again."

Fizzy looks up at me. "That's the answer you should have given me in your office."

"Answer to what?"

"When I asked you about what gave you joy."

My eyes move like magnets to her mouth. "But then how would I have monopolized all your time these past several weeks?"

She laughs.

"Besides," I say, "I never asked you what brings *you* joy."

Fizzy leans into me, bumping my shoulder. "This. Hanging out with you."

"But before I became the best thing that ever happened to you?"

"Jess and Juno. My family. Travel." She inhales deeply. "Sex. Writing."

"Still feeling stuck?"

She nods. "I can't remember the last time I opened a Word doc."

"To be fair, you've been busy. There's this whole reality show we're planning."

"But maybe that's a convenient excuse." She picks up a small piece of seaweed and drags it across the sand. "Every idea I come up with fizzles before I can even get started."

"I don't pretend I understand what this is like, but is it something you've been able to talk about in therapy?"

"Oh, for sure," she says. "But I got so tired of going over the same thing and not getting anywhere. I would do little writing exercises, but they felt pointless." She stares out at the water for a long moment. "I know I'll be okay if I don't write again. I know that the death of my writing wouldn't be the death of *me*. But I miss that me. I liked that me, and I'm not sure how to find her. Focusing on it in therapy started to make it worse, if that makes sense."

"It does."

"I'm normally pretty self-aware and can work through most things, but this—" She shakes her head. "It's got me beat. I'd all but lost interest in any man until yo—" She pauses, and then squints out at the ocean. "Until, you know, the show."

Until you, she was going to say. My heart twists uncomfortably.

She clears her throat. "But yeah, love stories. My current brain block."

"Maybe your brain needs to live one for a change."

"Look at you, producer." She smiles over at me. "Bringing us full circle."

I watch her tilt her face to the sky, eyes closed as she takes a deep breath. Finally, tonight, our last night before I endeavor to help her fall in love with someone else, I can admit it.

I am falling in love with her.

"What can I say," I murmur. "I try."

twenty-one

FIZZY

'll be the first to admit that I'm a talker, but I'm good with silence, too. Jess and I have spent many a workday sitting across from each other in productive quiet. I love the gentle moments with Juno on my couch, her little head in my lap while she reads. I love the big-sky serenity of a hike with my brother, Peter, or the leisurely peace of mah-jongg with my mother. Truth is, you'll never meet a book lover who hates the quiet.

But after the easy, overlapping flow of our conversation tonight, this silence with Connor is heavy. Side by side we sit in the sand, our legs stretched out before us, toes wiggling up at the sky. He's rolled his pants up, exposing feet, ankles, the lower half of his calves. His legs are tanned and lightly dusted with hair, muscled. The way he leans back on his hands, face tilted to the night breeze . . . it's like he's offering his body up for worship. That geometric, superhero chest. The long, corded neck, the bunching density of his shoulders. I feel my brain shrieking all the breathless, desperate thoughts, like *Your body is unreal*

and *I want your hands on me*

and *Fuck me into the sand.*

But what surprises me is that the silence has quieter thoughts, too. Things like *I really like you*

and *You're sort of my favorite person lately*

and *I want to be excited for tomorrow but all I can think is how I don't want tonight to end.*

Of course, this final thought lands just as Connor coughs into his fist, breaking the stillness. "So," he says, and smiles shyly over at me in a way that acknowledges how heavy things just got, how there is something hot and tangible in the air between us but maybe if we talk over it, it will dissipate. "You ready for tomorrow?"

Inhaling sharply, I sit up straighter. Right. Get yourself together, Fizzy. "I am. I hope I can sleep tonight. I really don't want to show up all puffy and shadowed tomorrow."

"I was going to say," he says, smiling, "you've appeared very calm for someone who's about to be on television."

"I won't deny that I've had regular facials since I agreed to do this and invested in some new gravity-defying bras." He laughs. "But I've also done so many signings where people have taken and posted photos of me from awful angles, there's really no point pretending to be a supermodel now."

"You don't have to pretend," he says. "You always take my breath away."

We both go still, staring straight out at the surf while the echo of his words spirals around us. My pulse goes quiet for a moment and then it roars to life, a walloping throb in my neck. And I can almost feel it in him, the way he wishes the waves would stretch up here and wash that moment away.

"Well—so. Anyway." His voice bursts out now, jazz hands, distracting. "You seem more excited for the first day of filming, at least. That's good."

I'm still raw from his declaration. Connor is an oak tree, and the more time I spend with him the more I register how frequently I feel like a stray leaf blown at the whim of my impulsive decisions and my roller-coaster job and even my own moods. *You always take my breath away*, he said. He doesn't do casual, isn't good at it. Of course he isn't. Unfortunately, that's partly why I like him. He moves steadily, with intent, through the world. I am so drawn to him it feels magnetic.

"I am excited," I admit carefully. "And I know you did an amazing job with casting. That said, I hope there's a contestant in the group who makes me feel even a fraction of what I'm feeling tonight."

I've kept my eyes fixed on the water, but I can feel him turn and look at me.

"What does that mean?" he asks.

Instead of answering, I shift and, slowly enough that he can stop me if he wants, I climb over him, settling on top of his thighs. "It means I'm, like, insanely attracted to you."

I feel something with Connor that I don't want to label quite yet, but it scares me to think I'd ever have to give it up.

"Fizzy."

"Yes?"

He stares at me, eyes shadowed, and adjusts his posture to set one warm palm on my hip. "Haven't we already decided this is a bad idea?"

His tone isn't accusatory. It's gentle and curious and maybe the tiniest bit hungry.

"Yes." I swallow, getting my longing under control. "But I was sitting here thinking how much I wanted to touch you and how scared I am at the idea of going home tonight and never feeling this way again."

Connor reaches up, coaxing a few flyaway strands of hair away from my face. "Do you really think that's possible?"

"I don't know," I admit. "I used to be attracted to people all the time. I used to love sex. I liked that fun and adventurous side of me so much. Being near you . . . it makes me feel like myself again, but a much more grounded version."

"That's a good thing, sweet," he says gently. "And may I add that maybe what you're also feeling lately is growth." The wind blows another strand of my hair across my eyes, and he gently tucks it behind my ear. "You are so much more than your playful, sexy, adventurous author persona. You are that, of course, but you are also a woman with thoughtful depth and sensitive layers, and I wonder whether the way you feel lately is less about me and more about connecting with a new side of yourself."

I can't blink away from his steady gaze. My blood seems to vibrate with what he's just said. "That's probably the deepest thing anyone has ever said to me."

He laughs at this. "In any case, I'm glad for you to be reminded before the show that you are a sexual person. That you can connect with someone this way."

"And here I am," I say, grinning. "Connecting with you."

His gaze searches mine for a second and his expression softens. "Mm-hmm."

"I'm not asking you to kiss me or do anything more than this. I just wanted to be close to you one time." I reach up, tracing the shell of his ear. "I'm going to miss you, starting tomorrow."

This makes him smile, but he directs it at my lips. "But starting tomorrow you'll see me more often."

"You know what I mean."

"I do."

"I'll have to share you," I say. "It'll be weird."

It's the way he tilts his chin, I think. He just lifts it slightly, a tiny, unspoken *come on, then.*

I lean in, slowly, so he can lean away. But he doesn't, and the second my lips meet his, I have the spiraling sensation of never having been kissed before. Connor is a mountain of a man, warm and massive, solid as bedrock beneath me. His mouth is soft and strong, commanding and pliable. Pleasure spears a sweet arrow through the center of my chest, and in a flash, our simple kiss flares, all the pent-up feelings pouring out as our mouths move together.

My God.

It is the best kiss of my entire lifetime.

He tilts his head, coming at me better somehow, and deeper, his lips parting to slot between mine, one hand wrapping around my hip to pull me flush against him, the other sliding up my neck, cupping my face.

I know passion—in the heat of many moments, I've collided with walls and broken furniture—but already this is something else. This is more than just urges and instinct; it's connection and longing uncorked. The feel of Connor's body beneath me leaves no doubt we could break anything in my house, but this hunger is intimate, too, sacred; burning me up from the inside. I am undone by the way his breath shakes against my lips and the quiet groans he strangles down when I sweep my tongue across his, when I wrap my arms around his neck, threading hands into his hair. I feel a desperate ache spiral through my torso when his hand leaves my hip and slides up under my sweater, big palm smoothing up my ribs, cupping my breast, coaxing my bra down as he kisses me with his hungry, teasing mouth. I sense that if we do this only once he wants to feel every inch of me. I want it, too, pressing into his hand, encouraging him with sounds, with my teeth scraping over his lower lip, his chin, down the sharp line of his neck.

The ocean roars behind us, waves rolling over themselves to break against the sand. My hands wander the width of his shoulders, down his chest to the flat plane of his stomach. His cheeks are flushed in the glow of the moon, lips full and bitten, eyes heavy with lust. A mark blooms on the skin of his throat, as clear as if I've graffitied my name there. *This spot belongs to Felicity Chen.* I want to put my mark all over his body, claiming. I reach between us, pressing a hand over the solid shape of him, my mind bottoming out when I register what I'm feeling. He's big, and my body clenches, suddenly, painfully hollow.

I roll my hips against him, but instead of bringing relief it only makes me wilder. His mouth chases my kiss, swallowing the sound I make when he rocks up, the thick line of his cock pressing exactly where I need him. His hands cup my ass, pushing me away and pulling me closer, back and forth, again and again. I know I could come like this. It's right there, shimmering on the edge of sensation, and I'm torn between letting my greedy body have its way and dragging him to the car so I can take my time.

But before I can unbutton his pants, he guides my hand away and pulls my hips closer again, arching into me.

"Take me home," I tell him. "I want you so bad, Connor. Just one time."

He breathes against my throat, mouth open, the shape of my name pressed into my skin. It seems to take monumental effort for him to pull away long enough to gaze up at me, only an inch between our faces, but it's enough for the cold, wet ocean air to invade the space. His eyes clear and he takes a deep, shaking breath. Bending, he rests his forehead to my shoulder, exhaling in a long, slow stream.

Finally, he says simply, "No."

Inside I am a beast with sharp, gnashing teeth. My clawed hands grab at the bars, shaking my cage. "Why?"

"Fizzy. We can't." But he doesn't let me go. He pulls me into his body, holding me. Connor takes a deep breath, chest expanding against me, and then he seems to deflate. "We just can't."

In his arms, with his deep breaths setting a rhythm for my own, my fevered dust settles.

"It wouldn't have to mean anything more than two friends scratching an itch," I whisper.

"Unfortunately, I suspect it might mean a good deal more than that."

I go still, feeling rattled by his words.

"Fizzy." A gentle surrender hangs between us. "I really need this show to work," he says quietly. "I don't regret this, but it can't happen."

Leaning back, I frown, drawing a line from his forehead, down the straight angle of his nose, over his lips, and release a low growl.

"Fine. Just take me home and I'll dig in my nightstand for the biggest vibrator I can find."

He laughs, and I hug him again, pouring all my gratitude into the embrace. Connor is awesome. I think about this friend I have now, this open, curious, steady man. I might not get to have him, but at least I get to keep him.

"I had fun on our quest for joy," I say into his neck.

"Yeah," he says. "Me, too."

"But you're the one who ended the insanely good groping, so you're obligated to carry me to the car."

"Is that right?"

"I don't make the rules, I just follow them."

I can feel the relief in his laugh that comes out warm against my hair. "Okay then."

It takes some awkward shifting, hard parts sliding against soft spaces and his face in my boobs, but he manages to stand up with my legs around his waist and my arms around his neck. With one tiny, final peck to my cheek, Connor carries our overheated bodies back to the parking lot.

twenty-two

CONNOR

I didn't sleep a wink last night. And I don't mean that I tossed and turned and eventually nodded off at some offensive hour. I mean that I dropped Fizzy at her place, had an internal crisis as she walked inside and closed the door, drove straight home, tried to read a few things for work and failed, went to bed, replayed every detail of the moment she climbed over me, had a wank—and then another in the shower—and not once from the moment I stepped inside to the moment I put the kettle on this morning did I enjoy a moment of blissful unconsciousness.

It's only six, but this day has already been a hundred hours long.

Thanks to our ridiculously padded budget, our set for the next few days is a cozy coffee shop in the Gaslamp Quarter. We've got the whole place to ourselves, but have paid the staff to supply craft services, and hired actors to unobtrusively chat in the background. It's a nice place with a green awning out front, local artwork on the walls, and quirky mismatched tables and chairs scattered throughout. The front counter is made from beautifully worn wood, and a pastry case is stuffed full of mouthwatering sweets. The baristas are being paid handsomely to keep everyone caffeinated, and the smell of coffee and sugar—along with the three espressos I've had since

I arrived—is nearly enough to make me forget that I could have fucked Fizzy into the California coastline last night.

Well anyway, let's find her soulmate, shall we?

Of course she looks fucking incredible today. She walks in and my heart drops down my body and through the floorboards. I'm relieved to see that she followed directions—with Fizzy you never know—and arrived in comfortable clothes, sans makeup. Yet somehow, seeing her sweetly disheveled, barefaced, soft, and warm makes this a thousand times harder.

The crew cheers for her, guiding her in and toward the back where hair and makeup has set up a little station out of the way. Three women flank her, one focusing on her makeup, another pulling a brush through her hair, and a third showing her wardrobe choices. Around me is a high-octane bustling energy, but I feel like the stagnant rock in the center of the whitecapped river, stuck in place.

Because amid the chaos, there's another observation to be made: she's not yet looked at me. Beyond a casual wave when she walked in, there's been nothing. Obviously, I need things to be easy between us on set. The last thing we want is for anyone to sense tension after we've been quite chummy for the past few weeks. But perhaps more important, I *like* her. I more than like her. I don't want things to be off between us.

Stepping up to the counter, I order two drinks and make my way to where she's scowling down at her phone.

"You all right?" I ask.

She closes the email app and slides the phone into her bag. "You don't happen to have a sexy manuscript completed and handy, do you? I'd only need to borrow it for, hmmm, forever, and permission to publish it under my name."

Deflecting with humor, how very Fizzy.

"Nah, sorry." I hand her a coffee. "But I do have this."

She tilts the cup, reading *Vanilla Latte* written in beautiful calligraphy on the side. These baristas are going all out. "How'd you know what I drink?" she asks.

"You ordered one of these after the Broad."

At this, the small team of beautifiers steps away—I wonder if there is a vibe that reads *Privacy, please* here—and I take a sip of my cappuccino before putting it down again. More caffeine is the last thing I need right now.

One of the sound guys approaches with Fizzy's small mic in his hand. "Ready?" he asks.

At her nod, he reaches for the front of her silk shirt and the words shove their way up my throat: "I've got it, mate."

He hands it over without any indication that he's heard the edge in my tone. But Fizzy has. Her smirk is louder than her bursting laugh could ever be.

"Quiet, you," I mumble, smiling, and hand her the cord. I motion for her to slip it under the hem of her top and out the neckline. Sensation echoes down my arm, sending electric pulses to my fingertips. I remember the way her breast filled my hand, the gasp she let out when I closed my finger and thumb around her tight nipple.

She brings the end of the cord up and out of her collar and holds it out for me.

I take it, and bend, attaching the clip to the front of her shirt as unobtrusively as possible. Speaking into her chest, I ask, "How are you, Fizzy?"

"I am fine, Connor," she says like a robot, and when I look up at her, she's smiling at me.

"Still a menace, I see." The backs of my fingers inadvertently skim her neck and collarbone, and she sucks in a quiet breath. "Sorry," I whisper.

"It's okay," she whispers playfully back, and I connect the cord to the mic.

Tension thrums between us. Her skin is so warm and soft, smooth and kissable. This close I can smell the subtle scent of her shampoo and body lotion. It makes me light-headed. Straightening, I adjust her collar to hide the mic.

"Should we talk about last night?" she blurts.

Behind me, there's a cough, a gasp, a snorted laugh, the clearing of a throat. A glance over my shoulder confirms that every headset-wearing member of the crew has just given us their undivided attention. "You mean our conversation about today's run of show?" I ask.

Awareness lands and Fizzy nods slowly, and then with more conviction, calling out loudly, "Yes! *Of course* that conversation! What other thing would we have to discuss?"

I gaze down at her, fighting a laugh as I reach forward to turn off the live mic. "I guess we don't need to test your sound levels."

She winces. "You should hold up a sign or something when you need me to be covert. Subtlety has never been my strong point."

"I think a safe rule of thumb is to be covert when we are together on the set of your dating show."

She snaps, pointing at me. "Good call. This is why you're the boss."

Pinned to the front of Fizzy's blouse is a custom-made tag with the logo for *The True Love Experiment*, and her name printed above the word HEROINE. Each of the Heroes will have a name tag, too, along with his archetype. It's all a fun gimmick to make the show stand out, but it's also a reminder of who *I'm* supposed to be. In fact, I should probably wear a name tag as well, though I'm not sure there would be enough space on it for all the reminders I'd need: Connor Prince III, Hot DILF only as an inside joke, Executive Producer, Not Boyfriend, Not Even Lover, Do Not Covet the Heroine

"But yes. About last night," I start, and her expression falls, worry creating a gentle crease in her forehead. Words evaporate from my brain. "Which is to say—that is, it was lovely, and I know you know this, I'm just confirming . . ." She stares up at me, waiting, her eyes softening as I struggle. "We should probably not do it again."

Fizzy nods. "I agree completely. In fact, I got home and didn't think about it again, not even once. Definitely not twice in a row."

I glare down at her. "Can we at least endeavor to go about this with sincerity?"

Rory calls that we're two minutes from rolling, and Fizzy does some sort of scout gesture.

"I am endeavoring, I promise. Besties only. But may I say one more thing before you go?"

"Of course."

She points to her mic. "We're sure this thing is off?"

I eye her warily and reach for the cord hanging limply from her open collar and show her. "It's disconnected."

"I promise you that I will do my very best today. You don't have to worry about my commitment to this project." A tiny, seductive smile curves her lips. "But let me just say—" Her eyes drift lazily down my body, lingering at my zipper, and then slowly back up. "Well done."

She pats my chest chummily, smiles, and walks toward her spot as I'm left staring after her.

I think . . . did she just compliment my dick?

It's crazy that my face can suddenly feel hot when I know for a fact that most of my blood has just been diverted in the opposite direction. Discombobulated, I take a moment to deposit my cup in the dish bin, where a barista cheerfully retrieves it. As shocking as Fizzy can be, it's refreshing to have someone simply say what they think. Things are weird? Let's talk about it. We'd like to fuck but can't? Let's admit it and both move on. I've never met anyone like her.

As Rory shouts directions, gives Fizzy a pep talk, and shows her her marks, a flurry of activity erupts. Makeup and hair rush in to do final touch-ups, Fizzy's mic is in fact tested once more, and background actors get into position. There is a vibration in the room, a pulsing thrum of excitement. It's all going to work. The show is going to succeed, I feel it in my marrow. It will be hard to move on from Fizzy, but I will manage.

I feel self-possessed, in control, creatively alive. Taking in a deep breath, I give myself a moment to appreciate that hard work has landed us here and to be proud that I stepped up to this challenge. Everything feels pretty fucking good.

And then the café door opens and Fizzy's first Hero walks in.

twenty-three

FIZZY

I am very skilled in the art of denial. For example, I am consistently surprised when it's time to pay quarterly taxes. I sing karaoke with Jess and Juno and am convinced that I sound exactly like Adele. I am confident that if I walk four blocks to get my morning coffee, I have also earned a cookie.

And today, too. I've known this show was coming for so long now, but it isn't until the makeup artist, Liz, comes in for touch-ups and the light warms my skin and everyone's chatter simmers down to a hushed hum throughout the room that I realize, *Oh shit, I might actually look terrible on TV. I might not have my mojo back. I might be awkward or boring or too old for this.*

Liz steps back, examining the makeup she applied earlier with such care and quantity that I started to feel like I was a wall being spackled. Just beyond her, I see Connor in the background, his attention fixed on one of the cameras as he quietly talks to the director. He looks so calm, so ready. He's probably been thinking about this moment, strategizing this entire shoot for weeks, and here I am, only now fully realizing that I am about to be on TV.

"Are we actually doing this?" I ask Liz, perched before me with a set of brushes fanned between her fingers. "This show? Today?"

"Y-yes?"

"Okay," I say numbly. "Cool cool cool."

I feel her studying me while I stare at the very interesting pattern of grain in the wood floor. "Are you okay, Fizzy?"

"No." I look up at her terrified face and realize what I just said. "Yes! I mean *yes*. I am great."

She disappears, unconvinced. Oh my God, I'm going to be on television. Why didn't I put on a sheet mask last night? Why did I let them put me in such tight pants? Why did I kiss Connor? Why am I looking at Connor right now? Cameras are aimed at me, preparing for my reaction to the first Hero to walk through that door. I should be breathless with anticipation, but my eyes are fixed on Connor's profile, fascinated by how hot he looks when he's concentrating.

Oh my God, this is going to end in a flaming disaster. *Focus, Fizzy.*

The director calls to me from her chair next to one of the larger cameras. I've already met Rory several times, but here, surrounded by cameras and lights, I'm struck again by how young she looks. She can't be more than thirty, and with her ripped jeans, Black Keys T-shirt, and long, dark curls covered by a faded baseball cap, she has the Hollywood laid-back vibe down perfectly. But my favorite thing about her—and the thing that seems to vex Connor the most—is the way she continually calls him *bro* without any intentional humor whatsoever.

"Okay, Fizzy," she says. "Just do what you'd normally do on a first date, and you'll be great."

Wild horses couldn't keep me from checking Connor's reaction to this potentially scandalous piece of advice, and just as I expected, he's biting back a knowing smile. He speaks into his mic: "Take that advice with a grain of salt."

My bursting laugh lands just before a hush falls over the set, and it echoes a few beats before everything goes silent. I'm sitting at a table for two in the middle of the room, primped and ready for the first of three dates today. Portable lights are set up just out of shot, and the heat is already suffocating, heightened under the pressure of everyone's expectations. I mean, listen, I've been the center of attention before. Usually, I thrive on it. I've delivered keynotes and been on panels at countless conventions, I've done small morning shows and spoken in front of readers all over the world. But this is different. This is glossy, big-scale, big-money fantasy television. This is the show where the pettiest among us will watch and critique and judge and think, *Why her?* I've taken on a huge responsibility, and sitting here when it's way too late to back out . . . I suddenly don't feel prepared.

With effort, I turn my face to the café entrance as a beautiful Asian man pulls the door open, stepping in with a heart-stopping smile. His eyes meet mine and that smile dials up, turning real at the corners.

He's dressed in black jeans and a black T-shirt, with full-sleeve tattoos on both arms and several winding up his neck from beneath his collar. When he gets closer, I can make out what's written on his name tag:

DAX: TATTOOED BAD BOY

I swallow the laugh, but the smile stretches wide across my face. It takes intense focus not to turn to Connor, to let him see in my face how much this delights me and to see, in turn, how proud he must be of getting this right. Connor worked so hard for this. He really listened.

But speaking of listening, Dax is here, and so I stand, greeting him with a half hug, receiving his gentle peck on my cheek.

With an understandable touch of self-consciousness, we settle into our seats across the table from each other and reach for our waters at the same time. Ice clinks against glass as we lift and take a sip. Hyperaware now of the cameras and crews and lights and complete unnatural spectacle of this all, Dax and I laugh into our drinks.

I didn't want any of this scripted, but now I'm wishing I'd practiced something—literally anything—to open this first date. Come Saturday, millions of people will sit down in their living rooms and watch me fumble my way through this moment.

But if there is an expert in dating anywhere, it's Fizzy Chen. So I shove this tiny, terrified instinct back into its dusty corner and look Dax right in the eye. "We're setting the bar high, I see."

He laughs and gives me a playful once-over. "I'll say."

I reach my hand across the table. "Nice to meet you, Dax."

"Nice to meet you, too, Felicity."

He holds on to my hand for a prolonged, flirty beat. His voice is naturally low and a little raspy, his fingers coarse and dry, palm calloused. Everything about him is rough around the edges, and I like it. He's a perfect balance of hot and sinful. Well done, Connor.

But do I tell Dax to call me Fizzy? I like the way Felicity sounds in his voice. It sounds dirty and playful, and that's the role he's been given, the one he's been sent to embrace. And I think of the audience watching, how they won't know my thoughts unless I say them aloud, and how I don't want them to think keeping things formal is a measure of my interest.

"Everyone calls me Fizzy," I tell him, releasing the handshake. "But I like the way you say Felicity."

"Felicity it is, then."

I smile in agreement. "So, Tattooed Bad Boy."

He nods.

"The tattooed part is self-explanatory. But why bad boy?"

"Let's see if you can guess."

I lean in, humming, studying. There's a sharpness to his gaze, an overt confidence. I think of his calloused hands. "Daredevil? I bet you're into extreme sports."

Dax laughs. "Skydiving, rock climbing, you name it, yeah."

"Holy shit." I smack the table. "I'm good."

A production assistant waves a red card just behind Dax's shoulder, a technique Connor set up to remind me not to swear like a sailor. It has the added effect of reminding me that Connor is right there watching, that *his* hands are enormous and warm, and of the way he sent one up under my sweater last night, cupping my breast, the pad of his thumb circling the tight peak as his kisses grew impatient and rough.

Focus, Fizzy.

"I want to know something," I say, leaning in closer to block out the shape of Connor's broad shoulders in the background.

Dax leans in, too, smiling coyly. "Anything."

"What is your ugliest tattoo?"

When he throws his head back and laughs in surprise, the old

Fizzy would notice Dax's long throat, that masculine spike of an Adam's apple, and about a hundred other things about him because he is gorgeous. Old Fizzy would be breaking the rules left and right, planning meetups with these contestants after hours. My trailer in the alley out back would do nicely.

Now, no matter how charismatic he is, no matter how much I appreciate his sex appeal, the idea of meeting up with Dax later leaves me feeling blank inside. All I can do is focus on not turning my eyes up to Connor in the background to gauge his expression while he watches us flirt.

But in the end, the date with Dax is objectively great. The glee he exhibits when he shows me a truly awful tattoo of a mermaid on his shoulder says so much about his sense of humor and willingness to be silly in front of the camera that I find myself genuinely enjoying talking to him. He's third-generation Korean American, has won all kinds of BMX trick competitions (which I'm sure are very impressive to those who know anything at all about BMX), and turns out to be a surprise foodie, with friends in the restaurant business all over town.

The next Hero date, if possible, is even better.

ISAAC: HOT NERD

He walks into the café, a bespectacled six-foot-three Black man, and an appreciative hush falls over the room.

He sits across from me, his Hero name tag slapped over a pectoral I can see outlined beneath his plain white T-shirt, and manages to make artificial intelligence sound only moderately terrifying before turning every ounce of genuine focus on me. When I finally find my words again, we discuss books, oldest sibling woes, favorite memes, and our shared disdain for having to go into the bank or post office in person anymore. For the first time in over an hour, I forget there are cameras capturing every single expression that passes over my face. I like him, and at the end of our time together I'm genuinely disappointed to see him go.

The third date is the first real miss.

BENJI: COWBOY

Physically, Benji—who goes by Tex—is great, but the energy is all wrong. I can see Connor pacing in the background behind a wall of screens as we struggle and jerkily interrupt each other, trying to fill silences in unison. When he asks me what my dad thinks about his daughter writing romance for a living, I ask him in return what his mom thinks about him riding horses for a living and watch the confusion play across his features.

When I'm blessed with the end of our date and Tex leaves, I'm on autopilot. Without thinking, I make a beeline to Connor where he's standing at a monitor, reviewing footage. He turns at the feeling of my hand on his arm, following me to a shadowed corner.

"What's up?" he asks, concerned. He bends a little, coming eye to eye. "You okay?"

I realize I don't need anything. I was just following an instinct to be near him, to feed this ghoul inside of me that is recharged in his presence. I want him to calm me down.

And this time I'm smart enough to turn off my mic. "Just wanted to say hi."

He smiles. "Hi."

"Are *you* okay?"

"Yeah," he says brightly. "Why?"

I see the lie in the tightness across his forehead, but maybe I'm reading too much into this and it isn't about watching me on dates after our orbit-bending dry hump but the pressure of, you know, having his livelihood hanging in the balance of this entire project.

"Nothing. Good." I look past him out the window of the café and to the street, where a few people loiter outside, clearly curious about what's going on inside, what all these cameras are doing here. "You seemed stressed when things with Tex were stalling."

Connor's deep laugh sends vibrations down my arm. "It was getting a little awkward—which doesn't make for good television. But you lecturing him about what BDSM really is circles us right back to great television."

I preen as if he's just paid me the greatest compliment. "So, I guess it's good to have a few duds?"

"Absolutely. There's no standout if you have chemistry with everyone." He scratches his chin. "You seemed to really hit it off with Isaac."

"Of course I did. Your casting skills are unmatched."

He smiles tightly. "Cheers."

"But," I say, "you know what only occurred to me today?"

"What's that?"

"You might know who my best DNADuo match is."

He shakes his head. "Nope."

"Really?" I'm relieved. I would be relentless, pestering him constantly.

Connor laughs. "Really. I know the range, know there are some good ones in here, but only Rory knows whose score is the highest." We both look over at the director, who seems to be using this break to talk Brenna's ear off. Connor looks back at me. "But you're welcome to speculate and think out loud in the confessionals."

"When are we doing that?"

"We'll shoot the first tomorrow night after the final date. Does that sound good?"

"Will you be interviewing me for these?"

"Me?" Adorably, he points to his chest. "Why?"

"Because you're hot and have an accent. This might surprise you, but chicks dig both those things."

"But I'm a producer."

"Wait, *what*?" I ask with mock alarm.

He laughs. "You'll be in the confessional trailer solo. You'll just need to give a recap of each date. We'll prompt you through an earpiece with questions, and—"

"You're going to put me alone in a room with a camera and trust that the entire thing won't go off the rails?"

Connor stills and pulls a deep breath in through his nose. He lifts a hand, waving it to Brenna, who jogs over immediately. "What do you think about having our host, Lanelle, interview Fizz—"

"I want you, Connor." Glancing at Brenna, I quickly say, "That came out wrong. This is purely a professional want."

"I have no idea what we're talking about," she says, "but you just pulled me away from hearing about the time Rory lost a contact in the mosh pit at a Social Distortion show and the entire mob stopped to help her find it. I'm just happy to be over here."

Connor and I both give this the sympathetic moment of silence it deserves, and then he turns and offers an apologetic smile. "Fizzy, I can't be on-screen. Have you met Lanelle yet?"

"I have, and she's great. But I know you better. That will come across on-screen."

"I'm not an actor," he says.

"Neither am I." I motion to him, from the top of his sexy head and all the way down the length of his solid bod. "And you're fooling yourself if you think all of this wasn't made to be in front of a camera." I turn to Brenna. "What do you think? Imagine the female audience's reaction."

Not realizing she was called over to referee, Brenna looks like she'd rather go back to listening to Rory's mosh pit escapades.

"I mean," she says with a wince, "Fizzy isn't wrong. You're just as hot as any of the Heroes—in a totally objective, still-my-superior-at-work kind of way, of course. And you two have chemistry."

I motion to her. "Give this woman a raise."

"I—" Connor says, but I jump in again, going for the kill.

"You said yourself that you didn't want the show to be overly produced. Wouldn't that include editing interviews to look like I'm talking to someone when I'm not? Let's talk it out for real! Viewers should see me hearing the questions and reacting in real time."

Connor runs an exasperated hand down his face and then turns his green eyes on me. "All right then. I have my own request."

"A quid pro quo. I respect it."

"I was thinking how great it would be if you could talk River into appearing in the first episode. Have him walk the viewers through the science."

I belt out a laugh. This poor, naive man. "You don't know River Peña. He'd sooner die."

"I assumed as much," he says. "But I also know how persuasive you can be."

There's an awkward beat of silence.

"I'm just going to . . ." Brenna points behind her before heading in the other direction.

I look at Connor again. "River is pretending that none of this is happening. *Nobody* is that persuasive."

"Based on personal experience, I disagree."

Connor gives me a knowing smile, and while I'd like nothing more than to stand around and flirt with him all day, he has a point. "I'm not sure I can convince River to do anything, but a good idea is a good idea. No promises, but I'll try."

"Likewise about the confessionals. I can't promise anything," he says, and extends a hand for me to shake, "but I'll try."

Connor wraps his hand around mine and we shake once . . . twice . . . and reluctantly let go. He glances briefly over his shoulder, then back at me. "You good?"

I nod and watch him walk over to Rory to discuss something. Liz comes to find me to ask if there's anything I need before we wrap for the day. I tell her nothing, but that's not exactly true. What I need is for Connor Prince III to do something that makes me not want to be near him every second, and I need him to do it soon.

twenty-four

CONNOR

I wake up before sunrise on Tuesday and get a brief shot of professional bliss before dread hits me like a shadow chaser. Yesterday's shoot was good—brilliant, really—but if I thought watching Fizzy flirt with a bunch of gorgeous, interesting men right in front of me would be difficult, I was only partially right. It was unbearable. And we've only just begun.

The truth is, if we thought we were onto something with the guys during the casting call, that awareness was amplified tenfold seeing them on camera with Fizzy. There were a handful of awkward moments, and not everyone clicked, but her chemistry with a couple of them was off the charts, palpable enough to feel all the way in video village, where some of the bigwigs were watching on the monitors. They congratulated me at the end of the day with dollar signs in their eyes, already feeling the tendrils of something great. I should be ecstatic, buoyed by their enthusiasm and plotting how to capitalize on it. And I am.

But I'm also a touch lovesick.

No better way to get my mind off things than exercise. And it's early enough that I have time to kill even after my run. I call Stevie and test her a bit and wish her good luck on her state capitals test.

I've just hung up and am walking out the door when my phone rings. Thinking it's Stevie again, I answer without thinking.

It's not Stevie.

"Hey, Dad." I jog down the stairs. "I'm on my way to work. Can I call you back?"

"I just need a minute."

At the driveway I pause, taking a calming breath. It's always the same shit: my time isn't important; his call is urgent. And I know what's coming. I climb in, the phone connects to Bluetooth, and my father's voice fills the car. "I talked to Stefania last week, and she mentioned you're doing reality TV now? That right?" I swear I don't have to tell anyone anything anymore, because my daughter will always do it for me. I'm also not sure if I'm more annoyed that he's been stewing about this for a week and is just now asking, or that the last time I talked to him was more than four months ago. I'm glad he has a better relationship with Stevie than he had with me—marginally—but everything with him comes with a cost. "When we spoke you said you were working on another conservation project."

This isn't a conversation I want to have with my dad on any morning, certainly not today. "The company is trying out a few new things this year. I'm a part of that."

"LA has plenty of better shops, Connor."

I stare out the windshield. "Dad, come off it. I don't want to live in LA. I'd see Stevie once a month, if that."

"Kids are adaptable," he says, and when I don't say anything in response, he continues. "Listen, you know how I feel. You could have easily come to work for me, C-suite from the get-go, seven-figure salary, but fine. You were doing important work." I hear his air quotes and swallow down an expletive. Getting into it with him is never worth it. "Now I have to stomach that my son spent a couple hundred grand on school so he could film a bunch of housewives?"

I bite back the rant on the tip of my tongue, knowing it won't make a bit of difference anyway. "It's not housewives, Dad. Anyway, this is a one-off. The company needed opportunities for product placement, and they asked me to take it on. It's a huge budget and they've already given me the green light to do my next doc when this show wraps."

I wince at the boast I can hear in my own voice, the pathetic attempt to earn his approval.

"And then what? You continue to be their cuck the next time they—"

"*Dad.* Enough."

He immediately falls silent. I rarely raise my voice to him.

Not long after he'd had his holiday fling with my mum, he'd married a woman he'd dated off and on in college, and they had a couple of kids. When I moved to the States, I lived with them for two years. My father is a multimillionaire who owns one of the largest real estate development firms in the States, and to me, a teenager raised by a poor single mum, money was power. He was intimidating and strict; Dad and I never butted heads because, like my two half siblings, I never dared talk back to him. He'd lecture us all while we sat there silently poking at our overcooked pasta. I moved out the second I could, got a partial scholarship to UCLA, and worked as a waiter to pay the rest of my tuition and to pay my way through film school at USC.

I thought that when Stevie was born, he might see this perfect little girl and magically turn into a decent human, but of course he didn't. He loves his granddaughter as much as he's capable of loving anything, but the only time he's ever told me I did a good job was when Nat and I split up, and apparently, I undid all of that by following her to San Diego. In his words: What kind of a man does that?

"All right," he says. "What's the show? *The Bachelor* version ten-point-oh?"

Does Fizzy get this when people find out she's a romance writer? The instant comparison to the one big property everyone is familiar with? "Yeah, Dad. Something like that. Listen, I've got to ring off. I'm about to head into the dead spot in Mission Hi—"

I end the call, letting him believe it's been dropped.

———————

By the time I walk on set, my blood pressure is as close to normal as it's likely to get today. And I'm surprised that I feel my pulse settling further by association: Fizzy can be found here.

It would be an understatement to say the set is similar to yesterday, because it is in fact *exactly* the same. We want it to look like the dates are taking place on the same day, so the pastries in the case have been replicated, the stacks of cups arranged just so, and the actors are in the same seats as when we called cut at the end of the day. Even Fizzy is in the same outfit, the soft silk top and tight black pants, looking—if possible—even more beautiful.

Despite the way my morning started, I am only mildly over-caffeinated when our first Hero enters.

EVAN: THE ONE THAT GOT AWAY

If there's one thing you can say about Felicity Chen, it's that she does not disappoint. When Evan steps through the door, Fizzy's eyes fall straight to his crotch before swinging wildly to me. I manage to contain a laugh, but Fizzy isn't quite so lucky. She lets out what can only be described as a guffaw that literally stops Evan in his tracks. A murmur of laughter ripples through the crew as Fizzy claps a hand over her mouth. Rory looks back at me. Without words she's asking whether we should reshoot Evan's entrance, and I shake my head, confident that Fizzy can save this with a joke and a moment of levity. But it's Evan who surprises me when he continues walking and stops in front of her table with an amused smile.

"Don't worry," he says with a self-deprecating laugh, and motions to his hip. "It's gone. Bart Simpson is no more."

She laughs. "It's for the best, trust me." Fizzy stands, rounding the table to embrace him. "There are probably a lot of confused people watching this right now," she says once they're sitting across from each other.

Evan smiles down at the table and blushes. A few feet behind me, one of the female crew members releases a breathy sigh.

Looking up again, he grins at Fizzy. "Then people should know that I had a rather unfortunate tattoo in a *very* unfortunate place, and Fizzy was the only person who was honest with me. In fact, I should thank her feedback for ninety percent of the sex I've had in the years since we broke up."

Fizzy laughs into her hands. "I'm happy for everyone involved."

"Speaking of happy for everyone . . ." He motions to the lights and cameras pointed at them. "How's this whole celebrity thing treating you?"

"You know," she says, "I get to sit here all professionally dolled up while scores of suitors are brought in one after another. I've been worse." She smiles, more at ease now. I don't sense any romantic sparks, but they already look comfortable together, which the audience will love. "What have you been up to lately?"

"After we dated and I picked up the pieces of my life," he says with a sly smile, "I tried my hand as a part-time barista while continuing to better myself as a student at UCSD. I've been there for about eight years now."

"Eight years is a lot of bettering yourself."

"Lots of people go to school for eight years," he says.

"And they have their own parking spaces at hospitals and the word *doctor* in front of their name."

Evan leans in. "Have you been talking to my mother?"

The crew holds in their laughter, and I let out a long, steady exhale. Fizzy is a bloody star.

ARJUN: MR. DARCY

Date two of the day shows up in a custom Gucci suit and alligator oxfords that cost more than most people's first car. Fizzy is visibly unimpressed. At the end of the date, she gives me a flat stare that, by now, I can correctly interpret as *Mr. Darcy was grumpy but kind. That guy was an egomaniac.*

Date number three is promising.

COLBY: NAVY SEAL

Colby is well over six feet tall and a wall of muscle. His black hair is cut short, his tan the combination of an olive complexion and early mornings spent battling the currents at Breakers Beach. When he takes a seat across from Fizzy, I have to tamp down a wave of pure jealous irritation over how good they look together. But their conversation is, well . . . frankly it's boring. To her credit, Fizzy really tries to carry the tepid back-and-forth, but lets out an audible gasp when he admits he hasn't read a real book since *The Da Vinci Code* was published in 2003.

The producer in me really needs this next one to hit it out of the park.

But the guy who kissed Fizzy two nights ago secretly hopes it all goes down in flames. Unfortunately for him, it doesn't. Enter:

NICK: CINNAMON ROLL

Nick is everything he was in his audition, and when he walks in, he drags along with him an aura of affability and a haze of sexuality that seems to shimmer across the room. Fizzy begins to stand, seemingly without realizing it, the second she spots him. They greet each other with a lingering hug, and I'm hit with the sense that I'm seeing something immediate and intimate. It's the kind of connection that makes me want to watch them have sex, and then my reflexes kick me in the mental balls for the thought.

The crew is spellbound. At some point Nick tells her about a litter of puppies they're expecting at his office, and Fizzy makes him promise that he'll keep her updated.

In an act of self-preservation, I manage to tune out the rest of their date.

Next, we get:

JUDE: VAMPIRE

I'm not sure what Fizzy was expecting when she put *vampire* on the list of archetypes, but I'm hoping Jude fits the bill. I think I might even surprise her. Jude walks through the door and crosses to Fizzy in a few strides. Beaming, she stands and greets him with a hug. His ears glitter with silver piercings, he has a lip ring *and* a nose ring, and he's dressed in expensive monochromatic black from head to toe. He has the same cool edge about him that Fizzy does.

Jude pulls out Fizzy's chair before moving to his own, and I am on tenterhooks waiting for the reveal.

"So, you're my Vampire." Fizzy gives him an appreciative once-over. One of the cameras is zoomed in close enough to catch the way she crosses her legs under the table, her high-heeled foot casually coming to rest against his leg. Great for ratings, terrible for my mental health.

"It would appear so," he says with a smirk. "It's nice to finally meet you, Fizzy. I was getting so nervous. I didn't think it was possible, but you're even more beautiful in person."

There isn't an ounce of insincerity detectable. Watching next to me, Brenna makes a tiny, infatuated squeak before quickly covering her mouth. On the outside I am completely impassive. Inside I am flipping off Vampire Jude.

He lifts his coffee in a toast. "Here's to hoping this is the first date of many."

Visibly charmed, Fizzy clinks her mug with his and they both drink.

"Tell me about yourself, Jude. What exactly does a vampire do for a living these days?"

"I'm a phlebotomist, actually," he says with a knowing grin.

And there it is. God, I've been waiting for this moment.

Fizzy slaps her hand on the table with a loud, surprised laugh, her eyes shifting just to the left of Jude to meet mine across the café.

That laughter is just for me.

twenty-five

Episode One Confessional Transcript

Connor Prince: Fizzy. How are you?

Fizzy Chen: I'm great now that you're here.

Connor: [laughs] Since this is our first show, we should explain to the viewers what we're doing. My name is Connor Prince and I'm one of the producers of *The True Love Experiment*. You'll have to forgive me for being a little nervous. I wasn't supposed to be on this side of the camera.

Fizzy: An oversight I'm glad I rectified.

Connor: As some of you watching may have discovered by now, Fizzy can be very persuasive.

Fizzy: You are not the first person to say that.

Connor: I believe it. You've met all eight of your Heroes by now. How are you feeling?

Fizzy: How am I feeling, let's see. In my book *Paradise Dreaming*, the main character, Jacqueline, has been shipwrecked for three years. She's tough, so she makes it through, but when she's rescued and in the safety of the ship captain's cabin, she's so famished and overcome by all the delicacies on board that she gorges herself until she can't remember her own name. I feel a little like that.

Connor: Too much of a good thing?

Fizzy: Maybe.

Connor: Isn't the hero of that book the ship's doctor?

Fizzy: He is! And he stays by her side all night and nurses-slash-bangs her back to health.

Connor: [laughs] This is a very Fizzy story.

Fizzy: I'll take that as a compliment.

Connor: Good, because it is. We don't want to sway our viewers, who will begin voting as soon as this episode airs. But tell me your first impressions of each of your Heroes. Let's start with Dax, our Tattooed Bad Boy.

Fizzy: Oh, poor Dax. He got straight-out-of-the-gate, awkward Fizzy.

Connor: You didn't look nervous at all. I'd say you two had a connection.

Fizzy: I think so, too. I'm definitely not going skydiving or rock climbing or bear wrestling with him, but he was great.

Connor: Next we had Isaac, Hot Nerd.

Fizzy: Also great. Did you see his arms?

Connor: I think all of America saw his arms.

Fizzy: All of America is lucky. Would it be too forward to ask that he be shirtless next time?

Connor: Maybe a bit. You two seemed to hit it off.

Fizzy: I think so, too.

Connor: Hero number three, Benji, aka Tex, our Cowboy.

Fizzy: I know I'm not supposed to influence the audience, so you can cut this part out, but he asked what my dad thinks about me writing romance. Inappropriate and weird.

Connor: Moving on! Next was Evan, The One That Got Away and the only one of our Heroes you've met before.

Fizzy: That's right. We dated for a few months when we were in our late twenties. He's a really good guy.

Connor: Who happened to have an unfortunate tattoo.

Fizzy: *Ay, caramba.*

Connor: Indeed. But he seemed grateful for your feedback.

Fizzy: [laughs] That's because Evan is easygoing. His glass is always half-full.

Connor: I'd wager to say yours is, too.

Fizzy: That depends on what's in the glass . . .

Connor: Cheeky. Let's move on to Arjun, our Mr. Darcy. Thoughts?

Fizzy: That I bet he color codes his sock drawer.

Connor: [laughs] What about Nick, the Cinnamon Roll?

Fizzy: This archetype is a bit more inside baseball, so for the viewers who don't know, a Cinnamon Roll is a hero who is sweet and supportive. He has the heroine's best interests at heart.

Connor: Right.

Fizzy: You know, underneath those suits you have some definite Cinnamon Roll tendencies. So many layers, Connor Prince III. One might even say I find you hard to peg.

Connor: You know me, like an onion.

Fizzy: Or a cake. But back to Nick. I liked him.

Connor: That's good, I'm sure it came across to the audience. Tell me about Colby, the Navy SEAL.

Fizzy: I would really like him to expand his reading choices.

Connor: [laughs] I'm sure he'd enjoy that, too. Then we had Jude.

Fizzy: The Vampire. He was very funny.

Connor: Is humor important to you?

Fizzy: Oh, absolutely. I need someone who doesn't take himself too seriously, who can let go and have fun even if it's out of his comfort zone.

Connor: Dance like nobody's watching?

Fizzy: Or sing at a boy band concert like nobody can hear.

[both laugh]

twenty-six

FIZZY

For the first twenty minutes after I arrive at Jess's on Friday night, I breathlessly download every detail I can remember about the eight dates. The Heroes' faces, clothes, voices, jobs, whether I liked them, what we talked about, what kinds of jokes they made.

When I describe the hilarious moment my ex walked into the café, a knowing grin painted on his pretty face—and an even bigger grin painted on Connor's—Jess nods in recognition.

"Is Evan the one with the tattoo you hated?" she asks. "Has that great laugh?"

"Update, he *was* the guy with the tattoo. He got it removed. And yeah, Chinese American, played softball with my brother. I put his name on the list because my dating past is littered with land mines, and Evan is a good guy, if not the sexual savior I need. But now I'm thanking past me for including him," I tell her. "He's great, and if all of these other men turn out to be duds, at least Evan and I can take a fun vacation together to Fiji."

"*Or* maybe things will be different this time without Bart Simpson standing between you."

"Maybe."

"So give me a rating, who's the top pick so far?"

"Probably Isaac. He was . . ." I pause for dramatic effect and give my head a shake to clear it. "He was so hot, Jess. And so interesting."

"I seeeeeeeee." She leans forward, eating this up. "And were there sparks? Fireworks? Bells ringing in the background?"

"Who knows. That's up to the audience to decide, I guess." If Jess senses the subtext there—that even after only the first round of dates I'm already considering I might not fall for one of these objectively fantastic Heroes because I can't stop looking over their heads at the executive producer in the background—she doesn't show it. She's too busy living vicariously through my crazy dating adventures. Just like old times.

"So are we watching the first episode together tomorrow?"

"I just need to make sure that Connor wasn't planning that I would watch it with him, but otherwise, yes."

Jess's eyes narrow. "Like, just the two of you?"

"No," I say, but the word sounds uncertain, like I might really mean *Maybe*.

"Fizz," she says in low warning.

"Well, maybe he was planning a thing!"

"Why would he plan to watch it just with you?"

"No, no, like—" I exhale, wincing. "Okay, I have something to tell you, but you absolutely cannot get mad at me."

"With that kind of lead-up I make no such promises."

"Then I won't tell you."

"Fine."

"*Fine.*"

We stare at each other in a silent standoff until I blink away, casually inspecting my nail polish. Usually, the odds of us each giving in are evenly split, but given that I'm the one with the juicy information—and I know she's spent the last eight hours doggedly running statistics on an enormous numbers thing—I'm confident I can win this one.

The silence of the room seems to hum with phantom sound. That spreadsheet must've been a doozy because she breaks much faster than I would have expected. "God, fine, just tell me."

"Sunday night," I say, leaning in, "the night before shooting started, Connor and I had our last joy excursion."

"Date."

"*Excursion.* We went to Torrey Pines to watch the bioluminescent waves."

Her *hmmm* is suspicious. She knows exactly where this is going.

"Well, spoiler alert, we ended up kissing."

Jess face-palms. "Fizzy."

I point an accusatory finger. "The agreed-upon terms stated that you can't get mad!" She drags her hand down her face, revealing a fake smile. "As I was saying, the kissing turned into making out and I was on his lap and—" I widen my eyes at her and lower my voice. "Jessica Marie, I am not positive because I did not *see* it, but I think Connor might have the biggest penis of any man I've ever touched."

Silence. Her expression flattens.

"Wait. I need wine for this." She disappears for a minute and then returns, setting two glasses of red wine down on the low coffee table and sitting across from me. "I don't want to encourage this, or for you to think I am somehow condoning it, but how big are we talking?"

I look behind me to make sure there are no impressionable ten-year-old ears listening in.

Jess quickly swallows a sip, shaking her head. "Juno's at Nana and Pops's house."

Reassured we're alone, I hold my index fingers an impressive—yet accurate—distance apart and then make a circle with the fingers of both hands to approximate girth. "Probably like this?"

She whistles. "Fizz, that's the diameter of your wrist."

"It is *fact!*" I smack a hand on the table. "It would be like fisting myself!"

Jess drops her head into a hand, sighing, and only then do I realize that River had just entered the room holding a tray of snacks for us. He makes a U-turn without pausing and silently exits.

"Wait, I need to talk to you," I shout at his retreating form. "His timing really is amazing."

"Well, good luck getting him back now."

"Oh please, like I can shock him anymore. Remember when he had to undress me?" On our group trip to Scotland, Jess was about to get into the shower, and in response to my panicked *Help me* text, she sent River, not realizing my emergency was being stuck in my dress. To his credit, River came in, tugged the offending garment up and off without hesitation, and walked right back out again. The man is unflappable. "Anyway," I continue. "As you can imagine, I will be unable to think about anything else until I touch it again."

She's already protesting. "You're actively on the show now!"

"Yes, but it doesn't have to affect the show! This isn't about feelings, it's a distraction. I have a taste for him now." I sigh. "I am a hunter."

She nods in understanding. "Like James in *Twilight*."

"Exactly like James in *Twilight*," I confirm.

"Except how Alice popped his head off."

I slap the table. "Why do you always intentionally miss my point!"

"The *point* is that this is going to end in disaster."

"I really don't think so. This is purely sexual. It's not like he and I are going to fall in love. I am a loud, romance-writing, adventure-seeking, opinionated woman. And he is a tall, sporty white man named Connor Prince III. I think we can all agree it's just a matter of time before I do something too shocking, or he'll do something to annoy and/or bore me."

My phone buzzes on the table between us. Connor's face lights up the screen and Jess sees it before I can flip it over and pretend it's my brother calling.

"You even put his picture in his contact info?" Her disgust is totally feigned. Under that baggy sweatshirt and sensible shoes, Jess is a giant drama queen. She is living for this excitement.

With a bright smile, I answer. "Hey, boss!"

"Hey, you. You have a few minutes for a postmortem?"

"That depends. Am I the dead body?" Across from me, Jess gives me a disapproving frown. I tap my forehead to remind her that face will give her wrinkles. I'm such a good friend and she never thanks me for these things.

Connor's laugh is a low vibrating tickle to my lady parts. "It's just a saying, Fizzy."

I hit Mute and whisper to Jess: "His voice is so deep. Did I always know his voice was this deep?" Returning to the call, I say, "I know, I'm only joking. Yes, I am free to examine a proverbial dead body."

He laughs again. "Cool. You home? I can come to you."

"I can be home in ten."

With a quiet "Great," he hangs up.

And shit. If we eliminate the possibility that I am excited to see Connor, there is no remaining explanation for the way I bolt up to gather my things.

Jess follows me to the door. "What are you doing?"

"He's meeting me at my house to do a debrief." I tuck my phone into my purse.

"Is that a good idea?"

"Is it a good idea to discuss the work we are doing together?" I pretend to ponder it. "I think so."

"Discussing it at your house," she says.

I open the door, stepping into my shoes. "Guess we'll find out." When her frown intensifies, I add, "Fine. I promise we'll stay out of the bedroom."

"As if you need a bedroom," she says.

I pause with my hand on the knob. "That is a great point. Okay, gotta go!"

"Wrist diameter!" she calls to me as I jog down the stairs.

"I don't need to walk tomorrow!"

"How's the writing going, Felicity?"

"This is research!" I call back.

I can practically hear her aggrieved groan as she waves from the front door.

twenty-seven

FIZZY

Connor beats me to my place and is waiting on the porch, one broad shoulder leaning against the column at the top of the steps. He's changed from the nice dress pants and button-down he had on earlier and is my favorite version of soft Connor: worn shirt, worn jeans, worn sneakers. In the moonlight and with the diffuse cone of light from the porch lamp overhead, he looks like a Hallmark cuddle come to life.

"How are you?" he asks as I approach.

"I'm great." I reach him and stretch to kiss his cheek before realizing that's not a thing I should do with my platonic producer bestie. His expression when I pull away is a mixture of amused and concerned.

"Sorry," I say, and why not be fully honest here: "I was happy to see you and unfortunately did not hit the mental brakes in time."

His face does a weird blip through a laugh and a grimace and finally settles on blankness. "No problem." Soft Connor is now stiff as a board. "I just wanted to check in to see how the first week of shooting went for you, and whether you needed anything."

"Me?" I ask, unlocking my front door. He follows me inside. "I'm fine."

"On our end, things are looking fantastic," he says, toeing off his Vans. "You really are a natural on-screen, Fizz. Today we cut all the sections we want from the dates and tonight we finished editing in the backstory intros and the testimonials."

"So the episode is done?"

"It's done. This is going to be great, and it's all you."

I turn to face him after setting my purse down and catch how his eyes have warmed. "Actually, it's *you*," I insist. "You're the one who took that hero archetype challenge and ran with it. The casting is perfect. They're perfect." I gently chuck his shoulder. "And hot. Well done. A veritable buffet of beefcake."

I say this to compliment him and his efforts, of course, but my words seem to drain the warmth from his eyes again. "Well," he says flatly. "Good. Would you be interested in watching the premiere to-gether at my place? With the crew, that is, not just me."

"Sure! I'm excited to see how it all looks on-screen. I don't think I had much of a connection with Arjun or Tex—"

"I think the audience will pick up on that, too."

"—but I think the others were okay. Any one of them could hop on the Fizzy Express." I grin at him as I do a dorky little *choo-choo* gesture. "This will be fun."

Connor blinks away, studying his shoes by the door, and it means I get to stare at him. I feel light, elated by the success of the first week of filming, and giddy to be alone in a room with him. The sneakiest of thoughts escapes, unguarded: *As great as these Heroes are, none are him.*

"Do you want a beer or anything?" I say, distracting myself from this truly awful voice in my head.

A short nod. "Sure."

He follows me into the kitchen, where I grab us each a bottle and lean against the counter. "Who is your favorite?" I ask him.

"My favorite Hero?" He takes a sip as I nod. "I don't have one."

"Come on." I make a buzzer sound. "Really? I see you as an Isaac fan."

"They all seem like nice blokes. It's why I cast them."

"Well, so far I like Nick, Dax, and Isaac. Jude is great but I'm not sure we click."

"Not Evan?"

"It didn't work the first time, but who knows?"

"Okay. Just keep an open mind."

"Oh, I will," I say, waving this off. "But if you're asking me right now who I'm most attracted to, that's my answer. That's all."

Connor looks like he's debating something before he finally opens his mouth. "So, this brings us to my one piece of feedback, which is perhaps to tone down the come-to-bed eyes a little."

I feel my smile slip from my face. "The— What?"

"Viewers want to see you forging a real connection."

"And that doesn't start with flirting? Have I been doing dating wrong this whole time!"

"It's the *way* you flirt," he says, unamused by my humor.

"The way I flirt," I repeat flatly, and set my bottle a safe distance away. I may need both hands to throttle him.

"Only thirty-three percent of *Bachelor* viewers tune in for *The Bachelorette*. Do you know why that is?"

Oh, I know this one. "The patriarchy."

"Yes. Viewers are far more accepting of a man dating multiple women than they are of a woman dating multiple men. It's not right, but that's the way it is."

"Look who's suddenly an expert on pop culture TV."

"I told you, I'm taking this seriously."

"So you want me to play harder to get? Romance has fought long and hard to get away from the ideal of virginal ingenue heroines. If you think I'm going to play into that stereotype on this show, you're going to be disappointed."

"I didn't say that."

"Then what *did* you say?"

He shifts on his feet, neck red. "I don't mean you can't— Listen," he says, trying again. "Never mind. You're fine just the way you are."

"Oh, well. *Thank you.*"

A quiet falls then, and it's like a match blown out, the way the energy evaporates from the room.

"Why are you suddenly mad at me?" I ask him. "What did I do?"

"I'm not." He shakes his head, looking briefly miserable. "I'm sorry."

"I said yes to this show because I wanted to take care of the audience in your clumsy hands—"

He laughs dryly. "You've made me well aware."

"—but it's fun because I'm doing it with *you*," I finish, reaching for his hand.

Finally, he looks up. And I think I get what's happening. God, I am so dumb sometimes.

"I have fun with you," I tell him, tugging him closer. "This first week on set was great because I'm comfortable with *you*. I insisted you do confessionals because I like being with *you*. I risked my life talking to River because I believe in your amazing ideas. You are doing your job so well, and I'm sorry if—"

My words are cut off when Connor steps forward, cupping my face. His mouth fits to mine and in an instant, every thought melts away.

It is a simple kiss, soft lips, firm pressure, and then he gives me another from a different angle before he pulls away. Connor's green eyes search mine, flickering back and forth in question. My thoughts scream to not let him retreat again, but before I think to tug him back to me, he's already resolved, stepping closer, crowding my space. I stand on my toes as he bends to meet me, his mouth softer and hungrier now, going after those angles we found last time, deeper, his tongue teasing and hot. Connor groans and the sound drops me into a pool of want, and all I can think about is diving down, finding more of that hoarse need he's hiding away. I keep expecting him to break it off, to pull away again and apologize, remind me that we weren't going to do this again, but the more we kiss, the more his intensity ramps up.

Connor lifts me, setting me in front of him on the counter, pushing my legs apart so he can step between them. His hand roams up my back, around my ribs, cupping my breast while the other pulls my hips forward, pinning me to his body. I'm rewarded with another groan, and another when I grind against him. He doesn't stop me as I unbutton his shirt, spreading it open, flattening my hands against the warm wall of his torso, broad and tight.

Connor's mouth is on my neck, his fingers curling around the strap of my tank top, dragging it off my shoulder and lower, stretching the fabric, pulling my bra with it to bare me to his mouth and teeth. The feel of his bite and kiss on my nipple is pleasure undiluted, making my vision spot black as my body greedily steals every available molecule of oxygen.

His hair is so soft in my hands, and he seems to like when I pull it, grunting into my skin, biting me in delicious retaliation when I'm rough. When I pull it hard enough, he moves with the gesture, standing again and claiming my mouth. I want his kiss for hours. I've never been kissed like this before, with such command and confidence, with an energy that's nearly angry. He shows no signs of stopping tonight, and adrenaline dumps heat into my bloodstream.

Connor's teeth are bared against my jaw, hands digging up my skirt to drag my underwear down my legs.

"All right, sweet?" he asks roughly into my neck, and I nod, keep nodding, because he has permission, frankly, to do whatever the hell he wants. I want to put together a coherent thought about what this feels like, the way his hands wrap so imposingly around my thighs, the heat and scrape of his teeth on my skin, but only later will I really be able to process anything but the flood of sensation, this feeling of what it's like to be completely consumed with wanting someone. We are live wires, bare nerves, moving on instinct.

His palm slips back up my thigh, teasingly slow, his kiss still rough and playful, teeth tugging my bottom lip. And then his fingertips graze over me, slippery and hot for him. His mouth goes soft and overcome against mine before he pulls away a fraction, balancing care and command, watching my face as he fucks me with one finger, and then two, maddeningly slow. I'm watching his mouth, the way it shapes these half-formed words, the way his teeth bear down on his lower lip when he presses his thumb to me, circling, the cocky smile that appears when I let out an involuntary cry.

Under my impatient fingers, his pants are soon down around his knees, beautiful cock finally in my hand, and I bring him to me, teasing us both until we're a fevered mess, kisses sloppy and biting, the head of him pressing into me and—

We pause, sensibility over sense, fumbling for that stray condom in the junk drawer, laughing into a kiss about how convenient that was, how being a mess is sometimes useful. He does it because my hands are shaking and his are steady, but I watch because I'm smart and naked Connor is the sexiest thing I have ever seen.

And when he steps forward again, I say his name, a question mark in my voice, but he kisses me, says, "Don't," against my mouth, "I can't say no again," as he pushes forward.

It's slow, perfect torture. Sanity is so fragile, I think, losing my mind in inches, one after another as he works his way into me, carefully, his focus on my expressions and sounds. But then it goes from careful to starving the second he's all the way in, like stone in silk, and I become a wind tunnel of thoughts, tiny particles and fragments flying by too fast for me to process. I am a selfish monster wanting more. I am a wizard toying with time to make this sex last an eternity. I am the first woman to ever be with a man, I'm sure of it.

I'm still sitting on the counter but it's a formality. His hands are under my ass, arms holding me up, angling me so that he can move in a way that makes us both gasp. There's so much power behind each thrust, so much pent-up need coursing between us. For all my talk about enjoying sex, I've never been a noisy lover, but with Connor there isn't room for anything else and there's too much sensation to hold inside, it has to escape somehow. Sharp, rhythmic gasps. Surprised cries. The sound of our sweat-slick skin coming together. I hear myself and wonder at it, feeling half out of control of my own body and brain. Maybe I am. I don't care. I'm not worried about anything, not wondering for a second if it's good for him because the answer is written in the furrowed lines of his forehead, the soft bow of his lip as he stares between us, slowing to watch, moving to touch me, thumb stroking.

"Like that?" he asks quietly.

I nod, whispering, "Come here," and pulling his face to mine.

We should take our time, but it's hard when everything feels strung too tight inside, ready to snap. He reaches up, pressing a flattened hand to the cabinet beside my head, closing me in, watching me take over for his touch. Almost immediately, I'm falling.

I should hold back, but it's too late. Pleasure hits me with euphoric devastation. I thought I'd only get this once; it was, after all, what I thought I needed. Just to clear my head of him.

But that was before. I mean, I've had all kinds of sex and this wasn't like any of those experiences. I wish I knew what this was.

twenty-eight

CONNOR

A perusal of my Google history from the early hours of Saturday morning will yield the following results:

- ✦ Why sex with a coworker is bad

- ✦ What to do if I slept with someone I shouldn't have and it was great

- ✦ How to avoid sleeping with someone you're attracted to

- ✦ How to avoid sleeping with someone twice

- ✦ Can my boss fire me in California?

- ✦ Producing jobs in San Diego

- ✦ Producing jobs near San Diego

- ✦ Jobs in San Diego

- ✦ The effect of an absent father on daughters

- ✦ Time machines

Unsurprisingly, none of these were much help.

I didn't go to Fizzy's intending to have sex. I went over wanting to celebrate a great first week of filming, to see what we could do better, see how we can make things more comfortable for her. But I also went over there already knowing that if I kissed her, she would kiss me back. And I went over there knowing that I want her intensely, have fallen a bit in love with her, and I don't manage jealousy well. I wanted her to be mine, still. She'd been right, what she said at the beach; I hadn't realized how hard it would be to share her once the show began.

In hindsight, I realize it was inevitable that we would have sex. And that sex inevitably would be messy, hard, tender, and spectacular. And now I am royally fucked, because all I can think about is doing it again.

A few hours before the premiere, I find Nat in my kitchen, where she's opening a bottle of wine. None of the Heroes will be joining us tonight—they won't spend any time with Fizzy that isn't captured on film for the show—but most of the crew is here. A few have already descended on the extravagant catering spread set up out back (another budget perk), and the rest are chatting among themselves, anxiously waiting to see if our little show will be a hit or if we'll all be looking for jobs tomorrow morning. There's so much money being poured into this that, success or failure, the scale will be massive either way.

Fizzy should be here any minute, which is why I'm hovering in the kitchen doorway like a creep.

Nat must sense me behind her because she glances over her shoulder. "Hey," she says, and pulls the cork free from the bottle.

I move to stand near the stove, not sure I want to have this conversation, but knowing I will go insane if I don't talk to someone. "Hey."

She reaches into one of the cabinets for a glass. "Where's the kiddo?"

"In her room." Stevie was prepared to wait in the front yard for Fizzy to show up, but I convinced her that Ocean Beach traffic is always bad this time of night, especially on the weekend. She relented but only after I promised I'd let her know the minute Fizzy arrived. "Who knew it only took a visit from Felicity Chen to get our daughter to finally clean in there?"

Nat snorts while she fills her wineglass. "Fizzy is a good sport. The hero worship is strong in our offspring."

The reminder twists my stomach because it's not just my life that will be affected if this all goes wrong, but Stevie's, even Nat's. We've never gone through this before, because I've never really been involved with someone. Not that we're *involved*-involved, I remind myself. It was sex. People have sex every day.

But . . . people do not have sex like that every day.

My silence earns another look in my direction. "Everything okay?"

"Sure, sure." Another moment passes and I change my mind no fewer than five times regarding simply turning around and dropping the whole thing. "I had sex with Fizzy last night."

Nat's mouth opens; she blinks. "I'm sorry, what?"

"Do you really need me to say it again?"

"I just . . ." she says, rightfully at a loss for words. "The last I heard, you turned her down because it wouldn't work. That was weeks ago." I grimace, because I haven't told Nat about the beach. "I thought you told me it was just a professional relationship."

"It was." But that's not entirely true. Our relationship was professional for approximately one millisecond; the crumbled boundaries look like a pile of rubble in the rearview mirror. "And then it wasn't."

I look up when my best friend Ash's voice booms down the hall. "Everyone relax, the chips are here!" I groan as he and Ella walk into the kitchen carrying at least a dozen bags of tortilla chips between them. He's also got his sweater on backward, but at the moment I'm too anxious to be entertained.

"You know there's only going to be fifteen people here, right?" I ask. "And you're two of them?"

"I was so excited I don't even remember being at the store!" Ella says. "We went on a shopping spree—" She mimes pulling everything off a shelf. "Straight into the cart!"

Oblivious to what they walked in on, she drops her collection of bags onto the counter.

But while Ash can't focus on physical details to save his life, he is far too observant when it comes to people. He's gone still beside Ella, looking from me to Nat. "What's with the mood? Did we interrupt something?"

Nat gives me a look that says it's my story to tell. This isn't how I wanted to do this, but I'm positive they'll find out eventually anyway. With a quick glance around to make sure there's nobody else nearby to overhear, I whisper, "I was telling Nat that I had sex with Fizzy last night." The silence that follows is so long, the depths of it so dark, I finally add, "Somebody say something."

"Fizzy?" Ella asks. "As in the star of the dating show we're all here to watch?"

Ash follows up with the hottest of takes: "That seems like a bad idea, Connor."

"I didn't intend to do it," I explain.

He frowns. "I'm trying to picture accidental sex and am confused by what I see."

"Okay, back up," Nat says. "You are the least impulsive person I know. You were dead set against this. What happened?"

"I'm not entirely sure," I say. It was like a drain stopper was pulled and every bit of my objectivity and reason went spiraling down. I had no right to critique her behavior; she's been fantastic. I had no right to feel jealous, I still don't. "I got a bit peeved when we were talking about the other blokes, and—"

"Other blokes meaning the men you cast as Heroes on the show?" Ash asks with a *you're such a dipshit wanker* lean to his voice.

"Right, fuck off, but then she seemed to get it," I say. "Honestly, she sees right through me."

Nat lets out a happy little whimper and I point at her. "Not helpful."

"Sorry, I just like the idea of her seeing through you."

"Well, it's got us in a fucking mess now, hasn't it?"

"You're not suggesting you put your dick in her because she's perceptive," Ash says, and Ella smacks his shoulder.

"No. It's because"—I scrounge around for an answer—"Fizzy is so . . ." I end the thought with a growl. "Fizzy."

"Connor," Natalia says gently. "You *like* her. A lot."

"I do." My shoulders go slack like I've been punched in the

stomach because now the truth is out there: my feelings are a pile of tangled complications and there is no way to safely maneuver myself out of any of it. "And I'm supposed to find her soulmate."

"What are you going to do?" Ella asks.

"My job," I say with a shrug. "What choice do I have? I'm definitely not having sex with her again."

"Unless it's another accident," Ash says.

"Fuck off."

He laughs. "Well, maybe the show will flop."

Ella smacks his shoulder again. "It's not going to flop," she insists. "Why would you say that?"

"Because maybe that's Connor's way out! He didn't want to do this. It was *their* idea. If it flops, then clearly it wasn't a *good* idea, and that's not on Connor, that's on Blaine!"

"Blaine was pretty clear about what I'm supposed to do. And they've sunk a fortune into this, so I have no excuse. It has to work."

When the doorbell rings, everyone freezes.

"Here we go," I say, pushing away from the counter. I stop in the doorway to the hall and turn to face them. "Please, don't stare at us the whole time. It's already going to be weird."

"Of course not," Nat says.

"Or ask her a ton of questions," I add. "On top of everything else, she's probably quite nervous."

"You look *quite nervous*," Ash says.

"Piss off," I say under my breath.

As I walk through the house, I give myself a little pep talk. I am thirty-three years old. I'm producing a show with an enormous budget that's about to premiere on national television. I've overseen entire productions under some of the worst conditions in the most inhospitable places in the world. I've helped keep an actual human child alive for over ten years and not lost or seriously mangled her once. I can do this. I can manage my feelings for Felicity Chen.

I open the door and immediately know I'm fooling myself. She's beautiful—she's always beautiful—but I register that the world is divided into people who know what it's like to make love to Fizzy Chen, and people who don't. I'm now one of the lucky, broken ones. I know how her skin tastes and what it's like to kiss her until she melts. I know her sounds and the way her eyes drift closed right before she comes. I don't know how to go about the rest of my life pretending I don't want her with a force that rivals the pull of the tides.

Last night we fixed our clothes and she walked me to her door. We stood facing each other, just like this. Her lips were swollen, her cheeks still flushed from exertion. I leaned forward and what was supposed to be a simple goodbye peck melted into something warm and greedy. Time tipped sideways. I immediately wanted her again, right there against the wall or maybe kneeling over her on the couch, her legs wrapped tight around my waist. I hadn't left yet and we'd already made a mess of things, what did it matter?

But it does matter. There's no room in my life—personally, or professionally—for a fling. And Fizzy has never indicated that this is anything more than that. Hell, I wouldn't even be involved in this show if Blaine hadn't forced me, and he couldn't have forced me if I didn't absolutely need this job. Having feelings for Fizzy doesn't change any of that.

With my hand cradling her jaw, I'd dragged my lips up her neck, placed a kiss to her cheek. I'd straightened to meet her eyes and saw the same want and confusion reflected back at me. Neither of us knew what to say, so we hadn't said anything. Instead, I'd walked out to my car knowing that if I didn't leave right then, I wouldn't leave at all.

"Hi," I say now, taking a step back and motioning for her to come inside.

"Hi." Her hair is in a sleek ponytail, her cropped pants and sweater both black but feet framed in bright orange heels that bring her a few inches closer to eye level. She's wearing a slash of dark eyeliner, her lips a screeching, house-on-fire red. I want to see that color smeared all over my skin.

I'm glad we're alone because the air pulses with shimmering want.

"Should we get the awkward out of the way," I ask, "or drag it out for peak discomfort later?"

She lets out a small, relieved laugh. "Let's take pity on everyone and kick the elephant out of the room now." She pulls in a steadying breath. "I've been practicing this."

"By all means, let me have it."

"Last night was one hell of a way to break a dry spell." She's close enough that anyone in a nearby room wouldn't be able to hear, and her eyes are molten and intimate. "But it's also really complicated. I think we both get that."

I nod. She's giving me this out and I'm going to take it. I'm going to take it and run with it and do my best to ignore how naive we're being and dig my head deep into the sand. "Absolutely."

"We'll just have to drive everyone nuts with all this unresolved sexual tension." She grins. "I've written about it, I'm an expert, you know."

"I'm pretty sure I know how those books end."

"Then let's agree this is a buddy comedy, not a romance." With a little wink and a squeeze to my forearm, she steps in past me. I follow the way her eyes move over everything and wonder what she sees. It's a nice place, with tall ceilings, weathered wood beams, a good-sized yard for the area, and a great kitchen. I bought it about three years ago, and while I've never had much of a need or a want to really decorate it, I've tried to make it feel like a home for Stevie.

Fizzy stops in front of a snapshot of twenty-three-year-old me holding a newborn Stevie. "Oh, this is unfair," she says, picking up the frame.

I look exhausted, young, and stupidly, naively happy. I had no idea what I was doing, or what it even meant to be a dad, but I instantly loved that little girl in a way I hadn't known was possible. There were already cracks showing between Nat and me, but I figured we could make it work. I'd find a way.

"Nobody told me that Fizzy was here!" Stevie races around the corner in her socks and wraps her arms around Fizzy in a tight hug.

"It just happened!" Fizzy says. "And I have something for you." Stevie steps away long enough for Fizzy to reach into her purse and pull out a small package with Wonderland's logo emblazoned in iridescent lettering. Stevie tears into it and I realize it's the only concert DVD she doesn't have.

"Thank you!" She squeezes her eyes closed and hugs Fizzy again.

"Make sure to watch it with your dad. He's got some dance

moves to work on before the next tour." Fizzy meets my eyes over Stevie's head and gives me a teasing wink.

"All right, that's enough. Come on." I pick Stevie up and swing her over my shoulder, trying to tamp down the confusing mix of anticipation and dread I feel at the prospect of the next few hours. Stevie squeals and I glance back to where Fizzy is giggling and following behind us. "We'll be starting soon, and there are some people I want you to meet."

The minute Fizzy is in the kitchen, it's clear Nat and Ella can't help themselves. Nat gushes about Fizzy's books, how she's read every single one, and how she can't wait for what's next. She sweetly, obliviously asks Fizzy when that might be, and to her credit, Fizzy gives an answer that she's clearly used many times before and that nicely balances "it's going to be a while" with "I'm so excited about it." Nat tells her all about walking in on me that first day mid–Fizzy googling before Ella interrupts to breathlessly explain that she isn't a big reader but knows everything about every dating show ever and cannot wait for the show to start tonight. Ash mostly stands off to the side smiling at the countertop and trying not to make direct eye contact.

I've been so wrapped up in the Fizzyness of the situation tonight I've barely let myself think about the show. But when it's time and everyone crowds into my living room, the nerves finally kick in. Likewise, Fizzy declines food or a glass of wine, saying she's not sure it will stay down. Everyone tries to get Fizzy to sit on the couch in the center of the room—she is the star, after all—but she insists it will only make her more anxious. She needs space to pace and possibly escape if needed. Everyone laughs, and that's how Fizzy ends up standing in the back with me.

The room falls into silence as the opening notes of the theme song play. The glossy *True Love Experiment* logo appears on the screen, followed by our host. Just as we hoped, Lanelle Turner is the perfect amount of funny and relatable as she introduces herself and explains the premise of the show. We'll meet our Heroine, and her eight Heroes. Along with Fizzy, each contestant has undergone the popular DNADuo screening, and the results have been sealed. Not even the producers know the outcome. It will be up to the audience to follow each date and vote for who they think is Fizzy's soulmate. Each week the votes will be tallied, and two Heroes will be eliminated. In the final episode, the DNADuo scores will be revealed, and we'll see if the audience or science has been a better predictor of Fizzy's soulmate. The Hero chosen by the audience will win a $100,000 cash prize, and, after the scores are revealed, Fizzy will have the chance to choose who she takes along for an all-expenses-paid trip to Fiji. Hopefully, the audience correctly chooses her true love and happily ever after.

But first, the audience gets to meet River. When Lanelle mentions his name, the room around me fills with applause, the loudest—including a few catcalls and whistles—from Nat and Fizzy. When I asked Fizzy how she managed to convince him, she first told me she used nature's credit card. When I didn't get it—

Sex, Connor. Oh my God, a dirty joke doesn't work if I have to explain it!

—she said she told him that by laying out the science himself, he controlled the narrative, and therefore how people would see it. It didn't mean he was necessarily backing the show, only his technology.

Now, footage of River walking through the halls of the Salk and working in a lab fills the screen, followed by a voiceover of him explaining the initial idea, and the years and years of research that went into developing it. He's careful to clarify that it isn't about finding people with similar DNA. Quite the opposite: it's about compatibility as predicted by hundreds of validated scientific and psychological evaluations. Despite his hesitance, he's thoughtful and charming while remaining completely impartial to the idea of the show. He's perfect.

With the format clear, Fizzy is introduced, and again, the room fills with noise, much more exuberant this time. There's a video montage that includes footage of her speech at UCSD, a brief breakdown of her impressive literary career, and then an interview with Fizzy on her couch at home.

"I have success and happiness on my own," Fizzy tells the camera. "I guess what I'm looking for is someone to be my best friend and lover. Someone with whom even the silly small things are fun because we're doing them together."

Next to me, Fizzy groans and covers her face with her hands. When she leans forward, I see a small bruise sucked into the skin behind her ear. The sight of it makes me go hot all over. "Are you kidding?" I nudge her and redirect my focus back to the TV. "Look at you. You're perfect."

On-screen, the Heroes are being introduced. Because Fizzy didn't have much of a connection with Arjun or Tex, we've edited it to show less of their stories and dates than the others. We won't always be so heavy-handed, but with eight guys to get through and limited time to show it, we took Fizzy's preferences into account and made the call. There are glimpses of the guys at home and snapshots of each of their backstories. We see Isaac with his mum and grandmother, and leading a research meeting in a glass-walled conference room. Stevie quickly announces that she wants Isaac to win. Most of Nick's intro takes place in his veterinary practice. There are shots of him with puppies and kittens, and it gets the predictable reaction of *awwwwwww* from almost everyone in the room. Dax is shown jumping out of an actual plane, hanging from a cliff somewhere in Arizona, and then at a table in his parents' home, talking about what he hopes to find on the show. We see Evan on the campus of UCSD, jogging up the steps to the engineering building. We follow him to the coffee shop where he works part-time, see him laugh with his coworkers as they good-naturedly tease him about being on a dating show. In just a few minutes on-screen, it's clear everyone loves him.

Beside me, Fizzy spends the first half of the show looking like she might be physically ill, but by the third commercial break, she's relaxed enough to want some wine. A good sign.

She follows me to the kitchen during commercials. The living room behind us is a rambunctious mix of voices, all shouting out their opinions and shared enthusiasm for the show. Any questions I had about its watchability and success are put to rest as the minutes go on and it's clearly an entertaining program. Brenna is monitoring social media and says people are loving it. The show's tags are trending. I can exhale for the first time in a fucking eternity.

Fizzy leans against the counter while I open a new bottle of wine.

"How are you feeling?" I ask.

"Better than I expected. It's really good, Connor."

"*You're* really good."

"I'm serious. You took my suggestions—which, let's be honest, were really just me starting a big game of power-play chicken—and turned them into something totally unique. A lot of people are going to watch this show and love every minute. Hell, I'd watch it. With someone else as the star, that is."

"That's a fucking relief, and I mean it."

Remembering the wine bottle in my hand, I reach into the cabinet behind her for a glass, and freeze. The moment is so reminiscent of the one last night: our bodies close, sharing the same breath, my hand on the cupboard door for leverage as I pushed into her over and over, harder and harder.

Her breath catches and I watch as goose bumps erupt along her neck. I could kiss her now, and I think she'd kiss me back. If I asked her to stay after everyone left, I think she'd do that, too.

In the other room, music cuts through the air, signaling the end of the commercial break. I follow her back just as the first confessional begins. The guys each have their turn solo, and each is charming and obviously interested in Fizzy. Frankly, the idea that any of these men wouldn't fall all over themselves to be with her is unfathomable, but our editing team—myself included—has done a good job of creatively tempering Tex's and Arjun's enthusiasm so no one feels too bad for them when they are likely voted off over the next twenty-four hours.

And then my confessional with Fizzy begins.

I'd neglected to mention this part to any of my family, and as my face appears on-screen, the room explodes with their noisy surprise. Nat is fucking delighted, Stevie is dancing on the couch and shouting that that's her dad, and Ash lets everyone know that he's just been issued a free pass to give me shit for the foreseeable future.

Next to me, Fizzy is as smug as I've ever seen her. "Do you see that charisma?" she calls to the room, glass held in front of her. "Hollywood, please hire me as your casting director."

When it quiets again during another commercial, she taps me and motions to the TV. "Is now when you tell me I was right?"

"Let's manage expectations." Most of the room has emptied out during the break, everyone waiting for the loo or off to the kitchen to refill their drinks. "We'll get numbers tomorrow. Your phone must be blowing up with messages. What's everyone saying?"

Fizzy drains her glass and leans back against the couch. "Not ready for that level of reality yet. Let me stay in this soft-launch enthusiasm bubble until at least nine tomorrow morning. Then I'll tiptoe into opinions. But for now"—she motions to the TV—"I was right about you. Say it."

"You are occasionally clever."

"Always."

"An average amount."

"Tell me I'm the best."

I smile. "You, Fizzy, are the best."

"Thank you, wow, I never expected such a compliment, but it means so much." She hands me her empty glass. "Now please, more wine."

twenty-nine

FIZZY

I get into my car, turn it on, and then sit idling at the curb, staring out at the dark street. This feeling I have right now—the jittery, hyper-adrenaline, restless feeling—most people would have this reaction to seeing themselves on a dating show, to witnessing how the masterful editing made the entire episode sing, and then, at the end of the night, getting the call that the show is on track to being the biggest reality show debut in a decade.

But I know myself and know that the reason I get these kinds of heart flutters is the same reason I became an author in the first place: I love romance. I love the swooping in my chest when I read a good kiss, the choking of my lungs when I get to the angst, the shaken-carbonated blast of joy reading the happily ever after. I just watched eight perfect men vying for my heart, and they're not even why I have the flutters. I have them because I got to see my new favorite person tonight.

Stretching, I find my reflection in the rearview mirror and glare at that harlot. "Listen up," I tell her forcefully. "It's a relief that things didn't go very, very wrong because you had sex with your producer. Be grateful you can be attracted to someone again. You did it to get it out of your system. Now get your act together and stop thinking about his eyes and his smile and his dick."

Satisfied, I put the car in gear and drive home.

I don't care how confident you are, nobody wants to run into someone when they're braless, wearing pajama pants, and buying single-serving canned wine at CVS. But as I step out of the booze and spirits aisle at the respectable hour of noon on Sunday, I collide face-first with the center of a very, very solid chest.

"I am so sorry," I say, quickly dropping to the floor to retrieve my scattered armload of canned rosé.

"Fizzy?"

I glance up, eyes traveling over miles of toned leg—momentarily bummed by the obstruction of black running shorts—until my eyes skip up to one of the best smiles I've ever seen. "*Isaac?*"

He kneels to help me retrieve my spilled treasures and it's a little embarrassing how many there are. I'm not sure how I managed to balance all of these in the first place.

"Stocking up for hibernation," I joke as we stand. Even I can appreciate the shame in wasting such soaring specimens of men on pocket-sized me, but who am I to question the universe?

Isaac grins adorably. "Rosé: the perfect winter wine." He carefully balances my last can on top of the teetering pyramid. "What are the odds of running into each other here?"

"I'm sure you could calculate them, Hot Nerd."

"Touché." He laughs and eyes my haul. "Grabbing some quality refreshments for what looks like some day-drinking fun?"

I eye the single Gatorade in his left hand. "We all choose to hydrate in our own way." He laughs again, and I add, "And it looks like you aren't suffering similarly, but I felt so mentally drained after the episode aired last night. I've been useless all day."

Isaac nods. "Yeah, I felt the same. I finally went for a run just to get away from every relative within fifty miles who showed up at my house this morning to talk about the show."

I groan. "My mom has been calling me nonstop since last night. Conveniently forgetting my phone at home while also procuring wine felt like killing two birds with one stone."

He laughs again, but this time it has a quiet huskiness, the tenor of an inside joke. The sound sends a heated thrill down into my stomach and . . . what's that? *Pants feelings?* For someone who isn't Connor? Right here in the middle of CVS? Holy shit, baby. I *am* back!

"While this has been the absolute highlight of a very weird day," he says, grimacing, "I'm pretty sure we're breaking at least half a dozen rules by seeing each other outside the show."

"Oh shit, you're right." I quickly glance down the nearby aisles. As contestants, we all signed contracts that, among other things, expressly forbid us from fraternizing outside of the show. We could be fined, fired, or even sued. And yet you don't see me going anywhere. "I half expect an alarm to go off and for Connor to come out with one of those cartoon nets."

"I could escape," Isaac says with a grin and a single backward step. "I've got better running shoes on."

"Don't discount me," I tell him. "I'm surprisingly agile."

"I bet." He gives me a very long once-over. "Does it give me an advantage with you that we frequent the same CVS?"

"I don't get to decide, remember?"

He snaps his fingers. "Shoot. All right, well, I'm gonna get out of here." With a sexy little wink, he turns and waves over his shoulder. "I'll see you tomorrow."

I watch Isaac until he's out of sight, my pants still aflutter down below. "As a professional writer," I mumble to his very nice retreating backside, "I must say I would absolutely verb the adjective noun out of him."

"Are you Felicity Chen?"

My entire body jerks around at the voice to my left, where two older teen girls stand holding snacks and Red Bulls. I clutch my collection of wine to my chest, willing my heart to slow. I've been recognized before, but it's usually in the context of something bookish, such as browsing in the aisles of my local indie, not when I'm dressed like a writer on imminent deadline and carrying enough wine for an entire football team.

And then it occurs to me. Did they see me talking to myself? Do I look like a horny hobo?

A more startling thought lands: Did they see me talking to Isaac? Shit.

"That's me!" I finally manage to say.

They look at each other in shared excitement, then back to me, eyes sparkling with barely contained glee. "Oh my God," they say in unison, and one adds a high-pitched "You were so good last night!"

The girl who spoke is taller, with an emerald-green hijab and makeup so flawless that it transforms her black-and-white tracksuit and sneakers into high fashion.

"Do you know if they're going to make all the episodes available to stream?" she asks. "I've already watched the first one twice and might die if I have to wait a week."

"Just the one episode a week," I say, not relishing being the person who pierces their joy bubble. "We're shooting it as we go."

She groans playfully, but her friend in a UCSD sweatshirt pushes on. "I love your books and legit lost it when I saw you were doing this. I've read *Base Paired* four times." Before I can say anything, she quickly adds, "Can we ask you something? I know you're super busy."

"Was it the pajamas or the armload of canned rosé that gave away my hectic schedule? Go for it."

She laughs, turning her phone to face me, and points at the screen. "Do you know if this is Connor Prince's Instagram?"

Connor comes up repeatedly that day: in the afternoon when my mom drags me along to H Mart and a woman recognizes me in the frozen food aisle, praising me for a moment before asking whether Connor has starred in anything else, and again in the evening, when another parent completely loses her mind in front of me and Jess at Juno's ballet recital. Both times I find myself wanting to text him to gloat about how smart I am.

I resist. I do check his Instagram, though. By Monday morning, his follower count has ballooned from his mom, Nat, Ash, and some random dude, to twenty-two thousand. I'd bet my entire canned rosé collection that it hasn't even occurred to him to look.

After hair and makeup on Monday, I am led into an industrial kitchen at the Hilton Bayfront hotel. We do the bad news first: As predicted, Arjun and Tex have been eliminated by the voting audience. But then, the remaining six—Dax, Isaac, Evan, Jude, Colby, and Nick—are called out one by one, dressed casually and wearing wide smiles as matching accessories.

Isaac gives me a little wink, and I bite the inside of my cheek to keep from grinning back.

Lanelle introduces this week's plan: I get to choose which Heroes I want for each of the scheduled activities, including preparing a gourmet meal for my bed-resting sister, planting trees in Balboa Park, taking a craft cocktail class, going deep-sea fishing, pampering with mani-pedis, and a beach cruiser ride around Coronado. Viewers will see the dates compiled sequentially, of course—although the six dates will take place over the next three days, with confessionals and loved-one interviews scheduled for recording on Wednesday.

First up, of course, is the meal prep date. I am given ten minutes to firm up a plan before the cameras will roll again, showing me "thinking it over" before spontaneously giving my choices. Of course, there's the schoolyard pick vibe—whoever I choose first is the one viewers will assume I am most eager to spend time with—but I also have to be strategic about the best way to get to know each of them outside of their natural elements.

I choose Colby, the Navy SEAL, to cook with. In part because I like the idea of watching his forearms flex while he chops vegetables for the lunch we're making for Alice, but also because at our date last week he told me his mother owns Querida, one of my favorite taco shops in San Diego County. I bet the dude knows his way around a kitchen.

He does, but unfortunately his expertise means he ends up

mansplaining a lot about knife handling—fitting, I suppose, given his profession—and how to debone a whole fish. I flirt and crack jokes and drop innuendo, trying to help him out because I'm sure a lot of this bravado is caused by nerves, but unfortunately, he keeps talking over me. I don't see an easy way for the editing team to make him look great.

Jude and I plant trees that afternoon in Balboa, and I joke that I am disappointed to discover that he doesn't sparkle in the sun. His sense of humor seems to have taken the day off, because he gives me an unsolicited monologue about what *Twilight* did to "legitimate vampire literature." I wonder whether, when it comes time to put the episode together, Connor will keep my unimpressed look directed at the camera.

Speaking of Connor, he's there. Jesus, he's so incredibly *there*. Being tall in the background, carrying equipment in those stupid, brawny arms. Laughing huskily when I hold up a zucchini and give the camera a knowing wink. Shaking his head in exasperation when I tell Jude our next date should be in Volterra and he readily agrees, clearly without knowing what that means.

At least *Connor* knows Volterra is where the sparkling vampires live.

During the craft cocktail class with Nick—complete with disastrous attempts at bottle throwing and a lot of puckering when I use way too much lime—Connor, Rory, and one cameraman are the only crew members nearby. It shrinks the sweet, stained glass–windowed bar down to a broom closet. When Nick feeds me a cherry, instead of looking deep into his eyes, I turn my gaze on instinct to where Connor stands behind the camera rig. They make us shoot it again.

If possible, the proximity issue is worse on the deep-sea fishing date with Evan. Connor is seated directly at my feet, holding the mic gear while Rory throws up over the side of the deck, and the two cameramen struggle with handhelds on the surprisingly turbulent boat ride. At one point, Connor reaches out and steadies me with his hands on my thighs, gripping me until I've successfully hauled a huge tuna aboard.

Evan notices, I'm sure, but has no time to question it because as soon as the briny scent of the fish lands at his feet he, too, loses his lunch over the side of the boat—which I am delighted to say is caught on video.

When Evan has recovered, we sit side by side on the now gently rocking boat while the crew changes battery packs. The thing is, the more time I spend with Evan the more I remember how much fun we had, how easy it was to be with him, to joke around and tease each other. But I also remember that, Bart Simpson aside, while there was a spark, there were never fireworks.

We only dated a few months, but Evan played on my brother's rec league softball team and even met my family once. It's crazy that in my many years of exuberant dating, only a handful of men have ever managed that.

"I got the invitation to Peter's wedding," he says. "I hope he knows I RSVP'd no because I had to"—he gestures around us, indicating the show—"but not because I don't want to attend."

"Don't worry, he knows."

"You like Kailey?"

"I suspect a love potion was involved because she's amazing."

Evan laughs. "I heard the guest list is over seven hundred people."

I nod. "I don't think I've met seven hundred people in my life."

He sets his reel in the cage mount and leans his head back to look up at the sky. "I'm sure the catering is going to be insane."

"It's the reason I've inquired about wearing elastic-waist pants instead of my bridesmaid dress."

He lowers his voice. "Can I admit that going out has been kind of weird since this thing started? Being recognized on the street is surreal."

"I'm dreading the million questions from my family members about why I need a show to find a husband."

"How are you managing the plus-one situation? I assume you can't take a date, but it's your younger brother's wedding." He winces. "That's a lot of attention on you for multiple reasons."

I shrug. I'd normally bring Jess with me, but she'll be in Costa Rica with River for a much-needed vacation. Of course, I'm fine going to family events solo, but Evan is right: this wedding will be different. Friends and relatives are flying in from as far away as Hong Kong for the occasion. Alice will be set up in a comfortable chair, very pregnant and very happily married. Peter's fiancée is a well-known dermatologist who also happens to be the daughter of the most successful plastic surgeon in San Diego. As comfortable as I would be going dateless, weddings are for family, and my mother would want me to attend with someone.

"I suppose I'll have to brave it without a date," I say.

"A date to what?"

Evan and I turn at the sound of Connor's voice, and of course this is the one time I don't have him on missile lock. "My brother Peter's wedding."

"It's this weekend, right?" Connor asks.

"Yeah," Evan says. "I met Fizzy through him. I'm not going, though, don't worry."

Connor glances over his shoulder and then squats down, lowering his voice. "I told Rory we are absolutely not shooting footage at the wedding, so don't remind her it's happening."

I salute him. "Got it, boss."

"Can you take Jess?" he asks me.

"She's on vacation." I wave it off. "Don't worry about me. I can go solo. I may be swimming with sharks all weekend, but I, too, am a shark."

With the popularity of the first episode, I know I won't be able to fly under the radar. In the past two days, I've been stopped at least four times each day. For the most part, the interactions are great. A few of them are readers, most are not. Some ask me about the guys, or the DNADuo, or just want an inside scoop, but every single one of them asks me about Connor.

In fact, according to Jess by way of Juno by way of Stevie, Connor is being bombarded. Ten-year-olds have a tendency to exaggerate, but if it's happening to me in the ladies' room at Barnes & Noble, it's got to be happening to him, too. The common theme: most viewers would like to ride him like a Peloton.

Connor's attention on me is like a heat lamp, and I'm relieved when it's time to start shooting. I'd rather watch Evan barf over the side of the boat again than think about Peter's wedding anymore.

I half expect Dax to take his socks off at the spa and reveal a missing toe or tattoo of a naked woman on top of his foot—both of which would be fascinating, but for very different reasons—but his feet are sadly intact and unmarked. Despite my concern that he might be bored or restless, he is a champ in the spa chair. He decides he wants his fingernails painted yellow, is ticklish when the pedicurist pulls out the pumice stone and gets to work on his calluses, and is shamelessly flirting with the woman doing his manicure— but sweetly, because she could be his grandmother.

When Connor told me last night at the marina that he'd be in the editing room this morning and his director of photography would be in charge for a few hours, I felt a pulse of relief like, finally, I'll be able to breathe.

But I was wrong. My brain knows he isn't here, but my reflexes don't. I keep looking up at the empty space where he would normally be and find myself scanning the area. It's a rude awakening to see how often I search for his reaction to things.

"You good?" Dax asks when we're sitting with our feet and hands held carefully still, nail polish drying. The crew is packing up, having gotten as much footage as they needed, I guess. But still no Connor.

Will he meet us in Coronado when we drive over for my afternoon bike ride with Isaac? Or is he editing all day?

"What's that?" I ask distractedly.

"Are you okay?" he repeats, smiling sweetly. "Are you in a hurry to get going?"

"No, no." I must've scanned the spa again unconsciously. Why can't I get my head in the game? I've done this before—slept with someone and then gone on dates with someone else later in the week! Sex is sex, it doesn't have to mean everything!

But, it also doesn't have to mean nothing.

Shit.

"Sorry," I say. "I was just thirsty."

Dax lifts a hand, waving to his new best grandmother-friend. "Can she get a cup of water, please?"

The adorable woman brings me some in a small plastic cup and Dax watches, concerned.

"Better?"

I nod. "Thank you."

"It's a lot of pressure, huh?"

"It is."

"I have about a million questions for you," he says, "about your job and your life."

"Yeah?" I smile over at him. Look at this man right here, attentive and fun. A thought hits me like a door blown open.

Dax could be my soulmate.

The cameras aren't even rolling, and he gives me a disarmingly kind smile. "I'm really hoping I get a third date."

Connor isn't in Coronado waiting for us. But the tandem bike is, and so is Isaac, with his knowing, crinkly-eyed smile and addicting belly laugh. We noodle around the island with cameras mounted on the bike frame and a cameraman ahead of us riding backward on a Vespa. Isaac is obviously a genius and makes me laugh the entire way, with the kind of off-the-cuff, quick-witted humor I find intensely sexy. It's impossible to ignore that there's something between us, and when he suggests we stop for spontaneous milkshakes I immediately agree. I want more time with him, face-to-face, close. Side by side, at a picnic table overlooking the ocean, we share stories from when we were kids, and for the first time on any of these dates, I forget that the cameras are right there.

I also realize, as I get to the bubbly bottom of my milkshake and Connor finally steps into view, sweaty and breathless, almost like he ran the whole way here, that I haven't thought about him since my date with Isaac began.

Isaac could be my soulmate.

And yet I still want Connor.

Get it together, Fizzy, I think, and turn my attention back to Isaac and his caramel milkshake and the cherry he's dangling for me to eat. No doubt viewers will compare this moment to the one with Nick yesterday, as I close my eyes and eat it with a smile. I tie the stem in a knot with only my tongue and open my mouth to flirtatiously display it. It gets the impressed reaction I'd hoped for—Isaac claps and gives me a sexy "Dang, girl"—but it takes every ounce of effort to not look at Connor to see what he thinks about it, and to wonder whether he's thinking about what that tongue of mine felt like gliding over his neck, his bottom lip, his jaw.

We'll have our confessional later, but my plan is to escape as soon as Rory says cut. My head is a mess, and I need to sift through my feelings for both men: my attraction to Isaac and the strange way it makes me feel like I'm betraying Connor, even though connecting with other men is literally the point of the show. But after the confessionals are all done and Isaac—who waited for me to finish— gives me a sweet hug goodbye and a gentle kiss to my cheek (pants feelings, we meet again), Connor's hand comes around my arm.

I think he'll ask me about Isaac, or tell me why he was late, or one of a dozen other possibilities.

What I don't expect is for him to quietly lean in and say, "Let me take you to Peter's wedding. It's easy to explain why I'd be there. I don't want you to have to face that alone."

thirty

Episode Two Confessional Transcript

Connor Prince: Well, here we are again.

Fizzy Chen: Hello, Connor Prince. You were away for some of our shoots this week. It was weird.

Connor: I know, and I apologize. Unfortunately for me, I had some things related to the show that I needed to take care of. Fortunately for you and our viewers, you had six handsome men to keep you company.

Fizzy: Am I allowed to say I missed you? Because I missed you.

Connor: That's very kind.

Fizzy: It was a hot day and you're really tall. We could have used the shade.

Connor: There she is. Brenna, please make a note to insert a rim shot in post.

Fizzy: Okay, stop, wait. All I want in life is a sparkle sound to announce my entrance into any room. If I knew we could add sound effects in edits, I would have gone insane in that editing booth.

Connor: This is precisely why you aren't allowed in the editing booth. Shall we get back to your dates? The week was quite a whirlwind.

Fizzy: It was busy, but the Heroes were great. I'm really hoping you cut when I slipped down the stairs at Balboa Park and my dress slid up to my neck and I showed everyone my butt, but I suspect you've already planned to include it.

Connor: You suspect correctly. But fear not, Felicity, we can also edit in small images to protect your virtue. Would you like the peach emoji or waving hand emoji over your bottom?

Fizzy: [stands and looks directly into the camera] America, are you seeing this?

Connor: [laughing, pulls her back to her seat] Let's get to the dates, shall we?

thirty-one

CONNOR

Come on up. Room 1402.

My brain stutters.

When I texted Fizzy to tell her I'd arrived, I expected her to meet me down in the lobby or direct me to the banquet hall. But meeting her in a hotel room feels like the exact problem I anticipated when I gave myself a stern lecture in the mirror at home.

"Escort her," I'd said to my reflection. "You're her handler, the executive in charge of her. You are not her date. You are not her lover. You are doing a job."

I can meet you down here, I type, but if she's upstairs and asking me to come to her, it's possible she needs help with something.

I delete it, typing, Is anyone up there with you? which sounds possessive and awkward. I delete that, too.

I see you typing, she texts. Don't be weird. I need your help.

Laughing, I delete everything again and type simply, On my way.

I hit the button at the elevator bank and suck in a deep breath; my pulse is climbing its way up my throat. Ideally, I need the elevator ride to take a half hour. Unfortunately, I suspect today will be a continuous series of reminders that I should not have offered to escort her to this event, because I am not equipped to handle being alone with her.

Her door, I see as I approach, is propped open with the dead bolt, but I knock anyway. A bright "Come in" drifts from inside.

Pushing it open just enough to peek my head in, I call out, "I could be anyone, and you just invite me in sight unseen?"

"You're statistically unlikely to be a criminal." Her voice echoes from the bathroom. "You just texted, and besides, half of the people on this floor are relatives or friends."

"Well, I'm glad the chances of someone you know seeing me walk into your hotel room are relatively high."

Her voice gets louder as she walks into the bedroom. "I'd just tell them you're delivering room serv—"

She stops for a breath when she sees me, but her next words are lost to the blank void of my cranium as I take in the strapless beaded gown poured over her body. It's gold, covered with intricate beading and formfitting until about midthigh, where it spills in a wave of shimmering fabric around her feet. She's wearing her hair piled in some complicated arrangement on her head, and a few dark strands hang loose, skimming her bare shoulders.

"Connor?"

I startle, having no idea how long I'd gone mute. "Yes—that's— I'm here."

When I drag my eyes to her face, she's fighting a smile. "I asked if you could help me?"

"Uh, right—with what, exactly?"

"My dress?"

She turns to show me what she means. Awareness lands, and

this view is infinitely worse. A long V of unmarred, honeyed skin is exposed in the space where the buttons lie open. I strangle down a groan but am not entirely successful, and it comes out like a whimper I must consciously rebrand into a frustration of a nonsexual variety: "A casual count tells me there are at least eighty thousand buttons here."

"There are forty," she tells me. "I realize I should have had an auntie do this before you got here, but alas, everyone is busy and here we are. For obvious reasons—the primary one being that I can barely bend over in this, let alone twist to button it myself—I need another set of hands."

The words *bend over* are a screeching train wreck in my thoughts. I blame the image they conjure for the way my voice shakes as I approach her with a casual "Sure, of course."

But then I do something without fully realizing it until a shiver runs down her back: I drag a knuckle down the length of her spine.

"If you do that, we're not getting this dress on." She turns and looks at me over her shoulder. "And I know how you feel about boundaries."

"It is frankly exhausting to be the only one erecting them," I mumble.

Fizzy laughs, delighted, and faces away again.

"You are reassuringly predictable."

"Well, you're the one who just stroked me and then said *erecting*."

I exhale a dramatically weary breath. "It was an unintentional, glancing touch."

"I'm starting to wonder if leaving this unbuttoned was an unfortunate oversight or happy accident."

The first button is a bitch. The holes are tight, and the buttons are satin covered and minuscule, making them exceedingly hard to grasp. But by the third I've got it mostly figured out. We fall quiet as I carefully make my way from the curve of her lower back up to the soft expanse between her shoulder blades. And just before each button comes together, I fight the urge to lean forward and kiss the skin beneath my fingers.

Hooking the final fastener at the top, I give myself one brief indulgence, and cup a palm to the back of her neck as I lean around to gaze at her. Her cheeks are flushed, pupils wide and black.

Jesus, she's as turned on as I am.

"Your chastity is assured," I tell her. "Because I am not doing that again."

Fizzy smiles and clears her throat before turning fully to give me an appreciative once-over. "You look hot."

"Thank you. You . . ." I swallow when my voice comes out a bit strangled. "You look breathtaking."

She reaches up, touching my bow tie. "I was hoping you'd arrive flustered over how to tie this so I could do it for you."

With a grin, I reach up and tug the end, untying it in a smooth pull.

Fizzy's answering smile is a bolt of sunlight.

"I figure you should do something in return after I fastened those seven thousand tiny buttons."

The unintended innuendo hangs heavy in the air between us. She steps toward me, still smiling as she takes hold of the tie, tugging it to align the ends evenly around my neck. "I didn't get the impression you were under duress."

"I'll send you the bill for my arthritis prescriptions."

She hums and her smile lingers, softening. "Are you ready for today? It might be overwhelming."

"I hope so. It's been a while since I attended a fancy wedding."

"Yours?"

I laugh. "No. I went as someone's plus-one."

"Did that night end with *your* chastity intact?"

I let out a hearty laugh. "Oh yes. She was a friend of a coworker and had recently relocated from Arizona. I knew from the moment I picked her up that something was off, but she insisted she was fine."

"Oh boy."

"Indeed. She cried during the ceremony—"

"Understandable."

"Absolutely, but then also cried during dinner and the first dance. When I finally asked if she really was all right, she admitted that her husband had left her for his assistant, and that's why she'd relocated to be closer to her parents." Fizzy's wince deepens as she focuses on the bow tie. "When the guests were invited to make toasts, she held her glass aloft and told the happy couple to enjoy the night because love is an illusion and men are incapable of keeping their dicks in their pants."

"You realize I'm stealing this story, right?"

I nod. "So, it's a low bar, but I'm guessing no matter what happens tonight, it will be better than that."

Fizzy laughs. "Glass half-full, I like it. But you have no idea how huge my family is. Statistically speaking, that's a lot of crazy."

With her focus still on the bow tie, I take the opportunity to openly stare at her. "Evan did pull me aside and give me some inside scoop."

Fizzy's hands go still. "He did?"

"What to give, some of the things you've probably been doing this morning, like the tea ceremony—"

Her bursting laugh interrupts me. "Did he tell you that Peter would be on a wild scavenger hunt?"

I shake my head, mesmerized by the way her lips plump into a sweet pout when she thinks over her explanation. "In our community, the tea ceremony is a big deal. It usually happens in the morning, and the bride and groom are kept apart. The groom is given a list of tasks to prove his love for the bride before the family decides he's worthy enough. It's all a game, but Kailey's three sisters were the ones to pull it all together and he had to do beer pong at seven this morning—"

"Actual beer?"

She nods, beaming. "Then they made him drink some kind of random fridge concoction—we were all gagging. He had to answer trivia about Kailey, and then dance and sing for everyone."

"The singing and dancing in front of everyone—"

"Am I describing your literal nightmare?"

I begin to say yes but then, for a feverish pulse, I imagine an alternate universe where it is me at this ceremony, proving my worth to this woman right here. My hesitation melts. "No" comes out instead. "If I was in love, I'd do it all."

"Carry ten gallons of water half a block using only leaky buckets?"

I reach up, dragging a strand of hair away from her bottom lip. "Of course."

"Drink a fridge concoction?"

"Easy."

"Easy?" She squints at me. "Hoisin, mayo, rice vinegar, almond milk, garlic paste, and mango juice."

"You act like it's cyanide." I laugh. "You think a man who loves a woman won't drink something minging to be able to see her walking down the aisle toward him?"

She looks up and meets my gaze. Her right eye has a spot of gold in it, like she looked up at the sun once and a tiny splinter of it became trapped there. I can see it shrink as her pupils dilate.

Fuck.

She blinks away. "Would you run three miles in the middle of the night for this hypothetical woman, too?"

"Only three?" Her smile falters, and I look down at her hands. She doesn't appear to have made much progress. "Do you have any clue how to tie this?"

"It's a weird angle because you're a giant Viking."

"I think, in fact, you've never done this before."

"You might be right," she says, frowning. "But I'm not a quitter."

I lift my chin, giving her better access, feeling happy to stand here all night. "Okay, it sounds like we might be here for a while. Tell me more about this tea ceremony."

"Well," she says, and pulls free whatever progress she's managed so far to start over. "After the groom proves his worth, he's allowed to see the bride. They both wear the most beautiful traditional garments, and the bride and groom pay their respects to the family members—oldest to youngest—and a cup of tea is offered in turn to each of them. The family gives the lai see, which are red envelopes containing money, and the elders give them advice . . ." She trails off. Tilting her head, Fizzy takes a deep breath. "Honestly, I love the tea ceremony."

An ache passes through me when I hear the wistful longing in her voice. She's so rarely vulnerable, it's both wonderful and devastating to see this tiny crack in her armor. "I can see that."

"Anyway," she says, straightening with a quick inhale, "we did that at Kailey's parents' house this morning, and got back here with just enough time to change, and that's when I remembered the eighty thousand buttons on my dress." She steps back, surveying her work, and frowns. "I'm going to be honest, the execution here is not great."

I look down, undo the floppy mess of a tie, and Fizzy glowers as I handily fix it. "You don't have to gloat, you mountain of jerkface."

"I'd been trying to make you feel useful here, but you've just told me we're in a hurry."

She runs her hand down my chest, spreading sparking warmth beneath my skin. Her hand stalls at my pocket and she pats it. "Is this what I think it is?"

I reach inside the blazer, pulling out the red envelope with cash inside. "Like I said, Evan helped me figure out what to bring for a gift."

She stares up at me. "That's very sweet."

"I like him," I admit begrudgingly. "He's a good guy."

"He is, but I mean you. *You're* sweet."

I scowl this away. "I am absolutely not *sweet*."

Fizzy reaches up, gently pinching my chin. "You, in fact, are the sweetest."

thirty-two

CONNOR

In the time that I was buttoning her dress and she was pretending to know what to do with my tie, the hotel lobby has turned into a madhouse. Black-tie wedding guests are everywhere, hugging, introducing, even crying in greeting. Looking around at the opulence that has spilled from the banquet hall into the lobby, I get the sense that the bride's family is the kind of wealthy that is hard for most mortals to comprehend.

"Seven hundred guests," Fizzy tells me sotto voce, leading me through the crowd. "Peter said they bought out several floors of rooms here for family on both sides flying in from all over the world."

I let out a low whistle, taking in the decor in the hallway outside the main banquet room—small cocktail tables with tasteful bouquets, glass bowls of wrapped chocolates, and wedding programs—and then inside, where I nearly trip over my own feet because the scale of the decor is unlike anything I've ever seen: cream silk is draped down walls; at least seventy tables are each decorated with tall vases dripping with red and orange blooms. Our destination is outside, where the ceremony will be held before what Fizzy promises to be a night of food and dancing and partying. But we are stopped every few feet as someone Fizzy knows steps into view and she greets them with her unfiltered enthusiasm. Women are hugged with a joyous cry; male relatives are embraced and teased. I am introduced to at least fifty people whose names I immediately forget because I am in awe of Fizzy in her familial element: warm, loving, quick with a story or anecdote.

A few people comment on my appearance on the show, and I quickly divert their attention back to Fizzy. Getting stopped by strangers and praised for being in front of the camera is still something I'm trying to get used to. It's not that I don't like doing the interviews; I do. Verbally sparring with Fizzy has quickly become one of my top-three favorite activities, and even I see that we play well off each other. But the public recognition is not something I'd mentally prepared for.

As we move through the crowd, all that lingers is the impression Fizzy gives that everyone I've met is the most impressive, or interesting, or adventurous, or creative person to have ever lived. And then, as we step out to the massive lawn resplendent with flowers and satin ribbons, there are Fizzy's parents, greeting guests as they come outside.

She takes my elbow, guiding me forward. "Connor, this is my mother, Lányīng Chen." If I had to do the math, I'd guess she was somewhere in her early sixties, but her skin is luminous, with only faint lines around her eyes.

The shift in Fizzy is subtle but noticeable to someone who can barely take his eyes off her: with her parents she softens, becoming more daughter than center stage, more caretaker than party girl, reaching up to straighten the pendant of her mother's necklace.

I expect a handshake, but am pulled in for a hug instead, and I carefully embrace her mother; she is smaller than her daughter. As I pull back to meet Mrs. Chen's smiling eyes, I think of my mother back home, how she looked exhausted day and night, how an event like this would make her panicked and uncomfortable.

Beside Mrs. Chen stands her husband, Ming, a lanky man I met at Fizzy's book signing, with a mischievous smile he passed down to at least one of his three children. "Here's my new friend who'll make my daughter a superstar!"

We shake hands in greeting as Fizzy leans in, mock offended. "Hello, Father, I'm *already* a superstar."

"When do I get my red carpet date, then?"

The two of them continue on as Mrs. Chen wraps an elegant hand around my forearm. "I like your show," she says. "You are very handsome on TV."

"Thank you," I say, grinning. "I'm surprised Fizzy lets you watch it."

Thankfully, she laughs at this. "You see her clearly, and I appreciate that."

I'm momentarily stilled by this. "I think most of the credit goes to your daughter. It's rare to find someone so genuine and natural in front of a camera. I'm beginning to think there's nothing she can't do."

"When she writes her real novel, you'll make it into a movie, okay?"

Now I'm confused for a different reason. "Her—"

Fizzy waves this off, breaking in. "When he's not finding my soulmate, he's saving the Earth, Mom! No time for romance adaptations!"

A woman who looks like she's probably the wedding coordinator catches Fizzy's eyes and points to her watch.

"Looks like it's time," Fizzy tells me.

We make our way toward the unending rows of white chairs tied with red ribbons. When a strand of Fizzy's hair blows across her forehead, I reach up and brush it away without thinking.

Our eyes meet and my heart sinks deeper into this warm, alluring place.

"What did your mum mean about writing a 'real' novel?"

She shrugs, turning to watch the guests move in large numbers now toward the seats. "She means a book with thoughtful suffering."

"Sounds engrossing."

"There are many people in the world who view romance as hobby writing," she says, and turns her face back to me. There's no tightness there, no hurt. "Pretty sure she thinks I'm still warming up to attempt my masterpiece."

Now might be the time to admit that I was once one of those people, or quietly contemplate the connection we share between our respective careers versus what our parents think we should be doing. But my first thought flies out instead. "I think *you* are the masterpiece."

She opens her mouth as if she's got a smart comeback, but nothing happens. With a wry twist to her lips, she shakes her head at me. "You're something else."

"Something good, I hope."

She points to the seats. "Groom's side on the left. That's where you'll sit. Go make friends."

"Got it."

"I'll see you after the ceremony." She gathers her dress and turns to head back inside to meet the wedding party. "Miss me," she calls over her shoulder.

I watch her walk away, quietly admitting, "I already do."

thirty-three

FIZZY

I have been to an inordinate number of weddings in my day. I have been maid of honor twice (Alice and Jess), a bridesmaid fourteen times, performed three weddings, and twice have done a reading during the ceremony (once was a passage from one of my books, and that was very weird). I'm sure a lot of people go to weddings and take note of what they like, what they would do differently. They think about the decor and the food and the number of guests. They lean in and whisper that they would never have put so-and-so and what's-her-name at the same table. They maybe even get business cards from the various vendors.

Not me. It's possible that the shine has been scrubbed off weddings in all my various experiences with them, but I think the wedding is the least romantic part of romance. Sure, there is splendor and catering and the opportunity to wear completely outlandish clothing. But there is also family politics and stress and the reality that many people spend the equivalent of a down payment on a house on a single day's celebration. Love is not found in a four-foot-high floral centerpiece or a seven-tiered chocolate cake. Real romance is in the quieter details. Who proposes, and how. The way they look at each other across a room. The anticipation of what it means to be married, the nights spent side by side, shaping their forever. The first moment alone after the commitment is made. The day after, when they get to finally embark on the adventure. And, of course, all the banging.

But these are things one never considers about one's brother. Yuck.

I blink away from Peter and over to his new wife, Kailey, just as she's kissed by a grown-up version of the person who more than once held me down and farted on my face.

He pulls away, smiling, and there—right there—is what I came here to see: that unadulterated look of awe. That first beat of eye contact, the silently squealed *We're really married?* Peter can be a selfish ass and I will never forgive him for cutting my ponytail off when I was thirteen, but he loves Kailey. He'll be good to her.

And hopefully he will knock her up soon and keep the focus off me and my continued single status. *That is,* I remind myself, *unless I end up happily ever after with one of my Heroes.*

The thought pings around in my mind, but it remains a tennis ball bouncing on empty walls. I look out to the cheering crowd of guests, my eyes zeroing in on Connor in the middle of the pack, standing like a skyscraper in the suburbs. And what do you know? He's looking right back at me.

———————

It takes ten minutes to make my way through the crowd to him, and in between catching up with family, being stopped for photos, and once directing someone to the closest restroom, I'm able to catch glimpses of him talking to people around him. God, I love that I can find him so easily, that he cleans up so well in a slim-fitting black tux, and that he left his hair soft and floppy instead of meticulously styled. But his looks aren't even the most interesting thing about him anymore. He's so personally warm, gives such sincere eye contact. I love the way he interacted with my mom, the way he was so excited to meet everyone who stopped us on our way out to the garden. The way he puts his whole self into whatever he does and lets himself be emotional when he talks about his daughter. Connor Prince III should be awarded a gold medal in the Active Listening event at the Romance Olympics. It's hard to believe I looked at him months ago and saw a plastic hero archetype. He's no longer Hot Millionaire Executive or Hot Brit or Soft Lumberjack or even DILF . . . he's just Connor.

How did I once find him boring and unpleasant and cliché? Now I'm struggling to not think of him as soulmate material.

And it's good that I'm succeeding, because by the time I reach him, he's standing with one of Peter's high school friends, a petite blonde named—I kid you not—Ashley Simpson. When I say Ashley is hanging on Connor's arm, I mean this: imagine a giant rock, and then imagine a barnacle. I like Ashley well enough—even though she toyed with Peter's heart for years when he believed looks were more important than brains, and then chased him relentlessly once he figured out that brains were more important than looks—but I step up behind them right as she asks Connor if she can steal him away for the first dance, and my gut fills with a shimmering, violent heat.

I jerk to a stop. He hasn't seen me. He should accept. I won't like it, but it would be a good way out of this weird, inappropriate, untenable thing we have going on. I'm supposed to like Isaac or Dax or Nick. (Maybe Jude. I think we can all agree Evan isn't it. But Connor is *definitely* not it.)

But then Connor says only a gentle "Sorry, tonight these dancing feet belong to Fizzy," and my heart takes a gasping, free-falling tumble into my stomach.

At Jess's bachelorette party, we were doing the drunk yet predictable swoon over all the big and small ways River is perfect for her. Given that everyone else was married, inevitably the topic turned to me, and the disaster of my love affair with Rob. The group was small—only about six of us—but everyone fell into overlapping reassurance that I'm amazing, that I deserve the best man alive, that whoever this magical human is, he's still out there for me.

I didn't believe it at the time, and despite doing this show, I'm not sure I totally believe it now. In the past couple of decades, I've dated a lot. I always assumed I wasn't picky; I liked to brag that I didn't have a type. I've had a thousand awesome first dates, and a handful of fun second dates. And then, that's it. I'm attracted to a lot of people, but rarely do emotions get involved. In hindsight, my feelings for Rob benefitted from standing in the residual glow of Jess and River. But truthfully, the relationship was embarrassingly superficial. I didn't know anything about his life (obviously), and he certainly never made me feel like *this*.

Oh *shit*, that's not bad. I open my clutch for my notebook but come up empty. Even if I had started carrying one consistently again, this clutch is the size of a Pop-Tart.

Standing behind Connor, watching him gently but firmly turn down an objectively gorgeous woman, knowing that he does not do casual relationships and that he understands and admires me enough to put his entire professional career in my hands, and that if he feels even a fraction for me of what I feel for him, he's putting his heart on the line to do this show with me, I realize that what I told him weeks ago is true, I don't have a *type*.

But maybe I do actually have a one.

Have you ever been slapped? By yourself? This feels a little like that. I close my eyes, really squeeze them shut, willing the panic to subside. If I were writing this moment, I would describe the tunneling awareness that the feelings I've been ignoring have been here all along. I'd maybe make the heroine stagger to the side or reach for a half-empty glass of champagne and down it to take the edge off the sudden appearance of dizzying anxiety. But in reality, epiphanies just feel like your soul opening a gaping mouth and lamenting, "Oh, I am *such* a dumbass."

I come up to the pair, swallowing down the thick ball of emotion in my throat. "Hey, you two, what's up?"

Connor turns, extracting his arm from Ashley's grip and setting a warm palm on my lower back. His answering "Hey" is low and warm, carrying a thousand meanings. I look up into his eyes and I know I can't be imagining it. That one word says *Hey, there you are*, and *Hey, did you hear that exchange just now*, and *Hey, I missed you*, and *Hey, remember when we had hard, fast sex and it was mind-blowing?*

Ashley leans around from his other side, smiling at me. "Hi, Fizzy."

I tear my gaze away from Connor's. "Hi, Ashley. Thanks for coming."

"Ohmygod, of *course*. I was just meeting your *producer*. Do I get a dating show next, and can *he* be on it?"

I smile tightly and look up at Connor like *Wanna field this one?*

He gazes down at me, sweetly amused. "I already told her I'm happier mostly behind the camera and you're the one who made me do the interviews."

Ashley rolls on. "It's seriously *unreal* that you are doing this, Fizzy. I heard about it, but I had no idea it was such a big *deal*. Connor said the second episode airs tonight."

"It's a big deal because Connor is doing an amazing job with it."

"It's so funny, though." Her laugh trills like tiny, spiked bells. "A few of us were talking earlier about how you're a romance author, like, shouldn't you know all the ways and places to meet people? If you can't meet someone the usual way, there is literally no hope for the rest of us, right?"

I sense the smile slipping from my face, and I can't do anything about it. An uncomfortable laugh escapes. Usually, I see these backhanded digs coming from a mile away. Usually, a smart comeback is right there on the tip of my tongue.

How is an expert in romance like you still single?

Gotta keep up with market research, you know.

It's hard to find the right man after writing the perfect hero.

Even the simplest "I don't have a lot of time for a relationship" doesn't come to me in time. I feel caught in the headlights out here in the clinking hum of cocktail hour at my younger sibling's wedding. In this gown that Connor so carefully buttoned up for me, and with my family all around me, and carrying these new, enormous feelings, I'd felt invincible—but oh, right. I'm the unmarried spinster. How easy it is to knock down and reshape someone with a few sharp words.

"I think it's hard for someone in the public eye to find a good fit." Connor steps in smoothly. "Fizzy is understandably careful."

Ashley snorts. "Oh my God, you are so sweet. But I mean Fizzy used to date literally everyone."

"Yeah," he says with a cute bursting laugh. "Because everyone wants to date her."

Ashley's face does a thing. It's a barely restrained *Uh, okay, buddy*. It's a laugh held in.

Connor's smile remains, but it doesn't look totally natural anymore. "Do you read her books?"

Ashley shakes her head. "Oh, I don't read books with just romance in them; I need there to be some plot, too."

He goes quietly stony. "There's plenty of plot. And Fizzy's are the gold standard." I stare up at him with fondness. This liar, still pretending he's read my books.

"Oh, I'm sure—"

He rolls on and somehow manages to cut her off without leaving an insult in the air. "People think romances are just about sex— and some are, which is fine—but they're also about social change and challenging the status quo, such as who the world thinks deserves a happily ever after."

"And pirates," I say, my heart glowing like a Vegas billboard inside my rib cage. "Don't forget pirates."

"And sometimes pirates." He smiles down at me before turning back to Ashley. "Fizzy's one of the best writers I've ever read, and has millions of readers." His hand makes a slow circle on my back.

Does he even know he's doing it? It's making me dizzy with want. "She did the network a favor by agreeing, and the ratings are entirely due to her on-screen charisma with every one of the contestants." He laughs, and it's smooth and round. "God, I sound like such a producer, don't I?" He waves himself away with a self-deprecating grin. "Well, anyway, I'll stop bragging about her now. It was very nice to meet you, Amy."

With a firm hand, he leads me away.

I allow myself to be guided back up the grassy path and indoors to where a band plays during cocktail hour. Connor nabs us two flutes of champagne off a passing tray and hands me one.

"That was swoony," I tell him.

"I literally just grabbed it from a tray. Christ, raise your bar a little."

Laughing, I smack his beefy shoulder with my free hand. "Not that. The way you gently dragged her back there."

Connor takes a sip, eyes on me, swallows. "I understand her preconceived notions because I used to share them. It wasn't based on anything factual—I'd never actually read a romance novel. I'm guessing she hasn't, either."

"So what happened?"

"Nat set me straight, and I read your books."

"Yeah, but only, like, one of them."

"I've read *almost* all of them." He smiles down at me. "There are quite a lot."

I pause with the flute pressed to my lips. Champagne bubbles pop and tickle my skin. "What?"

"I told you I would."

"Yeah, but that's just a thing people say."

He shakes his head. "Not me."

"And your preconceived notions?"

He takes a drink of champagne, head tipped back, neck flexing. Drink lowered again, he meets my gaze. "I can admit when I'm wrong."

I can hear my pulse in my ears. Is this thirty-seven-year-old Fizzy's kink? Honesty, accountability, and open communication? "That woman back there? Her name was Ashley, by the way, not Amy."

His grin is wicked. "I know."

I don't even know what to do with the infatuation ballooning in my torso. This bubble of joy rising in me is going to take me out, land me flat on my back if I don't get my arms around him somehow. Peter and Kailey are still outside, taking couples' photos post-ceremony. We have such a long night ahead of us, with dinner and toasts and dancing and cake, but I'm going to take advantage of this quiet lull. I take Connor's glass and set it down on a high-top table, and then lead him to the small dance floor where a few couples sway slowly to the music.

He looks quizzically down at me, but his arms go around my waist when I slide mine up his chest and around his neck. "This is a sexy posture," he says into my ear.

"Well, I feel sexy things about you."

"But publicly?" he asks.

"Just give me this one dance, you hot DILF."

He relaxes against me, hands warm on my lower back, and I rest my cheek to his chest. "You have nice muscles."

"Thank you."

"You are a very dapper brick wall."

A quiet laugh rumbles against my temple.

I close my eyes. "You make it very hard to want to fall for someone else."

The truth of this weighs me down, an anchor, dragging behind me.

He doesn't say anything to this, not for five or ten or thirty seconds. I keep waiting for the remorse to land or to feel rejected in his silence, but instead it feels like agreement. He's holding me so close.

"Maybe we can sneak out of here later and watch the episode," I say.

"I'd like that."

"No funny business," I add. "Despite what I just said. I know we can only be work homies watching the episode together." I notice he doesn't say anything to *this*, either. And then it occurs to me. "Wait. Should you be at the office or—I don't know—accessible somehow tonight?"

"No," he says. "Blaine's on it. He knew taking you here tonight was an important job."

"A *job*, huh?"

"I pretend you're a lot of work. It gets me points with the boss."

"I am a lot of work."

This makes him laugh. "Felicity, you are the easiest thing I've ever done." I look up at him, watch his words land on his own ears. A flush crawls up his neck and turns the tips of his ears pink. "You know what I mean."

"I do know what you mean, but you're also full of shit. Objectively speaking, I am a handful."

He tucks my head under his chin. "Get over yourself."

I laugh into his shirt and close my eyes. Fuck, he's perfect. This is awful.

thirty-four

CONNOR

Slow dancing with Fizzy is the last moment of quiet we have for the next four hours, because what follows is the most luxurious and impeccably planned event I have ever attended. There is an opulent eight-course meal, surprisingly tender speeches, riotous dancing, cake cutting, and woven throughout are endless people wanting to see Fizzy, hug her, take photos with her. Fizzy has jokingly described herself as the family disappointment, but it always felt like there was a kernel of truth there, and tonight, the internalized disconnect astounds me. It is clear from watching her that everyone in this room adores her beyond measure, and even though it isn't her wedding day, the attention she receives makes it seem that a soft beam of light follows her through the room.

Or maybe that's just my gaze.

Truly, I cannot take my eyes off her. And when she approaches me later, holding an unopened bottle of champagne and gesturing with a tilt of her head that she wants to escape, my heart does an aching dive in my chest. I didn't realize until the opportunity was before me how much I wanted to be alone with her again before the night ends.

"Do you have to head out or can you come up and watch tonight's episode with me?"

I know the right answer is that I should head home. I know, too, that when it comes down to it with this woman, it's always up to me to set boundaries, and my feelings for her are contained behind a very thin, very fragile wall. I should do a better job protecting my heart.

But with two glasses of wine in my blood and feeling drugged from her proximity on my arm all night, the wrong answer comes easily: "I don't have anywhere I need to be. Stevie is with Nat."

The crowd is still going strong in our wake, and the evening hush of the lobby wraps us in an echoing bubble. Fizzy reaches forward, pressing the call button for the lift, and we look up together, watching for the Up arrow to illuminate.

"Your family is amazing."

She laughs. "The funny thing is I think you really mean that."

"I do."

"Well, if you're looking for a wife, my auntie Cindy is here for you, in case the three hundred times she mentioned it wasn't enough."

Remembering, I pull from my pocket a cocktail napkin with a number I think is written in lip pencil and drop it into the bin. "I'm good."

"Was that Ashley's number?"

"It was."

Fizzy beams at me as the lift arrives, and we step in. "You're my favorite."

"I'd better be."

"Have you already seen tonight's episode?" she asks.

I stare quizzically down at her. "I edited most of it."

"Is it good?"

"Please."

"I'm gonna need you to unbutton me," she says, gesturing casually to her dress like she's informed me she'll need me to pluck a piece of lint away or pick up her dry cleaning.

My mouth goes dry. "I figured."

"I'll behave myself."

"No, you won't," I say, laughing.

"I promise to try, how's that sound?"

"Empty and foolish, but I appreciate the gesture."

The doors open and, still smiling, she leads me down the hall to her room, swiping the card at the door. Silence swallows us up as she drops her clutch and key on the table, and I'm consumed with a flushing panic. I'm not an idiot; I know this is exactly how sex starts. I've had sex with her already, am half in love with her at this point, and we're both high on party vibes and champagne. Coming up here was a bloody terrible idea.

Fizzy walks over, turning her back to me. "Get to work."

Luckily—or unluckily, depending on how you look at it—unbuttoning her gown goes infinitely faster than buttoning it did. But to my relief and true to her word, she does not immediately let it fall to the floor and face me in whatever complicated lacy underwear situation she's hiding under there. She steps away with a hand holding it up at the front, smiling over her shoulder at me. "I'm gonna change in the bathroom; you get the episode pulled up."

I find the remote, connect to the right app, and get it ready to play. With Fizzy still changing, I duck out onto the balcony to call Stevie. The cool sea air washes over my flushed skin, and I draw in a steadying breath before pulling my phone from my pocket.

When Nat answers, I can hear another breathless, adrenaline-fueled voice chattering in an excited stream in the background.

"Greetings from fangirl central," Nat says.

"Again?" I ask, laughing. I wasn't sure Stevie would still be awake but should have known better. The Wonderland concert DVD has been viewed no fewer than ten times in the week since Fizzy gave it to my kid.

"She's watching with Insu and giving him a blow-by-blow of the concert with you and Fizzy. You're a shoo-in for parent of the year, you jackass. How's the wedding?"

"Gorgeous."

"How's Fizzy?"

Ahh, the real question. "Equally gorgeous," I say on a pained exhale.

"I see."

"We're in her hotel room to watch the show. She's changing."

I can almost hear Nat's brows lift through the line. "I *seeeeee*."

I push away the image of Fizzy's bare back before she turned to grab her pajamas from the drawer and duck into the loo.

"It's fine," I tell her. What I don't tell Nat is that I slipped a couple of condoms into my wallet this morning. I'm not having sex with Fizzy. *I'm not.* But my lesson in being unprepared for this kind of thing turns eleven in January. You don't have to tell me twice.

I move to the railing on the balcony. During the day, Fizzy's room would have a stunning view of the ocean. I can see it now, but only as a dark mass of churning movement in the distance. The proximity is underscored by the loud tumble of waves as they crash. The unremitting turbulence mirrors what's happening in my chest. "Anyway,

I called to tell Stevie good night, but if she's busy, I'll just catch her in the morning."

"You sure? I can grab her."

"No, let her educate Insu. He must learn exactly what he's in for." I turn at the sound of Fizzy moving around in the room behind me. "I should go anyway. Make sure you watch tonight. Give me those ratings."

"Don't I always?"

I smile because, yeah, she does. "Tell the squirt I love her, and have a good night, Nat."

"I will. Love you."

"Love you, too."

I step inside and come to a stop with one foot in, one foot out. Fizzy said she was changing into something *comfy*. I foolishly hoped that meant long-sleeved flannel pajamas, not tiny shorts and a soft cropped sweatshirt. There's just . . . so much skin.

"What the fuck 'ave you got on?" I ask, accent turning coarse.

"They're my jammies. You want me sleeping in a snowsuit?"

"Yes."

She lifts her chin to indicate the balcony. "Everything okay?"

I get my head back on straight. "Yeah. Just telling Stevie good night."

"I bet she misses not getting her Saturday with you."

"Not really." I set my phone on the dresser, undo my tie, and unbutton my collar, hearing how that sounded. "I mean, don't get me wrong, we have a blast together, but she's not suffering alone. She's watching Wonderland with Insu tonight."

"A girl's dream."

"Right." Tossing the tie to the chair, I admit, "We've all had to learn how to roll with it when my schedule gets nuts. I'm lucky that Nat is so flexible about all of it, especially lately."

Fizzy grabs the bottle of champagne, twists it open with a pressurized pop, and climbs onto the bed, sitting cross-legged. "You two are the most well-adjusted divorced people I've ever met." She takes a swig. "I have a friend who only talks to her ex through her lawyer."

"It's something we've had to grow into." I glance around the room. Other than a bed and a dresser, there's only the fancy and very uninviting chair in the corner. I'm really going to have to sit on the bed with her. Fuck.

Fizzy must sense my hesitation because she pats the mattress. "Get over here," she says. "Let's watch this."

I sit down, leaving as much distance as possible between us— which is not much, considering that she's set herself in the direct center. With a playful gleam in her eyes, she hands me the champagne. I feel like I'm being hunted. I take a long drink.

The bubbles warm my stomach as Fizzy presses Play and the show opens. The theme music is catchy, an awful earworm if I'm being honest, but that works in our favor. It's been added to countless videos and memes on social media—as far as Brenna tells me, that is. Fizzy bounces in place a little when Lanelle enters. "I fucking love her."

"She's great." God, I love this energy. Just the two of us, watching this thing we created together.

Lanelle gives a brief recap of where we are in the show progression, and we get quick cuts of the previous, now-eliminated contestants. There's a smooth transition to Fizzy and the remaining Heroes meeting in the industrial kitchen. Lanelle explains what the week's activities will be, and the view closes in on Fizzy choosing which Hero will join her for which date. She's playful and sexy and oozes charisma.

"You really were made for television."

"It's so hard not to get caught up in critiquing myself," she says.

"I can see that." Before I can offer further reassurance, Colby appears, tying on his apron for the cooking activity. It was clear from the start that whatever chemistry he and Fizzy had during their first date didn't translate to their second, but we do a great job of making their time together look less painful than it was in person.

We cut to an ad, and Fizzy takes the bottle from me, swigging. "What do you think the reaction would be if I'd just punched Colby in his mansplainy face?"

"As your producer, I would advise against it."

"And as my friend?"

I take the bottle back and smile as I bring it to my lips. "I'd tell you to go at him again."

She laughs, shifting so that she's lying on her stomach with her feet at the head of the bed. I stare down at the view of her completely bare legs. I am well and truly fucked if I have to watch her go on dates with other men on television with the perky curve of her ass cheek right in front of me, peeking out the bottom of her tiny shorts.

Shifting, I lie beside her, mimicking her posture. "Bet Colby doesn't survive the week."

"Or Jude." She lifts her chin when he comes on-screen, walking toward her in the park where they'll plant trees. "I'm honestly impressed with how good you are at your job."

"How so?"

"This date," she says, nodding to the television. "It looks so intimate, like we're in this gorgeous park, completely alone. You've captured my expressions in a way that makes it seem like I'm swooning over him. And Jude—look at him. What is that filter? I need it in front of my face at all times. He looks so hot and not at all derpy here." She laughs. "In reality, it was eighty-nine degrees, humid, and crowded." She points. "Was I looking at him there or you? I swear that entire date I kept looking at you."

"We might have to work on that a little," I say with a nudge to her shoulder. "I appreciate the boost to my ego, but audiences need to imagine you falling in love with any one of them."

Fizzy rolls her eyes at the TV. "Nobody will believe I'm into someone who unironically used the phrase *legitimate vampire literature.*"

"Any true vampire expert would have understood your Volterra joke."

Fizzy sits up and turns to face me. "I knew you'd get that!"

"The movies alone made over three billion dollars worldwide. And Nat dragged our entire uni crew to see *New Moon.*"

Fizzy settles back as the show continues, and I can't help but wonder what the audience is feeling after watching Jude fizzle out almost as much as Colby. But then Isaac is on-screen.

I'd missed most of their date in real time, so I was surprised when I sat in the editing booth and watched it unroll in front of me. Even unedited, the footage of them together is brimming with sexual tension. When Fizzy loses her shoe somewhere along the bike path, it turns hilariously slapstick as they try to retrieve it without getting off the tandem bike, laughing the entire way. In every shot of Isaac listening to her speak, he looks smitten. Fizzy, too, seems to be enjoying herself, and it didn't take creative editing to do it. She's fun and funny and looks like she's genuinely trying to impress him. It hits me like a slap that I've never seen Fizzy try to impress anyone before.

"You two look good together," I say.

"I like him."

I bristle at the note of fondness in her voice. Of course she likes him, he's objectively wonderful, interested in her, and *available*. I should be encouraging it, not wanting to yell, "*Cut!*" each time he makes her smile.

I startle when she jabs me in the side with an index finger. "You look a little broody over there."

"Not at all. Just calmly watching this very well edited episode."

"Uh-huh."

My gaze snares on the way her lips come away wet from a drag of champagne and she swipes them clean with the back of her hand. I'm infatuated with the blast of her laugh when she does something newly embarrassing on-screen. Her complete lack of self-consciousness or pretense wrecks me. As does the absent way she kicks her feet behind us, her bare legs sliding against one another, so visibly soft and supple.

Fizzy does a double take when she glances at me. "You're staring."

"Because you're hogging the champagne." I know I should take it easy, but, truthfully, that ship has sailed. "Hand it over."

She passes it to me with a smirk and then adjusts her position, flattening down to rest her chin on her folded hands as she watches

Isaac's confessional moment with me toward the end of the show where he admits that Fizzy intimidates him, but he thinks that's a good thing for a man to feel when he really likes a woman. "He's a good guy."

The fire reignites in my rib cage. "He is."

She looks over her shoulder at me. "Wow, you really choked on that admission, didn't you?"

I point to my throat. "Champagne. I was swallowing a sip."

"Why is it so hot when you lie?"

I ignore this and she rolls to her back, staring up at me with the light from the television illuminating her face. "Who do you think will win?"

"No idea."

"You must have *some* idea. We'll be down to four next week."

"I think Isaac has a pretty good shot. Brenna tells me the Internet loves him."

"Brenna tells you? Don't you go online at all?"

"I'm *online* frequently. But I don't go on social media if it can be helped."

"This tracks." She takes the bottle again. "I stalked your Insta. You have a picture of Stevie's tiny feet on bike pedals and then a picture of a dog from, like, four years ago. That's it."

I laugh. "I don't need the world to know what I'm doing every second."

"Hot." She studies me. "But as the producer, don't you need to know what's trending?"

"We need some of us to watch the show as its own thing, in isolation, so the story arc about finding you an actual soulmate stays consistent and true." Her brows go up like I've just confessed to being a principled vegan. "Fizzy, I'm not altruistic. Others on the team track the voting. I just get the final numbers. It's really a giant mess until the window closes and I don't relish watching it in real time."

She rolls up to her side facing me. "So you want Isaac to win?"

There's no good way to reply to this honestly without sounding possessive or jealous or delusional. "I think he's the best remaining contestant."

"That's not really an answer."

"Too bad, because it's the only one I'm going to give."

"Are there any you wish hadn't been eliminated?"

"Jude—assuming he's ousted this week—and purely for the comedic factor." I tap her nose. "Colby because I like it when you're scrappy."

"Jude wouldn't have the slightest idea what to do with me."

"Sweet, *none* of these poor sods have the slightest idea what to do with you, and that includes the bloke who's already had a shot at it."

She laughs at this. "But you do."

"Course I do." I grab the champagne back and take a long, draining pull of it. "Take you as you are by day and fuck you till you're wrecked by night." I pass the back of my hand over my mouth and reach over to set the empty bottle down on the nightstand.

Beside me, Fizzy's gone silent. It's my turn for a double take; her eyes are soft, lips slack. "What's with you? Did I get that wrong?"

"No."

She looks like she wants to devour me, and I laugh. "I can't be the first to see through all the hilarity and impassioned lectures, Fizzy. You'd enjoy a man who understands that you just want a hot best friend who makes you laugh and come in equal measure. Honestly, it's not that hard."

She falls onto her back again, staring up at the ceiling.

"What?" I loom over her. "Is that offensive? Have I disrespected your hidden depths?"

"Enjoy," she says.

"What's that?"

She turns her eyes to me. "You said enjoy. 'You'd *enjoy* a man.' Not *want* or *need* or even *deserve*." She turns her attention back to the ceiling and smiles. "You're right. I'd really fucking enjoy a man like that. I just love that phrasing."

"Why do you think you're so complicated?"

"Because everyone else does."

I shake my head, rolling to my side to face her and propping my head on a hand. "Not me. You're a Rubik's Cube with four blocks."

She laughs, reaching across her body to smack my chest. "Hey."

"A maze with a straight line through the middle. It's just that most men are quite stupid."

I can tell she wants to be mad but the delight in her eyes burns bright. She reaches up, brushing my hair off my forehead. "Careful," she says.

"Careful what?" Her lips are soft and wet, her neck bare and stretching endlessly, soft for my mouth. I can see her pulse beating just beneath her jaw and want to press my face there and absorb the feeling of her fire thrumming under my touch. "You gonna rough me up for being straight with you that you're just a big, messy softie?"

She drags her fingers along my temple and down my jaw. "Are you trying to make me want you?"

"I think that's the problem," I say, adjusting my head in my hand. "I don't really have to try."

Fizzy smiles distractedly. "Because you're so sexy?"

"Obviously."

She rolls back to her side, tracing her thumb along my bottom lip, and not even an oncoming train could get me to evade her touch. I can see in her eyes, too, that she understood my true meaning. I don't have to try with her because everything between us is too easy. Too obvious. Too good. The idea that she'd end up with a Jude or even a Nick seems laughable now.

But so is the idea that she'd end up with me.

Trying to clear the fog of alcohol and desire, I pull away from her touch. Her eyes refocus and she blinks away from my lips.

"Uh-oh," she whispers. "The spell is broken."

"Nah, it's late. I'm sure you've got more wedding celebrations early tomorrow. I should head home."

Fizzy frowns. "Let's put on a movie or something. You've been drinking."

"I'll cab it." I move to climb from bed, but she cups a hand over my forearm, stilling me.

"Connor. You should stay here. I can behave myself. I promise."

I laugh. "You're not the only one who needs to behave, sweet. Historically I just have more self-control. I don't think I do tonight."

She sucks in a sharp breath and exhales it shakily. "I'll have it for us, then. I know we can't fool around."

"For about a hundred reasons," I say. "The most obvious one being the show. A second, equally important one being that for you it can be just sex, and for me it's something more sincere. I don't want one without the other, and unfortunately, sincerity seems to be off the table."

"Does it?" she asks quietly.

I stare at her, at her thoughtful pout and lashes fanned on her cheeks as she closes her eyes and exhales again. "What does that mean?" I ask.

"I don't think this is just about my sexual reawakening."

"No?"

She shakes her head. "I think I have capital *F* feelings for you."

My wine and champagne buzz comes slamming back into my skull, making my thoughts blur, my blood thicken. Fuck. Fuck fuck fuck.

"That right?" I ask.

Fizzy nods. "On the beach, when I talked about the way I felt reconnected to the part of me I missed?"

"Yeah?"

"It's you. The person my heroines choose is always the person who makes them feel like the best version of themselves. You make me feel that way."

"But that doesn't have to be romantic, Fizzy," I tell her, throat tight. "I do want to be your friend when all of this is said and done."

"What if I wanted you to be my *best* friend? The kind who also kisses me?" she quietly asks.

Maybe the champagne has disengaged my filter, but otherwise I've never felt more sober. This all suddenly feels inevitable. I can't even remember wanting to resist her. "You'd only have to ask."

Her gaze drops to my lips, and her mouth goes soft and hungry. "Kiss me."

With her hand cupping my face, she gently guides me to press my mouth to the full sweetness of hers for a single, lingering touch. I pull away.

"More," she whines sweetly, and her smile turns wicked. "With tongue."

I laugh at this. "Is that a good idea?"

"No, it's a terrible idea, but that's my brand." Fizzy stretches, dragging her lips up the column of my neck. "Holy shit you taste good." Her teeth graze the straining muscle there, and she scoots closer, pressing into me. "I want you, Connor, all the time."

Fire sears through my bloodstream and an ache pierces my groin. Surrendering, I let my hand do what it wants—gliding up that warm, honeyed thigh, over the curve of her hip, under the hem of those unbelievably soft sleep shorts to find even softer skin just beneath. The kind of sex we could have in here makes my imagination dissolve into white noise.

"How's this for a plan," she says, gently biting my neck. "What happens in this room stays in this room."

"I feel like I've heard this before." My voice is thick with desire. My fingers find the lush curve of her ass.

"We start with kissing," she continues, using her leg to coax one of mine forward. She rocks into me, clamping my thigh between hers. "If it feels good, we maybe take some clothes off. If you don't want to have sex with me, that's fine." Pulling back, Fizzy smiles up at me. "You can just eat my pussy and head home, and everyone is happy."

Laughter rises up out of me and I couldn't resist her even if I was shackled to the wall by my wrists and ankles. I am so fucked for this woman. So I do the only thing I can imagine: I give in, turning my face down to hers, and let the night dissolve between us.

thirty-five

FIZZY

I used to think first kisses were the most powerful of all the kisses. That first, hyperaware contact with such uniquely soft, responsive skin. The discovery of someone else's sounds and tastes and desire. The ultimate reveal: Is there real passion there?

But I was wrong. First kisses are great, but the one hundredth, the one thousandth kisses are better. There's familiarity and comfort, satiating a need but with enough knowledge to know how to tease and play. Whoever invented kissing is my favorite historical figure ever.

"I want to kiss you for the rest of the weekend," I mumble into his mouth.

With a laugh, he rolls over onto me, his hand running up and down my thigh, gripping and stroking until I arch into his touch, coaxing his fingers up my hip, along my ribs, over my breast.

I could be satisfied with kissing, but I want everything else. Being with Connor feels like a devastating inevitability. I have this pit-deep need for something not just fast and satisfying but slow and whole. I sense the same surrender in him, too. It's in the way he kisses me so slow and deep, the patient mapping of his hands across my body, over my clothes, before he drags one item of clothing at a time up over my head or down my legs with deliberate, patient purpose.

"You're so beautiful," he says into the sensitive skin below my ear, and then repeats it quietly into my neck, my shoulder, my breasts.

This isn't rushed foreplay. This is like someone put the whole world on pause. He's solid and strong above me, and I become a pliable, languid tangle of limbs and skin under his attention. His lips linger on my breasts, tongue and teeth teasing me expertly, mouth sucking. It hits me like a thunderbolt: only someone who knows me from the inside out can satisfy and torture me like this in equal measure.

I've never felt such a longing to be *someone's* the way I do with Connor. I want to eat his possessive, open-mouthed kisses for every meal. I want him to have a memory of kissing every place on my body. I want my hands to instinctively mold to the shape of him. I want him to know by the heat of my skin and the pitch of my sounds how close I am.

Connor tells me he can't stop thinking about me, that all he wants to do is touch me. He kisses down my body to settle between my open legs and reaches up, running his thumb over my lips, feeling the shape of my sounds as he works me over with his mouth, giving me something to suck and bite while pleasure pours out of me. I want to let my head fall back and lose myself in the wide swirls of his tongue, when he sucks, tight and determined, but I'm afraid to miss any of it. When I look down, I see the top of his head, his eyes closed in bliss. I tangle his soft hair in my hands, and when his name escapes on an exhale, he looks up, mouth still on me, fingers inside, his own sounds vibrating up my spine. I say his name, wanting to imprint on my memory that it's Connor making me feel this way, should only ever be him taking me to the edge, closer, closer, and then making me fall. Once I'm wrecked and boneless, he rolls me over, sinking fingers and teeth into all my curves, biting gently down my legs, his teeth grazing the swell of my ass, up my back to send shivers down my spine. A slow thrust against my thigh, and I feel how hard he is, his breath shaking against my skin.

I look over my shoulder at him, feeling kiss drunk and heavy-limbed. "You don't by chance have protection."

"I do." He kisses back down my spine and stands. "My wallet."

"Please tell me it hasn't been there since the divorce."

He laughs. "Only since this morning."

"How confident."

"ABC's," he says, tearing it open. "Always be prepared."

"That's ABP."

Connor huffs out a distracted laugh. "There's not so much blood in my cranium at the moment," he says absently, and we both watch him slowly roll it down his length, inch by straining inch.

"I'm seeing that."

He pulls me to stand, bending to kiss me, his urgency in the tight grip of his hands on my hips, the restraint when he pivots me and sits in a smooth movement coaxing me onto his lap.

"I want you in charge." Connor guides me closer. "Go slow."

But slow sounds awful. I want to impale myself and die a happy death.

He tempers my impatience, and I don't know how because he looks about as calm as I feel, flushed and tight all over. I want to bruise his thighs, eat him whole. The galaxy inside me expands, too fast, in a world-ending way. The feel of him—his patient, trembling hands on my waist and full mouth on my breasts and his urgent body filling me—sends me into a euphoric trance. I start slow, but eventually animal instinct takes over, slippery and wild. It's so good it's speechless, gasping sex. It's take up the whole bed sex, head hanging over the edge, sheets popping off the corners sex. It's screaming into his ear, laughing into kisses as we slow down and check in with each other sex. It's slow, shared breath, tiny movement and fast, headboard slapping sex. When he finally comes—behind me, curled over my back and trapping me in a savage, tender cage—the room falls still for the first time in an eternity. His massive body heaves in breaths, fists shaking where they're planted on the mattress beside mine.

"Holy shit," he breathes against my spine. His forehead is sweaty when he presses it between my shoulder blades. "Holy shit."

My ears are ringing, skin prickly and aware that I've taken a new shape. I can feel my heartbeat in my windpipe; my thoughts are warped with thrill and pleasure and the tight, hyperaware realization that I want him close to me every second of every day from here on out. I want to tattoo my name into his skin and shout his name a hundred times and make sure everyone hears.

He shifts back and away, standing at the end of the bed. I've never felt so physically drained and spiritually full all at the same time. I collapse forward onto the warm mattress, and roll to my back, staring up at the ceiling.

Connor gazes down at the situation around me. "This bed is a disaster."

"Let's put it back together so we can destroy it again."

He laughs. "I might need a minute."

"Okay." I throw an arm across my face. "But only one."

He leaves, bare feet padding across the tile into the bathroom. Quiet shuffling. Water running.

I feel like I'm floating.

He returns and gently touches his fingers to my inner thigh before pressing a warm, wet cloth there, drawing it up to where a pleasant ache throbs, cleaning me with slow, careful hands.

"Ready?" he asks.

I push up onto an elbow. "I am. Are you?"

He shakes his head but kisses me, distracting with the familiar drag of his teeth along my lower lip, and then presses a fresh, cooler cloth between my legs. The shock immediately shifts to a soothing bliss.

"We went at it quite a long time. I'm worried you're gonna be sore."

I hum into his lips. "Good sore."

The light from the bathroom sends gold along his arms, his fingers, and I feel like he's painting me with stardust. It's crazy, but I need him again. This is a choking, panicky feeling. I am infatuated, I am mesmerized by everything he does. When he stands to return the washcloths to the bathroom I grab his forearm, taking the damp cloths from him and tossing them somewhere to the side, out of sight.

"Don't go."

"I was just—"

"I don't care. I don't want you to leave my sight."

With a smile, he climbs back over me.

"Look at you," he whispers into my neck. "A needy cuddler. Who would have guessed?"

"I'm not usually."

"No?"

"What have you done to me, Connor Prince III?"

He aligns his body beside mine, pulling me right up against him, coaxing my leg over his hip. "Only a fraction of what I've thought about doing."

"You think about me when you're alone?" I ask.

Connor hums, the sound raspy and deep. "All the time."

"Me, too."

He pulls back, grinning at me. "You do?"

"Of course I do," I admit, and he tucks some of my tangled hair behind my ear. "Sometimes it's sexy stuff, and sometimes I just really want to hang out with you. I like you."

"I like you, too." His hand smooths down my side, over my thigh. "Christ, you're so soft."

It seems absurd to me that I haven't ever experienced such a basic building block of intimacy—post-sex languishing, lazy kisses and touches that are somehow more aware and more hazy—but I'm realizing I've been shitty at allowing any post-coital connection. These smaller kisses that lead nowhere, words spoken into skin, talking about the sex we just had with vulnerability and honesty and giddiness. Something creaks open inside me, a door to a secret room.

"That was the best sex of my life," I say.

He doesn't look surprised or skeptical. He says only, "Same," as his lips make a warm path down my neck.

"I want to do it again."

He laughs. "Do you see how sweaty I am?"

"Mmm, yes." I run my hands over his shoulders. "Let's go rinse off together."

We stand and I see he was right: the bed really is a disaster. Connor holds my hand even for the short walk to the bathroom, and it's good he does because my legs are shockingly wobbly. He presses his front to my back as we wait for the water to heat, his arms banded around my waist. He is a whole planet behind me, a sun.

Under the water, we share wet kisses and sudsy hands and it's not long before he's impatient again, too. He drips footprints on the bathroom floor as he rushes out to hunt for the second condom. Such confidence in this man who packed up his things earlier today.

This time the cold shower wall is at my back and his skin is hot, pressed all along my front. It's slow and careful, then hard and frantic, his fingertips gripping bruises into my thighs, his body thrusting so deep it obliterates every other sensation. I don't know how I'm going to function if I have to leave this room and act normal after this. I don't know how I'm going to pretend I don't want him with a clawing hunger every time I see him.

I finish him in the bed with my hands and mouth, his fingers a chaotic mess in my wet hair, his rough, filthy words scraping the walls as he comes. It's a long silent pause after, my face pressed to his stomach, his heart pounding through the entire length of his torso.

"I'm crazy about you," I say.

His voice is a low vibration reverberating down his body. "I'm out of my mind."

"I'll want you again tomorrow, and the next day, and literally every day after that."

Connor is quiet so long I think he's dozed off, but then his voice rises out of the darkness.

"Can we fake it?" he asks, finally. "I'm lying here wondering if we can do both. This and that."

"I promise to do the best acting of my life, and I played a sun in a fifth-grade play, so I can assure you I'm very good."

Laughing, he pushes up onto an elbow, looking at me with a pleasure-drunk blur to his gaze. "A sun?"

"I had to just stand there." I kiss his navel. "You know me. Trust me, it was very difficult to not join in the orbit dance."

He smiles, but it doesn't take over his face the way I expect. "I'll have to hide my jealousy."

Oh.

"I won't fall in love with any of them, Connor."

He drags me up his body, aligning me over him. Our hearts pound in tandem, recharging. "What if you need to, to make the show work? That's what I can't stop thinking about. You have chemistry with Isaac. I should let you pursue that. This—you and me— seems like such a terrible idea, but I want you so bad. I can't say no to you."

"Let's just take it one day at a time, okay?"

I haven't felt this way before. It's such a simple declaration, and for now I can only make it to myself. Any lie I ever said about keeping this easy, about being able to walk away and focus on the show, is obliterated into dust. There's a universe expanding in my rib cage, stars and planets and all kinds of dangerous sparking debris that could destroy me. I'm consumed by a distracting ache, a sharp want, a desperation for this thing I have already in my arms. I know what this is even if I've never felt it before. I'm falling in love.

thirty-six

FIZZY

'm falling in love, but I'm also falling asleep, in the warm circle of his arms, with the hard planes of his body somehow forming the perfect mattress. We both wake up with a jolt when someone drunk bangs on the door across the hall.

Overheated, I slide off Connor's body onto the cool, twisted sheets. He groans, rolling to reach for a bottle of water, offering me some and then taking a long drink.

"What time is it?" I ask.

"Around three."

We'd barely been asleep twenty minutes, but it felt like hours for how deep I'd been.

"I wonder if anyone noticed that we disappeared," I say.

"I'm sure."

"I'll get a lot of questions about it at the brunch tomorrow."

"Especially from your sister," he says, and I laugh. Connor rolls away to put the water back on the nightstand and I take the opportunity to run my hands up his back, mapping the broad expanse. He returns to me, and I'm just as happy rubbing my hands all over his front. "Easy enough to answer, right?" he says. "We were watching tonight's episode together."

"Mmm, I know you're saying words," I say, tracing his ribs, "but all I see is naked."

He puts a finger under my chin, tilting my face up so I look into his smiling eyes. "I meant to ask how the wedding was for you, but we got distracted."

My first instinct is to look away and make a joke about finding joy in thwarting familial expectations, but the new instinct, the bigger one, is to be bare with him. "It wasn't as hard as Alice's," I admit. "At her wedding, everyone felt sorry for me, and it completely caught me off guard because I was there to celebrate, and I got all this pity and concern instead that the younger daughter was getting married first. At least yesterday it felt like a meme that I'm single, rather than gossip."

He studies my expression for a few quiet beats, then just gives a quiet "Hmm."

"I'll get married, or I won't," I tell him. "It shouldn't affect anything anyone else does. But I know it isn't that simple. My parents worry because they love me. They want me to be married because *they* are happily married; they want me to have kids because they love having us. Even though it stings, I know in my heart the reason my mom always refers to my 'real novel' is because she is sure I'm the best writer alive, but knows the world looks down on romance. She doesn't want me to put myself in a position where I'm not valued for what I can do. It isn't because she doesn't value my skill, she just sees writing literary fiction as the more ambitious way to do it."

"I don't know," Connor says quietly. "Seems it's pretty hard to write a compelling book when the reader already knows how it ends."

Perfect, I think. *He's perfect*. I need a new track or I'm going to climb on him again and I don't think he can fit more than two condoms in that wallet.

"What about your dad?" I ask. "I assume he knows about the show now?"

"He talked to Stevie. She told him."

"And? Is he impressed that his son is being stalked on social media?"

"Not exactly." He picks up a strand of my hair and twists it absently. "Your mum might not understand romance, but she's proud of you. Her concern comes from a place of love and good intentions. The problem is that I'm not who my father wants me to be."

"I'm sure that's not true."

"I used to think it was something deeper, something unfulfilled in him, but I think he's honestly just a shitty human." His forehead furrows with a frown and I tip his face down, press a kiss there until the tension smooths out again. The idea that anyone could look at him and not see all the wonderful parts of who he is makes my insides boil. "But I have Natalia and Stevie," he says with a smile. "More than makes up for it."

"What was your wedding like?"

"To Natalia?"

"Yes?" I say, grinning. "Unless there's another wife somewhere in an attic."

He laughs. "It was at the courthouse. It was very simple."

"How old were you?"

"When we got married? Twenty-two."

"Oh. Babies."

"Yeah. And baby." He smiles at me. "She was pregnant."

"Oh."

Connor nods, rolling to his back and tucking one arm beneath his head. A bicep pops and I pretend that I'm not dying to touch it, because we're having a serious conversation. "We'd been really good friends for a couple years, but only been lovers for about six months by then. I think I already knew we weren't a great fit romantically, but it was a fun and easy hookup. I knew she'd had a thing for me almost since we first met. I mean, looking back I think I worried that I'd fuck up our group dynamic if I ended things."

"That's rough."

"So then she finds out she's pregnant, and she wants to keep the baby—which, totally her call, I never had any issue with her making whatever choice worked for her. But since my own father was absent and"—he sighs—"such a dick, really, I wanted to do the right thing, and immediately proposed."

"Ah," I say.

He shifts to his side, toying with a strand of my hair again. "Yeah." I sense this isn't a story he tells very often because he's taking longer than he normally would to put the words together. "It was nice at first. Stevie was a really easy baby. I loved the family Nat and I had made. I knew we would be good parents."

I make a sound of understanding.

"But I wasn't ever in love with her, and it got harder to pretend. I was sick with the decision about whether it was worse to stay, or leave and potentially make all the same mistakes my dad made. I never wanted Stevie to feel the way I did."

"Right."

"I'd love to say I talked about this with her," he says, "but I didn't.

I loved her, but I wasn't in love with her, and in hindsight I was just looking for a way to make her stop loving me. I was immature and not very evolved."

When he says this, I think I know. But the heat of his body and the sweetness of his fingers drawing delicate vines across my collarbones makes it feel like his next words are spoken with invisible ink.

"I cheated on her."

He lets the sentence sit and it penetrates me like poison, first with a sting at the surface and then with a flashing burn as it takes root inside, ulcerating.

"I have no defense." I feel him looking at my face, but I can only fix my gaze on a tiny scar on his shoulder. My heart is squeezing so tight I can barely swallow. I am all locked up inside. "We got in a fight while I was at work and I just . . . didn't go home. I went out, met a woman at a bar—whatever, it's such a boring story. I knew if I stayed out all night I couldn't lie about it the next morning. I sat in my car until the sun came up. Nat knew as soon as she saw me. And yeah," he says quietly, "that definitely ended things."

I'm still unable to figure out how to make sound. I nod numbly.

"Maybe it would have happened eventually. We'll never know. It was the worst thing I've ever done," he says. "I've done a lot of work on myself. A lot of therapy. Nat has forgiven me, but it took a long time." The shoulder I'm staring at lifts in a shrug. "It's why I don't think I can stomach casual relationships anymore. Like, I don't even remember the woman's name or her face. What a vile thing to do." He exhales slowly. "That feeling has never really left me."

I hear what he's saying; I even hear the emotional weight of his words, the regret and the self-flagellation and the sincerity. But the contradiction of him marrying Nat to do the right thing and ending it in the cruelest possible way feels like a hot and cold wire, twisted around my windpipe.

Suddenly I'm up,

I'm standing,

I'm searching through my open bag for my clothes.

Underwear, joggers, T-shirt. My joints move like they're programmed, muscle memory, locating everything and panic-dressing myself in the dark.

Connor pushes up. "Fizzy."

"I'm just realizing people are probably still down at the bar." I laugh like, *Duh me!*

His pause feels as deep as a canyon. "It's three o'clock in the morning."

"I know, but I'm the big sister and just left the wedding without saying goodbye to all my family."

"You did say goodbye."

"Not to everyone!"

He goes silent and I can't look at his face. My thoughts are a flurry of broken trust and fear and anger and sadness. I feel nauseated and frantic, but I see from a distance, too, how this is unfolding. How wild I must look to him right now.

Connor's voice is steady. "This is about what I just told you. I completely understand why this upsets you. But I need you to come back and talk this out with me."

I trip as I shove my foot into a shoe. "I swear it isn't about that.

And I'm sure that was super hard for you to share. I'm sorry to do this right now, I just really should check to see if anyone is up that I need to spend time with."

My card key is on the dresser and I grab it, shoving it into the pocket of my hoodie.

"Fizzy. *Please stop.*"

I take a deep breath and look at him. He's sitting up, has pulled a sheet over his lap to cover himself. His hair is a disaster, eyes bright even in the dim room. He's devastatingly gorgeous,

and I think I love him,

but I also think if someone can justify cheating once, they can justify it again. You're either a cheater or you're not.

"Fizzy. Come back."

"I can't."

"Talk to me about what's going on right now. I was a dumb kid. I'm not that guy anymore."

"It's fine. This isn't about that."

"It is. And it's okay. I don't like that I did it any more than you do, but I want us to be able to live with our fuckups. I want us to talk about them."

I look away, at the ugly bamboo wallpaper, but I don't even feel like I'm in the room with him anymore.

I'm in a crowded restaurant and Rob's wife is glowering down at me. I'm aware of my confused date slowly putting the pieces together across the table from me. I'm home alone later, devastated to discover that I am the worst of things: a home-wrecker.

Before Rob, I thought I was bulletproof. I thought I'd always be enough for myself, that I didn't need anyone, that no man could tank my feelings or sense of self-worth. And then Rob and the whole situation made me question it all. I promised myself I would never feel that way again.

Now I see that Rob was a paper cut. Connor could obliterate me, and it wouldn't take something as enormous as cheating.

I look over at him. "You want me to be honest?"

He nods immediately, forcefully. "Always."

"Okay, well," I say, clenching my jaw and grasping the first lie that comes to me. "I think we were both tipsy and then sex-drunk and we got way too heavy. I don't know what I was thinking. We barely know each other."

Connor gusts out a disbelieving breath. "We *do* know each other. Getting to know each other has been our *singular focus* for *months*."

The words fly out of me: "Then I was wrong about you. You're not the man I thought you were."

When he can't come up with anything to say in response, I turn and leave.

thirty-seven

CONNOR

I stare at the door, waiting for the telltale sound of the key card, of Fizzy coming back in to regroup, find her level head, talk this out. But the hotel is so quiet this time of night, the only sound I hear is the elevator ding down the hall, and the mechanical sound of the car descending.

What the fuck just happened?

I fall back onto the bed, staring up at the ceiling. I know Fizzy to be a lot of things—wild, brave, self-assured, assertive, intense—but I don't know her to be flighty like this. Fizzy is the heroine who turns around to face the oncoming danger head-on. She isn't the one who throws out bollocks excuses on her way out the door. Now I'm alone and stark naked on this sex-ravaged bed with the echo of our sounds still embedded in the four walls.

I sit up, shoving the sheets away. My former therapist's reminder floats up into my thoughts: *You don't have to deal with it right this second, but you* do *have to deal with it.* I'll give Felicity Chen the same courtesy. She doesn't have to deal with me this instant, but eventually, she will have to face this.

With deliberate patience, I shower again and get dressed. As much as I can, I put the room back together, ignoring the way images flash into my head as I straighten the sheets—*the long plane of her neck as she throws her head back and cries out*—as I hang up our towels—*water dripping from her lips as she stares between us and watches me fuck her*—as I put the champagne bottle in the recycling bin—*the view of her lips kissing down the length of me.*

And then I sit in the chair by the window and slowly count to one hundred and then back down to one. The entire time, I think she must be on her way back.

She must be—just now.

Maybe now. She'll walk in and I'll put aside this anger and we'll talk it out, one word at a time.

But when I leave just after four, the hallways are empty; the bar downstairs is predictably dark and silent. I have no idea where she went but am not going to chase her down with a text message or a call. Fuck this. The sleepy valet takes my ticket and pulls my car around. What a bloody mess.

thirty-eight

FIZZY

I need you to say that again," Jess says, cupping her warm mug of tea and tucking her feet under the blanket. "I want you to hear how insane it sounds."

"I admit I have feelings for him," I repeat robotically, pacing my living room floor. "We proceed to have the best sex of my entire lifetime. For hours. Twice. Then he tells me his marriage ended because he cheated. So I bolted."

"Yes, but specifically the next part."

"The part where I went and sat on the floor in an empty hotel ballroom for an hour?"

She nods, and then lifts her coffee to her lips to take a sip, letting my words ricochet off my silent living room walls. I did do this. I left Connor naked in my hotel bed while I bolted downstairs and hid in a dark ballroom for an hour, my mind spinning wildly out of control.

I sent up the bestie bat signal at five this morning and told Jess she had to come over as soon as she landed from Costa Rica and as soon as I got home from the Sunday post-wedding brunch. But given how much stuff there was to pack into cars, how many people there were to pay, and how many family members there were needing rides to the airport, it's now nearly ten o'clock at night. I feel panicky and nauseated, but I'm not sure if it's regret, resignation, or sheer exhaustion from a lack of sleep.

"He was trying to talk it out with you," she says over the steaming top of her mug.

I don't need reminding. Every regrettable, overreactive moment of my meltdown is imprinted in my brain like a bad, drunken tattoo.

I reach the end of my living room and turn to pace in the other direction, for the five hundredth time. "I know he was. And I know this all happened like eight years ago, and he was upset, and he's older and wiser, but the fact that he decided to not just end his marriage but explode it . . ."

"Fizzy, we are all dumb when we're young. I mean, you must see the parallels here: I got pregnant because Alec and I had unprotected sex in a bathroom at a party. Connor messed up, but then he stepped up. He went to therapy; he moved here to be present. Juno barely sees Alec once a year."

An ache passes through me, and I stop my pacing to wince over at her. "Shit. I know. I'm a dick for venting about this to you."

"No, come on, I'm the exact right person to vent to. Being hurt, being betrayed? It does weird things to us. I know this is your button and nobody would blame you for how you reacted."

I resume my stride, turning to walk to the other end of the room, feeling her eyes on me.

"But we have to believe that the people we care about are conscious, accountable people," she continues. "The fact that he told you, that he's really done the work to grow . . . I mean, most men aren't that evolved at thirty-three, let's be honest."

I groan, turning and heading the other direction again. "I *know*."

"If you were the same person you were at twenty-four, you'd have a different guy every week and wouldn't even be considering finding a soulmate, on a show or otherwise."

"Not *every* week."

"Stop pacing and tell me what happened next."

I stop abruptly, collapsing onto the other end of the couch. "Once I got my shit together, I told myself that if he was still in the room when I got back upstairs, I would apologize and talk it out."

She straightens. "And?"

"He wasn't." Jess deflates. "He'd left while I was gone. And maybe that's a good thing," I say, "because the other half of the deal I made with myself was that if he wasn't there waiting for me, it was a sign that this Connor thing was doomed, and to move on."

"You don't believe in signs."

"Yes, I do."

"Remember the time that black cat was sitting on the hood of your car when you walked out of Twiggs and barely two seconds after you put it in your car, you got that horrible *New York Times* review?"

"I really don't like this turn in the conversation."

"You then took the doomsday cat home with you, and called me to complain, all shocked and outraged that this stray, feral harbinger of doom shredded your curtains within, what, thirty minutes?"

"I think," I say, putting a single finger up as if to test the direction of the wind. "Yes, I think it's time I find a new best friend."

She laughs. "Should I even ask about Isaac? You said you saw a possible future there."

"You know I don't do love triangles!" I look up at the ceiling. "It's like she doesn't know me at all."

She reaches across the expanse of couch, pulling me toward her and into her arms. "Connor did something dumb when he was in his twenties. Fizz, you of anyone should understand that."

She doesn't mean it as a dig. She's paying homage to my battle scars, my medals of honor for adventure, my backlist of sexual exploration. And I went through this exact thought process, too, when I sat there on the floor in the dark. First, there was my indignation, my bright, hot panic that the person I had big heart and pants feelings for was a cheater. But then my blood cooled and the other things he said echoed a little louder: That it was the worst thing he's ever done. That he's done a lot of work on himself, gone to therapy. That Nat has forgiven him.

But even if I could view his past with some perspective, my fight-or-flight moment left me feeling unsteady, remorseful, and anxious. How are the heroines in my books so *sure* of themselves and the person they fall in love with? How does anyone really know what and who they want? It's all such a risk. Who chooses to fling their heart out into the blackness of uncertainty, blindly hoping someone catches it?

"The thing is," I say into her shoulder, "I signed a contract saying I wouldn't date during this show. They're paying me a lot of money to do this. And this isn't just a little lie. I could be in breach of contract if I'm caught with him. Like, actual Big Legal Trouble. He could lose his job. I haven't finished a book in more than a year, I'm avoiding my agent's phone calls like I'm hiding from the mob, and I'm starting to feel like I can't even do dating right. But last night in the hotel room, I didn't care about any of that because I just wanted to be with him."

She hums, listening.

"I've never felt that—that insatiable thing, you know? I want to be near him every second. If I eat something delicious, I want him there to take a bite. If I see something beautiful, I want to turn to him and point it out. If I hear something hilarious, I immediately want to call him and tell him everything."

"Oh, honey."

"But if it got out or I couldn't fake it well enough, it would mess up his life, and mine." I swallow as the hardest one bubbles to the surface. "I know that and still none of it mattered."

"We do crazy things when we fall for someone, Fizz."

"Yeah, but you know the only thing that scared me enough to get me to leave that room?"

"What?"

"That even if by some miracle everything goes right, I could still get hurt."

She sighs into my hair.

"And if Connor hurt me, I don't know whether I'd be able to write another love story."

I wait for the joke. One of us needs to make it; the moment is too heavy.

I guess you weren't kidding about his magical dong.

It's right there for the taking.

But Jess says the last thing I expect: "That's how you know he's the one, Fizz."

I fall asleep and Jess must have carefully extracted herself because it isn't her moving out from under my head that wakes me, it's me falling off the couch and landing in a pile on the floor.

I don't immediately move because I want to hold on to the dream I was having, cling to it for just a few minutes longer. Connor's arms were just here, banded around me on the couch. I was so warm, so content. We were breathing together, doing nothing but talking and laughing and falling into easy silence. While my body slowly wakes up, the remnants of a bone-deep sense of connection and intimacy lingers until the fog of sleep clears and it hits me what I just dreamed: Connor and I were living together.

That's how you know he's the one.

I've never wanted to live with anyone. Is Jess right? Is that what this is? This sense of being known, being loved, being safe in the quietest moments with him? But why does that feeling of safety and connection have to come intertwined with the outright terror of giving over to the powerlessness of it all, of putting my heart and well-being in Connor's hands?

I think about what it would feel like to never touch him again, and a raw stab of pain spears me. His hands, his lips, his laugh, his weight, his deep melodic voice, his steady gaze, yes—okay—his magnificent . . . presence. I want to dig my fingernails into the floorboards at the idea of giving that up.

It's midnight, but urgency floods my veins as I reach for my phone on the coffee table. There are no missed calls from him, no messages. I push on, not letting myself wonder what that might mean.

Are you up? I text him. I hope so because I'm on my way over.

I don't wait for a response. I don't stop to think. I shove my phone into my purse, stuff my feet into my shoes on the way out, and don't even bother to lock my front door.

Outside his place, I climb out of my car and look up at his dark porch, dark windows.

I'm here, I text.

Nothing.

I call but it rings, and rings, finally going to voicemail.

This is when I have a brief internal meltdown. It's Sunday night. I think Stevie's at Nat's because Connor came to the wedding with me, but what if he picked her up today? I don't want to wake her with a Romance Heroine Banging on the Door move, but if his phone is on silent I could pace out here at the curb until morning and he'd never know I was here. How do people in books and movies make their big-feelings confessions when there are potentially kids fast asleep in the house!

I tilt my face to the sky, groaning. Real life is so much harder!

There's nothing to do but text again. Hi. Yes, I really did drive over here at midnight. Please tell me you're up.

Finally, after I stare menacingly at my phone for a good thirty seconds, three dots appear. My heart leaps into my throat.

Just saw these. I'm up.

His porch light goes on as I jog up his walkway. Connor opens the door, leaning a shoulder in the doorframe. Does he know how good he is at this? No one leans like him: with patient confidence, one hand tucked into a pocket, one foot crossed over the other.

He has my favorite soft hair falling over his forehead, a gray crewneck sweatshirt, faded and worn jeans, and bare feet. But most of all, it's just *him*, the whole package: the solid mass of his body and his kind eyes and full mouth and the sharp line of his nose. Our eyes meet, and even with the carefully guarded wariness I see there, I think it would take an approaching semi truck to get me to look away.

Connor gives me a quiet "Hey" before he steps back, letting me in.

"Hey," I say when he turns to face me, shutting the door behind us. The air between us warps with heat. I want to sink to my knees and worship him. I have never in my life felt such attraction or such devotion.

"I'm glad you were up," I say, breathless—I hope from excitement and not the jog up eight steps to his porch.

"Sorry, I had my phone on silent."

"It's okay." I can't catch my breath. Bending, I put my hands on my knees, sucking in air. "Sorry, I think I'm just nervous." I straighten, finally getting my bearings. I've written this scene a thousand times but, wow, it is way scarier to live it. "I have two things I want to say," I tell him.

"Okay." He swallows, lifting his chin. "Let's go sit."

An excellent plan: apologies first, confessions second, sex third.

I lead us into the living room and sit in the middle of the couch, patting the space beside me. He eyes it for a beat before sitting, but it's hard to miss the way it feels like he's trying to keep as much distance between us as he can.

"I'm sorry about the way I left," I say immediately. I'm even more desperate to get this out of the way now given his strained body language. Connor is tall and muscular, of course, but always carries himself like someone in a much smaller frame. I've never been more aware of his size before.

Well, now and when he was *actually lying on top of me* with his giant—

Focus, Fizzy. "I freaked out," I say, regrouping. "You saw it, you called it. Infidelity is a hard limit for me."

There's only one lamp on, behind him, and it leaves his expression in shadow. "I know."

"But I shouldn't have left. I should have stayed and taken a minute to figure out what I want to say, and it's this: I feel awful for Natalia. But also for the anonymous woman who didn't realize she was part of a young guy's kamikaze mission. Who probably thought she was just having the luckiest night of her life."

"I think about her a lot."

My heart melts a little. "That woman was me once, and not only did it break part of my heart, but I had to reckon with being another woman's heartbreak, too."

He could tell me, *For what it's worth, she didn't know I was married,* but he doesn't. And even if it's true, I appreciate that he isn't trying to defend himself. He just listens, absorbing this.

"I'm sorry I reacted that way," I say.

Connor nods. "I'm really not that guy anymore. I'm nearly a decade older, Fizzy. Infidelity is a hard limit for both of us."

"I know. I wish I hadn't run off like that. I'm sorry I left after what we'd just done. After what we'd just said." I take another deep breath. "I spent a lot of time by myself downstairs, thinking."

Connor hums, an unspoken *Go on, then.*

"At first I was panicking," I say, my anxiety ratcheting higher with his silence. In any other situation, even patient, measured Connor would say something to lighten the mood, to make this easier for me, but he's being so still, like he's bracing himself for something. "But then I let myself process what you'd said, and I realized something. About my feelings for you."

His eyes are on the floor and I stare at his amazing face, giving myself a few beats to calm down. Getting these words out feels like fitting my whole body through a straw. I've never said this next part. "I've been fickle my whole life," I admit. "I've never been someone who could close her eyes and visualize what it would be like to be with one person forever. I thought I was doing more of the same when I bolted today, but—"

"Fizzy—"

"No, let me get this out."

"I don't think—"

"I promise I'm not gonna be a jerk again."

"No, no, it's not th—"

"I realized something important tonight."

"Fizzy, listen—"

I know how this exchange would be written in a transcript. *Overlapping*, it would say. The staccato of words coming out one after the other, crowding the space, drowning us in bursts of noise. I laugh, shoving past the way he doesn't want to hear what I'm going to say.

So I blurt it out, loud enough to drown out his protest: "I'm in love with you."

And it's a beat before I realize my words barreled right over his: "I can't do this."

Everything falls nuclear-winter-level silent. The stillness in the room is absolute. And then the sound of him carefully clearing his throat feels deafening.

"Oh God," I say, laughing awkwardly, but inside I'm shriveling up in humiliation. "Did you just say what I think you said?"

His gaze is soft but steady. "I'm sorry."

"If this is about the show," I quickly say, "we can go back to our original plan. We can be secret if we need to." Desperation rises in me the longer I face this stiff, cold version of Connor. "I'm not going to let anyone get in the way of this if you're willing to try. What I said in the hotel about being crazy about you? I meant it. I'm all in. We can sneak around. I'm very small; I can be stealthy. In fact, my high school guidance counselor gave me two career paths: romance author or secret agent."

I expect a grin but I don't even get a flicker of a reaction. Instead, he breaks his gaze away and turns it toward the dark fireplace. With his profile illuminated, I see how tired he looks. His chiseled cheekbones seem gaunt, and I realize that it's because there's no smile in his eyes.

Dread falls like a weight in my stomach. Of course. I broke this. The way I left the hotel room, the way I revealed my fickle, impulsive side . . . was the exact wrong way to handle Connor. I knew he was guarded, knew he entered into things only after cautious deliberation. Knew he was trusting me with something he probably hasn't told many people, and I smashed that laboriously constructed trust with the mighty Fizzy hammer.

"I fucked up, didn't I?" I say quietly. "Leaving you last night blew the whole thing up."

He inhales deeply and slowly. "I told you from the start," he says to his lap, "that I didn't want something if it was only sex."

"I know."

When he turns his eyes up to me, the distance in his gaze sends a chill down my arms.

"What we shared felt much deeper than sex, Felicity, but at the first sign of trouble you fled. I've spent the last twenty-four hours feeling angry and hurt and incredibly stupid for trusting you. It makes it very hard for me to believe you now."

Mortification isn't a swift punch to the gut; it is a slow seeping of ice-cold water into my veins. I can't imagine what Connor thinks about me right now—I wonder if he's regretting putting the Heroes' hearts in my hands, let alone putting his own precious heart there. I agreed to do this show in the middle of my worst and deepest writer's block, and I justified it by saying I was doing it for the audience. And now I'm telling him to date me in secret, putting his job and his life here in jeopardy after I fled the hotel room like a panicked idiot the first time he confessed that he might not be a perfect human. It was supposed to be us against the world, and I blew it all up.

I have never in my life felt like such a profound failure.

thirty-nine

CONNOR

This time when Fizzy leaves, I only feel blank inside. I'd wanted to hold on to this anger—had spent the day going from indignant to hurt to disappointed and back again—but as I watched the excited flush drain from her face, breathless hope replaced by grim understanding, my anger slipped away, and I just felt . . . tired. Now there's only the silence of my thoughts, and the flat bleakness of the door firmly shut, literally and metaphorically.

I should feel relief that it's finally over and I can get back to focusing on what got me here in the first place, namely my job and my family, but I don't. I feel like absolute shit.

And she told me she's in love with me.

Blaine is the last person I want to see Monday morning, but he barges into my office just as I'm packing up to leave for the set.

"I can tell you're on your way out, but we need to talk first," he says, closing my office door.

"Did the final numbers come in?" Brenna's text from about six this morning showed numbers up over week one, on track to break another record.

"Fuck the numbers right now," he says. "Just tell me I'm not going to have to deal with any fucking drama on your crew."

I go still, setting my car keys down on my desk. The possibility of photos of Fizzy and me together . . . "What's this about?"

"Social media is raking Trent's crew and *Smash Course* over the coals because of this doping bullshit."

My first reaction is relief. And then I frown, leaning in like I need to be closer to his words to process them. I was so wrapped up in the drama with Fizzy this weekend that I feel completely disconnected from anything beyond her, and us, and *The True Love Experiment.* "What doping bullshit? Trent wouldn't do anything like that." The man used to make library documentaries and low-budget sitcoms, for fuck's sake.

"What dope—?" Blaine asks, cutting off in abrupt disbelief. "Connor, he's been dealing with lawyers for weeks. As of this morning it's all over the goddamn Internet."

I look past him, remembering. Trent came back to San Diego for meetings with lawyers. It didn't even occur to me to ask why. "I haven't been online yet," I tell him. "I came straight here before heading to set."

Blaine gives me the brief rundown: a facilities manager at one of the venues used for Trent's show came forward with video proof that two of the other producers on the show were giving performance-enhancing drugs to a contestant.

"Okay, this is bleak, this is shit," I say. "But it's entertainment television, not the Olympics."

"Yeah? Not the Olympics? Well, what do we tell the execs at SuperHuman and Rocket Fuel? Should I call our biggest sponsors and explain why we're taking obscene ad money to promo their workout formulas during commercial breaks, but letting the contestants dope off camera? Oh, is that not enough for you?" He doesn't let me answer this rhetorical question, not that I'd bother. "Well, how about this: one of the producers was also *fucking* this contestant in the tour bus bathroom, so you tell me if it still doesn't matter."

My stomach drops. "Jesus."

"You're the juggernaut, Conn, but Trent's show also has the highest ratings in his time slot. You see now how the audience treats these things like their fucking lifeline. They get invested, and when you give them the power of a vote? They feel ownership. Let them have that kind of power and you're finished the second you step out of line. We put everything we've got into this goddamn show and cannot lose our viewers because Trent's team was breaking the law and banging the stars."

"Okay." I lean back against my desk, cupping my neck. "What do you need me to do?"

"I need you to reassure me that your shop is clean. I want to hear that these Heroes you cast are *perfect goddamn gentlemen*. That Fizzy could run for president if she wanted to. I want to hear that *no one* on your crew has wandering hands or a penchant for jerking off in front of people." Dread fills my gut with a leaden weight. "I want to hear that the only fucking happening is the fucking Felicity Fucking Chen will do with the winner of this goddamn Fiji trip we are spending a small fortune on!"

With wry defeat, I exhale a laugh. I reckon it's good we ended things; I'd have to end it now anyway. I fucking hate all of this.

Blaine takes a step closer, glowering. "Connor? I need the words."

I swipe a hand down my face. "Yeah. We're clean."

"No bullshit, Connor," he says, straightening. "You're the only thing we have left right now, and if your show tanks, we go under. And you know what that means: *you* go under."

Ash reaches across the table and tugs at my collar. "You look like me today."

I peer down to see what he means. The sweater I pulled on as I left the office is on backward, with the tab sticking up against the front of my neck. How nice that the two women who stopped me for a photo before Ash arrived didn't bother to tell me. I tug it over my head, putting it on the right way this time. "I'm a little distracted."

"I can imagine." He studies me for a beat. "You're not on set today?"

I shrug, poking at my plate. "I was headed over when Blaine found me. I just needed to get my head on straight. I'll head over in a bit. Shooting starts around three. Rory and Brenna've got things handled."

"Ah. You're avoiding her."

I take a bite of melon instead of answering.

"What you ought to do is go home and sleep. You look like crap."

I grunt in response, though I know I should do better. Ash has the day off for a teacher development thing that doesn't start until this afternoon, and instead of lounging in bed with his wife, he's here with me at brunch, listening to me explain *again* how my life is in the toilet.

I know it's a good thing I ended my relationship with Fizzy, but a part of me was hoping Ash would say what I know deep down, that I needed to give her time to work through what was probably the hardest thing for her to hear me say. Unfortunately, after hearing the entire story—the hotel drama, Fizzy's confession, and the situation with Trent's show—Ash agrees that I probably did the right thing.

But I've never, not once in my life, felt this way, never been so into a woman that I considered risking my livelihood to be with her. And I hate how last night went, hate that she now feels like she can't be straight with me if she's panicked, that she can't fuck up, too. I hate most of all that none of it matters anyway after Blaine's ultimatum this morning.

Ash ducks, trying to catch my attention. "Conn."

Meeting his eyes, I give a small "Yeah?"

"You know what Fizzy would say right now?"

"I'm dying to hear it."

"It's only hot for a hero to brood for, like, three-quarters of a book."

A real laugh bursts out of me. "That is exactly what she would say."

He grins at the compliment. "And you're ignoring the very obvious silver lining," he says brightly.

"Which is?"

"That now you know you're ready for a relationship."

I laugh again, but it's back to sardonic. I can't blame him for trying. Finding Ella was the best thing to ever happen to Ash. "There's not a solid batch of evidence, Ash. Fizzy and I had a seesaw fling for a few weeks and then it ended before it even began."

"But you were *open* to it."

I lift the spoon to my lips, murmuring, "I fell for her against my will," before taking a bite. "But yeah. I suppose."

"Maybe this time you try DNADuo," he says, slicing neatly into his omelet. "There are so many more users in the system now that it sounds like people are getting lots of good matches. A Gold Match isn't rare anymore—one of the teachers at school even got two! He can meet them both, find the perfect fit. Can you imagine just being handed a list?" He takes a bite and stares at me with unmasked curiosity. "I'd love to see who your perfect fit is."

I shove Fizzy's face out of my thoughts and give a noncommittal hum. A few months ago, I would have described her as loud and unrelenting. Now I can't imagine using those qualities as insults.

"Besides, now you're a hot commodity, Connor." He takes another bite and chews.

I'm still daydreaming about Fizzy's loud mouth and what she did with it, so this takes a second to penetrate. "You mean the confessionals? Ah, that's just a small bit."

"That *small bit* is likely a huge part of the reason Blaine's trying to put some fear in you."

I still, looking up at him. "What are you talking about?"

Ash appears to do a mental obstacle course before he carefully puts his fork and knife down. He lifts his napkin to his lips, tapping gingerly. "Are you unaware of what's happening online?"

"You mean our ratings?" I nod as I say it because Brenna sends them to me every morning. "They're great."

"No, I mean your fan base."

"I've had a few people stop me, but that's just because they recognize someone from TV."

"A few?" he says pointedly, and I follow his gaze to a group of women in a booth across the restaurant. As soon as they see me, their eyes snap back down to the table. "I'm talking about Connor Prince stans."

I shake my head. "It's not like that."

With a condescending chuckle, he pulls out his phone, mumbling to himself, "I tell him his phone is good for more than texting and reading the news, but does he listen? No." Ash taps his screen a few times with a flourish and then turns it to face me. "First of all, your Instagram. You have almost three hundred thousand followers."

I blink. I haven't posted anything in years. "What?"

He gives an exasperated sigh and swipes through his phone again before setting it on the table in front of me. "There."

I scan around, trying to orient myself. "What am I looking at?"

"It's Twitter." A finger comes down, pointing at a cluster of letters. "What does that hashtag say?"

"It says . . ." It takes me a minute to read because the words are all smushed together, no spaces. "'Daddy Prince The True Love Experiment'?" I look up at him. "Who's Daddy Prince?"

"You are. That's what the *True Love* fandom calls you."

"The—*fandom*—?" I break off, confusion deepening. "*Daddy Prince?*"

"Twitter blows up when confessionals start."

"I'm not even on-screen that much. There are more successful, better-looking, and frankly more agreeable men for them to get excited about."

"Can't argue with that," he says with a grin. "But they're writing you in anyway. Apparently, *Daddy Prince*, they love your deep voice and your sexy accent, and the way you and Fizzy banter." He glances up at the sound of my stifled mortification. "Oh, come on, stop looking so horrified. 'Daddy Prince' is pretty tame compared to some of the other stuff here." As he continues to scroll, his grin turns into a frown and he muses, "I didn't realize 'choke me' was such a common phrase."

I ignore this. "What does that mean, 'write in'? Can't they only vote for the contestants?"

"You wouldn't know this because you're a social media troglodyte, but no. The way your team has set it up, if the show is tagged, a tracking program considers it a vote and keeps a tally. It could be '#GiantAnacondaCock_TheTrueLoveExperiment' and Giant Anaconda Cock gets a vote."

I stare at Ash. "What?"

"Don't worry. Most people use it the way you intended. They hashtag Colby or Isaac or whoever. It's quite smart, really; lots of the big music award shows do it. I think the Oscars even started doing it for fan favorite and favorite movie moment. It's a great way to get engagement because the tags are visible to everyone, you can tweet—aka *vote*—as many times as you want, which means tweeting and retweeting puts it in everyone's feed. You can't buy exposure like that. It's all there on your pocket computer if you care to look."

This entire conversation has thrown me off-kilter now that it's sinking in what Ash is telling me. Viewers are voting for me? Blaine doesn't know as much as he'd like everyone to believe, and I have to assume that if he did know something about this—or, worse, about me and Fizzy—he would have mentioned it, right? Either way, I'll need to be very, very careful over the next few weeks.

"Of course, there are people writing in all kinds of names," Ash says. "Lots of *Your Mom* and other random things. I think Captain America had a pretty decent number one week."

"Great," I say dryly. "A flawless system."

"There will always be idiots," Ash says, dismissing this as he pushes his plate aside and leans in. "So far, Isaac has the most votes every week. But you're definitely gaining."

I lean back with a soft gusting exhale, feeling Ash's attention on me while I process this. "For sure Brenna sees this. Why didn't anyone tell me?"

"Maybe they're trying to ignore it." He picks up his water glass and takes a sip. "I mean, it's not like you can win this thing."

––––––––––

These words bounce around in my head.

It's not like you can win this thing.

He's right, of course. I'm not even a contestant. Still, there's a faint echo of pity party, too. I *can't* win.

I'm stuck in that tight mental squeeze where I have too many things on my mind and not enough time to devote to them. I could spend an entire week thinking about how it felt to have Fizzy on my arm at her brother's wedding, let alone everything that happened later that night. But add Fizzy's confession, Blaine's visit to my office, and everything that Ash told me about the votes . . . my mind is a blur.

All of that gets pushed aside, however, because there's a job to do. And somehow, Fizzy and I both manage to treat it like one. After the weekend votes have been tallied, we're down to four Heroes: Isaac, Nick, Dax, and Evan. I'm not sure if it's a reprieve or torture that the crew is rolling smoothly and I'm not necessary at Fizzy's cozy dinners with the Heroes, following them on their long walks on the beach, their dates bowling and apple picking and taking surfing lessons, but I take advantage of the space anyway, because we probably both need it. The only time I see her all week is for an awkward and forced confessional. Otherwise, I hole up in the editing room and piece together a narrative for each possible couple, blasting music through headphones in every moment of downtime I have so I can't hear the echo of her telling me she's in love with me. I create the most compelling episode yet, earning the top ratings for the network that week. But it is a truly hollow victory.

After a much-needed weekend with Stevie, I'm back on set the following week. I'd hoped it would be easier to see Fizzy, but it isn't. Monday brings the elimination of Dax and Nick, and the appearance of a Fizzy who spent her own weekend doing God knows what with God knows who. I don't imagine she's running around sleeping with blokes left and right—primarily because I know that her feelings for me are sincere, and also because she's contractually forbidden—but the rational part of my brain doesn't speak up when I see her walk into the restaurant for filming on Monday afternoon. I'm hotly possessive at the sight of her in tiny denim shorts and a thin white tank top. I want to put my hands on her body and my mouth on her skin and press her into a wall, coaxing a confession of love out of her again.

But I keep the mask firmly in place. These final two dates are the ones viewers will use to choose a winner, and tonight, Isaac is having dinner on camera with Fizzy and her parents. I was beside her with them only a week ago, pride heating my blood. Now I'm behind a camera, watching Liz dust powder on Mrs. Chen's forehead, watching Mr. Chen joke with Rory about his good angles, knowing Fizzy's parents are going to meet the handsome, accomplished, and deserving man who will likely win. If I know Fizzy—and I feel like I truly do—she will accept my rejection at face value and do everything she can to move on. She will embark on the trip with Isaac and do her very best to enjoy both of them to the fullest. When they're together in Fiji, will she forget what it felt like to be in my arms? Will she sleep with him simply because he's there? Or will their connection deepen, grow stronger than what she and I had?

I hate both scenarios, but honestly can't imagine what *stronger than what we had* looks like. I see Fizzy with these men and must continually repress the possessive instinct to claim her in small and large ways. And that instinct is back now, shaped differently but undeniable, as I watch the two people I realize I want to be *my* in-laws prepare to meet another man.

"You good?" Rory asks, walking back to the cameras.

The *no* is already forming on my lips when I pull myself back into awareness, blinking hard. "Yes. I'm great."

I stand from the table just as Fizzy steps from the makeshift dressing room in the back and into the dining area. Her hair is in two buns, tendrils escaping and framing her face. Eyes slashed with dark liner, a shredded T-shirt and ripped jeans capped with shit-stomping boots. Tonight, Fizzy has come prepared for battle. For a split second, a feverish pulse, I have never wanted anything the way I want her. And the feeling doesn't dissolve, not even when I step outside for a long, deep breath of fresh air.

forty-one

FIZZY

Because the universe is a bored cat, and I am but a powerless mouse, Connor is without his usual crisp suit and is in a tight black T-shirt and jeans today. Even though I put on all this armor to help prop up my tender insides, it's all I can do to not cross the room and paw all over him. I barely saw him last week and missed him so much I spent the entire weekend in my pajamas watching the first three episodes of *The True Love Experiment* over and over just to see him in the confessionals. Now his floppy hair, biceps, and pectorals outlined by soft cotton jersey are right in front of me. He's exuding that trademark calm patience as he discusses something with Rory and . . . *God*, look at him. I love him, and it really, really hurts.

Ergo, I have decided I hate love.

I outlined a new book last night. It's basically about a woman who falls in love with a man but she's a hot mess and he rejects her, so she walks off a cliff. Except at the bottom of the cliff is a big bed of pillows—because I'm not really into literary fiction or horror—and then she suffocates in the pillows. Except she doesn't suffocate, she just rolls around and feels sorry for herself until Uber Eats gets there with her Krispy Kreme order.

I also threw this outline in the trash.

And then I tried to sleep, because this week is probably the most important week of filming, but "sleep" mostly looked like me lying facedown on my bed crying into my pillow.

I want to go over to him, pull him aside, and tell him that I won't ever do that again, I won't run off like that. Does he know how much I admire his cautious side? He is the stillness to my storm, the shadow to my bright sunlight, the Styles to my Harry.

The date with Isaac is awesome. I mean outwardly, of course. Inside, I am all marionette strings and positive self-talk. Dad cracks his dumb, awesome jokes; Isaac talks about his job in AI research, and I can see my mother quietly losing her mind imagining a trio of smart grandbabies. I sip from my bottle of lime Perrier. Product placement deals for everything from sparkling water to sunblock to clothing retailers have started to crop up, so I am careful to keep the label turned out. See, Connor? I can be a team player.

My parents talk about what it was like to move to the U.S. from Hong Kong in their twenties, and the struggles of raising three kids with such different personalities. It will make for incredible, authentic television. In my quiet moments of dissociation, I can see this from above and know that we're all doing a really great job.

There's satisfaction in getting something right, I guess—I'm faking it like a pro while ignoring the hot giant behind the camera. Isaac is gorgeous and smart—my mom is half in love with him before we've even made it to entrées, and my dad keeps giving me that *Eh? He's pretty great, eh?* look that means he'll be asking me about Isaac for the next several months. This is exactly why I've never introduced my parents to a guy before. It would be one date and then six months of questions about how long I expect to wait for a proposal. I worry that they don't entirely understand the premise here—that we're just trying this dating thing out, and this isn't a Meet the Family meal in the way that it usually would be—but I can't even get it up to worry too much because I'm just so fucking sad, and right now every ounce of my focus has to be on getting through it.

"I like him," Mom pronounces into her still-live mic as soon as we're up and standing. "You should pick him. Think of how smart and pretty your babies will be." Called it.

The crew chortles in the background and I reach up, carefully unclipping her mic from her collar. "The audience decides the winner, Ma."

"But he should be your boyfriend," she continues, unaware as I fumble to turn it off. "You look so good together."

On instinct, my eyes turn to the row of cameras. Connor reaches up, slipping off his headset and placing it on the seat beside him before he picks up a clipboard and casually writes something down. No reaction, certainly no consternation. He doesn't even look up the way he used to, that reactive flash of jealousy heating his eyes. Now it's just relaxed Connor, not caring about the prospect of someone else being my boyfriend.

It's cool, I'm fine.

Allow me to fling myself off a cliff into a bed of pillows.

Hugging my parents, I see them out to the confessional trailer to meet with the man himself, and then I sit down, waiting my turn.

A half hour passes before my parents find me for goodbyes.

"We told Connor that we think you should marry Isaac!" my dad whisper-yells, and then kisses my cheek.

I give them the best smile I can produce. "Awesome, I'm sure he loved that."

Isaac leaves for the confessional and, honestly, I would pay a lot of money to be a fly on the wall in that room. I bet it's the size of a teacup with the combination of their two hulking bodies, Connor's quiet intensity, and Isaac's dazzling charm.

Or maybe it's fine. Maybe the room isn't cold at all, and Connor isn't weird with Isaac in the slightest, even though one of my favorite parts of Connor's body was inside my body one week plus forty-eight hours ago and a casual observer would say that we were both being pretty dramatic about our big emotions. But I've never been in love, so I've never fallen out of it before. Maybe it does happen like that for some people—a switch flipped down, a match blown out.

There's a shuffle behind me and I notice the crew start packing up gear. My heart feels like a mallet behind my sternum. Any second now one of the sweet PAs will call me in for my interview. I'll recap the date, talk about what I liked, what didn't feel right—even though I barely remember it, and I'm sure I'll be a monotonic, yearning mess, but I don't care, at least I'll be near him. It was the only thing that made last week bearable, even though he made eye contact for approximately fifty milliseconds in the entire ten minutes. I'm going through withdrawals; I want to be alone with Connor so bad it feels like a vine of thorns wrapped around my heart.

It's Brenna who comes over, eyes downward on her phone. "Looks like you're free to go home!"

I shake my head. "I haven't done my confessional yet."

She recites from the text in front of her. "Connor says we're skipping you tonight and covering both dates tomorrow."

"Wait—why?" On my call sheet it had a confessional for each night this week.

She only shrugs. "It's what he said." She scrolls back through her messages. "Looks like he's already left."

———————

Sleep is a fickle mistress. It probably doesn't help that I spend most of Monday night cheating on her with a neurosis named One Thousand Things I Did to Fuck Things Up. I forget to set an alarm, so it's a good thing I fall asleep with my phone under my pillow (in case Connor calls me in the middle of the night because he changed his mind and loves me, too) and that it starts vibrating beneath me.

It's Jess. I answer with whatever sound it makes when my mouth is pressed directly on the receiver.

"Well, good morning," she says back.

"Time is it?"

"Just after eight."

I push to sit up in my too-bright room. I hadn't bothered to close the curtains last night, and sunlight streams in like there's something to celebrate. "Shit."

"What time do you have to be on set today?"

I squint at the wall, thinking. "Ten, I think."

"You have plenty of time."

"I know." I reach up, rubbing my face. "I meant *Shit, I have to pretend to be fine again today*."

"You're forgetting something."

"What's that?"

Jess whisper-squeals through the phone: "Who's joining you for today's date with Evan?"

With a relieved groan I collapse back onto the bed. "Ohthankgod, that's right." Despite the dark cloud following me everywhere, I giggle. The date with Evan was originally supposed to be with my brother and his new wife, before we realized during scheduling that they'd be on their honeymoon. My sister was the second obvious choice, but has been shifted from "taking it easy" to official bed rest. I have a pool of about a zillion aunties I could choose from, but that would honestly be a circus, and even with all of this self-loathing, I don't hate myself *that* much.

"How's River feeling about being on TV again?"

"Grouchy, but stoically resigned."

"My favorite version of him."

She laughs. "I'll see you soon. Go get 'em, tiger."

I give my most pathetic roar.

———

Of course, the first thing that happens when I go from the bright sunshine outside to the dim elegance of the restaurant is I collide directly with a wall of Connor. It is not unlike running face-first into brick—physically, emotionally, spiritually.

We do one of those terrible bursting, overlapping apology dances before abruptly turning in opposite directions: me, to hair and makeup in the back, and him to the row of cameras setting up for the day of shooting.

The restaurant is quiet; I'm the first to arrive. Up front, it is just

Connor and Rory huddled around the cameras. I swear I hear every rumbling murmur of his voice, feel it like a vibration down my spine. Liz has to keep reminding me to tilt my chin up and turn my face to her, because I keep unintentionally turning my head toward the front of the restaurant, drawn to him in these unconscious, aching ways.

My entire life I've felt grounded in who I am and what I want, but lately . . . lately it feels like I have no identity anymore. I'm not a writer, I'm not a wild date, I'm not even a pesky best friend or bawdy aunt. And in all this quiet in my mind, the *who am I really?* shouts the loudest. One of my favorite things about Connor was that he didn't need me to be anything. I could be silly and loud or thoughtful and contemplative and it was all just . . . me. He told me that I was more than my playful, sexy, adventurous author persona. He said I had thoughtful depth and sensitive layers. It felt like he had a pocket Fizzy Decoder (and I am not just talking about his dick).

(Though the dick helped, too.)

Evan arrives in a suit and looks objectively hot. I'm so conflicted. On the one hand, I could choose him for the trip. It's not going to happen with us—I think we both know that—and maybe a relaxing ex-to-friend trip together to Fiji is just what I need. But on the other hand, with the show's popularity, I don't want to do the public "breakup," don't want to have to pretend to have been in love and fallen out of it.

But if I choose Isaac, I'd be doing us both a disservice. Isaac is exactly who I would have expected to fall for, but in this reality, I now only feel very platonic things for him. Are his feelings genuinely romantic? Would a trip with him be the most excruciating, awkward ten days? Could I maybe learn to like him?

I groan, and Liz gives my chin a gentle pinch, reminding me to hold still while she applies eyeliner.

"What's with you?" she asks, her breath sweet and minty near my cheek. "You seem stressed."

"I am."

"Are you worried the audience won't choose the one you want?"

Liz has never asked me anything about the show. I always assumed it was a don't-ask-don't-tell kind of thing, but maybe it's as simple as everyone not being a nosy asshole such as myself. A smart woman would say yes. A dumb one—me—says, "I don't think I want either of them."

She straightens, and her voice comes out in a whisper. "Which one do you want most?"

I go for broke: "The one who's seven feet tall with the god-tier bone structure."

She laughs but seems completely unsurprised. "Yeah, you two are a trip."

I don't immediately know what she means, and a self-conscious flush flashes through me. Because then I *do* know. She means what I feel, too, which is that the real story has been the friendship that has bloomed between me and her boss, Connor Prince. The cameras haven't captured this most beautiful of all story arcs: how this towering, intentional man and this small, chaotic woman came together first with friction and then with mutual admiration and then with something that felt a lot like love. I had the real story right in front of me this whole time, and blew it.

"He's been so off," Liz says, breaking into my thoughts. "Everyone feels it."

These last words pull me up to the surface again, newly aware. "What do you mean?"

She shrugs, sweeping one last pass of blush to the tops of my cheeks. "Oh, you know." I can't press for more without making it weird.

Liz steps back and surveys her work, pulling the protective cloth from my collar. "You're good," she says. She lifts her chin, and I turn to see a PA standing behind me.

"Ready?" he asks, and gestures to the trailer outside. Panic ignites in my bloodstream. "Rory wants a confessional first. You can head on out. Connor's waiting for you."

forty-two

FIZZY

've been in this trailer a dozen times over the past few weeks, and until today it has been my favorite hunting ground. It's small but comfortably furnished, with cameras secured in consistent places that make it easy to film these interviews no matter where the set takes us every day. There are two couches: one for Connor, one for whoever he's interviewing. The shades are pulled, the lighting soft and designed to feel private and intimate. Bottled water (labels facing out!) and a box of tissues are helpfully within arm's reach. This is where I give my thoughts on how things are going, how I'm feeling, my impressions of the Heroes. It's also the only time each episode where viewers get to see Connor as he walks us through each of the dates. I don't follow the show hashtags, because I'm not a masochist (and also, it's in the honor code that I don't track how the voting is going), but Jess mentioned again the other day that Juno told her that Stevie said people are loving him. Our little gang is like the Pony Express, but with gossip.

I don't blame these Internet women. Who could see this man on their TV and *not* fall for him? Hopefully it shows Blaine what a valuable asset Connor is, and it puts the ball in Connor's court for a change.

I've settled on the couch when the small trailer door opens and Connor ducks inside. His presence shrink-wraps the space, sucking up all of the oxygen.

No *hi* or *hello*. Just a quiet "Test your mic, please."

So we aren't going to be friends today. Noted.

Connor makes his way to his seat and slides a hand down the thigh of his dress pants. It really is taking a Herculean effort to not launch myself facedown into his lap. "One, two. One, two. Down with the patriarchy, up with romance, let women love who and what they love."

A pause while he waits for confirmation in his earbud. "You're good."

It takes him a moment to meet my eyes and arrange his face into a suitably pleasant—though not *too* pleasant—expression. "How are you feeling today heading into your last date?"

"Aren't you going to ask me about last night?"

He pauses, clearing his throat. "Yes. Right. Let's start over with that. How was last night for you?"

"It was hard," I say.

He waits uneasily for me to say more, like he knows I'm a live bomb. I should wax on about the date yesterday; that's my job, to talk. But everything goes blank inside.

Finally: "Hard, why?"

I want to laugh at this. *Hello, Connor, last night was hard because you barely looked at me and I want this show to be amazing so that your career takes off and you fall back in love with me.* But sadness is an ache I feel I need to continually swallow around, and turns out, sadness also makes it hard to laugh.

I reach for the water off to the side and twist off the cap, taking a sip. *Count to ten, one more sip, and do your damn job, Fizzy.*

"Last night was hard because I realize it might have been the last date ever with Isaac."

There. Just there. A tiny tic in his jaw. "Unless he wins, which it seems your parents would like very much." He's making his voice warm and amiable, leaning into his accent and that honeyed charm, but I know him. I see the tightness in his expression.

We do *know each other*, he'd said. *Getting to know each other has been our* singular focus *for months.*

I try to put on a natural grin. "Yes, my parents loved him."

He swallows. "We had a long conversation last night about why Isaac would be perfect for you."

"Is that right?"

Connor reaches for his own water, strangling down some unreadable expression. "They've met Evan before, right?" I am genuinely impressed—and annoyed—with how quickly he reined that in. I'm trash for his jealousy. I want to eat it slathered on toast.

"Yes," I say. "He's my brother's friend."

"And what did they think?"

"I don't think he made much of an impression at the time. But he is objectively amazing. And hot."

"Well, as producer and part of the team who cast him, I'll take that compliment," Connor says smoothly, the little gleam in his eye telling me he sees exactly what I'm doing. "As our One That Got Away, he'll be having dinner with your best friend, Jessica, and her husband, River Peña, who also happens to be the inventor of the DNADuo technology."

"That's right. Make sure to mention that *a lot*. River loves attention."

Connor laughs, shoulders relaxing. "You're going to be in top form tonight, I see."

"It's my last date night. How disappointed would everyone be if I was tame and well behaved?"

"We would all be devastated." The heat of his smile warms me to my marrow. How can he not see how good we are together? "How are you feeling entering this final date?"

"Relieved."

"Relieved why?"

"Because it means soon I can stop pretending I want someone other than you."

Connor goes silent, looking jerkily around at the cameras aimed at each of us. "Fizzy, you—you can't say that."

"Edit it out, then."

He reaches forward and gently switches one camera off, then the other. We both reach up, turning off our mics. Connor removes his earpiece and lets out a long exhale. "Shit."

"I miss you," I say once I know we're really alone. "I wish I could tell you how sorry I am for what I did. I know I said you aren't the man I thought you were, but I was just scared."

"I know."

"You're exactly who I need you to be."

He doesn't say anything, but the light catches the top of his hair when he bends to rest his head in his hands.

"I hate this," I say. I suck in a deep breath. "I hate the thought of ending up with someone other than you. I'm fickle about everything but this, Connor. I'm sorry I hurt you. I meant what I sai—"

"I know." His voice is calm, but resolute, and I realize what's coming when he sits up and meets my gaze. He's going to find a new way to let me down easy. How many times am I going to ask this man to reject me? "And I'm so sorry I've put you in this position," he says. "I'm sorry that I've contributed to what you're struggling with. I'm sorry you have to pretend to want one of these remaining Heroes. But you're so good on this show, Fizz. Every day I feel like the smartest man alive for casting you." We stare at each other for a long pause. I silently repeat over and over that I love him. I'm making up for a lifetime of never having said it, and even if he doesn't feel the same, it feels so good to shout it with my gaze.

Finally, he exhales. "For what it's worth, this is hard for me, too."

Everything inside me goes strangely quiet. I don't know why him saying that makes it possible for me to continue, but it does. "I really needed to hear that. You've seemed so composed. You seemed so . . . over me."

"I'm *not*—" He breaks off. "I don't feel composed." Connor closes his eyes, swallows. "I'm not made of stone." He reaches forward, hesitating before he turns the camera on, as if asking my permission.

So, I give it. "Go ahead. Sorry for the interruption. I'm ready."

———

River's surly face when he walks in and is approached with a makeup brush and fawning crew goes a long way toward pulling my mood up from the basement. When Brenna asks for River's autograph on the palm of her hand, the laugh I let out at his horrified expression echoes through the room, lightening it all somehow. *What does one do with an autographed hand?* his face appears to silently wonder. *Cast it? Tattoo it? Never wash it again?* River isn't down with any of these possibilities and instead scribbles his name on napkins and coasters and business cards for the background actors and crew while Jess and I play a one-minute game of whisper catch-up.

"We were just alone in the confessional trailer," I say into her ear. "It was so perfect—just *us* together—and we started to relax and then I said I missed him, and that I hate having to be with someone other than him, and he admitted that it's hard for him, too!"

She gasps. "What!"

"I know!" I whisper-yell. "He said, 'I'm not made of stone.'"

Jess lets out a low whistle. "That's *hot.*"

Unfortunately, we have no more time to process what this means because Brenna collects us, fetches Evan and River, and leads the four of us to a table in the center of the restaurant, in perfect lighting. What a weird feeling, to be at a standstill in every other aspect of my life and yet feel like everything is moving too quickly all around me.

When I meet my best friend's eyes, I feel the tight knot of sadness and regret loosen.

I am here for you, her eyes say.

I know and I love you, mine say back.

I mean, hers say, *I am here for you tonight for dinner, and you owe me.*

Your husband is a riot.

Her gaze turns wry. *He complained all day.*

River complaining about being social! I do not believe you!

River clears his throat. "Stop doing that."

"Doing what?" Jess asks.

"That thing where you converse without words," he mutters.

I go to throw my napkin at him when, from behind the cameras, Connor clears his throat in reminder. "We're rolling."

There's some scripted conversation we're required to have referring to River's last appearance, about GeneticAlly, the technology, and reminders to viewers about River's involvement in the inception of the entire thing. But then dinner devolves into something easy where we forget for small stretches that we're being filmed, where we tell stories from our past that we may have told a hundred times or never heard before—it doesn't matter because even if I'm not romantically interested in Evan, I like him. I know the cameras are catching the easy familiarity we have. It bodes well for Evan, which bodes well for Connor.

But, God, I wish it were Connor beside me.

forty-three

CONNOR

Natalia's text message is only five words, but I study each of them for a good ten seconds.

"Fuck," I say aloud in the sealed silence of my car parked outside of her house.

She's with Juno at Fizzy's

In the madness of the show, my weekends with Stevie have been sporadic at best. Tonight was the perfect night to pick her up and have a cozy night relaxing at home. But there is nothing relaxing about the prospect of driving over to Fizzy's. I know it probably isn't true—and it certainly isn't fair—but it feels like my ex-wife is forcing me toward Fizzy on a night when I'm not sure my emotional storm doors are sturdy enough to weather any more alone time with her. Today was hard. The confessional was brutal, and watching an easy, chatty double date I wished I were a part of was even worse.

But Nat couldn't know that, so here we are.

I don't bother going up to say hi to her anyway, even though I'd love to vent it all out to someone who knows as well as I do what's on the line for me here. Instead, I turn my car around at the end of the street and head toward the little cream-and-blue bougainvillea-covered house just over two miles away. And once I'm at the curb,

I feel frozen again, even though my kid is inside and what I'd really like is to get my daughter, grab a pizza, and make a pillow fort on the couch for some quality television time. I don't want to think about the show, or the woman who runs constant laps around my mind, or the way she looked earlier when she confessed her feelings again. I was seconds from crumbling. I'd never known that kind of sensation, the way my heart felt heavy but airborne inside my rib cage. I'm so fucking in love with her I can barely take a full breath.

I'm out of the car, I'm up the steps, I'm closing my eyes at the door and taking a deep, calming breath before knocking. Greet everyone, grab my kid, head home.

Protect my heart. Protect Stevie. Move on.

At my knock, three voices yell out a cheerful "Come in!" and I open the door to find them piled on the couch beneath a mountain of fuzzy blankets.

"I could have been a bad guy," I tell them, frowning.

"We saw your shadow on the porch through the window," Stevie says.

Juno nods. "You're taller than everybody."

Fizzy gives me a playful *I mean, they're not wrong* face, but I can't engage. I realize it as soon as I lay eyes on her. There is so much pent-up longing and desire in my chest that it feels like if I say anything else, it will come out as a bellow. And if I take one step deeper into her house, I'll drag her into her room, lock the door, and fuck her into the floor.

"Grab your stuff, squirt." I lift my chin to where her backpack sits across the room, papers and colored pencils and bright colorful erasers spilling out everywhere.

The room goes quiet; exuberant energy drains. Great, now I'm the moody dick who spoiled the party.

"You okay, Dad?" Stevie asks, carefully extracting herself from the tangle of limbs and blankets. "Are you mad at somebody?"

I go for relaxed but knackered, rubbing a hand down my face. "No, Sass, just tired."

"Are you sure?" She stares at me. "You're doing that face Fizzy says is going to make you need Botox."

I ignore this and try to keep us on task. "Do you have your things together?"

"Because if you are mad," she barrels on, "remember that you told me people aren't the same as fruit. You don't look for new ones if they're bruised." I can ask this child a hundred times to pick up her wet towels or to stop using glitter on my bed, but *this* she retains?

Juno scrunches her nose. "I don't like bruised bananas," she says.

"Well, now I'm tired *and* hungry," I say, putting my hands on Stevie's shoulders and trying to steer her toward the door. "Let's get out of here so we can grab something to eat."

"Fizzy got pizza!" Stevie says, pointing excitedly to the kitchen. "There's a ton left because she always orders too much."

"It is one of my many superpowers," Fizzy agrees, and I feel the way she's staring at me, willing me to look at her, but I just can't. Not after the emotional gut punch of the confessional earlier today.

"I'm good." I shake my keys in my pocket. "Come on, Sass."

"Connor," Fizzy says in this low voice that feels like seduction. It's too familiar, so knowing. "You don't have to rush out. There's tons of food. Come sit for a bit, you had a long day."

"Thank you, but I'm good," I say again.

Juno stands, following Stevie to where she's shoving stuff into her bag. Her little husky voice is hilariously incompatible with whispering: "Is your dad one of the guys dating my Auntie Fizzy on that show?"

I resist the urge to groan, pretending I haven't heard this. With Fizzy's eyes on me, I pull my phone from my pocket and open the first app my thumb finds on the home screen, simply needing something to do. Calculator. I punch in a few random numbers and divide it all by two.

"No." God. Stevie's whisper is just as bad. Under any other conditions, Fizzy and I would be making eye contact and absolutely losing our shit. "He's the producer."

"What does that mean?" Juno asks.

Trying to look very preoccupied, I randomly multiply everything by four and subtract 15.6.

"He makes it," Stevie whisper-yells. "He's the *boss.*"

Thanks, Stevie, but I don't feel like the boss of anything right now. I feel like I'm a weather system, under pressure, about to crack wide open.

"Do they hate each other or like each other?" Juno asks, and my stomach drops.

Before Stevie can field this one, I call out from the doorway. "Squirt, let's go."

Finally, Fizzy climbs from the couch and pads over to me. She's wearing sweats and a Wonderland hoodie and looks like brunch and holiday and post-sex euphoria rolled into human form. My body and brain had already started paving the road ahead together and it's so hard to put the entire operation in reverse. I had already committed.

She tilts her head to meet my gaze, and after a split second of her concerned eye contact, I look back down at my screen.

"Are you . . ." Fizzy comes around to my side and looks down at my screen. "Why are you doing math?"

With a grimace, I slide the phone back into my pocket. "Just fidgeting."

"You're standing here doing math and being grumpy," she says, and the sunshine in her voice makes me want to kiss her once, lick her lip, so sweet.

Finally, Stevie jogs over, grinning up at me. I see the question in her eyes and pour every bit of love into the smile I give her so she knows I'm okay. "Say thank you to Miss Fizzy."

"Thank you, Auntie Fizzy."

Auntie Fizzy.

I smile at Juno as Fizzy kisses Stevie's forehead and then steer my kid out the door. Bad news: this heartache feels like a permanent stain in my thoughts. Good news: only a few more days of this and I never have to see Fizzy again.

forty-four

FIZZY

I stare after Connor and Stevie as they climb into the car, wondering if terse silence is going to be our new vibe from here on out. I have to admit, I don't love it. Turning, I close and lock the door before facing the mess of our girls' night shenanigans. I'm aware that a pair of eyes tracks me across the room when I go to fold up the blankets. Most kids are barely aware of how many grown-ups are in a room, let alone what interpersonal sparks are flying. But Juno Merriam is an incredibly perceptive child, and there is no way I'm getting out of this night without some interrogation.

"Mom said she'd let me watch your TV show when it was done," she says, squinting down at a colorful eraser in her hand as if it requires careful consideration.

Here we go.

"Oh yeah?" I tilt my head for her to follow me into the kitchen. "It's pretty tame. Stevie's watching it. Why's she making you wait?"

She jogs after me and grabs a cookie before I can put the box away in the cupboard. "She wants to see how it all turns out first."

"Her and me both, kiddo."

Juno takes a bite and chews, biding her time like a velociraptor. "So, whoever wins this weekend will be your boyfriend?"

"Only if he and I decide we want that." I pull out a chair at the small kitchen table and practically crumple down. I am suddenly pass-out exhausted.

She sits down across from me and draws spirals on the tabletop with her fingertip. "Do you like the boys that are left?"

"I do . . ." My voice trails off, and the *Just not in that way* follows in a droopy echo.

Juno nods for a few long seconds. "What're their names?"

"Evan and Isaac."

"Do you like one of them more than the other?"

Her very normal question makes me sad again. "Isaac, I guess."

"What's he like?"

"Nice," I say, and look up to the ceiling, thinking. "Attractive." God, pull it together, Felicity. Isaac is an amazing man and you're describing him the way you would a new couch. I look at Juno and take a deep breath, trying to infuse some enthusiasm into my words. "He's a scientist, just like your dad."

"He's a geneticist, too?" she asks, squinting skeptically.

She's smarter than I am. "No, I think he makes robots or makes sure robots don't take over the world or something related to the reason I'm nice to my Alexa."

Juno laughs. "That's not the same thing as genetics, Auntie Fizzy."

I throw a wadded-up napkin at her. She ducks out of the way and the flash of her laughter propels her question out, so sneakily: "Do you think Mr. Prince wants Isaac to win?"

I hold on to my smile, leaning closer. Juno is a worthy sparring partner. Pride and unease battle it out in my pulse. "I don't think Mr. Prince cares who wins as long as the show is successful."

"I think he cares who wins." She goes for broke: "I think he likes you."

"Yeah?"

"Mm-hmm. Like at the concert? I could tell he liked you. He stared at you the whole time."

"That's because I'm fascinating, Juno. Keep up."

She giggles. "I bet he doesn't like seeing other boys on dates with you."

I hum, studying her. She doesn't flinch or shrink at all. "And—okay, you know Aiden R.?" she continues. I nod, because there are, like, four Aidens in her class. "He likes Stevie, and they always sit together at lunch, but today Stevie was assigned to Indonesia for World Cultures Day with Eric, and Aiden was quiet-sad the same way Mr. Prince was tonight."

"Oh yeah? How's that?"

She points to her face. "You know how boys clench their jaw like this?" She does a pretty solid impression. "He was doing that and just, like, ignoring her at lunch. But it wasn't like Stevie had a choice about who she does World Cultures Day with. It's assigned."

"Right," I agree sympathetically. Ugh, this metaphor is pretty great. I redirect: "Who did you get assigned to work with?"

"Kyle Pyun," she says, and gives a vague grimace. "He's really hyper but at least he gets good grades."

"Totally." I lean in, grinning. "Is he cute?"

Juno looks genuinely disgusted. "Auntie Fizzy, we're in fifth grade."

"I'm not asking if you're engaged, Junebug, just whether he's got potential."

"Mom says boys are dumb until high school."

"Wow, that's generous."

"So if Isaac wins," Juno says, doing her own redirection, "does he get money or something?"

"In theory he gets me."

She laughs like this is funny. "Yeah but . . . you know. Like a real prize."

Pressing my lips together, I give her a flat "I get to choose who I'm taking to Fiji, and there's a cash prize for the Hero who wins the most votes, if that's what you mean."

Her eyes are planets. "A trip together?" I nod. "Sleeping in the same room?"

"We can have separate rooms if we want."

Juno's lip curls a little. "Would you want to share a room with him?"

"I'm not averse to sharing a room, but I'm not sure I want to share it with him yet. It will be our decision once we get there."

She nods, looking to the side, thinking. I look down at my phone. It's almost nine. Time for River to come get her and save me from this laser interrogation.

"What if Lucas Ayad was one of the contestants?" she asks.

I playfully scowl at the mention of my favorite Wonderland member. "I mean obviously if Lucas was a contestant and he didn't win fairly, I'd invent a time machine to go back and rig the results."

"We should start a petition to write him in," she says. "Tell everyone to start tagging Lucas Ayad in the votes."

"You just want that so I don't marry Suchin and steal him from you."

Juno beams. "Suchin belongs to me, he just doesn't know it yet."

This kid cracks me up. "How can you talk about Suchin like this but can't even tell me whether World Cultures Day Kyle is cute?"

"Because I actually know Kyle—gross." She leans in now, too. "But what if we vote for Mr. Prince?"

I knew her checkmate was coming, but it still catches me unaware.

"I knew you were up to something, you little shi—" I pull back just in time, correcting to "Silly child," but it doesn't matter. Juno giggles knowingly, all puppies and rainbows in the delighted sound, holding out her hand.

"One dollar, please."

I lean back in my chair, opening the junk drawer and digging for some change. Dropping four quarters into her palm, I say, "I'd rather talk about Lucas and Suchin."

"Because you like Mr. Prince, too?"

"Juno Merriam, mind your business."

"Some of the girls in my class and their moms like Mr. Prince."

Get in line, ladies.

I hum in acknowledgment and make a mental note to tease him about it, then remember he probably doesn't want me to tell him anything. And now I'm sad again.

"My dad says if you want something, it doesn't matter how scared you are, you have to try."

I stare at her, wondering for the one hundredth time where this child came from. "Your dad said that, eh?"

Juno nods. "He said my mom scared him at first. But then he

was more scared of not seeing her again." She smiles at me. "So, if that's how you feel about Mr. Prince or . . . what was his name?"

I stare at her. Juno doesn't forget anything. This sneaky faker is too smart for her own good. "Isaac?"

"Right," she says slyly. She's becoming more like her mother every day. "If that's how you feel about Isaac, then don't let being scared get in the way."

Three sharp knocks land on the front door, not a moment too soon. With one more wry grin at Juno, I push back and stand, walking to the living room.

"You couldn't have arrived three minutes earlier and saved me the Spanish Inquisition?" I ask.

River laughs out a breath. "Oh boy. Better you than me."

"You know once they start outsmarting me, I charge forty-five dollars an hour to babysit."

With her backpack slung onto her shoulder, Juno joins her dad at the door. "Thanks for dinner, Auntie Fizzy."

"Yeah, yeah, I love you, get out of here."

She giggles, leaning into my embrace, and I watch them turn to leave.

But River stops at the edge of the porch. "Hey," he says, uncharacteristically unsure. "I wanted to ask something."

"This sounds ominous." It becomes more so when he bends to Juno, murmuring for her to go wait for him at the curb.

"Is everything with the show okay? With Connor," he clarifies.

"What do you mean?"

"With that other North Star show going up in flames last weekend for the doping scandal, and the producer being fired and—"

"Sorry, wait. What other show?"

He frowns. "I don't watch it, but apparently they have another show that's got all kinds of physical challenges in arenas."

I have a vague memory of Connor mentioning another program they were doing to bring in a younger, male demographic. "Oh, right. *Big Mouth* or *Smash Face* or something."

"*Smash Course*," he says. "I guess the producers were giving a lead contestant performance-enhancing drugs. One of the producers was apparently sleeping with him on the road, too, and it blew up online."

"Oh shit."

"Yeah. The show is being canceled." River reaches up to scratch his neck, adorably uncomfortable putting his nose in anyone else's business. "With everything that happened between you and Connor, I just wanted to make sure he was okay."

It's like a fog has cleared as everything since my confession on Connor's couch suddenly comes into crystalline focus. If North Star has lost one of its two cash cows due to scandal, they'd definitely turn the pressure up on Connor to make sure he's running a tight ship. If word got out that we'd been together, basically making the show a sham, it wouldn't just end his career, it could take down the entire company.

And Connor would be blamed for it all.

forty-five

CONNOR

The penultimate episode of *The True Love Experiment* rakes in the highest prime-time rating for any reality show in nearly a decade. At an early meeting with the entire crew, it's clear that the numbers defy comprehension. If we had champagne in the office at nine in the morning, it would be popping.

As we walk back to my office, Brenna jogs behind me, excitedly telling me about the TikTok trends, the viral edits and reels—and she sends me a few, but I think by now she knows that seeing evidence of the true hysteria online will make the pressure to execute this live finale too intense. It doesn't help that the furor over *Smash Course* hasn't died down. Today's twenty-four-hour news cycle means the public's memory is often short for these sorts of things, but it seems every day a new detail emerges to get people riled up again. It all hits close enough to the situation with Fizzy that one might think it would reassure me that I'm doing the right thing, and make being away from her easier to bear. One would be wrong.

When he arrives just after ten, Blaine is an overstimulated hound, circling continually, making laps around the offices. He's crowing about the little guys showing Hollywood how it's done, about knowing he chose wisely putting me on this and how I should trust him next time. The adulation is bittersweet: Of course I'm thrilled that Fizzy and I managed to create something that has resonated with so many viewers, but the obvious conflict of falling for her is a shadow that lurks behind my celebratory mood. My failed marriage would have been the easiest relationship to maintain—without passion, but convenient and amiable—and yet building something with the one woman I'm truly lost for has proven to be impossible.

Maybe in a few months, I think, after the spotlight has turned away and the world has moved on to the next shiny thing, we can make a go of it. But that isn't how love works. No matter what poetry tells us, love isn't always patient; it is urgent and hungry, eating up all of the blank space in my head.

I escape to the editing room, hoping to drown everything else out and spend the day helping put together the retrospective clips of all the Heroes for the recap portion of the live finale this weekend. But it is in this quiet retreat that Blaine finds me and slaps a piece of paper down on the mixing board.

"Blaine—"

"Contingent on you not shitting the bed," he says, ignoring that he's just inadvertently deleted the clip we were working on, "here's a contract for you to produce and host season two of *The True Love Experiment*."

Sensing the storm brewing, Pat, our editorial producer, pushes back from his computer and makes his escape. "Think I'll go grab a cup of coffee."

The door closes behind him and I peer down at the paper.

I knew it was coming—frankly it would be stupid of us to not green-light a second season—but seeing it in black and white stuns me silent for a moment anyway. I am sure, with the structure we've built, the crew and I could do it again with another Heroine or Hero at the center, and even if it's half as successful as this first season has been, it would be a financial success for the company. And for me.

I just can't imagine doing it with anyone but Fizzy beside me. Not to mention another season keeps me in the public eye and pushes a possible relationship between us even further out of reach.

"Can I think about it?" I ask.

"*Think about it?*" Blaine pokes the third paragraph with an insistent finger, pressing a bunch of buttons underneath it. "Kid, do you see what we're offering you? We're talking more money, more time, more staff, and a bigger production budget."

I do see. What they're offering me is part of the reason I want to consider this carefully.

Gingerly, I guide his hand away and swivel in my seat to face him. "I see the financial incentive, and I know we could do the show again quite easily. But, for as crazy as this might sound—because I know we are absolutely the biggest thing on television right now— money is not the only thing I care about. I enjoyed what I was doing before. I'm not sure I'm ready to abandon the documentary world quite yet."

He waves this off. "Fine. We'll give you the $40K for your ocean thing. You can do one of those and one of these a year. Is that what it will take for you to sign?"

"This wasn't our agreement, Blaine."

"I'm offering you a huge opportunity. You're a natural in this space."

"I just need a moment," I tell him. "It's not a no or a yes, it's a 'let's talk about this after the final episode.'"

Blaine lets out a short laugh and narrows his eyes at me. "I see. Okay. You're angling for more, and I respect that."

"It isn't that. I—"

He winks and slaps my shoulder. "I'll see what I can do."

It takes active focus to shove the thoughts of money and pressure and Blaine and my career and my family and—most of all—Fizzy out of my mind and simply focus on the task in front of me. Between the various cameras, there are over two hundred hours of footage to go through for all the clips and retrospectives we'll need for the finale. It's pretty much an all-hands-on-deck situation. We want to share moments of each Hero being unguarded, unfiltered, and as appealing as each of them is in real life. I feel like we've captured the essence of a handful of truly amazing people—without irony or mockery in our tone—and that feels monumental. Maybe it's this element that has resonated with so many people, the authenticity of it all. I want this last, full episode to be emotional and funny, genuine and inspiring.

But given that we're editing clips of Fizzy or about Fizzy, there's no escape from her. Worse, in front of me are hours and hours of unfiltered proof that she meant what she said: she doesn't want any of these other men. By now I know her smiles, and she gives them ones that are bright and sincere but ultimately platonic. I know her laughs and those, too, are genuine, but the Heroes don't get the one that comes from the depths of her, the round, joyful belly laugh of Fizzy being absolutely lost in the moment. I know her touch, too—fuck, do I know her touch—and while she gives them friendly affection, never is there heat in her fingertips or her gaze. There is nothing overtly sexual about any of it.

We need to edit this reel together, but shit, all I can see is her falling for me. Her eyes flicker to the cameras constantly—looking for my reaction, anticipating some quiet inside joke, or seemingly of their own volition as if when her mind wanders, it wanders to *me*. But that's only what I want to see.

I can't help with this. I'm not objective anymore.

Pulling my headphones off, I toss them down to the mixing board just as Rory steps in.

"All good here?"

I scrub my hands over my face and then nod. "I've lost all fucking objectivity. We've edited the Arjun, Jude, Tex, Colby, and Dax segments for the retrospective. Those are fine. But I'm stalling out on Nick, Isaac, and Evan. Honestly, Ror, I'm having a hard time imagining how we pull this off at the end. Fizzy is great, but am I insane? There's no actual love story here."

Rory stares down at me for a long beat. "You're not seeing it?"

"No."

She looks past me to the frozen image of Isaac laughing on-screen. "Don't worry, bro, it's all there."

"I just don't want to arse it right at the end."

She laughs. "There is no fucking way."

"I'm glad you're so confident."

"I think right now you're just too close to it."

Well, Rory, no shit.

forty-six

FIZZY

Tuesday afternoon, the bell chimes over the door at Twiggs, and everything about it—the force of the chime, the footsteps that follow, the jostling of keys latched to a purse—is so familiar that I know without even looking up who it is.

"Fizzy?" Jess asks.

I don't blame her for the bright surprise in her voice; I'm surprised, too.

I type the end of the sentence and then look up at her, reaching for my latte. "Hello, bestie."

"Hi. What am I seeing? A laptop? Notebooks with frantic scribbling?" Her eyebrows inch up. "Are you . . . writing?"

"I had an idea this morning." In fact, I woke up with a scorching sex scene in my head and thought . . . maybe I'd try to write it down. If I'm being honest, it's a filthy fantasy about Connor's mouth, but the inspiration hit me the way it used to, in this sort of fevered excitement, and I didn't want to let the moment pass me by.

I packed up my laptop, came here, and of course what was clear and perfect in my head on the drive over is a mess of words on the page, but I'm forcing myself to remember that it's okay for a draft to be awful. It's better than nothing, and I've had enough nothing to last a lifetime. Terrible can be edited.

Jess sits down across from me. "That's fantastic."

"No, it's garbage," I say, "but I'm just happy to be typing words that aren't hate mail to myself." I shrug before remembering something. "Oh my God, I eavesdropped on the best conversation today."

She leans in. "Hit me, I've missed gossip."

"These two women were sitting at the front table with the wobbly leg—"

"I hate that table."

"—and one of them said her husband fired the nanny after recognizing her on an escort site."

"Wait," Jess says. "Why was he cruising an escort site?"

"Exactly! Wouldn't that make a great opening for a book? Scumbag husband sees familiar face on an escort site and is too stupid to realize he shouldn't tell his wife? Wife leaves him and falls for the handyman who comes to fix the toilet her ex never got to." I tap my chin, turning the idea around in my head. "Scratch that, make it the roof so he can be shirtless."

I reach over to jot it in my notebook before I forget.

Satisfied, I turn back to Jess. "What are *you* doing here anyway?"

"Working." She winces. "I'm bored at home. River is planning a new start-up with Sanjeev and . . . I miss it. The idea of not working anymore is sort of depressing to me. I didn't get into math for money, I got into it because it's *fun*."

"Maybe we're getting our mojo back?"

She grins. "Fuck, I hope so." The moment lingers, our gazes hugging, and slowly, Jess's smile straightens as, I presume, she reads the shadow in my eyes. "Hey." She reaches across the table and takes my hand. "I'm sorry that things with Connor fell apart. That really sucks about the other show tanking."

I nod. I've got nothing useful to add. It does suck.

"But does it help to know it wasn't just about what happened at the hotel, that there were other things at play?" she asks. "I'm guessing he didn't have much of a choice."

"I guess?" I laugh and it comes out a little watery; I didn't realize I'd gotten teary. "I know this situation is complicated. I know he has different pressures and responsibilities. It's bigger than me and my feelings."

"Look at this character growth. Five stars," she says, grinning. Pushing back to stand, she says, "I'm going to order coffee. Need a refill?"

"I'm good." I'm so close to finishing this terrible document. I'll probably never show it to another human, but it isn't even about that.

Two hours ago, my agent called to let me know she expects several of my backlist titles to hit the bestseller lists this week. Apparently new readers have been discovering my books, and posting photos and hilarious challenges, videos, and reviews. She sent me a few and I laughed through teary eyes as I watched. Writers can work for years and never know how a story will land with an audience. Being reminded that my words really affect readers made me want to get back to it immediately. Book people are just better, I swear by it. She also scolded me for avoiding her calls (valid), but said that she cares about *me* first, and if I never want to write another book, that's fine. I won't be letting her down, and she won't take it personally. I have to do what's best for me. Four months ago, the idea of hearing that would have been a relief, a weight lifted, but the moment Amaya said I could quit if I wanted, all I felt was a devastating bleakness.

It made me realize I'm not ready to give up writing. I did the show to find myself, not for fame, and if I have to give up Connor, I want to at least hold on to what makes me *me*. And what I am is a writer. So even if every word in this doc is garbage, I'm not quitting.

And tomorrow, I will put on my mental blinders and sit down and try to make a diamond out of a hunk of coal. Because tomorrow, I will do everything I can not to think about Connor and the show and how in just over four days I will be expected to embark on a trip with a man who isn't the man I want.

When my phone buzzes on the table, my immediate hope is that it's him. I need to work on that. But then it buzzes again. And again. I turn it over and my heart takes off in a gallop for a very different reason. It's a text from Alice.

Fizzy.

Fizzy oh my god

Meet us at the hospital

I'm in labor

Everyone says newborns are ugly, that they look like grumpy old men or tiny, unfurled leaves. They're wrinkled and red-faced; fuzzy and grouchy. They do nothing but sleep and eat and cry and poop.

That might be true for other babies, but at only six hours old, Helena Ying Kwok is already, hands down, the most beautiful and entertaining human ever to grace this planet. Baby Lena—I chose the nickname—has her mother's tiny button nose and her father's permafrown. She has her maternal grandmother's full lips, her paternal grandfather's long neck, and her maternal grandfather's gassiness. But the dimple in her left cheek is all mine. This one is going to be a rascal. From this moment forward, I have no choice but to lay down my life for her.

Petting her tiny fist, I gently uncurl her tight little fingers, kissing each one. The sweet crescent moons of her fingernails are a miracle. My heart is too small for these feelings; the sense of choking on happiness, of drowning in it, hits me every few breaths. "I'm your Auntie Fizzy," I whisper. "I will never let you suffer an ill-fitting bra. I'll tell you when you have food in your teeth. I'm the one you come to when you need clothing advice or spending money. I only ask that you let me vet every person you want to date."

"Okay, okay. Give her back."

I make a strangled, infatuated noise and pass her back into Alice's outstretched arms. I've been in this room for just over forty-eight hours and am going on roughly three hours of sleep, but I've never felt more energized. Alice, though, looks like she's about to drop.

Labor was intense. My sweet baby sister spent twenty-six hours pacing the room in early labor before fifteen hours of active labor and an epidural that didn't take. An obstetrician himself, her husband, Henry, was on the verge of insisting the doctor wheel her in for a C-section, but as if little Helena heard her daddy and decided enough was enough, she came out with one more push, bright-eyed and with only a tiny, shocked cry of protest. She's not even a day old, but already the room is packed with people and flowers, gifts and balloons.

Mom comes up behind me, sliding her arms around my waist from behind, and we peer together at baby Lena in Alice's arms.

"She is perfect," Mom whispers.

"She redefines the word *perfection*," I agree.

"I remember holding you," she says, "and this new feeling pushing everything else away. I had everything I needed in that moment. It's still like that, every time I look at you."

Bittersweet warmth threads through me. I never feel so loved as when I'm with my family . . . and I hate knowing I might never give my mother this magnitude of a gift: a grandchild, someone else to love unconditionally in the way only she can.

But being the mother she is, she already knows what I'm thinking. She turns me to face her. "You were perfect then, too, and you are perfect now."

Eyes watery, I laugh. "You are not a credible source."

"I am the *only* credible source. I've known you every second of your life."

I have no walls left up to hold things in. I clutched my screaming sister's hand for the past day, watched her experience brutal pain and blinding joy. With nearly everyone I love packed into this room, crowding around Alice and Henry and Helena, I feel stripped down, a live wire. "I might never do what Alice just did," I remind Mom. "I might never even get married. I might never write the kind of book you want me to write. I might always be exactly like this."

"So?"

"So?" I repeat. "So I don't want to disappoint you."

Mom cups my face in her hands. "You look in the mirror and see all of the ways you are letting me down. I look at you and see everything I've ever wanted you to be. That admiration is where expectations come from, dai leu, not from disappointment. And if I want something for you, like marriage or a baby, it's because these things have made me happier than anything else in life. You spend so much time working to make other people happy, and all I care about is that *you* are happy."

The way these words drag Connor's face front and center in my mind's eye is startling. He is, without question, the current seat of my happiness, and if there is anything about the show ending that makes me sad, it's the reality that I won't see him every day.

And then a new jarring thought crashes in.

"Mom," I ask, "what day is it?"

She blinks at me, confused. "Thursday."

I look at the clock. It's a quarter to five in the evening and if it is indeed Thursday, then I am an hour away from the wrap party that begins in fifteen minutes.

I lean over Alice, kissing her forehead. "I'll be back later tonight."

"Where are you going?" she asks without taking her eyes off her newborn.

"Wrap party."

Finally, Alice turns her dark, tired eyes to me. "Tell him you love him."

I've started to turn, but pause at her words. "What?"

"You know what I'm talking about."

I stare at her. I haven't talked about Connor with anyone but Jess, too worried about it getting out, too worried about stressing out my pregnant sister, too worried about my show already outshining my brother's wedding, too worried that the show was yet another embarrassing stain on my résumé as far as my family was concerned. But in the end, the people who love you see through all the subterfuge anyway.

"It's not that simple," I tell her. "I wish it were, but it isn't just about me."

"Even so." My exhausted sister lifts her hand. I lean forward, like she might cup my cheek. Instead, she lightly slaps it. "Say it anyway."

forty-seven

CONNOR

For all her outward chaos, Fizzy is always on time. This punctuality, in fact, was the first hint I had that much of her "hot mess" persona is only an act. The second hint was the highly detailed list of terms her team sent me, and ever since then I've only ever known her to be entirely dependable. So the fact that she is forty-five minutes late to the wrap party has me worried.

And apparently, I'm not the only one. Brenna materializes at my side, her gaze fixed on the stairs leading up to the space we've booked at Stone Brewery for tonight's event. The crew mills about, sipping drinks, nibbling food, chatting. But even though we've all been here long enough to be loud and a little rowdy, there's an undeniable vibe that the party hasn't yet started.

"Where is she?"

I shake my head. "Dunno."

"Have you texted her?"

"I haven't," I say. And I haven't, but not for any good reason. At least, not for any reason I can tell my assistant. I haven't texted Fizzy because the longer she fails to appear, the more I grow worried something bad has happened to her, and the longer I put off knowing exactly what it is, the longer I can maintain my life as I know it, with sanity intact.

I become aware that Brenna has leaned over to get a good look at me at the same time I register I'm staring at the stairs up to our party space like a sniper tracking a target. Inhaling sharply, I bring my pint glass to my lips.

"You okay?" she asks.

"Fine."

"You look a little tense."

"No."

"You sure?"

"Yep."

"Okay, cool, because I think I just saw her walking through the restaurant."

I bolt forward, reaching the railing in two long strides, curling one hand around the wrought iron and staring down into the busy restaurant. Almost immediately, I spot her messy bun and her bright smile as she bobs through the crowd near the bar. Everything inside me unclenches; adrenaline washes through me, hot and frantic. As Fizzy weaves through the room, she's stopped by a woman wanting to take a picture with her.

"She's safe," Brenna says, again having materialized silently at my side.

"What? Of course she is," I mumble distractedly, frowning down at where two men approach, waiting for their turn. They stand far too close.

"It's just," she says, tapping the back of my hand with the tip of her finger, "you're gonna break that railing."

I loosen my grip but don't take my eyes off what's happening in the bar below. Not that I should worry; Fizzy is nothing if not self-sufficient. When they catch her attention, she lets them take a photo and then politely but firmly shakes her head at whatever they ask next, pointing to the stairs. I track her the entire time she jogs up to us.

As she steps into view, everyone turns and a roaring cheer begins and then sort of . . . tapers off as we take in her appearance. It's not a formal party—this isn't the kind of event with fancy champagne flutes being carried on trays or the expectation of cocktail attire. Even so, casual Fizzy is usually more polished than most of us at our best. Today her hair isn't just in a messy bun, it looks slept on and tangled. Her clothes look slept in, too. She looks tired and pale. Concerned murmurs shimmer across the group.

That is, until a smile breaks across her face like the sun rising, and she shouts, *"I am an auntie!"*

The cheers break out anew, a roar really, and everyone rushes forward to surround her. Fizzy disappears in the circle of bodies and I try to soak this moment in because I've been in the business long enough to know that not every crew is this tight, not every project is this magical, and when this type of chemistry exists, it's something to be treasured. But I also know that the magic is *her*, that she's taken this group of strangers and built a family. Isaac is here, Evan is here, yes—but so are Dax and Nick, Jude and Colby. Contestants who have been eliminated have come back because even if they aren't on the show anymore, they're still part of this thing that we all created.

I watch Fizzy hug everyone, show photos of the newborn on her phone, and the impulse to burst forward and monopolize her time takes an unexpected back seat to the pride I feel watching her command the room and be so adored. Maybe there is a way for us, after everything ends. Maybe it won't be a scandal if we come together in a few months; maybe us falling in love won't tank the credibility of a second season of the show. I know it isn't true, but I yearn for her with a tight, simmering ache, this slight, scrappy, ball-busting woman who has my heart and my mind and my entire fucking body wrapped around her smallest finger.

forty-eight

FIZZY

I know Connor is over there. I can feel him watching, like a proud dad in the background rather than the mastermind behind all of this. I want him to wade in, find his way into the middle of this affectionate scrum. Doesn't he know that the only reason all of this worked so well is because of him? It was his vision. His competent energy and relaxing presence, his hands-on management of the entire crew, and his spot-on casting. Not to mention his hot-as-sin self and the unexpected hit of having him interview us all in the confessional trailer.

But with my emotions at an eleven, and my adrenaline so high it feels like a strobe light inside my veins, maybe now is not the time for Connor to approach. I think Alice is right, and maybe this really will be my last chance to tell him that I love him no matter what the outcome is on Saturday, but I know myself. In my current state of mind, I'll lose my cool and tell him I know about North Star, and fuck anyone who thinks they get a say in what we do.

Which is exactly why he didn't tell me in the first place.

But there are two important conversations I realize I *do* need to have tonight, and both are with the men I won't be able to contact between now and Saturday. One of them will win, and I suspect it's going to be Isaac, but if it isn't, I have to manage Evan's expectations, too. I'm down for a trip to Fiji with either of them, but in each scenario, I will be sleeping alone.

I'd have every eye in this place tracking me if I head straight for them, so I spend some time talking to everyone. Dax and I make plans to grab dinner—just for fun, he insists, totally platonic—once all of this chaos has settled down. Jude informs me that he understood the Volterra joke and just didn't find it to be all that funny.

"That's okay, Judie," I say with a smile. "There's no accounting for taste."

Colby mansplains how he wasn't actually mansplaining things to me in the kitchen, but after we laugh about it, I sense that being away from the cameras results in a much more relaxed Colby. Everyone has their guesses about who will win, who *should* win, and whether either of the two remaining men is my true Gold Match.

It's an unseasonably chilly evening and most everyone is inside, getting drunker and louder and sloppily nostalgic and affectionate. I know I'm breaking the rules by drawing Isaac outside alone onto the patio, but he comes eagerly, with a note of relief in his expression.

"Do you want my jacket?" he asks, motioning to take it off.

I shake my head, zipping up my hoodie. "Thanks, though. I still feel a little flushed and high from the excitement of being crowned World's Best Auntie overnight."

"I bet," he says with a laugh, resting his folded arms on the railing and looking out over the beer garden. "I remember when my little sister had her first baby. I never *got* babies before, you know?"

He looks at me. "Didn't get what the big deal was. But it's different when it's one you're related to."

"I've always loved kids, but this feeling is next level. It's wild to have someone so tiny who belongs to me this way. I don't want to mess it up."

He laughs. "You won't."

We fall quiet and it's weird being with him all alone. Other than our CVS moment, we've never been alone; truthfully, we don't even know each other that well. Other shows have the contestants living together, spending hours and hours in forced proximity. Some shows even give them privacy to sleep together. I love that this show has been different, love that it relies on personalities and energies in a way that matters in the real world, but I also think there are things about getting to know someone behind closed doors that bring out real chemistry. I wonder if Isaac and I would have worked had we met by chance.

He turns his head, resting his chin on his shoulder to look at me beside him. "I know why I'm out here, by the way."

Mimicking his posture, I ask, "Do you?"

"Mm-hmm." He smiles. "I want you to know, I'm cool with it."

"With what?"

"This—us—not working out, even if I win."

"Why do you think that's what I'm going to say?"

He stands and turns so he's leaning back against the railing, facing me. "Come on, Fizz. You've obviously been holding back."

I allow this with a nod, studying him. "Why do I sense that you are, too?"

Isaac takes a deep breath and turns his face up to the sky. "About three days after we filmed the first date, I got a text from my high school girlfriend. She'd moved back to the area."

Relief is warm and golden coursing through me. "Ah."

"We haven't seen each other yet. I'm not about to break the rules." He laughs. "But we've been texting and, yeah. I feel like it could be something, you know?"

"That's amazing, Isaac."

"So, if I'm right, and you are holding back, I wanted to say that it's okay." I nod. "And if I'm wrong, and you're feeling real things here, I wanted to be up front. Don't need you getting hurt." He reaches forward, sending his thumb gently along my cheekbone. "You're honestly one of the coolest people I've ever met. This is probably the only woman alive who could keep me from going after you with everything I've got."

He's put it perfectly. I like Isaac so much. In a parallel universe where there was no Connor, Isaac might be perfect for me. "I totally get it," I say.

"I know you do."

"What's happening, my homies?"

Isaac and I turn to see Evan walking out with three full pint glasses balanced in his hands. He passes one off to Isaac, one to me, and then lifts his in a toast. "To my very long shot of winning this thing, and to the most beautiful woman I've ever dated."

We all laugh, clinking glasses, and take a sip. I swipe away the foam from my upper lip. "I think the two of you are probably neck and neck."

"No way." Evan quickly swallows a sip to disagree with me. "He's gonna win, and I want you to know, it's okay."

"Evan—"

"No, really, Fizz. We had our shot and it didn't work out. I'm glad I got you back in my life again. And that I lasered off that terrible tattoo. Goldschläger is the devil's sauce," he says by way of explanation, and lifts his beer for another toast. "Whatever happens, it's been a crazy ride."

Inside, Connor is easy to find because he's a giant surrounded by a group of his adoring fans—I mean the crew, but let's be honest, everyone is at least eighty percent in love with him. As if he senses that I've walked back inside, his eyes immediately meet mine across the room. I cannot ignore the way they go all soft and relieved, like he didn't relish letting me out of his sight.

Or maybe that's the hope talking.

I do my best to temper that hope. I hurt him, and even if Connor decides he can trust me with this again, rational Fizzy knows that doesn't really change anything. If Connor was warned not to fuck things up, then that's still going to be true tomorrow, and next week, and three months from now, because the magnifying glass we're under due to the show's popularity suggests no sign of letting up. In the end I must allow that maybe it's for the best that we didn't sleep together again, because I very likely would have figured out a way to drag him and his big ring finger and big dick all the way to Vegas to make it official.

Squaring my shoulders, I ready myself for what is probably a hard conversation, and tilt my head to the side so he knows I want to talk to him in private. With a little nod, he bends to say something to the two women he's talking to, and tracks my movement across the room, into the far corner where an empty table sits in the shadows.

I sit with my back to the wall, watching him as he walks toward me. It's so strange to have experienced these feelings only by writing them, never in reality. When I say that my heart aches and feels like it's being stretched in opposite directions by two fists, I realize now that isn't hyperbole. Love hurts.

He sits across from me, setting his half-finished beer down on the table. "Hi."

I take a moment to reply with the same greeting because there are so many other words at the surface pushing forward. Finally, I go with a safe "Hey."

"What's up?"

I decide to cut to the chase: "I heard about *Smash Course*."

His eyelid twitches, jaw ticks. "Yeah?"

"Yeah. I'm sorry. Things must be stressful for everyone over at North Star."

He nods, lifting his beer and frowning down at it. "It's been rough, yeah, thanks." Connor takes a long drink.

"Since we aren't going to see each other like this anymore, and it would probably be unprofessional to call you after the show airs on Saturday, I had a few things I wanted to say."

"Fizzy," he says, leaning forward on his forearms.

But I hold up a hand. "I'm not asking you to change your mind. I get it. But I've never been able to deliver a romantic declaration be-fore, and the last time I tried—at your house—it was interrupted by your rejection. So I just want to get it off my chest, because I think it will feel good." I raise my eyebrows at him. "Is that okay?"

He nods, swallowing heavily. It draws my focus to the long line of his neck, and I watch the flush crawl from beneath the collar of his shirt and up to his jaw.

"I love you," I say to his neck, and finally manage to drag my gaze to his. His fresh-leaf eyes are in shadow; he's backlit with the room behind him, but even so, I can see the way they flicker back and forth between mine, searching. "I have never, not once in my life, felt this way for anyone. When you were getting ready to cast the show, and you asked me what I wanted in a partner, I said I wanted someone who cares about the right things, who is good and works hard, who doesn't take himself too seriously. You are all those things and more. You are kind, and hardworking. You are patient, and honest, and loyal. I admire you so much."

He stares at me so intently, and I know him well enough to know that he won't interrupt me, won't crash across the table to kiss me senseless even if that's secretly what I want. I love that he's respectful even if I crave being disrespected by him, and only him.

"I also said I wanted someone that I was just fucking hot for," I say, "and I've never wanted someone the way I want you."

He swallows again, only now breaking eye contact and staring down at his beer.

"I won't detail that," I tell him, "because we're in public and I also realize that it's not cool to have one-sided verbal sex with someone who has explicitly said that he does not want to be with me."

Connor laughs a little at this, turning his heated gaze back up to mine. There's a challenge there. Hope translates it as *I don't recall ever saying that I didn't want to be with you.*

"But I'm saying that I love you," I continue, "because I sometimes think we as a society hold too many things back. We're afraid of being vulnerable or rejected, we're scared that we're weird or say things that no one else thinks. And that's okay. I'm not scared of that with you. I *know* I'm being rejected, I *know* I'm weird, and I know for a fact that no one else thinks exactly what I'm thinking right now because no one knows you the way I do. No one loves you in this exact, perfect, consuming way."

"Fizzy," he says quietly, his fingers twitching on the table. Carefully, he reaches one hand forward and brushes his fingertips over the back of my hand.

"So, when you're home later, and feeling however you feel about this conversation—whether it's grossed out, happy, sad, or confused—I just want you to know that there is someone on this planet who loves you unconditionally and deeply because of who you are and how you carry yourself. I'm so glad to have known you, Connor."

He looks down again, taking a slow, deep breath. "I don't know what to say right now."

"I know. That was a lot. You don't have to—"

"No," he says quickly. "I mean, there is so much I'd *like* to say, and I'm not sure how to articulate any of it."

I bite my lips, willing myself to not speak over him.

"If you know what happened with *Smash Course*," he says slowly, "then I presume you understand why I had to continue to stay away."

Hope flares alive, hot and thrashing behind my ribs. "Yes."

Connor looks at me quizzically. "I expected you to tell me it's all bollocks."

"It *is* bollocks," I say. "But you get to choose how you handle it. You clearly knew that I wouldn't care what Blaine or anyone else has to say about it, and you made the decision that's best for you. How can I be upset about that?"

He looks at me, surprised.

"Don't you get it, Connor?" I say. "I'm telling you I love you. I want what's best for you, even if that isn't me."

Connor opens his mouth to reply but Brenna approaches behind him. I cut him off. "Brenna's coming over."

Turning in his seat, Connor smiles at her. "What's up?"

She looks shaken. "Do you have a second?"

"Join us." I pat the seat beside me.

But she shakes her head. "Sorry, I—I think I need to cover this one with Connor solo." She lowers her voice to him. "We have the results."

I lean in. "*My* results?"

Neither of them looks at me, but Brenna nods at him. "I want—" she says, and then gives a shaky smile. "You and Rory will need to figure out the edit plan, that's all."

"Oh, right." Connor turns back to me.

I try to read the forecast in his expression. "Is everything okay?"

"Everything's fine." His smile is only a flicker across his lips. "We need to finish this conversation, but can we do it another time?"

This entire change in vibe has me jittery and uncomfortable. "Yeah, totally." I stand.

"Fizzy," Connor says.

"All good." I move around him, but he stops me with his hand on my forearm.

"I mean it. We need to finish this."

I nod but don't say anything else. It would come out strangled and broken anyway. I'm glad I told him everything I wanted to say, but I don't feel better the way I expected to. If anything, I feel worse, especially with the prospect of truly *finishing this* to look forward to.

forty-nine

FIZZY

I'm not surprised that I don't hear from Connor before the live finale begins, but I would be lying if I said the last day and a half wasn't lonely and stressful. Everyone in my life assumed I'd be busy with something or someone else, but in reality, I was alone in my living room, eating ice cream out of the gallon container, replaying my conversation at Stone with Connor over and over, and watching old episodes of *Breaking Bad* to feel better about my life. Sure, I confessed my love to a man for the third time without any reciprocation, but at least I don't have a dead body in the bathtub upstairs.

I dutifully show up at the television studio downtown at noon on Saturday for hair and makeup, and hold out hope that I'll get a glimpse of Connor at some point—even from across the room, I'm not greedy—let alone some time to speak to him in private. But if he's in the building with us, I never see him.

I do see Brenna, Liz, Isaac, Evan, and all of the Heroes who've been voted off but will return for the reunion portion of the show. We're ushered around from room to room, being powdered and coiffed and prepped for the interview. Being in the studio feels like we've leveled up in importance; gone is our cozy little coffee shop, sweet dates in the park, and the illusion that what we're doing here is some small indie production. This is big. Somehow, even with the new followers, being stopped in public, bestseller lists, and calls for interviews, I never quite comprehended just *how* big this has gotten. There are security guards who walk us from trailer to studio. The entire building hums with energy, and a line of people hoping for tickets to the live finale wraps around several city blocks.

I'm given four choices for outfits, but the truth is, I don't really care what I'm wearing. I feel oddly numb as I step into the dressing room and pull on the red A-line dress I know my mother will love, because I realize that facing my life after this isn't going to be easier. I did this show for some sort of jump start, inspiration, a change of perspective. I found something new inside me—the feeling of genuine love and passion—but unattended, I already feel it turning into a sharp spur in my thoughts, souring. In all of my visions for the show, never did I come out of it sadder than I was before.

From our prepping, we're told that the run of show will go a little something like this: The Heroes will be interviewed as a group, with short videos shown for each of them. After this, I'll be brought out to talk about my experiences with them. Finally, the audience vote will be revealed, followed by the DNADuo scores. The winner will be crowned and he'll pick me up in a fireman's carry to take me out of the building and aboard the plane to Fiji.

I might have fictionalized that last part a bit.

Brenna sets me up offstage so I can watch the first portion from the wings as well as on a monitor nearby. From the other side of the set, the men file in to roaring applause, and Lanelle gives a brief introduction to the show, how it started, how it grew in popularity beyond anything we ever imagined.

Inside my chest, my heart feels like a wind-up toy cranked too tight.

Nick, Dax, Colby, Jude, Arjun, and Tex are seated on the long couches on either side of Lanelle's chair, with Isaac and Evan in the positions closest to her.

"These eight Heroes were invited to join the show and date the much-beloved romance novelist Felicity Chen." Cheers rise again, and I peek out, trying to find Jess, River, Juno, and my family out in the dark mass of bodies. "The goal was not to pull them out of their day-to-day lives but to see who clicked, who connected . . . and who didn't. Every week, you—the audience—voted on which Hero you believed was Fizzy's soulmate. And tonight, we've assembled the entire cast to discuss their experiences, their hopes, and most of all, their thoughts on *The True Love Experiment!*"

The theme song plays, there's a vaguely cheesy light show, and they cut to the first commercial. When we return, the segment opens with a montage reel introducing each of the Heroes' archetypes and showing them in their daily lives, on the show, and talking about meeting me. There are wolf whistles when we see a clip of Colby doing shirtless pull-ups, some laughter as Arjun gets his shoes polished by a street vendor, fangirl screams when Dax launches himself out of an airplane, and the sound pitches higher when the video transitions to a clip of Isaac walking down the hall with a piece of robotic equipment I'm sure they had him hold as a prop so he would appear very Hot Nerdy.

The audience laughs as Dax exits the café after our first meeting and exhales a breathless "Holy [bleep], she's sexy."

I clap a hand over my mouth, holding back a cackle.

"Fizzy has this aura, you know?" Nick says in the video. "Confident, strong, grounded. But [long bleep], she's hot."

More laughter, and then it doubles when Arjun says: "Yeah, I don't think we connected."

The audience cheers when Isaac appears. "Fizzy is the kind of woman a man could wait his whole life for and never meet. You look at her and think, 'Damn, she's fine,' and then you start a conversation and realize she's got you running in circles and you didn't even realize it."

"I knew even when we first dated that she was something special," Evan says. "A word of advice: don't get a Bart Simpson tattoo."

The crowd roars. The video makes me feel this tight tangle of emotions high in my throat. Why couldn't I fall for one of them?

When the footage ends, Lanelle waits for the applause to die down before she comes in for the salacious part of the show.

She asks the Heroes who were eliminated early vaguely cutting questions with a smile—didn't Tex think it was a bit sexist to ask me what my father thought of my romance career? Why did Colby think the audience voted him off? Did Arjun watch his episode, and how did he feel he came across?

But then she dials up the charm with Dax and Nick, flirting shamelessly, asking them whether they'd change anything they did or said on the show, whether they think they'd do a show like this again. And then there's a surprise announcement: both Dax and Nick will be back as the leads in the second season.

"Holy shit," I murmur to myself. "Holy *shit!*"

I wonder whether Connor is producing it, or if he's free now. If he can do exactly what he wants without fear of losing his job and his life in San Diego. I want to ask him, but I have no idea what happens after tonight.

"Hi," a deep whisper comes from right behind me, and I startle, clapping a hand over my mouth and turning. I'd given up thinking I would see Connor at all tonight, assuming he was watching all of this up in some bird's-eye-view editorial suite. The instinct to throw my arms around his neck is strong, but even stronger is the desire to drink in the sight of him. His hair is soft and falls across his forehead, but he's wearing a crisp black suit with a thin black tie. He looks soft and devilish, cuddly and powerful. He is everything in one man, every hero right in front of me, and it takes all my willpower not to uselessly declare my love for a fourth time.

"That's amazing about Dax and Nick!"

He nods. "I think so, too."

"Are you EP again?"

"I haven't decided." His voice is steady, but there's something in his eyes, some tightness that I've never seen before.

I step a little closer. "You okay?"

"Yeah." He tugs at his shirtsleeve in his suit jacket, smooths his hands down his chest, then over his hair. Fidgety Connor is a surreal sight. He glances at me and away. "You?"

"I would say I'm comparatively chill. What's with you?"

"Finale," he says simply. "Just nervous."

"Everything is going great," I tell him. "Haven't you been watching?"

"Yeah—just—" Connor sucks a deep, jagged breath and then blows it out. "The hard part is coming."

I turn to face him fully and set my hand on his chest. This, I know: "Everything is going to be amazing," I promise him. "You don't have anything to worry about. I will not let you down."

He nods, and his gaze falls to my mouth, drifting unfocused.

My heart decides to evaporate from my body.

"Whatever happens," I whisper, forcing the words out, "we did this spectacular, brilliant, once-in-a-lifetime thing together, and I will never regret it. I will never regret *you*."

Before the words are fully out of my mouth, he's already leaning down, lips on mine, warm and urgent, his hands cupping my face. Surprise pulls a cry from my throat, but my instincts send tight, possessive fists to the lapels of his jacket, and I stretch up onto my toes, eager for his mouth, desperate for the addicting balance of domination and tenderness in his touch. I don't know what this is, but I'm no fool. I'll take anything this man will give me.

With a quiet groan, Connor tilts his head, deepening the contact into a decadent slide, sending a hungry hand down my body, cupping the curve of my ass, and pulling me tightly against him. The other threads fingers into my hair until he's holding the back of my head and pouring everything he has into the kiss. It is the perfect balance of soft and hard, wet with teasing licks and sucks. He catches my bottom lip between his teeth, drags slowly away, and I chase the contact, but he stops me, pressing his thumb over my lips.

He stares at his finger, conflicted, before sliding it away for a final, lingering kiss.

"Connor."

"You're right," he says.

"About what?"

But applause breaks out in a blast of sound behind me. We are back from commercial and that's my light cue illuminating overhead.

Connor turns me bodily, gently pushing me forward, and in a daze, I walk onstage—hair mussed, lipstick gone—to find out who I'm meant to spend the rest of my life with.

fifty

FIZZY

The roar of the audience feels like a hive of bees inside my head. I glance out, trying to gauge how many people are here, but the stage lights are blinding. I can't see anything.

What just happened?

Did Connor just kiss me goodbye?

The set has been restructured, with a love seat inserted beside Lanelle's chair, and the two sofas with all the Heroes put off to the side, one next to what I presume is my love seat, and the other behind, on a riser so they sit in two rows of four. I presume whoever wins the audience vote will come sit beside me, but the moment I sit down alone on the two-seater, I feel weirdly exposed and self-conscious.

My lips still tingle from the fever of Connor's mouth.

I have a couple of minutes to get myself together as the video montage of my life plays; in the darkness, a SWAT team of hair and makeup artists rushes in to fix the damage. On-screen, I'm shown writing (LOL), jogging (there's a lone cackle from the front row; I'll discuss that with you later, Jessica Marie Peña), and body surfing in Pacific Beach (welp, that's quite a wedgie). God, in hindsight, why didn't I say no to any of these ideas! An accurate portrayal of my life would be me double-dipping tortilla chips into a giant bowl of guacamole with *Crash Landing on You* playing on the television for the seventieth time and my laptop gathering dust in the corner. But I guess that doesn't scream Heroine material.

When the video ends, we cover what we already know: that I previously dated Evan and hated his tattoo; that Arjun and I had no chemistry; that Tex and Jude rubbed me the wrong way; that Dax and I looked like we wanted to eat each other but didn't actually have that much in common; and that I had great chemistry with Nick, Isaac, and Evan.

We all banter, we all bicker playfully. We break for commercial, and while everyone is joking and chatting, I feel my pulse start to climb. We're almost there. Almost there. Odds are good I'm going to puke on live television.

I want to be done with this, but also never want it to end. I don't know how to maintain a relationship with Connor after the show is over, or even whether I should. It's weird to be thirty-seven but only now learning how to do this: confess my feelings, go after who and what I want in my romantic life, manage rejection. I never expected to be the kind of person to have a hard time letting go.

The lights rise, signaling we're back. My palms are sweaty and I resist the urge to wipe them on my dress because I'm sure it would be very obvious that I'm freaking the hell out right now. We're going to find out the audience vote. We're going to find out our scores. We're going to find out the name of my soulmate.

But then Lanelle surprises me.

"Well, the eight of you weren't the only Heroes with ardent fans," she says. "There was also the surprise fan favorite; isn't that right, Fizzy?"

The crowd goes insane.

I blink, caught off guard, but manage to recover. "I assume you're talking about the hot producer, Connor Prince III?"

Lanelle laughs. "That's exactly who I mean. Before we get to the big reveals, let's spend a little time with the mastermind behind this show. Connor, come on out."

If I thought the audience was loud before, it's nothing compared to the greeting he gets. The reaction to the Heroes was cheering; this is cheering mixed with pockets of outright *screaming*, the kind of high-pitched hysteria I last heard at the Wonderland concert.

Connor steps onstage with a shy smile, all six foot five of him managing to look humble, and I am a real idiot because only now do I realize the other spot on this love seat is for him.

The entire time he walks across the stage toward me, his gaze is fixed on mine.

He sits down and smiles over at me. "Hi."

His long, muscular thigh is pressed along mine, and not to be dramatic, but it is the most erotic sensation of my entire life.

"Hi, yourself," I say, plummeting deeper into this intense eye-contact thing we're doing. "I didn't know we got to embarrass you on live television."

Connor's green eyes twinkle. "I had to give you one last go of it before the season ended."

Lanelle cuts in. "This is the chemistry we're talking about," she says, gesturing to us. "Fizzy, I heard that the only reason Connor did the confessionals was because you put it in the contract?"

"In a sense," I say, still smiling at him. "On our first day of filming, I told him I'd walk if he didn't do it."

Lanelle frowns dramatically. "That's pretty extreme."

"It's also a lie," Connor says, laughing. "She's only saying that so she looks tough."

"Let me have this!" I playfully shove him, and the audience breaks out into laughter. "He never lets me get away with anything."

"In all sincerity, the lesson here is for me to never doubt Fizzy," Connor says, and the audience *Awwwwws*.

"But listen," Lanelle says. "The two of you really had an amazing connection on-screen."

Unease thrums beneath my skin. I don't want her to put Connor on the spot like this. "A corpse would have chemistry with this man, Lanelle. Be serious."

The Connor fangirls in the audience scream.

"No, no, this is something special. Take a look." She gestures to the screen, where a montage of photos begins and takes my breath away: Connor and me on set, huddled around a monitor; the two of us side by side at the café that first week, him holding his iced coffee for me, letting me drink from his straw. One where I'm feeding him a bite of pasta at a crew lunch break; another where I'm standing behind him making a screwball face and bunny ears while Connor and Rory stare at something on a clipboard.

I look over at him, wondering what the hell this is, what is going *on*, but he's smiling giddily up at the screen and doesn't turn at the pressure of my attention on his face.

Then the screen cuts to a photo we asked a passerby to take of us at the Broad—

My heart army-crawls up my throat, seeking emotional cover.

—then a selfie at *The Rocky Horror Picture Show*, then to me screaming as I dangle from a harness at the climbing gym and Connor laughs his ass off with his two feet planted safely on the floor. There's a photo of the day we each tried to eat tacos on set in one bite (he won), and another from when he lifted me upside down and carried me to the confessional trailer because I was being too chatty with Liz and Brenna. There's a moment I don't even remember where I'm watching footage from the day's shoot and Connor is behind me, both hands on my shoulders. When the slideshow cuts to an image of the two of us with Juno and Stevie just before the Wonderland concert started, the crowd's cheering takes on a different tenor. Reality is setting in for them—and for me.

They're watching us fall in love.

The girls' faces aren't blurred out, meaning Nat, Jess, and River had to have given permission for this to be shown, and I feel my shock spread into a canyon of confusion inside me. What's happening? I look out into the audience, searching for where I know they'll be, right up front, but it's a mass of darkness. My pulse is gunfire in my throat, relentless.

"A real friendship," Lanelle says as the screen stills on a photo of me laughing hysterically in Balboa Park and, just to the side, Connor gazing at me with unmasked adoration. "Some fans even thought the *real* love story was right here."

The audience bursts into screaming cheers. A lone woman's voice rises out of the dark theater, "Kiss her, Daddy Prince!"

I turn to look at Connor, who slowly turns to meet my gaze.

Lanelle asks, "Do you know how many fans the two of you have online?"

It takes a beat before I realize she's asking me. I break my gaze from his, turning in slow motion back to Lanelle, shaking my head. My cranium weighs seven thousand pounds. "I'm not supposed to track the show's activity online, and frankly it was a good excuse not to go on Twitter at all." A ripple of amusement spreads through the room.

"Connor? What did you make of all of this?"

"Well, obviously I didn't plan to be in front of the camera." He swipes a hand over the top of his soft hair. "I admit it's not where I'm most comfortable."

A chorus of sympathetic coos drifts out from the audience.

"But Fizzy was right," he says, holding up his hands as if defending me. "It worked. It was *fun*, wasn't it?" He turns to look at me, and his eyes drop to my mouth. "Everyone knows it. Fizzy is smart, and funny, and makes everyone feel good." He exhales slowly. "She is the best mood."

The crowd absolutely loses its shit over this, and I gaze at him like *No, seriously, what are you* doing?

"I barely go on social media," he says to me as if we're the only people in the room. "But even I started to realize that people liked our dynamic." He smiles. "I like it, too."

Fuck, my heart.

"And from the sound of it," Lanelle says, "there are quite a bunch of Cizzy shippers in this theater!"

"*Cizzy?*" I mouth to Connor, who shrugs sweetly. Into the mic, I say, "I had no idea we had a shipper name, Lanelle."

"Can we turn the houselights up a bit?" Lanelle asks, and the audience becomes softly illuminated. "Raise your hand out there if you're a Cizzy stan," she calls out.

I blink in amazement at all of the hands that shoot up, and then turn when there's movement beside me. Tex, Colby, and Dax are all holding up their hands, too.

Lanelle turns to them, laughing. "You three?"

Dax nods with a giant grin on his face. "It was easy to lose when I knew I didn't have a shot to begin with."

"I voted for them," Tex admits.

"Me, too," says Colby.

"We don't even know the results yet!" I cry, struggling to maintain a grasp on what's happening. "What is going on here?"

I look over at Connor, who reaches for my hand and folds it between his. A hush falls over the vast theater. "What's going on is that I'm throwing my hat in the ring."

Pandemonium rises, all around us. Most people in the front few rows are even on their feet.

Backstage he said, *The hard part is coming,* and I know now that he meant this: putting himself in the spotlight for me, inserting himself not only as a hero but The Hero, risking everything for us. Devotion squeezes my heart in a tight fist.

"Is this going to be okay?" I ask him quietly. His job, his life here, everything.

He leans forward, whispering in my ear, "I told you back there that you were right." He's read my mind. Connor pulls back just enough to smile at me. "Thank you for reminding me: Everything *is* going to be amazing."

It hits me like a physical shove: He trusts me as much as I trust him. He came to me in the wings for the same reassurance I've always sought out in him. Somehow, even in front of millions, we have found a safe space in each other.

I can't handle this, can't handle what this is doing to my heart. If this is a grand gesture, I could never have written it, never have imagined the feeling that would swell inside me until I feel like I can't speak, can't even *think*.

Connor squeezes my hand, saying to the audience, "We figured I should get equal screen time, but of course that isn't possible. So, I made you something myself." Lifting his chin, he gestures to the screen again, and the houselights dim back down. The opening notes of my favorite Wonderland song, "Joyful," begin, and I feel a swell of emotion I'm not sure I'll be able to hold back.

There are video clips of the two of us joking on set, me throwing a wadded-up napkin at him. Footage of us eating lunch together, always separated by a few feet from the rest of the group; in another clip we're sitting at a table alone, noodling on our phones but silently together. There's footage of us trying to learn a TikTok dance together and cracking up, and then a quick-cut compilation of footage of me poking him in the ribs every time I walk past that has the audience in hysterics.

The next few clips show Connor patiently giving us feedback on set while I watch him with trusting, wide eyes, nodding. My love is as subtle as a brick to the face, and I'd be embarrassed by the way I'm obviously infatuated with him if it weren't so obviously reciprocated. Whoever captured the footage of him watching me cook in the industrial kitchen and plant trees with Jude is a genius; Connor looks like he's watching his favorite show.

The song ends, the screen turns black, and I think that's the end of it until the starkly clear sound of my own voice surprises me, backed by quiet music: "Should we talk about last night?"

The audience laughs at the implication, and oh *God*. I know what this is. The very first day of shooting, when my mic was live. Mortification washes icy cold through me. I slap a hand to my forehead and the audience vibrates with excitement over the salacious things to come.

The video on-screen is still black, but Connor's answering pause and then measured reply over audio leaves no question that he's trying to cover for what I really meant: "You mean our conversation about today's run of show?"

My blasting, "Yes! *Of course* that conversation! What other thing would we have to discuss?" sends the audience into waves of laughter.

Brenna appears on-screen, sitting beside Rory on the sofa in the confessional trailer. "Honestly, that those two were head over heels was obvious to all of us from the beginning."

Now Rory: "God. She was *constantly* looking at him."

This is followed by a hilarious quick-cut montage of all the times I glanced at Connor during filming. Sitting at the café table, in the industrial kitchen, at the park, in the spa looking for Connor when he wasn't even there. The video speeds up, clip after clip of scores of times where I'm glancing over, looking for him. More than I ever imagined I'd done, and I knew I looked for him *a lot*.

It's hilarious.

I bend, pressing my head into my hands as the audience cheers.

But then I straighten at Brenna's voice again: "Yeah, but Connor was just as bad."

Now there's a montage of Connor's face every time a Hero touched me, leaned in close, made me laugh, flirted with me. The compilation is hilarious—Dax and me on the first date, and a quick cut to Connor scowling at the monitor; Nick feeding me a cherry, and Connor appearing to breathe deeply with his eyes pointed at the ceiling; Evan braced behind me on the fishing boat, and Connor staring daggers at his back. The audience is eating it up, screaming with amusement. The Heroes, too, are in hysterics.

Isaac appears on-screen. "I think we all noticed it, but at first it didn't feel like they were dating so much as just really good friends."

Then Dax: "Those two are definitely hitting it."

The audience cheers bawdily.

Nick says, "I think he tried to fight it, but there's no doubt he's got a thing for her," and Colby, standing beside him some unknown night, says, "And Fizzy didn't want any of us because she wanted him. It's hard to be mad when you see two people falling in love."

I look over at Connor and realize he's been watching me. Of course he is; he said he put this together. And then it hits me—I've seen these outfits on Nick and Colby before. They wore them to the wrap party.

"You did this?" I ask quietly. "Just on Thursday?"

He nods, and then lifts his chin to the screen for me to watch what's next.

We're sitting in the confessional trailer, facing each other. We both look miserable and my heart bottoms out in my chest. It's the first bit of footage from that agonizing confessional on our last day of filming.

The part of that confessional that never aired.

"How are you feeling entering this final date?" Connor asks.

"Relieved," I say, and stare at him squarely. I remember that feeling, shoving my devotion out into the air between us, trying to get him to see how much I loved him. It's written plainly on my face.

Connor's expression tightens, his eyes searching mine. Seeing him like this, I don't know how I kept it together.

His mask slips again. "Relieved why?"

"Because it means soon I can stop pretending I want someone other than you."

"Fizzy," he says, glancing in panic at the camera, "you—you can't say that."

I lift my chin. "Edit it out, then."

With a long, slow exhale, Connor reaches to turn the camera off. The screen goes black.

The houselights come back on and it's a silent beat before the audience erupts, thunderously, standing in their seats.

My hand is so slippery in Connor's grip that I want to wrench it free and wipe it, but I don't dare; he subtly turns it over, pressing it to his leg. The audience screams again as they watch him flatten my hand to his upper thigh.

These people would suffer from cardiac arrest if they ever saw this man perform in bed.

"Well, Connor, looks like you've officially entered this competition," Lanelle says coyly, and for some reason my heart drops, like

I'd forgotten why we're all here. "I guess we need to find out how the audience voted."

She explains that voting took place on social media, where it was tracked by an objective third-party contractor, and rattles off the statistics about how many votes came in the first week and how many came in for the finale. The numbers are staggering. The lights dim and then slowly turn red for, I guess, suspense. And then Lanelle says, "With 41.2 percent of the vote . . . the audience chose Isaac!"

There is a pause, and then loud—but polite—applause.

"However," Lanelle says, smirking at the crowd, and I realize that of course she's in on this, too. "There was a bit of a surprise. Anyone know what it is?" The audience shouts out about a hundred different unintelligible things before she motions for them to quiet down and makes a show of examining her cue cards. "In a completely unprecedented turn of events, Connor Prince appears to have received 38.6 percent of the vote, and he wasn't even a contestant." Mayhem erupts and she has to shout over the roar of the audience. Even the crew behind the cameras is cheering.

I don't need Jess's nerdy math skills to know that 38.6 percent of the vote is *millions* of people. Millions of people who want Connor to be with me. But the only two that matter are sitting together on the couch. I look at him; his smile hovers somewhere between shy, smug, and completely overwhelmed.

I lean in, which only makes the uproar around us intensify. "Did you know about this?"

Connor lifts a single shoulder, his smile widening, and my heart swells, way too big in my body.

"All right, all right," Lanelle says, trying to get the show back on track. "But the real question is still in front of us: Did the audience—that's all of you—predict which of these Heroes is Fizzy's soulmate, as determined by the DNADuo?"

She goes in order of elimination. Surprising no one, Tex is a Base Match. However, Arjun turns out to be Silver. Jude and Colby are Base; Nick and Dax are both Silver. Sadly, Evan is a Base Match, but the audience vibrates, knowing what that means: Isaac is my Gold Match. With 41.2 percent voting for him, the audience got it right.

Lanelle confirms it; confetti blasts from hidden cannons in the stage. The bulbs on the retro logo flash and cycle in time with music; a cacophony of small, glittery fireworks goes off behind us. The camera zooms in on Isaac, whose handsome face appears on-screen. He throws his arms up in the air, waves at the audience, hams it up, and trades high fives and handshakes with the other Heroes. I stand up and give him a big hug. Even Connor is applauding.

But amid all the celebratory chaos, more questions linger.

Did Connor do the DNADuo, too? Do they have our *score?*

The audience settles and an anticipatory hum fills the theater. We all take our seats again, and Lanelle turns to me and Connor on the couch. "You've probably guessed there's one more thing we need to discuss: Connor also submitted a sample for the DNADuo."

My heart feels like it's going to jackhammer its way out of my body. "I suspected that might be where this was heading."

"So here we are," she says with a small smile. "The moment of truth. How are you feeling?"

The answer is simple, and I direct it to Connor: "I don't care what it is."

"I don't, either." But then he grins.

"Do *you* know what it is?"

He nods.

"Do *I* want to know?"

The audience laughs.

"I can't tell you that," he says. "It's up to you, sweet." Connor takes my hand, setting it back on his thigh. "I certainly won't force you to find out on live television."

The audience protests vehemently, and I know that even if he doesn't force me to, I have to. I'm not a dummy. If I leave this a mystery, I'll get shivved in the alleyway behind the studio.

"What if it's low?" I ask.

Connor reaches out and strokes a thumb across my cheekbone. He smiles, seeing only me in this enormous theater full of people, and in every grand gesture or emotional climax I've ever written, *this* is the expression I was going for. Being looked at this way is so much better in reality. "A smart woman explained to me that you're many thousands of times more likely to find your soulmate with a Base Match than ever get a Diamond Match."

It sinks in that this means he talked it out with Jess, that he went to her for context, or simply for reassurance, and I feel lit up like a flare inside.

My mind races through my last list of DNADuo matches, and how certain I was that knowing the scores would influence how I felt. But even if Lanelle told me we had the first zero in history, I would still choose Connor tonight and every night for the rest of time.

"Honestly, I'd be okay with anything as long as I have you."

"You have me." He reaches into his jacket pocket and pulls out the envelope. "You want to find out?"

I take the envelope with a hand that shakes like a feather in a hurricane.

Connor swallows, saying quietly—and very ardently, "No matter what it says, please know that I love you madly."

And then, accompanied by the wild screams of the crowd, he leans in and sets his mouth on mine.

It is a kiss that starts small, mindful of the fact that we are on television, sharing this moment with millions. But a cocktail of emotion rises in me—infatuation, relief, elation, and desire—and I can't help the way my hand rises to his neck, the way my mouth softens against the full bow of his upper lip, the delectable swell of his lower lip, the curved, amused corner. Without question, it will be clear to everyone watching that we have done this before.

As soon as our eyes open, a blast of a smile takes over my face. "I love you, too."

And then I suck in a breath and rip the envelope open.

fifty-one

Post-Finale Confessional Transcript

Connor Prince: Well. Felicity Chen. Here we are.

Fizzy Chen: Here we are.

Connor: How are you feeling?

Fizzy: I'm feeling like I was driven across town to film a confessional in this trailer when I should have been driven to your house to film our first sex tape.

Connor: [laughs] I mean about tonight, the finale, and the revelation of our score, you muppet.

Fizzy: Oh, it was the best night of my life. The surprises, the celebration with everyone onstage, the after-party.

Connor: God, there are going to be some *horrendous* hangovers tomorrow.

Fizzy: Tex was drinking beer out of his hat.

Connor: I don't think Nick ever found his shoes.

Fizzy: Yes, well, some poor choices were made, but not by us.

Connor: Indeed. Our night is only going to get better.

Fizzy: Promise?

Connor: Oh, I promise.

Fizzy: In that case, I think it's fitting that our score falls in the category of Titanium Matches. [winks at the camera]

Connor: I believe that's an erection joke and I'm going to move on.

Fizzy: You always assume I'm being dirty. Maybe it was just a joke about the strength of our bond.

Connor: Was it?

Fizzy: No, it was an erection joke.

Connor: You are ensuring that this footage never sees the light of day, aren't you?

Fizzy: When were you going to show this anyway? The finale was live!

Connor: I presume there will be demand for a follow-up or reunion episode of some sort. Brenna said "trending" and "viral" about seven hundred times tonight.

Fizzy: Okay, then just edit my boner joke out with bleeps and eggplant emojis; what's so hard?

Connor: Ah, note to self to add a cymbal crash there.

Fizzy: See, I didn't even mean to make that pun! You're as bad as I am.

Connor: Maybe that's why this is true love.

Fizzy: I think with a score of eighty-eight, there are a *lot* of reasons why this is true love.

Connor: Why don't you come over here and show me one?

[Editor's note: Minutes three to twenty-seven have been intentionally cut from footage.]

Connor: Right. We'll cut that.

Fizzy: You've got lipstick on your . . . just there.

Connor: Ah. Cheers. All right. Where were we?

Fizzy: True love.

Connor: True love.

Fizzy: Our happily ever after.

Connor: The one thing you promise your readers when they pick up one of your books. You know more about the importance of an HEA than most everyone watching this.

Fizzy: You know, it makes me a little sad that all these people watched the show, they wanted us together, and they won't be able to see it play out. Our future is going to be amazing. [looks at the camera] I am not volunteering for another reality show, Blaine.

Connor: Well, you could tell the viewers all about it right now.

Fizzy: All about our happily ever after?

Connor: Sure. What's it look like, do you reckon?

Fizzy: Oh, wow. Okay, well, we wrap this up and go back to my place, where we don't leave the bed for a full twenty-four hours.

Connor: I like this future already.

Fizzy: We spend next week with friends and family. Isaac enjoys his prize money, and I choose you to go with me to Fiji.

Connor: Not sure that's going to fly with the North Star executives.

Fizzy: Technically, I get to choose who I'm taking.

Connor: I don't doubt your ability to argue your case with Blaine.

Fizzy: When we get back, it's better than we could have ever imagined. People give us our privacy and we take a couple months off before beginning prep on the second season.

Connor: We?

Fizzy: I'm your new co-producer, don't you know?

Connor: Ah. Noted.

Fizzy: You cosplay as Luke Skywalker at Comic-Con and I'm your Yoda backpack.

Connor: A dream come true for me to carry you around in a dense, sweaty crowd.

Fizzy: We move in together next summer.

Connor: When it feels right, I ask Stevie how she would feel about having a fellow Wonderland stan for a stepmother.

Fizzy: I accept your proposal before the question is even out of your mouth.

Connor: Our wedding is the best party ever thrown.

Fizzy: Debauchery is my brand.

Connor: And every day of my life from this point forward, I will be able to sincerely say I love and cherish you with every fiber of my being.

Fizzy: Jesus Christ that's swoony. Can we get started on this future now?

Connor: Yes, my darling. We can.

acknowledgments

When we finished *The Soulmate Equation* in 2020, we assumed we'd written everything we intended to in that world. Jess, River, and Juno found their happily ever after, and that was that. You, dear readers, had other plans. *Soulmate* was released in May of 2021, we (virtually) headed out on tour, and at literally every event we got the same question:

Is Fizzy getting her own book?

We were a little thrown. We create secondary characters for lots of reasons—to puncture moments of tension with comedy, to challenge the heroine on her journey, or to provide a satisfying B-story arc—but rarely are they there to become stars in their own right. We never had a good answer to this, but the more people asked, the more we realized we really needed one; saying "Never say never" didn't fly with many of you. And then, one day, the right idea appeared. It probably didn't happen like a light bulb going on, but in hindsight it feels a little like that, like the beginning of Fizzy's story just popped up in a conversation between the two of us: she had lost her joy, and finds it again in the most unlikely place—with a man who evades all of her attempts to slap a convenient label on him, who sees her many layers and depths, and who finds his own joy in her infectious exuberance.

To be clear, if we had planned on writing a romance author as a main character from the get-go, we would have probably created Fizzy a bit differently in *The Soulmate Equation*. Romance authors are, to put it bluntly, given a lot of shit for what we do. We get asked in interviews whether we are writing our fantasies; we get asked what our fathers and husbands think of our careers; we get asked if we've done everything we describe in our books. So, for obvious reasons, we struggled at first to know how much to lean in to Fizzy's sex-positivity and exuberant dating life. We didn't want to play into those outside stereotypes. But it turns out that it was as easy as typing the word *Prologue*. Fizzy flowed out of us like we were exhaling. It meant that the real trouble blindsided us: What hero could possibly deserve her?

It took a while to find Connor in the pages. He's a quieter hero, a sturdy, bedrock presence. We wrote him in layers, carefully carving him into the story with each passing revision until he was as fully formed and dimensional as was our bold and bright Fizzy. And tonight, as we read it through one last time before it goes to press, we think it is the best thing we've ever done. *The True Love Experiment* is the thirtieth book we've written together and is our love letter to romance and fandom and fangirls everywhere.

And as always, although we write the words, it takes an enormous team of wonderful people working tirelessly behind the scenes to get it into your hands.

Holly Root, our Diamond Match, we must always put you first. You found us in the slush pile almost exactly eleven years ago; twenty-nine published books later and we still stare at you with heart-eyes. You are wise and kind, funny and intuitive, ruthless and brilliant—perfect for us in all ways. Kristin Dwyer is our PR Rep, our Precious, our safe space. Thank you for getting our books into the world, for wearing dorky hats with us at Disneyland, and always being up for book tour hotel breakfast. Dracarys.

Jen Prokop is one of the most brilliant freelance editors we have ever worked with; she finds the weak spots in our manuscript like it's her superpower. Thank you for your careful reads, your wonderful insights, and always having the perfect book recommendation at your fingertips.

We've said it before, we'll say it again: Gallery / Simon & Schuster has been the best home to us for every single one of our books. Jen Bergstrom is the rare kind of publisher who manages to balance mentor, champion, coach, friend, and businesswoman without ever losing an ounce of professionalism. We are truly in awe of the team you've built. Hannah Braaten, working on Fizzy with you has been the most fun; thank you for perfectly representing us in every room and helping us make this one exactly what we hoped it would be. Enormous thanks to the rest of the brilliant editorial team, Abby Zidle, Aimée Bell, Andrew Nguyễn, Sarah Schlick, Mia Robertson, Frances Yackel; sales powerhouses Jen Long, Eliza Hanson, and all of the reps we promised our firstborns to—hope they're behaving themselves, LOL; our amazing publicity team, Lauren Carr and Sally Marvin; marketing geniuses Mackenzie Hickey and Anabel Jimenez; the ever-patient and brilliantly creative art directors Lisa Litwack and John of the Mustache Vairo (you can never shave it; think of all the acknowledgments we'd have to edit). Our brilliant copyeditors find our mistakes and make sure the world never learns that we can't correctly place a comma or ever use a calendar. Production editor Christine Masters is called "the amazing Christine" in pretty much every email and deserves it. The Simon Audio team is full of stars: Sarah Lieberman, Chris Lynch, Louisa Solomon, Tom Spain, Desiree Vecchio, Gaby Audet, Taryn Beato, and Sophie Parens. Thank you to every person who touches our books, whether with a computer or doing the physical work of putting them together and getting them where they need to go.

Heather Baror-Shapiro, thank you for getting our words into the hands of readers across the globe. Mary Pender-Coplan, you are pure magic. Your calls are our favorite. Matt Sugarman, thank you for always representing our interests with the deepest commitment; you are a badass. Molly Mitchell, thank you until the end of time for managing the calendar and keeping us organized. You are GOLDEN.

To the friends, colleagues, and author idols who inspire us, share our fangirl screams, or who keep us from being messy all over the Internet, we love you: Erin Service, Katie Lee, Kate Clayborn, Sarah MacLean, Ali Hazelwood, Susan Lee, Jennifer Carlson, Jessica McLin, Brie Statham, Amy Schuver, Mae Lopez, Laura Wichems, Kian Maleki, Bianca Jimenez, Jori Mendivil, Cathryn Carlson, Ysabel Nakasone, Adriana Herrera, Katherine Center, Jen Frederick, Diane Park, Kresley Cole, Erin McCarthy, Sally Thorne, Sonali Dev, Alisha Rai, Christopher Rice, Sarah J. Maas, Sarah Wendell, Tahereh Mafi, Ransom Riggs, Stephanie Perkins, Helen Hoang, Tessa Bailey, Rachel Hawkins, Rosie Danan, Rachel Lynn Solomon, Rebekah Weatherspoon, Leslie Phillips, Alexa Martin, Jillian Stein, Liz Berry, Brittainy C. Cherry, Andie J. Christopher, Candice Montgomery, and Catherine Lu.

To Lo's Blue Flowers: I adore you all so much.

Thank you to our UK pre-readers for helping us with Connor's voice and vocab: Lindsey Kelk, Katy Wendt, Lia Louis, and Paige Thompson. Hopefully he sounds like a good Northern lad, but if he doesn't, blame us.

After publishing *The Soulmate Equation*, we were thrilled to hear from so many of you who deeply hoped Fizzy would get her own book, and at the same time, we are very conscious that a story of cultural identity or self-discovery for a character of color isn't ours to tell. It is hugely important to us that our books look like the world around us, and we hope we have balanced these two priorities: telling a love story for Fizzy that feels authentic, but which doesn't feel to our readers like a co-opted story of Chinese American identity. If you are part of this community, thank you for picking up our book and giving it a try. Our deepest debt of gratitude goes to our Chinese American pre-readers: Jennifer Yuen, Patty Lai, Eileen Ho, Kayla Lee, and Sandria Wong. These women answered every question we had and read through multiple versions of this book. They shared their time, their memories, and most importantly, themselves. Jen, Patty, Eileen, Kayla, and Sandria: We are forever thankful. We hope we made you proud. Anything that we got wrong is entirely on us.

By now, our families know almost as much about publishing as we do. They have seen us through the drafting, editing, and publishing of over two dozen books, hundreds of events, and countless flails and celebrations. We couldn't do any of this without them. Thank you, K and R, for celebrating our victories with gusto, commiserating through the struggles, and being proud, feminist husbands to your exuberant, fangirl wives. And thank you, C, O, and V, for being truly the most amazing kids, but thank you most of all for knowing how to make your own dinners when required. We love you more than words.

In case you couldn't tell, Fizzy is obsessed with her readers, and so are we. Our characters rarely speak for us, but when Fizzy talks about seeing her books impact people, watching their TikToks and Reels, and seeing all their beautiful photos? That's straight from us. We are nothing without all of you, and whether you found us at book one or book twenty-nine, whether you're a reader, a blogger, a BookTokker, a Bookstagrammer, or a podcaster, or you just love shouting into our DMs about our stories, we are so grateful.

If you are a bookseller or a librarian, we love the hell out of you. May your skin always look great, and may you always fly through the Ticketmaster queue. Thank you for all your work and for helping our books find new readers.

If you follow us, have met us, or attended one of our events, you know that we treat fangirling like a professional sport. It runs in our (purple) blood, and when we love something, we love it with every fiber of our being. Fizzy and Stevie's favorite band isn't officially BTS, but the euphoric joy they bring people was absolutely inspired by them. We've thanked BTS in four books now, but the happiness and inspiration they give us could fill every one of these pages. Kim Namjoon, Kim Seokjin, Min Yoongi, Jung Hoseok, Park Jimin, Kim Taehyung, and Jeon Jungkook, you inspire us to love better, to be kinder, to collaborate with passion, and to grow as individuals. Thank you for your hard work, for your dedication to each other, and for sharing your boundless talent with the world.

BTS and ARMY may be apart for a little while, but we will always be here, ARMY bombs ready for whatever comes next.

Christina, sunshine in human form. You are the glaze to my doughnut, the dimple to my smile, the Namjoon to my Jungkook, the exclamation point at the end of every one of my fangirl screams. I love this life we have made together, and sometimes still can't believe it. Thirty books and we just wrote one that fills our hearts to the brim. What a ride.

To my Lolo, I have been the proudest bestie this year. You put out your own book (*Scandalized* by Ivy Owens, available wherever books are sold) and were the best coauthor/mom/wife/daughter/BFF anyone could wish for. To say I love you isn't enough, but I think you know. I hope we write thirty more books together, go to five hundred more concerts, and find zero headless squirrels. IYKYK. You are forever my left quote.